GIDEON'S SWORD

By Douglas Preston and Lincoln Child

Fever Dream
Cemetery Dance
The Wheel of Darkness
The Book of the Dead
Dance of Death
Brimstone
Still Life with Crows
The Cabinet of Curiosities
The Ice Limit
Thunderhead
Riptide
Reliquary
Mount Dragon
Relic

In answer to a frequently asked reader question:
The above titles are listed in descending order of publication. Almost all of them are stand-alone novels that need not be read in order, except for the pairs *Relic*/*Reliquary* and *Dance of Death*/*The Book of the Dead*, which are ideally read in sequence.

By Douglas Preston

Impact
The Monster of Florence (with Mario Spezi)
Blasphemy
Tyrannosaur Canyon
The Codex
Ribbons of Time
The Royal Road
Talking to the Ground
Jennie
Cities of Gold
Dinosaurs in the Attic

By Lincoln Child

Terminal Freeze
Deep Storm
Death Match
Utopia
Tales of the Dark 1–3
Dark Banquet
Dark Company

GIDEON'S SWORD

DOUGLAS PRESTON

&

LINCOLN CHILD

GRAND CENTRAL PUBLISHING

NEW YORK   BOSTON

This book is a work of fiction. Names, characters, places, police departments, government agencies, corporations, religious institutions, and incidents are the product of the authors' imagination or are used fictitiously. Any resemblance to actual events, locales, or persons, living or dead, is coincidental. Falun Gong as portrayed in this novel is entirely fictional, and the authors extend their apologies for any inaccuracies in their depiction of this spiritual practice.

Grand Central Publishing
Hachette Book Group
237 Park Avenue
New York, NY 10017
www.HachetteBookGroup.com

Printed in the United States of America

First Edition: February 2011

10 9 8 7 6 5 4 3 2 1

Grand Central Publishing is a division of Hachette Book Group, Inc.
The Grand Central Publishing name and logo is a trademark of Hachette Book Group, Inc.

Library of Congress Cataloging-in-Publication Data

Preston, Douglas J.
Gideon's sword / Douglas Preston and Lincoln Child. — 1st ed.
p. cm.
Summary: "At age 12, Gideon Crew witnessed the brutal murder of his father. More than 20 years later, Gideon gets his revenge. But then a mysterious witness steps forward to confront Gideon on his crime—and offer him the chance of a lifetime"—Provided by publisher.
ISBN 978-0-446-56432-8 (regular ed.) — ISBN 978-0-446-57372-6 (large print ed.) 1. Children of murder victims—Fiction. 2. Revenge—Fiction. I. Child, Lincoln. II. Title.
PS3566.R3982G53 2011
813'.54—dc22

2010015235

We dedicate this book
to our most excellent literary agent,
Eric Simonoff.

MELVIN CREW

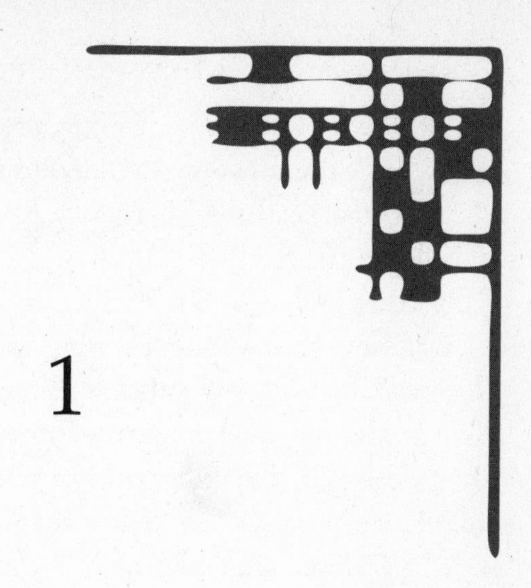

1

August 1988

Nothing in his twelve years of life had prepared Gideon Crew for that day. Every insignificant detail, every trivial gesture, every sound and smell, became frozen as if in a block of glass, unchanging and permanent, ready to be examined at will.

His mother was driving him home from his tennis lesson in their Plymouth station wagon. It was a hot day, well up in the nineties, the kind where clothes stick to one's skin and sunlight has the texture of flypaper. Gideon had turned the dashboard vents onto his face, enjoying the rush of cold air. They were driving on Route 27, passing the long cement wall enclosing Arlington National Cemetery, when two motorcycle cops intercepted their car, one pulling ahead, the other staying behind, sirens wailing, red lights turning. The one in front motioned with a black-gloved hand toward the Columbia Pike exit ramp; once on the ramp, he signaled for Gideon's mother to pull over. There was none of the slow deliberation of a routine traffic stop—instead, both officers hopped off their motorcycles and came running up.

"Follow us," said one, leaning in the window. "Now."

"What's this all about?" Gideon's mother asked.

"National security emergency. Keep up—we'll be driving fast and clearing traffic."

"I don't understand—"

But they were already running back to their motorcycles.

Sirens blaring, the officers escorted them down Columbia Pike to George Mason Drive, forcing cars aside as they went. They were joined by more motorcycles, squad cars, and finally an ambulance: a motorcade that screamed through the traffic-laden streets. Gideon didn't know whether to be thrilled or scared. Once they turned onto Arlington Boulevard, he could guess where they were going: Arlington Hall Station, where his father worked for INSCOM, the United States Army Intelligence and Security Command.

Police barricades were up over the entrance to the complex, but they were flung aside as the motorcade pulled through. They went shrieking down Ceremonial Drive and came to a halt at a second set of barricades, beside a welter of fire trucks, police cars, and SWAT vans. Gideon could see his father's building through the trees, the stately white pillars and brick façade set among emerald lawns and manicured oaks. It had once been a girls' finishing school and still looked it. A large area in front had been cleared. He could see two sharpshooters lying on the lawn, behind a low hummock, rifles deployed on bipods.

His mother turned to him and said, fiercely, "Stay in the car. Don't get out, no matter what." Her face was gray and strained, and it scared him.

She stepped out. The phalanx of cops bulled through the crowd ahead of her and they disappeared.

She'd forgotten to turn off the engine. The air-conditioning was still going. Gideon cranked down a window, the car filling with the sounds of sirens, walkie-talkie chatter, shouts. Two men in blue suits came running past. A cop hollered into a radio. More sirens drifted in from afar, coming from every direction.

He heard the sound of a voice over an electronic megaphone, acidic, distorted. *"Come out with your hands in view."*

The crowd immediately hushed.

"You are surrounded. There is nothing you can do. Release your hostage and come out now."

Another silence. Gideon looked around. The attention of the crowd was riveted on the front door of the station. That, it seemed, was where things would play out.

"Your wife is here. She would like to speak to you."

A buzz of fumbled static came through the sound system and then the electronically magnified sound of a partial sob, grotesque and strange. *"Melvin?"* Another choking sound. *"MELVIN?"*

Gideon froze. *That's my mother's voice,* he thought.

It was like a dream where nothing made sense. It wasn't real. Gideon put his hand on the door handle and opened it, stepping into the stifling heat.

"Melvin..." A choking sound. *"Please come out. Nobody's going to hurt you, I promise. Please let the man go."* The voice over the megaphone was harsh and alien—and yet unmistakably his mother's.

Gideon advanced through the clusters of police officers and army officers. No one paid him any attention. He made his way to the outer barricade, placed a hand on the rough, blue-painted wood. He stared in the direction of Arlington Hall but could see nothing stirring in the placid façade or on the immediate grounds cleared of people. The building, shimmering in the heat, looked dead. Outside, the leaves hung limply on the oak branches, the sky flat and cloudless, so pale it was almost white.

"Melvin, if you let the man go, they'll listen to you."

More waiting silence. Then there was a sudden motion at the front door. A plump man in a suit Gideon didn't recognize came stumbling out. He looked around a moment, disoriented, then broke into a run toward the barricades, his thick legs churning. Four helmeted officers rushed out, guns drawn; they seized the man and hustled him back behind one of the vans.

Gideon ducked under the barricade and moved forward through the groups of cops, the men with walkie-talkies, the men in uniform. Nobody noticed him, nobody cared: all eyes were fixed on the front entrance to the building.

And then a faint voice rang out from inside the doorway. "There must be an investigation!"

It was his father's voice. Gideon paused, his heart in his throat.

"I demand an investigation! Twenty-six people died!"

A muffled, amplified fumbling, then a male voice boomed from the sound system. *"Dr. Crew, your concerns will be addressed. But you must come out now with your hands up. Do you understand? You must surrender now."*

"You haven't listened," came the trembling voice. His father sounded frightened, almost like a child. "People died and nothing was done! I want a promise."

"That is a promise."

Gideon had reached the innermost barricade. The front of the building remained still, but he was now close enough to see the door standing half open. It was a dream; at any moment he would wake up. He felt dizzy from the heat, felt a taste in his mouth like copper. It was a nightmare—and yet it was real.

And then Gideon saw the door swing inward and the figure of his father appear in the black rectangle of the doorway. He seemed terribly small against the elegant façade of the building. He took a step forward, his hands held up, palms facing forward. His straight hair hung down over his forehead, his tie askew, his blue suit rumpled.

"That's far enough," came the voice. *"Stop."*

Melvin Crew stopped, blinking in the bright sunlight.

The shots rang out, so close together they sounded like firecrackers, and his father was abruptly punched back into the darkness of the doorway.

"Dad!" screamed Gideon, leaping over the barrier and running across the hot asphalt of the parking lot. *"Dad!"*

Shouts erupted behind him, cries of "Who's that kid?" and "Hold fire!"

He leapt the curb and cut across the lawn toward the entrance. Figures raced forward to intercept him.

"Jesus Christ, stop him!"

He slipped on the grass, fell to his hands and knees, rose again. He could see only his father's two feet, sticking out of the dark doorway into the sunlight, shoes pointed skyward, scuffed soles turned up for all to see, one with a hole in it. It was a dream, a dream—and then the last thing he saw before he was tackled to the ground was the feet move, jerking twice.

"Dad!" he screamed into the grass, trying to claw back to his feet as the weight of the world piled up on his shoulders; but he'd seen those feet move, his father was alive, he would wake up and all would be well.

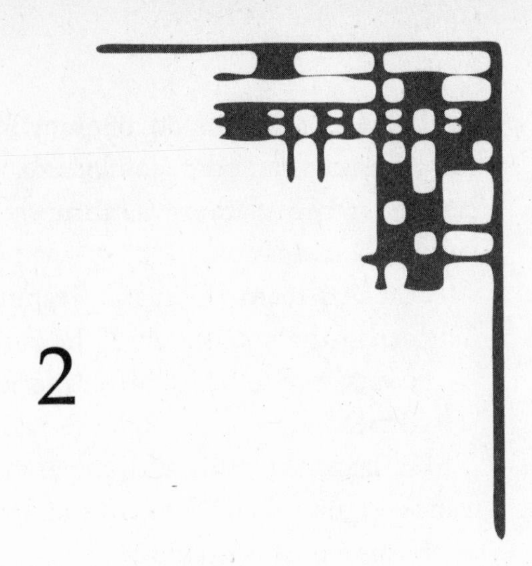

2

October 1996

Gideon Crew had flown in from California on the red-eye, the plane sitting on the LAX tarmac for two hours before finally taking off for Dulles. He'd hopped a bus into the city, then taken the Metro as far as he could before switching to a taxi: the last thing his finances needed right now was the unexpected plane fare. He'd been burning through cash at an alarming rate, not budgeting at all—and that last job he'd done had been higher-profile than usual, the merchandise difficult to fence.

When the call came he'd hoped at first it was one more false alarm, another attack of hysteria or drunken plea for attention. But when he arrived at the hospital, the doctor had been coolly frank. "Her liver is failing and she's not eligible for a transplant because of her history. This may be your last visit."

She lay in intensive care, her bleached-blond hair spread over the pillow, showing an inch of black roots, her skin raddled. A sad, inept attempt had been made to apply eye shadow; it was like painting the shutters on a haunted house. He could hear her raspy breathing through the nasal cannula. The room was hushed, the lights low, the discreet beeping of electronics a watchful presence. He felt a sudden tidal wave of guilt and pity. He'd been absorbed in his own life instead of tending to her. But every time he'd tried in the past, she had retreated into the bottle and they'd ended up fighting. It wasn't fair, her life ending like this. It just wasn't fair.

Taking her hand, he tried and failed to think of anything to say. Finally he managed a lame "How are you, Mom?"—hating himself for the inanity of the question even before he'd finished asking it.

She just looked at him in response. The whites of her eyes were the color of overripe bananas. Her bony hand grasped his in a weak, trembling embrace. Finally she stirred weakly. "Well, this is it."

"Mom, please don't talk like that."

She waved a hand dismissively. "You've talked to the doctor: you know how things stand. I have cirrhosis, along with all the lovely side effects—not to mention congestive heart failure and emphysema from years of smoking. I'm a wreck and it's my own damn fault."

Gideon could think of no response. It was all true, of course, and his mother was nothing if not direct. She always had been. He found it puzzling that such a strong woman was so weak when it came to chemical vices. No, it wasn't so puzzling: she had an addictive personality, and he recognized the same in himself.

"The truth shall make you free," she said, "but first it will make you miserable."

It was her favorite aphorism, and it always preceded her saying something difficult.

"The time has come for me to tell you a truth—" She gasped in some air. "—that will make you miserable."

He waited while she took a few more raspy breaths.

"It's about your father." Her yellow eyes swiveled toward the door. "Shut it."

His apprehension mounting, Gideon gently closed the door and returned to her bedside.

She clasped his hand again. "Golubzi," she whispered.

"I'm sorry?"

"*Golubzi.* A Russian salt-cabbage roll."

She paused for more air. "That was the Soviet code name for the operation. The Roll. In one night, twenty-six deep-cover operatives were rolled up. Disappeared."

"Why are you telling me this?"

"Thresher." She closed her eyes, breathing rapidly. It was as if, having decided to take the plunge, she couldn't wait to get out the words. "That's the other word. The project your father was working on at INSCOM. A new encryption standard...highly classified."

"Are you sure you should be talking about this?" Gideon asked.

"Your father shouldn't have told me. But he did." Her eyes remained closed and her body looked collapsed, as if it were sinking into the bed. "Thresher needed to be vetted. Tested. That's when they hired your father. We moved to DC."

Gideon nodded. For a seventh grader, moving from Claremont, California, to DC had not exactly been fun.

"In 1987, INSCOM sent Thresher to the National Security Agency for final review. It was approved. And implemented."

"I never heard any of this."

"You're hearing it now." She swallowed painfully. "It took the Russians just months to crack it. On July 5, 1988—the day after Independence Day—the Soviets rolled up all those US spies."

She paused, releasing a long sigh. The machines continued beeping quietly, mingling with the hiss of the oxygen and the muffled sounds of the hospital beyond.

Gideon continued to hold her hand, at a loss for words.

"They blamed your father for the disaster—"

"Mom." Gideon pressed her hand. "This is all in the past."

She shook her head. "They ruined his life. That's why he did what he did, took that hostage."

"What does it matter now? Long ago I accepted that Dad made a mistake."

The eyes opened suddenly. "No mistake. He was the *scape-goat*."

She pronounced the word harshly, as if she were clearing her throat of something unpleasant.

"What do you mean?"

"Before Operation Golubzi, your father wrote a memo. He said Thresher was theoretically flawed. That there was a potential back door. They ignored him. But he was right. And twenty-six people died."

She inhaled noisily, her hands bunching up the bedcovers with the effort. "Thresher was classified, they could say whatever they liked. No one to contradict. Your father was an outsider, a professor, a civilian. And he had a history of treatment for depression that could be conveniently resurrected."

Listening, Gideon froze. "You're saying... it wasn't his fault?"

"Just the opposite. They destroyed the evidence and blamed him for the Golubzi disaster. That's why he took that hostage. And that's why he was shot with his hands up—to silence him. Cold-blooded murder."

Gideon felt a strange sense of weightlessness. As horrifying as the story was, he felt a burden being lifted. His father, whose name had been publicly vilified since he was twelve, wasn't the depressed, unstable, bungling mathematician after all. All the taunting and hazing he'd endured, the whispering and sniggering behind his back—it meant nothing. At the same time, the enormity of the crime perpetrated against his father began to sink in. He remembered that day vividly, remembered the promises that were made. He remembered how his father had been lured out into the sunlight only to be shot down.

"But who...?" he began.

"Lieutenant General Chamblee Tucker. An INSCOM deputy chief. Group leader of the Thresher project. He made a scapegoat of your father to protect himself. He gave the order to fire. Remember that name: *Chamblee Tucker.*"

His mother ceased speaking and lay in the bed, covered with sweat, gasping as if she had just run a marathon.

"Thank you for telling me this," he said evenly.

"Not finished." More labored breathing. He could see her heart monitor on the wall, registering in the one forties.

"Don't talk anymore," he said. "You need to rest."

"*No,*" she said with sudden forcefulness. "I'll have time to rest...later."

Gideon waited.

"You know what happened next. You lived through it, too. The constant moving, the poverty. The...men. I just couldn't pull it together. My real life ended that day. Ever afterward I felt dead inside. I was a terrible mother. And you...you were so hurt."

"Don't you worry, I survived."

"Are you sure?"

"Of course." But deep within, Gideon felt a twinge.

Her breathing began to slow, and Gideon felt her grasp relax. Seeing she was going to sleep, he eased her hand from his and placed it on the bedcovers. But when he bent down to kiss her, the hand shot up again, grasping his collar with claw-like fingers. Her eyes pinned his and she said, with manic intensity: "*Even the score.*"

"What?"

"Do to Tucker what he did to your father. Destroy him. And in the end, make sure he knows why—and by whom."

"Good God, what are you asking?" Gideon whispered, looking around in sudden panic. "Mom, you don't know what you're saying."

Her voice fell to a whisper. "Take your time. Finish college. Go to graduate school. Study. Watch. Wait. You'll figure out a way."

Her hand slowly relaxed and she closed her eyes again, the air seeming to run out of her forever, like a final sigh. And in a way it was; she lapsed into a coma and died two days later.

Those were her last words, words that would resonate endlessly in his mind. *You'll figure out a way.*

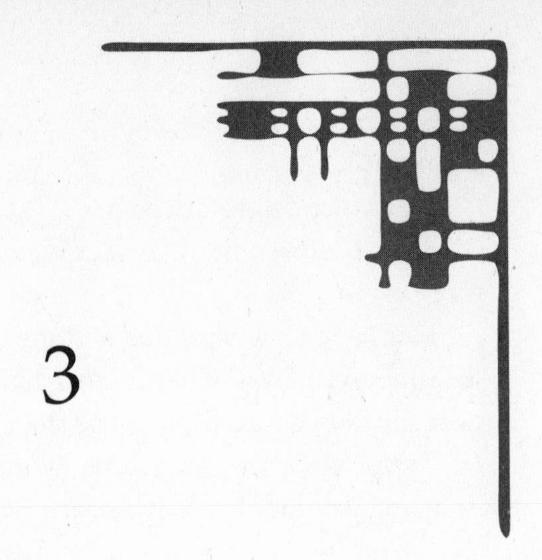

3

Present day

Gideon Crew emerged from the ponderosa pines into the broad field in front of the cabin. In one hand he carried an aluminum tube containing his fly rod; a canvas bag was slung over his shoulder, two trout inside, nestled in wet grass. It was a beautiful day in early May, the sun mild on the back of his neck. His long legs swept through the meadow, scattering bees and butterflies.

The cabin stood at the far end, hand-adzed logs chinked with adobe, with a rusted tin roof, two windows, and a door. A rack of solar panels poked discreetly above the roofline, next to a broadband satellite dish.

Beyond, the mountainside fell away into the vast Piedra Lumbre basin, the distant peaks of southern Colorado fringing the horizon like so many blue teeth. Gideon worked on "the Hill"—up at Los Alamos National Lab—and spent his weeknights in a cheesy government apartment in a building at the corner of Trinity and Oppenheimer. But he spent his weekends—and his real life—in this cabin in the Jemez Mountains.

He pushed open the cabin door and entered the kitchen alcove. Shrugging off the canvas bag, he took out the cleaned cutthroat trout, rinsed them, and patted them dry. He reached over to the iPod sitting in its dock and, after a moment's reflection, dialed in Thelonius Monk. The percussive notes of "Green Chimneys" floated from the speakers.

Blending lemon juice and salt, he beat in some olive oil and freshly cracked pepper, then basted the trout with the marinade. Mentally, he checked off the rest of the ingredients of *truite à la provençale:* onions, tomatoes, garlic, vermouth, flour, oregano, and thyme. Gideon usually ate only one real meal a day, of the highest quality, prepared by himself. It was an almost Zen-like exercise, both in the preparation and the slow consumption. When further sustenance was necessary, it was Twinkies, Doritos, and coffee on the run.

After washing his hands, he walked into the living area and placed the aluminum fly-rod case into an old umbrella stand in one corner. He flopped down on the ancient leather sofa and kicked his feet up, relaxing. A fire, lit for cheeriness rather than warmth, crackled in the large stone fireplace, and the afternoon sun threw yellow light across a pair of elk antlers hanging above it. A bearskin rug covered the floor, and old backgammon and checkers boards hung on the walls. Books lay strewn about on side tables and stacked on the floor, and a wall of shelves at the far end of the room was crammed with volumes stuck in every which way until no space remained.

He glanced toward another alcove, covered by an improvised curtain made from an old Hudson's Bay point blanket. For a long moment, he didn't move. He hadn't checked the system since last week, and he felt disinclined to do it now. He was tired and looking forward to dinner. But it had been a self-imposed duty for so long that it was now a habit, and so at last he roused himself, raked back his long straight black hair with one hand, and slouched over to the blanket, from behind which came a faint humming sound.

He drew back the curtain with some reluctance, the dark space releasing a faint smell of electronics and warm plastic. A wooden desk and a rack of computer equipment greeted his eye, LEDs blinking in the dimness. There were four computers in the rack, of varying makes and sizes, all off-brand or generic, none less than five years old: an Apache server and three Linux clients. For what Gideon was doing, the computers didn't need to be fast; they just had to be thorough—and reliable. The only brand-new and relatively expensive piece of equipment in the alcove was a high-performance broadband satellite router.

Above the rack was a small, exquisite pencil sketch by Winslow Homer of rocks on the Maine coast. It was the one remaining artifact from his previous profession: the one he simply hadn't had the heart to sell.

Pulling back a ratty office chair on an octopus of wheels, he seated himself at the small wooden desk, kicked his feet up, dragged a keyboard into his lap, and began typing. A screen popped up with a summary of the search results, informing him he had not been in attendance for six days.

He drilled through to the results window. Immediately he saw that there had been a hit.

He stared at the screen. Over the years, he'd refined and improved his search engine, and it had been almost a year since the last false positive.

Dropping his feet to the floor, heart suddenly hammering in his chest, he hunched over the desk, banging furiously at the keys. The hit was in a table of contents released to the National Security Archives at George Washington University. The actual archival material remained classified, but the table of contents had been released as part of a large, ongoing declassification of Cold War documents under Executive Order 12958.

The hit was his father's name: L. Melvin Crew. And the title of the archived, still-classified document was *A Critique of the Thresher Discrete Logarithm Encryption Standard EVP-4: A Theoretical Back-Door Cryptanalysis Attack Strategy Using a Group of φ-Torsion Points of an Elliptic Curve in Characteristic φ.*

"Mother of God," Gideon murmured as he stared at the screen. No false positive this time.

For years, he'd been hoping for something. But this looked like more than something. It might be the brass ring.

It seemed incredible, unbelievable: could this be the very memo his father had written criticizing Thresher, the memo that General Tucker had supposedly destroyed?

There was only one way to find out.

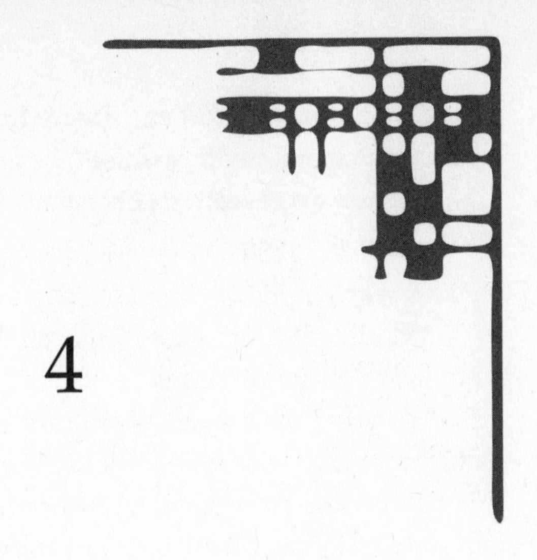

4

Midnight. Gideon Crew slouched down the street, hands in his pockets, baseball cap turned backward, filthy shirt untucked beneath a greasy trench coat, baggy pants hanging halfway down his ass, thinking how lucky he was that today was trash day in suburban Brookland, Washington, DC.

He turned the corner of Kearny Street and passed the house: a shabby bungalow with an overgrown lawn surrounded by a white picket fence only partially painted. And, of course, a lovely overflowing trash can sat at the end of the walkway, a fearful stench of rotting shrimp hovering in the muggy air. He paused at the can, looking about furtively. Then he dove in with one hand, digging deep, groping among the garbage as he went. His hand encountered something that felt like french fries and he pulled up a handful, confirmed they were fries, tossed them back.

He saw a flash of movement. A scrawny, one-eyed cat came slinking out from a hedge.

"Hungry, partner?"

The cat made a low meow and crept over, tail twitching warily. Gideon offered it a fry. It sniffed at it suspiciously, ate it, then meowed again, louder.

Gideon tossed the cat a small handful. "That's all, kiddo. Any idea how bad trans-fatty acids are for you?"

The cat settled down to nosh.

Gideon dove in again, stirring the garbage with his arm, this time turning up a wad of discarded papers. Quickly sorting through them, he saw they were some little child's math homework—straight A's, he noted with approval. Why were they thrown away? Should be framed.

He pushed them back in, dug out a chicken drumstick, and set it aside for the cat. He reached in again, both hands this time, wriggling downward, encountering something slimy, fumbling deeper, his fingers working through various semi-solid things before encountering more papers. Grasping them and working them to the surface, he saw they were just what he was looking for: discarded bills. And among them was the top half of a phone bill.

Jackpot.

"Hey!" He heard a shout and looked up. There was the homeowner himself, Lamoine Hopkins, a small, thin African American man, excitedly pointing his arm. "Hey! Get the fuck outta here!"

In no hurry, glad of the unexpected opportunity to interact with one of his targets, Gideon shoved the papers into his pocket. "Can't a man feed himself?" He held up the drumstick.

"Go feed yourself somewhere else!" the man shrilled. "This is a decent neighborhood! That's my trash!"

"Come on, man, don't be like that."

The man took out his cell phone. "You see this? I'm calling the cops!"

"Hey, no harm done, man."

"Hello?" said the man, speaking theatrically into the phone, "there's an intruder on my property, rifling my trash! Thirty-five seventeen Kearny Street Northeast!"

"Sorry," Gideon mumbled, shambling off with the drumstick in one hand.

"I need a squad car, right now!" shrilled the man. "He's trying to get away!"

Gideon tossed the drumstick in the direction of the cat, shuffled off around the corner, and then picked up his pace. He quickly wiped his hands and arms as thoroughly as he could on his cap, discarded it, turned his Salvation Army coat inside out—revealing an immaculate blue trench coat—and put it on, tucked in his shirt, then slicked back his hair with a comb. As he reached his rental car a few blocks off, a police cruiser passed by, giving him only the briefest of glances. He slipped in and started the engine, rejoicing at his good fortune. Not only did he get what he'd come for, but he'd met Mr. Lamoine Hopkins in person—and had such a lovely chat with him.

That would come in handy.

From his motel room, Gideon began cold-calling the numbers on Hopkins's phone bill the next morning. He worked his way through a succession of Hopkins's friends until on the fifth call he struck pay dirt.

"Heart of Virginia Mall, tech support," came the voice. "Kenny Roman speaking."

Tech support. Quickly, Gideon turned on a digital recorder plugged into a line-splitter on the phone line. "Mr. Roman?"

"Yes?"

"My name is Eric, and I'm calling on behalf of the Sutherland Finance Company."

"Yeah? What do you want?"

"It's about the loan on your 2007 Dodge Dakota."

"What Dakota?"

"The loan is three months overdue, sir, and I'm afraid that Sutherland Finance—"

"What are you talking about? I don't have any Dakota."

"Mr. Roman, I understand these are difficult financial times, but if we don't receive the amount currently overdue—"

"Look, buddy, dig some of the wax outta your ears, will you? You've got the wrong person. I don't even own a pickup. Suck—My—Dick." There was a *click* as the line went dead.

Gideon hung up. He snapped off the digital recorder. Then he listened three times to the exchange he'd just recorded. *What are you talking about? I don't have any Dakota,* Gideon mimicked aloud. *Look, buddy, dig some of the wax outta your ears, will you? You've got the wrong person. I don't even own a pickup.* He repeated the phrases many times, in different combinations, until he felt he had the inflections, tone, rhythms down just about right.

He picked up the phone and dialed again: this time, the IT department at Fort Belvoir.

"IT," came the response. It was Lamoine Hopkins's voice.

"Lamoine?" Gideon said, whispering. "It's Kenny."

"Kenny, what the hell?" Hopkins sounded instantly suspicious. "What's with the whispering?"

"Got a fucking cold. And... what I got to say is sensitive."

"Sensitive? What do you mean?"

"Lamoine, you got a problem."

"Me? I got a problem? What do you mean?"

Gideon consulted a sheet of scribbled notes. "I got a call from a guy named Roger Winters."

"Winters? *Winters* called you?"

"Yeah. Said there was a problem. He asked me how many times you'd called me from work, that kind of shit."

"Oh my God."

"Yeah.

"He wanted to know," Gideon-as-Kenny asked, "if you'd called me on your office computer, using VoIP or Skype."

"Christ, that would be a violation of security! I've never done that!"

"Man said you had."

Gideon could hear Lamoine breathing heavily. "But it isn't true!"

"That's what I told him. Listen, Lamoine, there's a security audit going on over there, I'll bet you anything, and somehow they're on your case."

"What am I going to do?" Hopkins fairly wailed. "I haven't done anything wrong! I mean, I couldn't make a VoIP call from here even if I wanted to!"

"Why not?"

"The firewall."

"There are ways to get around a firewall."

"Are you kidding me? We're a classified facility!"

"There's *always* a way."

"For Chrissakes, Kenny, I *know* there isn't a way. I'm IT, remember? Just like you. There's only one outgoing port in the entire network, and all that it allows past is passphrase-encrypted packets from specific nodes, all of which are secure. And even then the packets can only go to certain external IPs. All the classified documents in this archive are digitized, they're super-paranoid about electronic security. There's no way in hell I could call out on Skype! I can't even send out e-mail!"

Gideon coughed, sniffed, blew his nose. "Don't you know the port number?"

"Sure, but I don't have access to the weekly passphrases."

"Does your boss, Winters, have access?"

"No. Only, like, the top three in the organization get the passphrase—director, deputy director, and security director. I mean, with that passphrase you could pretty much e-mail out any classified document in here."

"Don't you guys in IT generate the passphrases?"

"You kidding? It comes down from the spooks in a secure envelope. I mean, they *walk* the sucker over here. It never enters *any* electronic system—it's written down by hand on a piece of frigging paper."

"Problem is that port number," said Gideon. "Is that written down?"

"It's kept in a safe. But a lot of people know it."

Gideon grunted. "Sounds to me like you're being framed. Like maybe one of the top guys screwed up and is looking for someone else to take the fall. 'Let's pin it on Lamoine!'"

"No way."

"Happens all the time. It's always the little guys who get shafted. You need to protect yourself, man."

"How?"

Gideon let the silence build. "I have an idea...it might be a really good one. What was that port number again?"

"Six one five one. What's that got to do with anything?"

"I'll check some things, call you back at home tonight. In the meantime, don't say anything about this to anybody, just sit tight, do your job, keep your head down. Don't call me back—they're no doubt logging your calls. We'll talk when you get home."

"I can't believe this. Listen, thanks, Kenny. Really."

Gideon coughed again. "Hey, what are friends for?"

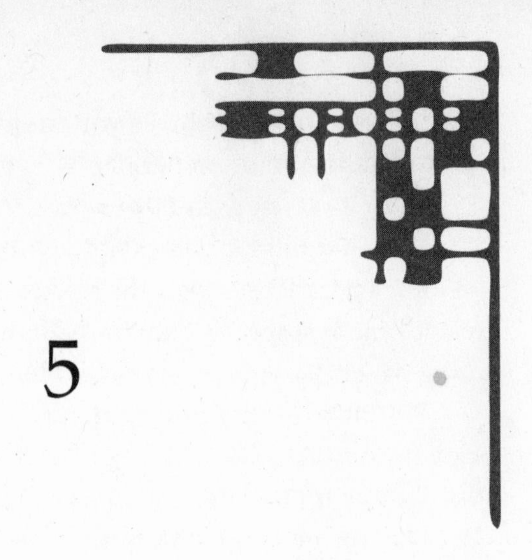

5

Hanging up the phone, Gideon Crew began flinging off his clothes. He slid open the closet door and laid a garment bag on the bed. From it he removed a fragrant, custom-cut Turnbull & Asser shirt, shifted his lanky frame into it, and buttoned it up. Next came a blue Thomas Mahon bespoke suit. He pulled on the pants, belted them, whipped on a Spitalfield flower tie (where did the English get those names?), tied it with a crisp tug, shrugged on the jacket. He massaged some hair gel between his palms and used it to slick back his floppy hair. As a final touch, he combed a smidgen of gray into his sideburns, which added an instant five years to his age.

He turned to look at himself in the mirror. Thirty-two hundred dollars for the new persona—shirt, suit, shoes, belt, tie, haircut—twenty-nine hundred for travel, motel, car, and driver. All on four brand-new credit cards obtained and maxed out for just this purpose, with virtually no hope of being paid off.

Welcome to America.

The car was already waiting for him in front of the motel, a black Lincoln Navigator; he slipped into the back and handed the driver the address. Gideon settled himself into the soft kid leather as the car pulled away, arranging his face, composing himself, and trying not to think of the three-hundred-dollar-an-hour price tag. Or, for that matter, the much higher price tag attached to the scam he was about to perpetrate, if he were to get caught...

Traffic was light and thirty minutes later the car pulled into the entrance to Fort Belvoir, which housed INSCOM's Directorate of Information Management: a low, 1960s-modern building of exceptional hideousness set amid locust trees and surrounded by a huge parking lot.

Somewhere inside the building sat Lamoine Hopkins, no doubt sweating bullets. And somewhere else inside the building was the classified memo written by Gideon's own father.

"Pull up to the front and wait for me," said Gideon. He realized his voice was squeaky with nervousness, and he swallowed, trying to relax his neck muscles.

"I'm sorry, sir, but it says *No Standing.*"

He cleared his throat, producing a smooth, low, confident voice. "If anyone asks, say Congressman Wilcyzek is meeting with General Moorehead. But if they insist, don't make a scene, just go ahead and move. I shouldn't be more than ten minutes."

"Yes, sir."

Gideon exited the vehicle and headed down the walkway; he pushed through the doors and headed for the reception/information desks. The broad lobby was full of military personnel and self-important civilians briskly coming and going. God, he hated Washington.

With a cold smile, Gideon went up to the woman at the desk. She had carefully coiffed blue hair, neat as a pin, clearly a stickler for procedure—someone who took her work seriously. Couldn't ask for better. Those who followed the rules were the most predictable.

He smiled and—speaking into the air just a few inches above

her head—said, "Congressman Wilcyzek here to see Deputy Commander General Thomas Moorehead. I'm..." He glanced at his watch. "...three minutes early."

She straightened up like a shot. "Of course, Congressman. Just a moment." She lifted a phone, pressed a button, spoke for a moment. She glanced at Gideon. "Excuse me, Congressman, can you spell your name, please?"

With a sigh of irritation he spelled it out, making it abundantly clear that she should have known the spelling already—indeed, he was careful to cultivate an air of someone who expected to be recognized, who had only contempt for the ignorance of those who did not.

She pursed her lips, got back on the phone. A short conversation followed, and then she hung up. "Congressman, I'm terribly sorry, but the general is out for the day and his secretary has no record of the appointment. Are you sure...?" She faltered when Gideon fixed her with a severe look.

"Am I *sure*?" he asked, raising an eyebrow.

Her lips were now fully pursed, her blue hair beginning to quiver with suppressed offense.

He looked at his watch, looked up at her. "Mrs....?"

"Wilson," she said.

He slipped a piece of paper out of his pocket and handed it to her. "You can check for yourself."

It was an e-mail he had concocted, allegedly from the general's secretary, confirming the appointment with the general he'd already known would be out. She read it and returned it to him. "I'm very sorry, he doesn't seem to be in. Shall I call his secretary again?"

Gideon continued to glare at her, fixing her with a subzero stare. "I should like to speak to his secretary *myself*."

She faltered, removed the phone from its cradle, and handed it to him, but not before dialing the number.

"Excuse me, Mrs. Wilson, but this is a classified matter. Do you mind?"

Her face, which had gradually darkened, now flushed rose. She stood up silently and took a step away from her desk. He put the receiver to his ear. The phone was ringing, but turning to block her view, he depressed the button and, almost imperceptibly, dialed another extension—this time, the secretary to General Shorthouse, the director himself.

Only, like, the top three in the organization get the passphrase—director, deputy director, and security director...

"Director's office," came the secretary's voice.

Speaking quietly and rapidly, and summoning the voice of the man who'd confronted him at the trash cans the night before, he said: "This is Lamoine Hopkins in IT returning the general's call. It's urgent—a security breach."

"Just a moment."

He waited. After a minute, General Shorthouse came on. "Yes? What's the problem? I didn't call you."

"I'm sorry, General," said Gideon, speaking like Hopkins but now in a low, unctuous tone, "about the lousy day you must be having."

"What are you talking about, Hopkins?"

"Your system being down, sir, and the backup not kicking in."

"It's not down."

"General? We're showing your whole grid as down. It's a security violation, sir—and you know what *that* means."

"That's preposterous. My computer's on right now and working perfectly. And why are you calling me from reception?"

"General, that's part of the problem. The telephony matrix is tied into the computer network and it's giving false readings. Log off and log back on, please, while I trace." Gideon glanced over at the receptionist, who was still standing to one side, making a conscientious effort not to overhear.

He heard the tapping of keys. "Done."

"Funny, I'm not reading any packet activity from your network address. Try signing off again."

More tapping of keys.

"Nothing, General. Looks like your ID might have been compromised. This is bad—it's going to require a report, an investigation. And it *would* be your system. I'm so sorry, sir."

"Let's not get ahead of ourselves, Hopkins. I'm sure we can fix it."

"Well . . . we can give it a shot. But I'll have to try resetting, and then accessing your account from down here. I'm going to need your ID and passphrase, please."

A pause. "I'm not sure I can give you that."

"You may not realize this, but in the case of network resets the passphrase is automatically changed, so you're allowed to release the passphrase internally to IT. If you feel uncomfortable with that, sir, I understand, but then I'll have to call the NSA for a passphrase override, I'm really sorry—"

"All right, Hopkins. I wasn't aware of that regulation." He gave Gideon the passphrase and ID. Gideon jotted it down.

After a moment, with huge relief in his voice, Gideon said: "Whew. That reset did it, sir. Apparently, it was just a hung screen. No security breach. You're good to go."

"Excellent."

Gideon depressed the key and turned to the receptionist. "Sorry to bother you," he said, handing her the receiver. "Everything's straightened out." He walked briskly out of the building to the waiting car.

Thirty minutes later he was back in his motel room, stretched out on the bed, laptop connected to an unsecured computer in the bowels of the General Services Administration that he'd remotely hijacked. He had chosen to target the GSA—the vast government bureaucracy that handles supplies, equipment, procedures, and the like—because he knew it would be a relatively easy mark, and yet one still within the government security perimeter.

Hopkins had explained—unwittingly, of course—that the INSCOM archive could only send documents to previously authorized IP addresses, and unfortunately most of those were also inside classified perimeters...except for one: the National Security Archives at George Washington University. This private archive, the largest in the world outside the Library of Congress, collected vast amounts of government documents, including virtually everything being routinely declassified as part of the Mandatory Declassification Review: the government's program for declassifying documents under several laws requiring them to do so. A veritable Amazon of information flowed into this archive on a daily basis.

Via the GSA computer, Gideon sent an automated request to the INSCOM secure archive at George Washington via port 6151, directing that a PDF file of a certain classified document be transmitted out through the same port, authorized via General Shorthouse's passphrase, to be added to a routine dump of Cold War declassified documents headed for the National Security Archives daily batch files. The file was duly transmitted; it passed through the firewall at the sole authorized port, where the passphrase was examined and approved; and the document was subsequently routed to George Washington University and stored with millions of others in one of the archive databases.

Thus, Gideon had successfully arranged for the erroneous declassification of a classified document and hid it within a huge stream of data leaving the secure government perimeter. Now all that remained was to retrieve the document.

The next morning, at around eleven, a certain rumpled yet undeniably charming visiting professor by the name of Irwin

Beauchamp, dressed in tweeds, mismatched corduroys, beaten-up wing tips, and a knitted tie (thirty-two dollars; Salvation Army) entered the Gelman Library at George Washington University and requested a slew of documents. His identity was not yet in the system and he had lost his temporary library card, but a kindly secretary took pity on the scatterbrained fellow and allowed him access to the system. Half an hour later, Beauchamp departed the building with a slender manila folder under his arm.

Back in the motel, Gideon Crew spread out the papers from the folder with a trembling hand. The moment of truth had arrived—the truth that would make him either free, or merely more miserable.

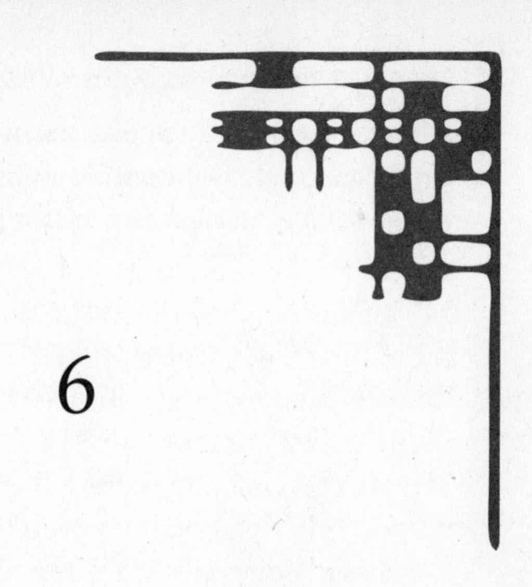

6

A Critique of the Thresher Discrete Logarithm Encryption Standard EVP-4: A Theoretical Back-Door Cryptanalysis Attack Strategy Using a Group of φ-Torsion Points of an Elliptic Curve in Characteristic φ.

Gideon Crew had studied plenty of advanced mathematics in college and, later, at MIT, but the math in this paper was still way over his head. Nevertheless, he understood enough to realize what he had in his hands was the smoking gun. This was the memo his father had written to critique Thresher, the memo his mother said had been destroyed. Yet it hadn't been. Most likely, the bastard responsible—believing it too difficult or risky to destroy the document outright—had stuck it into an archive he believed would never be declassified. After all, what American general in the era of the Berlin Wall would have believed the Cold War could ever end?

He continued reading, heart racing, until, finally, he came to the final paragraphs. They were written in the dry language of science-speak, but what they said was pure dynamite.

> In conclusion, it is the author's opinion that the proposed Thresher Encryption Standard EVP-4, based on the theory of discrete logarithms, is flawed. The author has demonstrated that there exists a potential class of algorithms, based on the theory of elliptic functions defined over the complex numbers, which can solve certain discrete logarithm functions in real-time computing parameters. While the author has been as yet unable to identify specific algorithms, he has demonstrated herein that it is possible to do so.
>
> The proposed Thresher standard is therefore vulnerable. If this standard is adopted, the author believes that, given the high quality of Soviet mathematical research, codes developed from this standard could be broken within a relatively short period of time.
>
> The author strongly recommends that Thresher Encryption Standard EVP-4 not be adopted in its current form.

That was it. Proof that his father had been framed. And then murdered. Gideon Crew already knew all about the man who had done it: Lieutenant General (ret.) Chamblee S. Tucker, currently CEO of Tucker and Associates, one of the high-profile defense industry lobbying firms on K Street. They represented many of the country's largest defense contractors, and Tucker had leveraged himself to the hilt in order to finance the firm. He was raking in huge bucks, but they managed to go right back out the door thanks to his extravagant lifestyle.

By itself, this document meant little. Gideon knew that anything could be counterfeited—or be claimed to have been counterfeited. The document wasn't an endpoint; it was a starting point for the little surprise he had planned for Chamblee S. Tucker.

Using the remote computer he had previously hijacked at the General Services Administration, Gideon stripped the document of its classification watermarks and sent it to a dozen large computer databases worldwide. Having thus secured the document from destruction, he sent an e-mail directly from his own computer to chamblee.tucker@tuckerandassociates.com with the document as an attachment. The covering e-mail read:

General Tucker:

I know what you did. I know why you did it. I know how you did it.

On Monday, I'm sending the attached file to various correspondents at the Post, Times, AP, and network news channels–with an explanation.

Have a nice weekend.

Gideon Crew

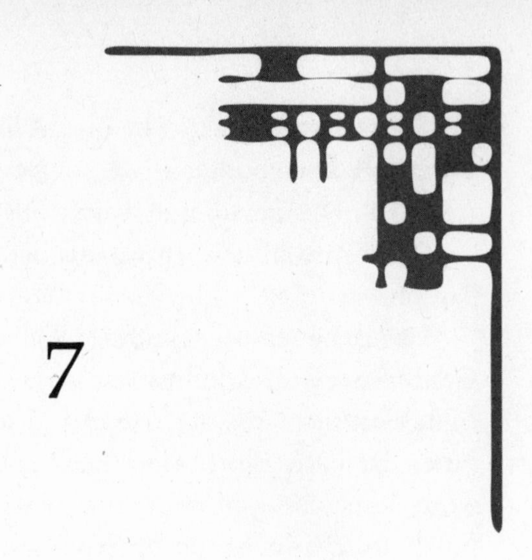

7

Chamblee S. Tucker sat behind an enormous desk in the oak-paneled study of his house in McLean, Virginia, thoughtfully hefting a four-pound Murano glass paperweight in one hand. At seventy years old, he was fit for his age and proud of it.

He shifted the paperweight to the other hand, pressed it a few times.

A knock came at the door.

"Come in." He set the paperweight down with exquisite care.

Charles Dajkovic entered the study. He was in civilian clothes, but his bearing and physique shouted *military*: whitewall haircut, massive neck, ramrod posture, steely blue eyes. A grizzled, close-clipped mustache was his only concession to civilian life.

"Good morning, General," he said.

"Good morning, Charlie. Sit down. Have a cup of coffee."

"Thank you." The man eased his frame into the proffered chair. Tucker indicated a silver salver on a nearby side table with coffeepot, sugar, cream, and cups. Dajkovic helped himself.

"Let's see now..." The general paused. "You've been with Tucker and Associates for, what, ten years?"

"That's about right, sir."

"But you and I, we go way back."

"Yes, sir."

"We have a history. Operation Urgent Fury. That's why I hired you: because the trust built on the battlefield is the finest trust that exists in this crazy world. Men who haven't fought together in battle don't even know the full meaning of the words *trust* and *loyalty*."

"That's very true, sir."

"And that is why I asked you to come to my home. Because I can trust you." The general paused. "Let me tell you a story. It has a moral but you'll have to figure it out on your own. I can't be too specific—you'll see why."

A nod.

"Ever hear of John Walker Lindh?"

"The 'American Taliban'?"

"Right. And Adam Gadahn?"

"Isn't he the guy who joined al-Qaeda and makes videos for Bin Laden?"

"Right you are. I've come into possession of some highly classified information regarding a third American convert—only this one is far more dangerous." Tucker paused again. "This fellow's father worked for INSCOM when I was there. Turned out the man was a traitor, passing information to the Soviets. You may remember the aftermath: he took a hostage over at the old HQ. Our snipers took him down. His kid witnessed it."

"I recall that incident."

"What you don't know, because it's also classified, is that he was responsible for exposing twenty-six operatives. They were swept up in one night and tortured to death in Soviet gulags."

Dajkovic said nothing. He set down the now empty coffee cup.

"That's just background. You can imagine what it was like to grow up in that kind of environment... Anyway, just like Lindh and Gadahn, this fellow converted. Only he didn't do anything stupid like go off to a training camp in Afghanistan. He went on to MIT and now he works at Los Alamos. Name's Gideon Crew. C-R-E-W."

"How'd he get security clearance?"

"Powerful friends in high places. He's made no mistakes. He's good, he's totally convincing, he's sincere. And he's al-Qaeda's pipeline to getting the Bomb."

Dajkovic shifted in his seat. "Why don't they arrest him? Or at least cancel his security clearance?"

Tucker leaned forward. "Charlie, are you really that naive?"

"I hope not, sir."

"What do you *think's* going on in this country? Just like we were infiltrated by the Reds during the Cold War, now we're being infiltrated by jihadists. *American* jihadists."

"I understand."

"Now, with the kind of high-level protection this fellow has, he's untouchable. There's nothing concrete, of course. This information fell into my lap by accident, and I'm not one to shy away from defending my country. Imagine what al-Qaeda would do with a nuke."

"It's unthinkable."

"Charlie, I know you. You were the top Special Forces guy in my command. You've got skills no one else has. The question is: how much do you love your country?"

The man seemed to swell in his chair. "You don't ever need to ask me that question, sir."

"I know that. That's why you're the only one I'd dare share this information with. All I can say is, sometimes a man has to take his patriotic duty into his own hands."

Dajkovic remained silent. A faint flush had suffused his weathered face.

"Last time I checked, the fellow was in DC. Staying at the Luna Motel out in Dodge Park. We believe he's going to make contact with a fellow jihadist. He may be getting ready to pass documents."

Dajkovic said nothing.

"I don't know how long he's going to be there, or where he's going next. He's got a computer with him, of course, which is as dangerous as he is. Do you understand what I'm saying?"

"I understand *completely*. And I thank you for giving me this opportunity."

"Charlie, thank you. From the bottom of my heart." He grasped Dajkovic's hand and then, in a spontaneous display of emotion, pulled him in and gave him a crushing hug.

As the fellow left, Tucker thought he noted tears in his eyes.

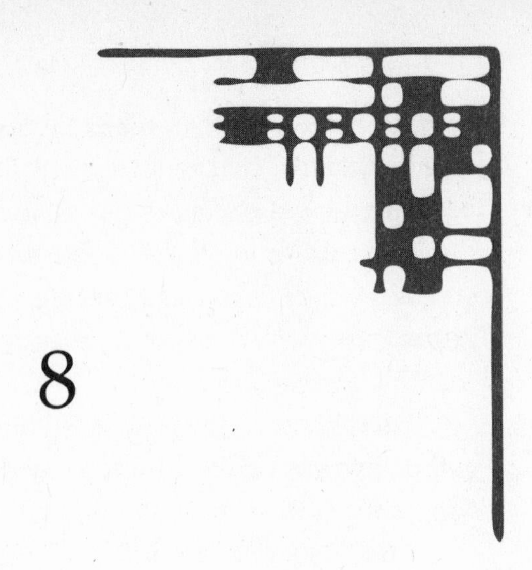

8

Skyline Drive swept around the curve of Stormtower Ridge, and the Manahoac Lodge and Resort came into view, a collection of condominiums and A-frames surrounding a hotel and golf course at the base of Stormtower Mountain. The Blue Ridge Mountains, layer after layer, stretched off behind into the hazy distance.

Dajkovic eased his foot off the pedal as the car approached the entrance to the resort, and he came to a stop at the gate.

"Just checking in," he said, and was waved through.

Crew had left this forwarding address at the Luna Motel, written it down "in case someone needed to find him," according to the clerk. He was staying at this resort now—isolated, long drive to get to, no doubt with security cameras up the wazoo. So either, as Tucker had said, Crew was getting ready to meet a fellow operative... or this was a trap. The latter seemed more likely. But a trap for whom? To what purpose?

Dajkovic swung into the entry drive and parked in front, giving the valet a five-dollar bill. "I'll be back in five minutes."

"Oh yes," said the lady at the front desk in response to his query. "Gideon Crew checked in this morning." She clicked away at a keyboard. "Left word for you he was climbing Stormtower Mountain—"

"For me?"

"Well," she said, "the message he left says a man would be coming to meet with him, and we were to tell him where he'd gone."

"I see."

"It says here he's climbing Stormtower by the Sawmill Trail, expects to be back by six."

"How long is the climb?"

"About two hours each way." She looked at him with a smile, her eyes running up and down his physique. "For you, probably less."

Dajkovic checked the time. Two o'clock. "He must have just left."

"Yes. The message was left at the front desk...just twenty minutes ago."

"Do you have a map of the mountain?"

"Of course."

She produced a map—an excellent topographic one, with the trails clearly marked. Dajkovic took it back to his car and climbed in. The Sawmill trailhead was down the road, and the map showed it to be a winding path going up the ridge of the mountain, apparently following an old fire road.

It was entirely possible Crew had left the directions so his contact could find him. Yet it seemed unlikely. No one involved in espionage would be so ham-handed as to leave such a trail. Yes, it seemed more likely that this was a trap. Not a trap for him, specifically, but for anyone who might be pursuing Crew. And if so, then Crew would be on the mountain—waiting along the Sawmill Trail to ambush anyone coming up behind him.

He examined the map. A much quicker, more direct way to

the summit led straight up the main ski lift cut, on the back side of the mountain.

Driving through the resort and past the golf course, Dajkovic came to the parking lot for the ski area. He got out and opened the trunk, removing a gun case. Back inside the car, he unlocked the case and removed an M1911 Colt and a shoulder holster, donned the holster, tucked the loaded weapon into it, and pulled on a windbreaker. A fixed-blade knife went into his belt and a smaller one into his boot, and a Beretta .22 was slipped in his trouser pocket. Into a small backpack he threw some extra ammunition, binoculars, and two bottles of water.

Once again he examined the map. If Crew was planning an ambush, there were a couple of obvious places for it where the Sawmill Trail passed through an area of exposed knobs.

As he stared at the map, he became convinced this was where the ambush would take place.

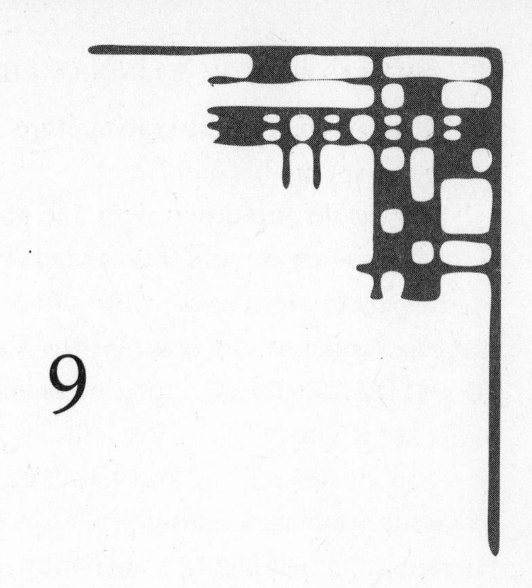

9

Dajkovic started up the ski lift cut, moving fast. It was half a mile to the top, and unrelievedly steep, but he was in peak physical condition and could make it in ten minutes; then, cresting the mountain, he would head down the Sawmill Trail, bushwhack to the summit of a secondary peak he'd identified on the map, an ideal place from which to surveil the area of exposed knobs, locate the ambusher—and then ambush him.

Five minutes later, halfway up the slope, a maintenance hut for the ski lift, shuttered for the summer, came into view. Dajkovic churned up the slope, detouring around it. As he moved past the hut he heard a tremendous *boom!* and suddenly felt a violent blow to his upper back—which, with his upward momentum, pitched him forward onto the slope and knocked the wind from him.

As he struggled for his .45, fighting the pain in his back and gasping for breath, he felt a boot press down on his neck and the warm snout of a weapon touch his head.

"Hands spread-eagled, please."

He stopped, his mind racing, trying to think through the pain. Slowly he spread his hands.

"I knocked you down with a load of rubber," came the voice, "but the rest are double-ought buck."

The barrel remained on the back of his head while the person—he had no doubt it was Crew—searched him, removing the .45 and the .22 and the knife in his belt. He did not find the knife in Dajkovic's boot.

"Roll over, keeping your hands in sight."

With a wince, Dajkovic rolled over onto the dirt of the trail. He found himself facing a tall, lanky man in his mid-thirties, with straight black hair, a long nose, and intense, brilliant blue eyes. He was gripping a Remington 12-gauge with a practiced hand.

"Fine afternoon for a walk, isn't it, Sergeant? Name's Gideon Crew."

Dajkovic stared.

"That's right. I know a fair amount about you, Dajkovic. What sort of story did Tucker tell you to get you out here, looking for me?"

Dajkovic said nothing, his mind still working furiously. He was mortified the man had gotten the drop on him. But all was not lost—he still had the knife. And though Crew was a good fifteen years younger than he was, the fellow looked thin, weak—not a good physical specimen.

Crew gave him a smile. "Actually, I can probably guess what the good general told you."

Dajkovic didn't answer.

"It must have been quite a story, to turn you into a hired assassin like this. You're not normally the kind of person to shoot someone in the back. He probably told you I was a traitor. In league with al-Qaeda, maybe—that would be the treason du jour, I guess. No doubt I'm abusing my position at Los Alamos, betraying my country. That would push all your buttons."

Dajkovic stared at him. How the hell did he know that?

"He probably told you about my traitor father, what he did getting those agents killed." He laughed mirthlessly. "Maybe he said traitorousness was a family tradition."

Dajkovic's mind was clearing. He had fucked up, but all he had to do was get his hands—one hand—on that knife in his boot and Crew was a dead man, even if he did manage to get off a shotgun blast.

"May I sit up?" Dajkovic asked.

"Slow and easy."

Dajkovic sat up. The pain was mostly gone. Broken ribs were like that. Stopped hurting for a while and then the pain came back, twice as bad. He flushed at the thought of this weenie knocking him down with a load of rubber.

"I've got a question for you," Crew said. "How do you know old man Tucker told you the truth?"

Dajkovic didn't answer. He noticed for the first time that Crew's right hand was missing the last joint of the ring finger.

"I was pretty sure Tucker would send an underling after me, because he's not the kind to put himself on the front lines. I knew it would be someone he trusted, who'd served under him. I looked over his employees and figured you'd be the one. You led a marine SOF team in the Grenada invasion, securing the American medical school in advance of the main landing. Did a good job, too—not one student was hurt."

Dajkovic remained poker-faced, waiting his opportunity.

"So: is your mind made up about me? Or are you willing to open your ears to a few facts that might not quite jibe with what General Tucker told you?"

He didn't respond. He wasn't going to give the scumbag an inch of satisfaction.

"Since I'm the one with the loaded shotgun, I guess you're going to have to listen anyway. You like fairy tales, Sergeant? Here's one for you, only nobody lives happily ever after. Once upon a time, back in August of 1988, there was a twelve-year-old boy..."

Dajkovic listened to the story. He knew it was bullshit, but he paid attention because a good soldier knew the value of information—even false information.

It only took five minutes. It was a pretty good story, well told. These types of people were always amazing liars.

When he was done, Crew pulled an envelope out of his pocket and tossed it at Dajkovic's feet. "There's the memo my father wrote Tucker. The reason why he was murdered."

Dajkovic didn't bother to pick it up. For a moment, the two just remained where they were, staring at each other.

"Well," said Crew at last, shaking his head. "I guess I was naive to think I could convince an old soldier like you that his beloved commanding officer is a liar, coward, and murderer." He thought for a moment. "I want you to bring Tucker a message. From me."

Dajkovic remained grim-jawed.

"Tell him I'm going to destroy him like he destroyed my father. It's going to be nice and slow. The memo I've released to the press will trigger an investigation. No doubt a news organization will put in a FOIA request to confirm the document is genuine. As the truth comes out, bit by bit, Tucker's integrity will be impeached. In his line of work, even though everyone is corrupt, the *appearance* of integrity is pure gold. He'll see his business dry up. Poor Tucker: did you know he's leveraged up the wazoo? The mortgage on his McLean McMansion is swimming with the fishes. He owes a shitload on that tacky Pocono golf-club condo, the apartment in New York, and the yacht on the Jersey Shore." Crew shook his head sadly. "Know what he calls that yacht? *Urgent Fury.* Funny, isn't it? Tucker's one weak-ass moment of glory. The Poconos, McLean, the Jersey Shore... the general can't be accused of good taste, can he? Of course, the Upper East Side girlfriend was a step in the right direction, but she's a hungry little bird, her beak open day and night. He hasn't saved his money like a good boy should. But bankruptcy will only be the beginning, because the investigation will eventually show everything I just told you: that he framed my father and was himself responsible for the death of those twenty-six agents. He's going to end up in prison."

Dajkovic found Crew staring at him. Again, he said nothing. He could see Crew was getting frustrated at his lack of reaction.

"Let me ask you another question," Crew said finally.

Dajkovic waited. His chance was coming—he felt it in his bones.

"Did you actually see Tucker under fire? What do you know of the guy as a soldier? I'll bet Tucker didn't set foot on land until the beachhead was totally secure."

Dajkovic couldn't help but remember how disappointed he'd been that Tucker seemed to be the very last soldier onto Grenada. But he was a general, one of the top commanders, and that was army protocol.

"Fuck it," said Crew, taking a step backward. "It was a mistake to expect you might actually be capable of *thinking*. You got the message: go deliver it."

"May I get up?"

"By all means, get your sorry ass up and out of here."

The moment had arrived. Dajkovic placed his hands on the ground and began to rise to his feet; as his hands passed his boots he slipped out the knife and in one smooth motion threw it, aiming at Crew's heart.

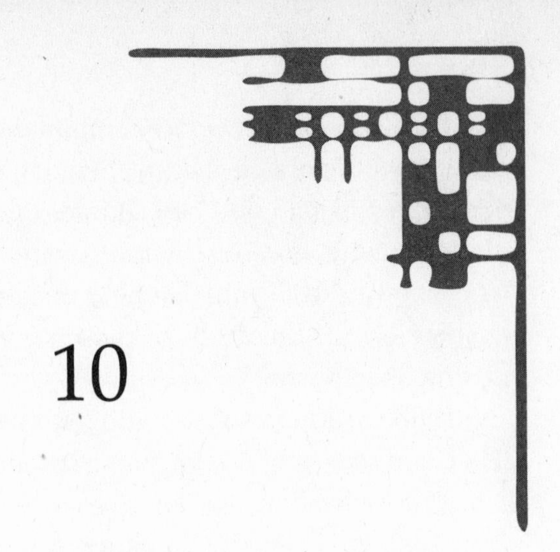

10

Gideon Crew saw the quick movement, the flash of steel; he threw himself sideways but it was too late. The knife slammed into his shoulder, burying itself almost to the hilt. As he fell back, trying to bring the shotgun up, Dajkovic leapt for him, ramming him backward with immense power and wrenching the shotgun from his hands. He heard a crack as his own head caromed off a stone.

For a moment, all went black. Then the world came back to him. Gideon was sprawled on the ground, staring into the barrel of his own shotgun. He could feel the knife in his shoulder, searing hot, the blood seeping out. He reached to pull it out.

"No." Dajkovic stepped back. "Keep your hands away from your body. And say your prayers."

"Don't do this," Gideon said.

Dajkovic racked a shell into the chamber.

He fought to think straight, to clear the fogginess from his head. "What do you know about me besides what Tucker said? Christ, can't you think for yourself?"

Dajkovic raised the gun and looked him in the eye. Gideon felt desperation take hold: if he died, his father would never be vindicated, and Tucker would never get his comeuppance.

"You're not a killer," he said.

"For you, I'm going to make an exception." Dajkovic's finger tightened on the trigger.

"If you kill me, at least do me this one favor: take that envelope. Look into the story I told you. *Follow the evidence*. And then do what you think is right."

Dajkovic paused.

"Find someone who was there in 1988. You'll see. My father was shot down in cold blood—with his hands up. And that memo—it's real. You'll discover that, too, eventually. Because if you take my life you'll also have to take on the responsibility of finding the truth."

He found Dajkovic peering at him with a strange intensity. He wasn't pulling the trigger—yet.

"Does it sound likely to you? Not that a guy with a top-secret security clearance at Los Alamos would be passing secrets to al-Qaeda—that's possible. No—that General Tucker would know about it? And ask *you* to take care of it? Does that really make sense?"

"You have powerful friends."

"Powerful friends? Like who?"

Slowly, Dajkovic lowered the shotgun. His face was slick with sweat, and he was pale. He looked almost sick. Then—kneeling abruptly—he reached for the knife in Gideon's shoulder.

Gideon turned away. He'd failed. Dajkovic would cut his throat and leave his body in the dirt.

Grasping the knife, Dajkovic pulled it from the wound.

Gideon cried out. It felt as if his flesh had just been seared by a hot iron.

But Dajkovic didn't raise the knife to strike again. Instead, he removed his own shirt and used the knife to cut it into strips. Gideon, head swimming in mingled pain and surprise, watched as the man used the strips to bind his shoulder.

"Hold that down," Dajkovic said.

Gideon pressed the strips against the wound.

"We'd better get you to a hospital."

Gideon nodded, breathing hard, gripping the bandaged shoulder. He could feel the blood soaking through already. He tried to overcome the searing pain, worse now that the knife was gone.

Dajkovic helped Gideon to his feet. "Can you walk?"

"It's all downhill from here," Gideon gasped.

Dajkovic half carried, half dragged him down the steep slope. In fifteen minutes, they were back at Dajkovic's car. He helped Gideon into the passenger seat, blood smearing over the leather.

"Is this a rental?" Gideon asked, looking at the car. "You're going to lose your deposit."

The old soldier shut the door, came around and got in the driver's seat, started the car. His face was pale, set, grim.

"So you believe me?" Gideon asked.

"You might say that."

"What changed your mind?"

"Easy," Dajkovic said, backing out of the parking spot. He threw the car into gear. "When a man realizes he's going to die, everything is stripped down to essentials. Purified. No more bullshit. I've seen it in battle. And I saw it in your eyes, when you believed I was going to kill you. I saw your hatred, your desperation—and your sincerity. I knew then you were telling the truth. Which means..." He hesitated, gunned the engine, the rubber squealing on the macadam, the car shooting forward.

"Which means," he resumed, "Tucker lied to me. And that makes me angry."

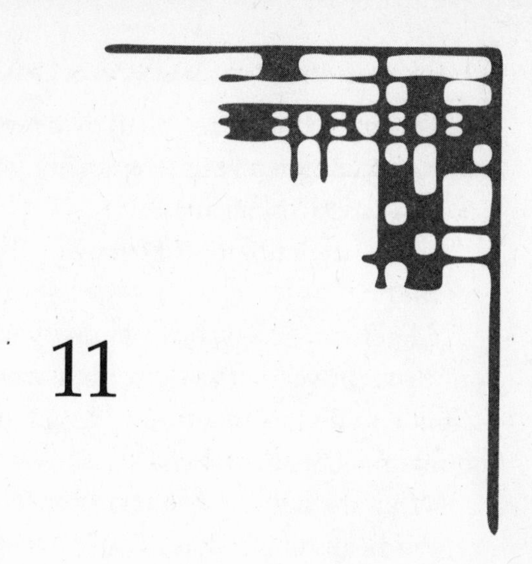

11

What the hell's this?"

Tucker rose quickly as Dajkovic pushed Gideon into the study, hands cuffed. The general stepped around from behind his desk, pulling a .45 and training it on Gideon.

For the first time, Gideon came face-to-face with his nemesis. In person, Chamblee Tucker looked even more well fed and well watered than in the dozens of pictures he had studied over the years. His neck bulged slightly over a starched collar; his cheeks were so closely shaved that they shone; his hair was trimmed to crew-cut perfection. His skin bore a spiderweb of veins marking the face of a drinking man. His outfit was pure Washington: power tie, blue suit, four-hundred-dollar shoes. The soulless study was of a piece with the man—wood paneling, interior-decorator antiques, Persian rugs, power wall plastered with photos and citations.

"Are you crazy?" Tucker said. "I didn't tell you to bring him here. My God, Dajkovic, I thought you could handle this on your own!"

"I brought him here," Dajkovic replied, "because he told me something completely different from what you said. And damned if it didn't sound plausible."

Tucker stared hard at Dajkovic. "You'd believe this scumbag over me?"

"General, I just want to know what's going on. I've covered your back for years. I've done your work, clean and dirty, and I'll continue to do it. But a funny thing happened on the side of that mountain—I began to believe this guy."

"What the hell are you trying to tell me?"

"I'm beginning to have doubts, and the minute that happens, I'm no longer an effective soldier. You want me to get rid of this man? No problem. I'll follow your orders. But I need to know what's going on before I put a bullet into his head."

Tucker stared at him for a long time, then broke eye contact and passed a hand over his bristly scalp. He stepped over to a well-polished cabinet, slid open a drawer, pulled out a glass and a bottle of Paddy, slammed them on the mahogany, and poured himself a few fingers. He swallowed it in one gulp. Then he glanced back at Dajkovic.

"Anyone see you come in?"

"No, sir."

Tucker looked from Dajkovic to Gideon and back again. "What did he tell you, exactly?"

"That his father wasn't a traitor. And that he isn't a terrorist, or in league with them."

Tucker carefully set down his glass. "All right. Truth is, I did tell you a bit of a story. His father didn't pass secrets to the Soviets."

"What did he do?"

"You got to remember, Dajkovic, we were in a war, a Cold War. In war, ugly things happen. You get collateral damage. We had a problem: an error was made. We rolled out a flawed code and some operatives died as a result. If that had come out, it would have taken down the entire cryptology section at a time when we desperately needed a new set of codes. His father had to be sacrificed for the greater good. You remember what it was like: them or us."

Dajkovic nodded. "Yes, sir. I remember."

"So now this fellow here, Gideon, more than twenty years later, is threatening me. Blackmailing me. Trying to tear down everything we've built, to destroy not only my reputation but the reputation of an entire group of dedicated, patriotic Americans. That's why he has to be eliminated. You understand?"

"I get it," said Dajkovic, with a slow smile. "You don't have to work around the facts to get me to do something for you. I'm with you one hundred percent, whatever you need."

"Are we clear what needs to be done?"

"Absolutely."

Gideon said nothing and waited.

Tucker glanced down at the bottle and glass. "Drink on it?"

"No, thanks."

Tucker poured himself another, slugged it back. "Trust me that this is for the best. You're earning my eternal gratitude. Take him out through the garage and make sure no one sees you."

Dajkovic nodded and gave Gideon a little push. "Let's go."

Gideon turned and headed toward the door, Dajkovic following. They passed into the front hall and headed toward the kitchen, walked to the back where a door evidently led out into the garage.

Gideon placed one handcuffed hand on the knob, realized it was locked. At the same moment he saw a quick movement out of the corner of his eye and instantly realized what was happening. Throwing himself sideways, he pitched himself into Dajkovic's shoulder just as Tucker's gun went off, but the round still caught Dajkovic in the back, slamming him forward into the closed door, the gun knocked from his hand. He sank to the floor with a grunt.

As Gideon spun and dove, he caught a glimpse of Tucker in the kitchen doorway, isosceles stance, pistol in hand. The gun barked again, this time aimed at him, blasting a hole in the Mexican tiled floor mere inches from his face. Gideon leapt to his feet, making a feint toward the general as if to charge.

The third shot came just as he made a ninety-degree lunge, throwing himself atop Dajkovic and grasping the .45 that lay against the far wall. He swung it around just as a fourth shot whistled past his ear. He raised the .45 but Tucker ducked back through the doorway.

Wasting no time, Gideon seized Dajkovic's shirt and pulled him to cover behind the washing machine, then took cover there himself. He thought furiously. What would Tucker do? He couldn't let them live; couldn't call the cops; couldn't run.

This was a fight to the finish.

He peered out at the empty doorway where Tucker had been. It led into the dining room, large and dark. Tucker was waiting for them there.

He heard a cough; Dajkovic suddenly grunted and rose. Almost simultaneously, rapid shots sounded from the doorway; Gideon ducked and two more rounds punched through the washing machine, water suddenly spraying from a cut hose.

Gideon got off a shot but Tucker had already disappeared back into the dining room.

"Give me the sidearm," Dajkovic gasped, but without waiting for a reply his massive fist closed over the .45 in Gideon's hand and took it. He struggled to rise.

"Wait," said Gideon. "I'll run across the room to the kitchen table, there. He'll move to the doorway to get off a shot at me. That'll put him right behind the door frame. Fire through the wall."

Dajkovic nodded. Gideon took a deep breath, then jumped from behind the washing machine and darted over behind the table, realizing too late how badly exposed he really was.

With an inarticulate roar Dajkovic staggered forward like a wounded bear. Blood suddenly came streaming from his mouth, his eyes wild, and he charged the doorway, firing through the wall to the right of the door. He pulled up short in the middle of the kitchen, swaying, still roaring, emptying the magazine into the wall.

For a moment, there was no movement from the darkened dining room. Then the heavy figure of Tucker, spurting blood from half a dozen gunshot wounds, tumbled across the threshold, landing on the floor like a carcass of meat. And only then did Dajkovic sag to his knees, coughing, and roll to one side.

Gideon scrambled to his feet and kicked Tucker's handgun away from his inert form. Then he knelt over Dajkovic. Fumbling in the man's pockets, he fished out the handcuff key and unlocked the cuffs. "Take it easy," he said, examining the wound. The bullet had gone through his back, low, evidently piercing a lung but, he hoped, missing other vital organs.

Suddenly and unexpectedly, Dajkovic smiled, bloody lips stretching into a ghastly grimace. "You get it on tape?"

Gideon patted his pocket. "All of it."

"Great," Dajkovic gasped. He passed out with a smile on his face.

Gideon snapped off the digital recorder. He felt faint and the room began to spin as he heard sirens in the distance.

GIDEON CREW

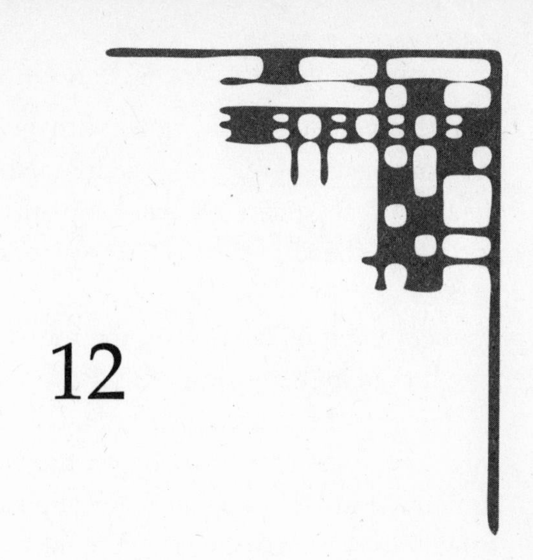

12

Gideon Crew picked his way down the steep slope toward Chihuahueños Creek, following an old pack trail. He could see the deep pockets and holes of the stream as it wound its way through the meadow at the bottom. At over nine thousand feet, the June air was crisp and fresh, the azure sky piled with cumulus clouds.

There would be a thunderstorm later, he thought.

His right shoulder was still a little painful, but the stitches had come out the week before and he could move his arm freely now. The knife wound had been deep but clean. The slight concussion he'd suffered in the tussle with Dajkovic had caused no further problems.

He came out into the sunlight and paused. It had been a month since he'd fished this little valley—just before going to Washington. He had achieved—spectacularly—the singular, overriding, and obsessive goal of his life. It was over. Tucker dead, disgraced; his father vindicated.

For the past decade, he had been so fixated on this one thing that he'd neglected everything else—friends, a relationship, career advancement. And now, with his goal realized, he felt an immense sense of release. Freedom. Now he could start living his life like a real person. He was only thirty-three; he had almost his entire life ahead of him. There were so many things he wanted to do.

Beginning with catching the monster cutthroat trout he was sure lurked in the big logjam pool in the creek below.

He breathed deeply the scent of grass and pine, trying to forget the past and to focus on the future. He looked around, drinking it in. This was his favorite place on planet earth. No one fished this stretch of creek except him: it lay far from a forest road and required a long and arduous hike. The wild cutthroats lying in the deep pools and under the banks were skittish and shy and hard to catch; a single false move, the shadow of a fly rod on the water, the heavy tread of a foot on the boggy grass, could ruin a pool for the rest of the day.

Gideon sat down cross-legged in the grass, far from the stream, shucked off his pack, and set down the fly-rod case. Unscrewing its end, he slid out the bamboo pieces and fitted them together, attached the reel, threaded the line through the loops, then sorted through his case for the right fly. Grasshoppers were scarce in the field, but there were enough that a few might have hopped into the water and gotten eaten. They'd make a credible lure. He selected a small green-and-yellow grasshopper fly from his case and tied it on. Leaving his pack and gear at the edge of the meadow, he crept across the grass, taking care to place his feet as lightly as possible. As he approached the first big pool, he crouched and twitched the rod, playing out a little line; and then, with a flick of the wrist, he dunked the fly lightly into the pool.

Almost instantly there was a heavy swirl of water, a strike.

Leaping to his feet, he raised the tip, putting tension on the line, and fought the fish. It was a big one, and a fighter, and it tried to run for a tangle of roots under the bank; but raising the tip farther, he used his thumb to increase the drag on the line, keeping the fish in the center of the pool. He slacked the line as the trout flashed for the surface, leaping and shaking its head, drops of water scintillating in the sun. Its muscular, brilliantly colored body caught the light, the red slash under its gills looking very much like blood; and it fell back and tried again to run. Again he increased the drag, but the fish was determined to get into the roots and fought him to the point where the leader was straining almost to the breaking point...

"Dr. Gideon Crew?"

Gideon jerked his head around, startled, and released the line. The fish took the slack and ran for the tangle of sunken roots; Gideon tried to recover and tighten the tension, but it was too late. The leader got wrapped around a root, the trout broke free, and the tip popped up, the line slack.

Overwhelmed with annoyance, he stared hard at the man standing twenty feet behind him, dressed in pressed khakis, brand-new hiking boots, a checked shirt, and sunglasses. He was an older man, in his fifties, with salt-and-pepper hair, olive skin, and a face that looked very tired. And a bit scarred, as if he'd survived a fire. And yet, for all its weariness, the face was also very much alive.

With a muttered curse, Gideon reeled in the slack line, examined the fluttering leader. Then he looked up again at the man, who was waiting patiently, a faint smile on his lips. "Who the hell are you?"

The man stepped forward and held out a hand. "Manuel Garza."

Gideon looked at it with a frown until the man withdrew it. "Excuse me for interrupting you during your time off," Garza said. "But it couldn't wait." He continued to smile, remaining unnaturally composed. The man's whole being seemed to radiate calmness and control. Gideon found it irritating.

"How did you find me?"

"An educated guess. We know this is where you sometimes fish. Also, we fixed a position on you when you last used your cell phone."

"So you're Big Brother. What's this all about?"

"I'm not able to discuss that with you at this time."

Could this be some blowback from the business with Tucker? But no: that was all over and done with, an unqualified success, the official questions all answered, he and his family's name cleared. Gideon looked pointedly at his watch. "Cocktail hour is at six in my cabin. I'm sure you know where that is. See you then. I'm busy fishing."

"I'm sorry, Dr. Crew, but, like I said, it can't wait."

"It? What's *it*?"

"A job."

"Thanks, but I've got a job. Up at Los Alamos. You know—the place where they design all the nice nuclear bombs?"

"Frankly, this job is more exciting and it pays a great deal more. A hundred thousand dollars for a week's work. A job for which you are uniquely suited, which will benefit our country—and God knows you need the money. All those credit card debts..." Garza shook his head.

"Hey, who doesn't have maxed-out credit cards? This is the land of the free, right?" Gideon hesitated. That was a lot of money. He needed money—bad. "So what'll I be doing in this job of yours?"

"Again, I can't tell you—yet. The helicopter is waiting up top—to take you to the Albuquerque airport, and from there by private jet to your assignment."

"You came to get me in a *chopper*? Sink me." Gideon vaguely remembered hearing the chopper. He'd ignored it; the Jemez Mountains, being remote, were often used for flight training from Kirtland AFB.

"We're in a hurry."

"I'll say. Who do you represent?"

"Can't tell you that, either." Another smile and a gesture with his arm, palm extended, toward the pack trail to the top of the mesa. "Shall we?"

"My mother told me never to take chopper rides with strangers."

"Dr. Crew, I'll repeat what I said earlier: you will find this job to be interesting, challenging, and remunerative. Won't you at least come with me to our company headquarters to hear the details?"

"Where?"

"In New York City."

Gideon stared at him, then shook his head and snorted. A hundred thousand would get him well started on the many plans and ideas he'd been working up for his new life.

"Does it involve any illegality?"

"Absolutely not."

"What the hell. I haven't been to the Big Apple in a while. All right, lead the way, Manuel."

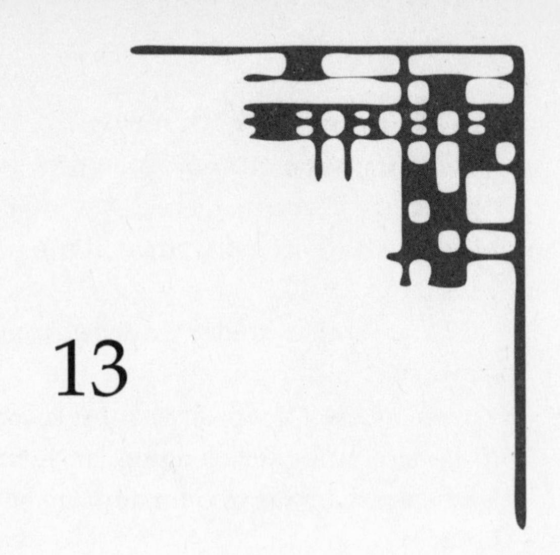

13

Six hours later, the sun was setting over the Hudson River as the limousine pulled into Little West 12th Street, in the old Meatpacking District of Manhattan. The area had changed dramatically from what Gideon remembered during his graduate school days, when he'd come down from Boston for some occasional R&R: the old brick warehouses and covered walkways, with their chains and meat hooks, had been transformed into ultra-hip clothing stores and restaurants, slick high-rise condos and trendy hotels, the streets crowded with people too cool to be real.

The limousine bumped down the refurbished street—bone-jarring nineteenth-century cobblestones re-exposed—and came to a halt at a nondescript building, one of the few unrenovated structures within view.

"We're here," said Garza.

They stepped onto the sidewalk. It was much warmer in New York than in New Mexico. Gideon stared suspiciously at the building's only entrance, a set of metal double doors on a loading dock plastered with old posters and graffiti. The building was large and imposing, some twelve stories tall. Near the top of the façade, he could just make out a painted legend: PRICE & PRICE PORK PACKING INC. Above it, the grimy brickwork gave way to glass and chrome; he wondered if a modern penthouse had been built atop the old structure.

He followed Garza up a set of concrete steps on one side of the dock. As they approached, the loading doors slid open on well-oiled hinges. Gideon followed Garza down a dim corridor to another set of doors, much newer, of stainless steel. Security keypads and a retinal scanner were set into the wall beside them. Garza put his briefcase on the floor and leaned his face into the scanner; the steel doors parted noiselessly.

"Where's Maxwell Smart?" said Gideon, in full wiseass mode, looking around. Garza looked at him, no smile this time, but did not reply.

Beyond lay a vast, cavernous room, an open shell four stories high, illuminated by seemingly hundreds of halogen lights. Metal catwalks ran around the upper levels. The floor—as big as a football field—was covered with rows of large steel tables. On them rested a confusing welter of disparate items: half-dissected jet engines; highly complex 3-D models of urban areas; a scale model of what appeared to be a nuclear plant undergoing a terrorist attack by airplane. In a near corner was an especially large table, displaying what looked like a large, cutaway section of the seabed, showing its geological strata. Technicians in white coats moved between the tables, making notes on handheld PDAs or conferring in hushed whispers.

"This is corporate headquarters?" Gideon asked, looking around. "Looks more like Industrial Light and Magic."

"I suppose you could call it magic," Garza said as he led the way. "Of the manufactured variety."

Gideon followed him past table after table. On one was a painstaking re-creation of Port au Prince, both before and after the earthquake, tiny flags on the latter marking patterns of devastation. On another table was a huge scale model of a space facility, all tubes and cylinders and solar panels.

"I recognize that," Gideon said. "It's the International Space Station."

Garza nodded. "As it looked before leaving orbit."

Gideon looked at him. "Leaving orbit?"

"To assume its secondary role."

"Its *what*? You must be joking."

Garza flashed him a mirthless smile. "If I thought you'd take me seriously, I wouldn't have told you."

"What in the world do you do here?"

"Engineering and more engineering, that's all."

Reaching the far wall, they rode an open-cage elevator up to the fourth-floor catwalk, then passed through a door that led to a maze of white corridors. Ultimately, they reached a low-ceilinged, windowless conference room. It was small and spartan in its lack of decor. A table of exotic, polished wood dominated the space, and there were no paintings or prints on the white walls. Gideon tried to think of a suitable crack, but nothing came immediately to mind. Besides, he realized it would be wasted on Garza, who seemed immune to his rapier-like wit.

At the head of the table sat a man in a wheelchair. He was perhaps the most extraordinary-looking human being Gideon had ever seen. Closely cropped brown hair, shot through with silver, covered a large head. Below a deep brow gleamed a single fierce gray eye which was fixed on him; the other eye was covered with a black silk patch, like a pirate's. A jagged, livid scar lanced down the right side of the man's face, starting at his hairline and running through the covered eye, continuing all the way to his jaw and disappearing under the collar of his crisp blue shirt. A black, pin-striped suit completed the sinister picture.

"Dr. Crew," the figure said, his face breaking into a faint smile that did nothing to soften its hardness. "Thank you for coming all this way. Please sit down."

Garza remained standing in the background as Gideon took a seat.

"What?" Gideon said, looking around. "No coffee or Fiji water?"

"My name is Eli Glinn," said the figure, ignoring this. "Welcome to Effective Engineering Solutions, Incorporated."

"Sorry in advance for not bringing my résumé. Your friend Garza was in a hurry."

"I don't like to waste time. So if you'd be kind enough to listen, I'll brief you on the assignment."

"Does it have anything to do with that Disney World downstairs? Plane crashes, natural disasters—you call that engineering?"

Glinn gazed at him mildly. "Among other things, EES specializes in the discipline of failure analysis."

"Failure analysis?"

"Understanding how and why things fail—whether it be an assassination, an aviation accident, or a terrorist attack—is a critical component to solving engineering problems. Failure analysis is the other face of engineering."

"I'm not sure I understand."

"Engineering is the science of figuring out how to do or make something. But that's only half the challenge. The other half is analyzing all possible modes of failure—in order to *avoid* them. EES does both. We solve very difficult engineering problems. And we dissect failures. In both these tasks, we have never failed. *Ever.* With one minor exception, which we're still working on." He flicked his hand as if waving away a bothersome fly. "Those two things, engineering and failure analysis, form our primary business. Our visible business. But they are also our *cover*. Because behind our public façade, we use these same facilities to carry out, from time to time, highly unusual and confidential projects for special clients. *Very* special clients. We need you for one of these projects."

"Why me?"

"I'll get to that in a moment. First, the details. A Chinese scientist is on his way to the United States. We believe the man is carrying the plans for a new, high-technology weapon. We're not certain, but we have reason to hope he may be defecting."

Gideon was about to make a sarcastic quip, but the look in Glinn's eye deterred him.

"For two years," Glinn went on, "US intelligence has been aware of a mysterious project going on in an underground compound inside the Lop Nor nuclear testing zone in far western China. Staggering amounts of money and scientific talent have been devoted to this effort. The CIA believes they're developing a new weapon, a kind of Chinese Manhattan Project, something that would change the balance of power completely."

Gideon stared. "More destructive than the H-Bomb?"

"Yes, that's the information we have. But now, one of the project's chief scientists seems to have stolen the plans and is on his way to the United States. Why? We don't know. We hope he might be defecting to the US with the plans for that weapon, but we can't be sure."

"Why would he do that?"

"Apparently, he was the victim of a successful honey trap at a scientific convention in Hong Kong."

"Honey trap?"

"Surely you've heard the term. An attractive woman is employed to get the target in a compromising position, pictures are taken, pressure is then applied... But this honey trap went awry and triggered the man's panicked flight from China."

"Right. I get it. So when is this scientist supposed to arrive?"

"He's on his way now. The man's on a Japan Airlines flight to

New York from Hong Kong. He changed planes in Tokyo nine hours ago and will land at JFK at eleven ten PM—that's in four hours."

"Jesus. Okay."

"Your assignment is simple: tail the man from the airport and, as soon as possible, take those plans away from him and bring them here."

"How?"

"That's for you to figure out."

"In four hours?"

Glinn nodded. "We don't know what format the plans are in or where they're hidden. They could be computer code in his laptop, hidden in a steganographic image, on a flash drive in his suitcase, or on an old-fashioned roll of film, for all we know."

"This is a crazy assignment. Nobody could pull this off."

"It is true that few could do this. That's why we've reached out to you, Dr. Crew."

"You're kidding—right? I've never done anything like this before. My work at Los Alamos is in HE. No doubt you've got dozens of better-qualified people downstairs."

"As it happens, you are uniquely suited to this assignment. For two reasons. First is your *former* career."

"What career would that be?"

"As a thief. Robbing art museums."

There was a sudden, freezing silence.

"Not the bigger museums, of course. The small private ones, generally, with less sophisticated intrusion-detection systems and lower-profile artwork."

"I think you need to up your medication," Gideon said in a low voice. "I'm no art thief. I don't have even the slightest criminal record."

"Which shows just how good you were. Such skills can be very valuable. Of course, you dropped this profession when a new and overriding interest came into your life. And with that we get to the second reason. You see, we followed with great interest your deft little operation against General Chamblee S. Tucker."

Gideon tried to recover from this second surprise. He mustered up his most puzzled look. "Operation? Tucker went nuts and attacked me and one of his employees in his house."

"So everyone thinks. I know better. I know that you spent the last ten years improving yourself, finishing college and getting your doctorate at MIT, all the while looking for a way to bring Tucker down and vindicate your father. I know how you managed to 'liberate' that top-secret document from the Directorate of Information Management, and how you used it to get at Tucker. He was a powerful man, and he had protected himself well. You showed enormous and varied skills setting up that operation, and then great self-possession in the aftermath of the shooting. You spun the business just right. Nobody doubted for a moment your narrative, even as you vindicated your father."

Gideon felt sick. So this was what it was all about: blackmail. "I don't know what you're talking about."

"Come, come. Your secret is safe with me regardless. We ourselves were looking for the best way to bring Tucker down. For a special client of ours, naturally. You saved us the trouble. And that's how you came to our attention."

Gideon could think of nothing to say.

"Earlier you asked me: why you? The fact is, we know *everything* about you, Dr. Crew. And not just your burglary skills or run-in with General Tucker. We know about your difficult childhood. About your work at Los Alamos. About your proclivity for gourmet cooking. Your fondness for Hawaiian shirts and cashmere sweaters. Your taste in jazz. Your weakness for alcohol. And—when under the influence—women. The only thing we haven't been able to learn is how you lost the top joint of your right ring finger." He raised the brow of his good eye quizzically.

Gideon flushed with anger, took a few deep breaths, and got himself under control.

"If you won't answer that, perhaps you'll answer something else: did you plan to turn Dajkovic from the beginning?"

Again Gideon said nothing. It was unbelievable, incredible.

"You have my word whatever you say will stay within these walls. We are, as you might imagine, rather good at keeping secrets."

Gideon hesitated. The truth was, Glinn had him by the short hairs. But he sensed, behind the hard, blank façade, that the man was truthful. "All right," he finally said. "The whole thing was planned from beginning to end. I set up the ambush knowing Tucker wouldn't come himself—the man was a coward. I'd studied his company and the people who worked for him. I figured he'd send Dajkovic, who was fundamentally a decent guy. I knew I could catch him and hoped I could turn him. It worked. We finished the... operation together."

Glinn nodded. "As I thought. A masterpiece of social engineering on many levels. But you made one mistake. What was it?"

"I forgot to check his boot for that damn knife."

Finally Glinn smiled, and for the first time his face seemed to be almost human. "Excellent. But the operation ended rather messily. Dajkovic got shot. How did that happen?"

"Tucker was no dummy. He realized Dajkovic was lying."

"How?"

"Dajkovic failed to share a drink with him. We think that's what tipped Tucker off."

"Then that was Dajkovic's mistake, not yours. I proved my point. You made only one mistake in that whole operation. I've never seen anything quite like what you did. You're definitely the man for this job."

"I had ten years to figure out how to take down Tucker. You're giving me four hours for this one."

"This is a far simpler problem."

"And if I fail?"

"You won't fail."

A silence. "Another thing: what are you going to do with this Chinese weapon? I'm not going to do anything to harm my country."

"The United States of America is, in fact, my client."

"Come on, they'd be using the FBI for a job like this—not hiring a firm like yours, no matter how specialized."

Glinn reached into his pocket and removed a card. He laid it on the table and pushed it toward Gideon with his finger.

He peered at the card, emblazoned with a government logo. "The Director of National Intelligence?"

"I would be dismayed if you believed anything I'm telling you. You can check it out for yourself. Call the Department of Homeland Security and ask to speak to this gentleman. He'll confirm that we're a DHS subcontractor doing legitimate and patriotic work for our country."

"I'd never get through to a guy like that."

"Use my name and you'll be put through directly."

Gideon did not pick up the card. He gazed at Glinn, and a silence built in the office. A hundred thousand dollars. The money was nice but this job looked fraught with difficulties. Danger. And Glinn's confidence in him was sadly misplaced.

He shook his head. "Mr. Glinn, until a month ago my entire life was on hold. I had something I had to do. All my energy went into that one thing. Now I'm free. I've got a lot of catching up to do. I want to make friends, settle down, find someone, get married, have kids. I want to teach my son how to cast a dry fly. I've got all the time in the world now. This job of yours—well, it sounds dangerous as hell to me. I've taken enough risks for one lifetime. You understand? I'm not interested in your assignment."

An even longer silence enveloped the room.

"Is that final?" Glinn asked.

"Yes."

Glinn glanced at Garza and gave him a short nod. Garza reached into his briefcase, removed a file, and laid it on the table. It was a medical file, labeled with a red tab. Glinn opened it up to reveal a stack of X-rays, CT scans, and dense lab reports.

"What's this?" said Gideon. "Whose X-rays are those?"

"Yours," said Glinn, sorrowfully.

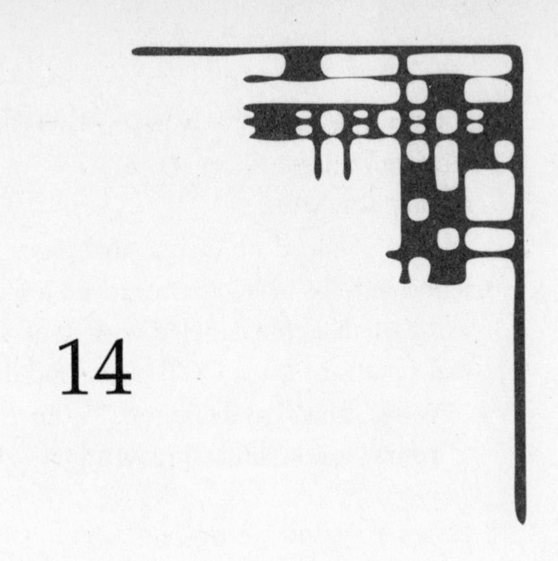

14

With a feeling of trepidation, Gideon reached over and took the file. The names had been cut out of the X-rays and scans, blacked out in the reports.

"What the hell is this? Where did you get these?"

"They came from the hospital where you were treated for your knife wound."

"What's this supposed to mean?"

"In the course of diagnosing and treating your injury, the usual tests were done: X-rays, MRIs, and blood work. Since you were suffering from a concussion, among other things, some of this work focused on your head. And the doctors made what is known as an incidental finding. They diagnosed you with an arteriovenous malformation—specifically, a condition known as a 'vein of Galen aneurysmal malformation.'"

"What the hell's that?"

"It's an abnormal tangle of arteries and veins in the brain involving the great cerebral vein of Galen. It's usually congenital, and usually asymptomatic until the age of twenty or so. And then it, ah, makes its presence known."

"Is it dangerous?"

"Very."

"What's the treatment?"

"In your case, the AVM is in the Circle of Willis, deep in the brain. It's inoperable. And invariably fatal."

"*Fatal*? How? When?"

"In your case, the best estimate is that you have about a year."

"A year?" Gideon's head spun. "A *year*?" He choked trying to get the next question out, and swallowed. Bile rose in his throat.

Glinn continued matter-of-factly, his voice neutral. "To speak in more precise statistical terms, your chances of survival twelve months from now are about fifty percent; eighteen months, thirty percent; two years, less than five percent. The end typically comes very fast, with little or no warning. There's typically no impairment or symptoms until that time, nor does the condition require any sort of physical or dietary restriction. In other words, you will live a normal life for about a year—and then you will die very, very quickly. The condition is incurable and in your case, as I said, there is no treatment whatsoever. It's just one of those terrible finalities."

Gideon stared at Glinn. This was monstrous. He felt a rage take hold, almost ungovernable. He leapt to his feet. "What is this, blackmail? If you sons of bitches think that's the way to get me to do your bidding, you're brainless." He stared at the file. "It's bullshit. Some sort of scam. If all that was true, they would've told me in the hospital. I don't even know if these X-rays belong to me."

Still speaking mildly, Glinn said, "We asked the hospital not to tell you; that it was a matter of national security. We wanted to get a second opinion. We passed the file along to Dr. Morton Stall at Mass General in Boston. He's the world's expert on AVMs. He confirmed both the diagnosis and the prognosis. Believe me, we were almost as shocked and dismayed to learn this as you are. We had big plans for you."

"What's the point of telling me this now?"

"Dr. Crew," said Glinn, a kindly note in his voice, "trust me when I say that our sympathies are very much with you."

Gideon stared at him, breathing hard. It was some ploy, or a mistake. "I just don't believe it."

"We looked into your condition with all the means at our disposal. We had been planning to hire you, offer you a permanent position here. This horrible diagnosis put us in a bind, and we were debating what to do. Then the news came in about Wu. This is a national security emergency of the highest order. You're the only one we know who could pull this off, especially on such short notice. That's why we're laying this on you now, all at once—and for that I am truly sorry."

Gideon passed a shaking hand over his forehead. "Your timing really sucks."

"The timing is never right for a terminal illness."

All his anger seemed to have evaporated as quickly as it had come. The horror of it made him sick. All the time he'd wasted...

"In the end, we had no choice. This is an emergency. We don't know precisely what Wu is up to. We can't miss this opportunity. If you decline, the FBI will jump in with their own op, which they've been eagerly pushing, and I can tell you it will be a disaster. You've got to decide, Gideon, in the next ten minutes, and I hope to God you will say yes."

"This is fucked up. I can't believe it."

Silence. Gideon rose, walked to the frosted window. He turned. "I resent this. I resent the way you dragged me here, laid all this shit on me—and then have the gall to ask me to work for you."

"This is not the way I would have wished it."

"One year?" he asked. "That's it? One fucking year?"

"In the file is a survival graph of the illness. It's a matter of cold probabilities. It could be six months, a year, two on the outside."

"And there are no treatments at all?"

"None."

"I need a drink. Scotch."

Garza pressed a button, and a wood panel slid to one side. A moment later a drink was laid on the table in front of Gideon.

He reached down, grasped it, took a slug, then another. He waited, feeling the numbing creep in his system. It didn't help.

Glinn spoke quietly. "You could spend your last year amusing yourself, living life to the fullest, cramming it in till the end. Or you could spend it in another way—working for your country. All I can do is offer you the choice."

Gideon drained the glass.

"Another?" Garza asked.

Gideon waved his hand in a no.

"You could do this one job for us," said Glinn. "One week. Then decide. You'll at least be able to walk away with enough money to live out your time in relative comfort."

There was a pause. Gideon looked from the file, to Glinn, then back to the file.

"All right, Christ, I'll take the assignment." Gideon swept up the medical file. Then he looked once more at Glinn. "Just one thing. I'm going to take this with me and have it checked out. If it's bullshit, I'm coming after you, personally."

"Very well," said Glinn, sliding a second folder toward him. "Here is information about your assignment. In there, you'll find background information on and photographs of your target. His name is Wu Longwei, but he also calls himself Mark Wu. The adoption of a Western name is a common practice among Chinese professionals." He leaned back. "Manuel?"

Garza stepped forward and laid a heavy brick of hundred-dollar bills on the table with one hand, and a Colt Python with the other.

"The money will cover your incidental expenses," said Glinn. "You know how to use that firearm?"

Gideon scooped up the money and hefted the Python. "I would have preferred the satin stainless finish."

"You will find the royal blue is better for night work," said Glinn drily. "You must not, under any circumstances or for any reason whatsoever, try to make contact with us during the operation. If contact is necessary, we will find you. Understood?"

"Yes. Why?"

"An inquiring mind is an admirable quality," said Glinn. "Mr. Garza, please show Dr. Crew out the back way. There's no time to waste."

As they headed toward the door, Glinn added: "Thank you, Gideon. Thank you very much."

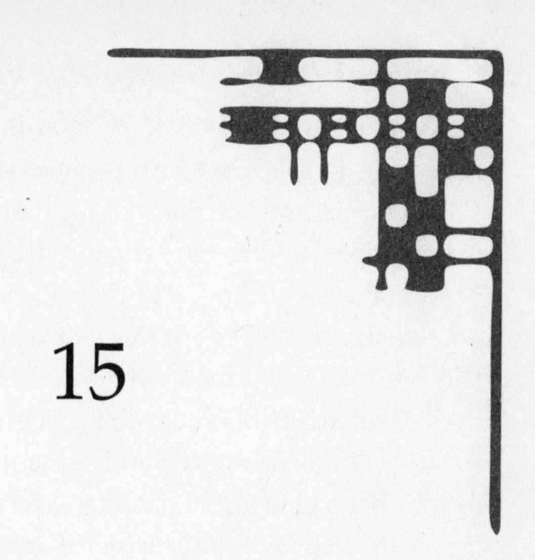

15

Gideon eased the stretch limo into an illegal space behind the taxi queue at the Terminal 1 arrivals level. He was still thinking about his call to the Department of Homeland Security, which he'd made from a pay phone as soon as he'd left EES. Avoiding the number on the business card, he'd called the general number, got some lowly operator, dropped Glinn's name—and was immediately put through on a secure line to the director himself. Ten astonishing minutes later, he hung up, still wondering how in the world, out of everyone, they had picked him for this crazy assignment. The director would only repeat: *We have complete faith and trust in Mr. Glinn. He has never failed us.*

He shook off these thoughts, and then tried—less successfully—to shake off the far darker ones related to his health. There would be time for that later. Right now, he had to stay focused on one thing: the immediate problem at hand.

It was almost midnight, but Kennedy airport was frantically busy with the last wave of flights arriving from the Far East. As he idled at the curb, he saw two TSA officers staring at him. They strode over, scowls on their self-important faces.

He climbed out of the limo, his dark suit itchy in the sticky summer night, and favored them with an arrogant smirk.

"What do you think you're doing?" said the first cop, small, thin, and aggressive as a ferret. He whipped out his ticket book. "The limo waiting area's over there!" He gestured sharply, the leaves of the ticket book trembling with his irritation.

The second cop arrived huffing, and he was a big one. Big and slow. "What's going on?" he asked, already apparently confused.

Gideon folded his long arms, propped a foot up on the fender, and gave the big one an easy smile. "Officer Costello, I presume?"

"Name's Gorski," came the reply.

"Ah," said Gideon. "You remind me of Costello."

"Don't know anyone by that name," said Gorski.

"There *is* no Officer Costello," said the thin one. "We've got no idea what you're talking about. You're not supposed to stop here."

"I'm here to meet the VIP arrival... You know all about it... right?" Gideon winked and slid a pack of gum from his pocket. He peeled off the wrapper, eased out a stick, offered the pack around.

The fat one took a stick.

"Let's see your hack license," said the thin one, waving away the gum and shooting an annoyed glance at his partner.

Gideon slipped out the license he had "rented" along with the limo—at significant expense—and handed it over. The thin cop snatched it, stared, passed it to the other. The fat one pursed his lips, looking it over intently. Gideon folded the stick of gum into his mouth, chewed meditatively.

"You know you can't stop here," said the thin cop, his voice high. "I'm giving you a ticket, and then you better get over to where you belong." He flipped open the book and began to write.

"Don't do that," said Gideon. "Tickets make me break out in hives."

The officer scoffed.

"Guess you didn't get the message," said Gideon, with a shrug.

"Message?"

He smirked. "About who I'm meeting."

"I don't give a rat's ass who you're meeting. You can't stop here. No exceptions." But the pen had halted. The fat one was still perusing the hack license, wet lips pursed in concentration.

Gideon waited.

"So who *are* you meeting?" the thin one finally asked.

Gideon's grin broadened. "You know I can't tell you that." He checked his watch. "His plane's arriving now. From the Far East. He'll get the VIP treatment at customs, breeze right through and be expecting me. *Inside.* Not out here, on the curb, arguing with a couple of flat—I mean, security officers."

Gorski handed him back the license. "License and stickers seem to be in order," he said to no one in particular.

"We never got a Security or VIP arrival notice," said the thin one. His tone was now several notches less confrontational. "I'm sorry, but the rules are the rules."

Gideon rolled his eyes. "Nice. So you guys know nothing. No skin off my back. On second thought, go ahead and write the ticket. I'll need it for my memo." He shook his head sadly and started to get back in the limo.

The thin cop stared at Gideon, eyes narrowed. "If this is a security VIP arrival, we should've been told. Who is he, some politician?"

Gideon paused at the open door. "Let's just say he's one of your own. The Jefe. A man known to be just a *tad* irritable when there's a fuckup."

The two cops looked at each other. "You talking about the commissioner?"

"You didn't hear it from me."

"We should've gotten a VIP notification," said Gorski, now in full whine.

Gideon decided it was time to get tough. He let the good-humored look fall from his face and glanced at his watch. "I guess I need to spell it out for you. It's a simple story, easy to follow. If I don't meet the Man at the bottom of the escalators in one fucking minute, the loose diarrhea is gonna hit the fan. And you know what I'm going to do about that? I'm going to write a memo that says I got shortstopped by two dumbass TSA cops who forgot to check their inbox for a VIP notification." He pulled a notebook and pen from his pocket. "How do you spell your name, Gorski?"

"Um..." Gorski looked over at the other cop, unsure what to do.

Gideon turned to the thin one. "How about you? You want to be in the memo, too? What's your name? Abbott?"

He gave them both a withering stare, first one, then the other.

They caved immediately. "We'll keep an eye on your limo," said the thin cop, nervously smoothing the front of his uniform. "You go ahead and meet him."

"Right," said Gorski. "No problem. We'll be right here."

"Good move. Why don't you practice the 'Who's on First' routine while you wait? I love that one." Gideon brushed past them and walked briskly through the doors into the vast baggage claim area. Luggage carousels rumbled and creaked on both sides. In front stretched a double pair of escalators, people streaming down. Gideon joined the small group of fellow limo drivers waiting at the bottom of the escalators, each holding up a small sign with a name.

The escalators continued to pour down their river of human cargo. Gideon scrutinized each Asian face. He had memorized the two photos Glinn had given him of Wu, but there was always the danger that he was one of those people who photographed differently from how he looked.

But no—there he was. A small, intense-looking man with a high domed forehead, a fringe of hair, wearing old-fashioned black-framed glasses and a professorial tweed jacket. He descended the escalator, eyes cast down, shoulders slumped, looking as timid and inconspicuous as possible. He wasn't even holding a carry-on bag or laptop.

Wu hit the bottom of the escalators, but instead of going to baggage claim he went straight ahead, walking fast, passing Gideon and heading out the doors toward the taxi stand.

Taken by surprise, Gideon hustled after him. There was no line at the taxi queue. Wu ducked under the waiting-line stanchions, grabbed a ticket from the dispatcher, and slipped in the first cab, a Ford Escape.

Gideon sprinted back to his limo.

"Hey! What's up?" cried the thin guard.

"Wrong terminal!" Gideon shouted. "I made a mistake! Man, I'm really fucked now!" He snatched out a fifty-dollar bill he had tucked in his front suit coat pocket for emergencies and tossed it at them, leaping into the limo.

They scrambled for the bill as a summer breeze tumbled it along the sidewalk, and Gideon tore away from the curb and went after the rapidly vanishing cab.

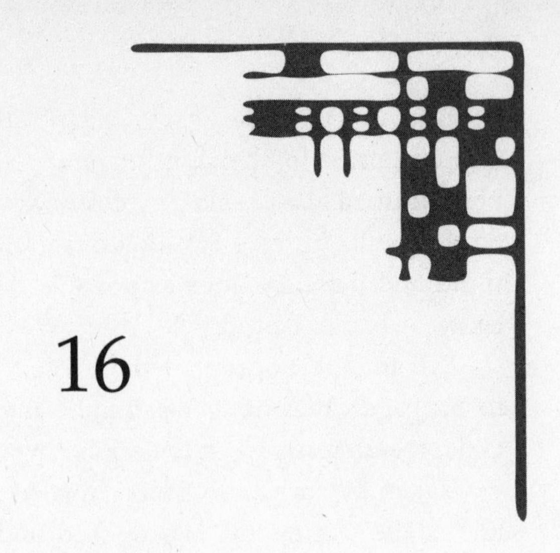

16

Gideon sped down the terminal exit road, finally catching up to the cab as it looped onto the Van Wyck Expressway. He slowed down and continued at a measured pace, keeping the cab half a dozen car lengths ahead in the moderate late-night traffic. From time to time he switched lanes, dropping back and then moving forward, in case Wu was suspicious.

It was almost routine. Neither the cabdriver nor the scientist seemed to be aware they were being followed, despite the conspicuous stretch limo he was driving. Following the standard route into Upper Manhattan, the taxi merged onto the Grand Central Parkway and passed Citi Field, then La Guardia Airport. As they passed the RFK Bridge, the skyline of Midtown Manhattan came into view like a tapestry of glittering gems, shimmering over the dark waters of the East River. Entering Manhattan via the Third Avenue Bridge, the taxi bypassed FDR Drive, instead heading along 125th Street in East Harlem, until finally turning downtown at Park Avenue.

Wu probably has an Upper East Side destination, Gideon mused.

Mentally he once again rehearsed his plan. He'd follow the taxi to its destination, then park nearby and...

Suddenly he noticed a black Lincoln Navigator with smoked windows approaching from behind, speeding down the slow lane and rapidly closing in.

The Navigator narrowed the gap until it was aggressively tailgating the taxi, although it could have easily passed. Gideon hung back. Despite the obviously new condition of the vehicle, the license plate light of the Navigator was burned out, the plate itself dark and unreadable.

Moving into the left lane, Gideon accelerated briefly to get a view inside the SUV through the windshield, but this late at night it was hopeless and he eased back, dropping behind once again, his sense of apprehension increasing.

The taxi, tailgated by the Navigator, accelerated, but the Navigator kept pace; the taxi then braked slightly and slowed, but the Navigator did the same, still refusing to pass.

This was not good.

The Navigator now crept forward until its massive chrome bumper touched the rear bumper of the cab—and then it accelerated with a roar, shoving the cab forward and sideways. With a terrific squeal of rubber the cab swerved, then recovered, fishtailing as it veered into the left lane. The Navigator swung in behind it and accelerated again, trying to ram it.

To avoid being hit, the taxi swerved back into the right lane and tried to slow down, but the Navigator, in a deft maneuver, swung in behind and rammed it again, this time with real force, and again the taxi driver had to accelerate to correct the deflection. The sound of his horn wailed across the wide avenue.

The Navigator jumped forward to ram the taxi again, but the cabbie swung into the left lane and then slewed around the corner onto East 116th Street, heading east. Here, in one of the main commercial districts of Spanish Harlem, there was suddenly more activity, the broad boulevard lit up and thronged with people despite the hour, the bars and restaurants open.

The Navigator made the turn with a howl of rubber and Gideon followed, the limo going into an awkward four-wheel power slide. Heart pounding, he accelerated after them. The Navigator's driver wasn't trying to force the cab to pull over; he was trying to kill its occupants by causing an accident.

The taxi accelerated in an attempt to outrun the Navigator. The two vehicles shot eastward on 116th, weaving in and out of traffic, provoking a furious blaring of horns, screeching tires, and yells. Gideon followed as best he could, sweaty hands slick on the wheel.

They tore past Lexington and approached the bright cluster of lights where 116th crossed Third Avenue. As they drew near at over seventy miles an hour, the light turned orange. Gideon braked the limo hard; there was no way they were going to make it. Suddenly the Navigator swung out and accelerated down the wrong side of the street, coming up alongside the taxi. Just before the intersection it swerved and gave the taxi a brutal sideswipe. With a billow of smoke the taxi slewed sideways through the intersection, clipped an oncoming car, flipped into the air, and went flying into a crowd outside a Puerto Rican lechonera. There was a dreadful sound, like the smack of sheet metal into meat. Bodies rag-dolled through the air, tumbling about the intersection. With a final shuddering crash the cab shattered the glass façade of the restaurant and came to rest with a death rattle and a burst of steam. Cooked meat came cascading out from racks and trays that had been on display in the window: roasted sides of pork, trays of cracklings, and spits of suckling pigs, all tumbling over the smashed taxicab and rolling about on the sidewalk.

There was a split second of terrible silence. And then the intersection exploded into an eruption of screams and shrieks as the crowd fled. To Gideon, looking on in horror, they resembled ants on a burning log.

He had pulled the limo over just before the intersection, and now he leapt out and ran toward the accident—just as a northbound city bus came roaring up Third Avenue, going at least fifteen miles over the speed limit. Halting at the crosswalk, Gideon watched helplessly as the bus blew on through; the driver, suddenly seeing bodies in the intersection, jammed on the brakes, but it was too late and he was unable to stop. The massive wheels thudded over several of the prostrate bodies, smearing them on the asphalt, and then the driver lost control. The bus skidded with a great shriek of burning rubber. Gideon watched helplessly as the careening bus T-boned a car on the far side of the intersection and came to rest on its side, the engine bursting into flame. Windows and the rear door of the bus were bashed open by screaming people and they spilled out, falling to the pavement, clawing and treading over one another in an attempt to get away.

Gideon looked around wildly for the Navigator. Then he spotted it, stopped partway down the next block. But the vehicle paused only for a moment: with a roar it tore off down 116th and swung south on Second Avenue, disappearing.

He sprinted across the intersection to the taxi. It lay upside down, its front partly inside the restaurant. Bodies were everywhere, some moving, some still. Gasoline ran over the sidewalk in a dark stream, moving down the gutter toward the burning bus—which exploded with a terrific roar, the force jumping the bus into the air. The flames mounted up, two, three, four stories, casting a hot lurid glow over the hellish scene. Hundreds of people from surrounding buildings were opening windows, craning necks, pointing. The air seemed to be alive with noise: screams and shrieks, pleas for help, agonized wails, the endless horn of the bus, the crackle of flame. It was all Gideon could do to keep a clear head.

Dropping to his hands and knees, he peered into the wrecked taxi. The driver's side was totally mangled and he could get a glimpse of the cabbie, his body literally merged into the twisted metal and glass of the car. He scrambled around to the passenger rear side and there was Wu. The man was alive; his eyes were wide open, and his mouth was working. When he saw Gideon, he reached a bloody hand out to him.

Gideon grabbed the door handle, tried to open it. But the door was far too mangled to budge. He got down on his belly and reached inside the broken window, grasping the scientist by both arms. He hauled him out and onto the sidewalk as gently as he could. The man's legs were horribly mangled and bleeding. Half dragging, half carrying Wu away from the spreading fire, he found a safe place around the corner and laid him carefully down. He took out his cell phone to call 911, but already he could hear, over the cacophony, sirens converging from every direction.

He vaguely became aware of a huge crowd of people behind him, rubberneckers keeping at a safe distance, watching the unfolding scene with prurient fascination.

The scientist suddenly grasped Gideon with a bloody hand, balling up the fabric of his chauffeur's uniform in his fist. He had an expression in his eyes that was lost, puzzled, as if he didn't know what had happened to him. He gasped out a word.

"What?" Gideon leaned closer, ear almost pressed to the scientist's lips.

"Roger?" the man whispered in heavily accented English. "Roger?"

"Yes," said Gideon, thinking fast. "That's me. Roger."

Wu said something in Chinese, then switched back to English. "Write these down. Quickly. Eight seven one zero five zero—"

"Wait." Gideon fumbled in his pockets, extracted a pencil and a scrap of paper. "Start again."

Wu began gasping out a list of numbers as Gideon wrote them down. Despite the heavy accent, his voice was thin, precise, punctilious: the voice of a scientist.

87105003302201401047836415600221120519715013
51010017502503362992421140099170520090080070
04003500278100065057616384370325300005844092
060001001001001

He halted.

"Is that it?" Gideon asked.

A nod. Wu closed his eyes. "You know... what to do with those," he rasped.

"No. I don't. Tell me—?"

But Wu had lapsed into unconsciousness.

Gideon stood up. He felt dazed and stupid. Blood from the scientist had stained his chest and arms. Fire trucks and police were arriving now, blocking the avenue. The bus was still afire, clouds of acrid black smoke roiling up into the night air.

"Oh my God!" a woman beside him said, crying openly, staring at the restaurant. "What a tragedy. What an awful tragedy."

Gideon looked at her. Then—as police and paramedics and firemen rushed past him, sirens filling the air—he stood up and, abandoning his borrowed limo, now hemmed in by emergency vehicles, walked slowly and inconspicuously toward the subway entrance two blocks away.

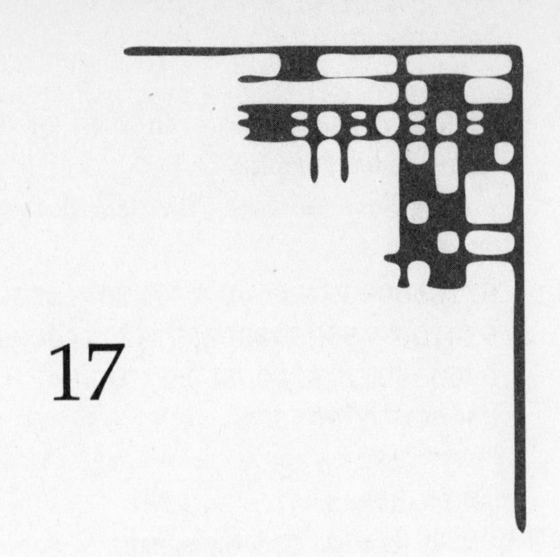

17

Henriette Yveline lowered her clipboard, took down her reading glasses, and gazed at the young, bedraggled man in the dark suit who had come stumbling up to the emergency room admissions station. He was a fine-looking fellow, lanky, jet-black hair askew and flopping over his brilliant blue eyes. But my goodness, what a state he was in—hands, arms, and shirt caked with blood, eyes wild, stinking of gasoline and burned rubber. He was trembling all over.

"May I help you?" she said, firmly but not unkindly. She liked to keep an orderly ER waiting area—not an easy task at Mount Sinai Hospital on a hot Saturday night in June.

"God, yes, yes," the man said all in a rush. "My—my friend, he just came in. A horrible car accident. Name's Wu Longwei, but he calls himself Mark Wu."

"And you are?"

The fellow swallowed, trying to get himself under control. "A close friend. Gideon Crew."

"Thank you, Mr. Crew. May I ask if you're all right yourself? No injuries, bleeding?"

"No, no, nothing," he said distractedly. "It's... it's not my blood."

"I understand. Just a moment, please." She replaced her reading glasses and picked up the admissions clipboard, perused it. "Mr. Wu was admitted fifteen minutes ago. The doctors are with him now. Would you care to take a seat and wait?" She gestured toward the large, spare waiting room, half-filled with people, some crying softly, others with the long stare. A large family huddled in one corner, comforting a sobbing three-hundred-pound woman.

"Tell me, please," said Gideon, "how is he?"

"I'm afraid I'm not authorized to release any information on that, Mr. Crew."

"I need to see him. I've *got* to see him."

"He can't see anyone right now," said Yveline, a little more firmly. "Trust me, the doctors are doing all they can." She paused, and added a line that never failed to comfort: "Mount Sinai is one of the finest hospitals in the world."

"At least tell me how he is."

"I'm sorry, sir, but hospital rules won't allow me to release medical information to anyone but family."

The man stared. "But... what does that mean, family?"

"A relative with identification or a spouse."

"Yes, but... you see, Mark and I... we're... partners. *Life* partners." Even under his bloody, dirty face, she could see him blushing at this intimate detail.

Yveline laid down the clipboard. "I understand. But I can only release information to a relative or legal spouse."

"Legal? For God's sake, you know perfectly well same-sex marriage is against the law in New York!"

"I'm so sorry, sir. The rules are the rules."

"Is he dead?" The man's voice suddenly became loud, very loud.

She looked at him, faintly alarmed. "Sir, please calm down."

"Is that why you won't tell me? Oh my God, *is he dead?*" He was shouting now.

"I need a piece of paper, some proof of your relationship..." Her voice trailed off. This had happened several times before: conflicts over gay and lesbian hospital visitation rights. The whole issue was under endless policy review—leaving it to people like her to run the gauntlet with the public. It wasn't fair.

"Who carries around a wad of official documents?" The man began to cry. "We just got in from China!" He swiped the shock of hair out of his face, his eyes bloodshot, his lips trembling.

"I know you're upset, sir, but we can't give out medical information to someone claiming to be a domestic partner without some sort of proof."

"Proof?" Gideon held out his bloody hands, his voice climbing into a shriek. "There's your proof! Look at it! His blood on my hands! I'm the one who dragged him from the car!"

Yveline couldn't even find the words to respond. The whole room was listening. Even the three-hundred-pound woman had stopped crying.

"I need to *know*!" And with this last wail, his knees buckled and the man collapsed on the floor.

Yveline pressed the emergency intercom, summoning the triage head nurse. The crowd stared at the man on the floor, but his collapse had been more emotional than medical and she saw he was already reviving. He rose to his knees, hyperventilating, and some members of the crowd rushed over to help him up.

"Help him to a seat," said Yveline. "The nurse is on her way." More people in the group responded, helping the man to a seat against the wall. He fell heavily into it, covering his face and sobbing loudly.

"Come on, lady," said a woman. "What's the harm in telling him how his friend is?"

A murmur of agreement rose from the crowd. Gideon Crew rocked in the chair, his face in his hands.

"He's dead," he said. "I know it. He's dead."

Yveline ignored the people and went back to her clipboard. It was a damn shame the rules forced her to be this way. But she was determined not to show vacillation or weakness.

"Why don't you just tell him how his friend is?" persisted the woman.

"Ma'am," said Yveline, "I don't make the rules. Medical information is private."

A harried nurse arrived. "Where's the patient?"

"He's upset—collapsed." Yveline indicated the man.

The nurse went over, suddenly putting on a smooth voice. "Hello, my name's Rose. What's the problem?"

The man choked up. "He's dead and they won't tell me."

"Who?"

"My life partner. In the ER. But they won't tell me anything because I don't have a piece of paper."

"You're in a long-term domestic partnership?"

A nod. "Five years. He's everything to me. He doesn't have any family here." He looked up suddenly, beseechingly. "Please don't let him die alone!"

"May I?" The nurse took the man's pulse, slapped a cuff on him and took his blood pressure. "You're okay. Just upset. Just slow down your breathing and let me talk to the admitting staff."

The man nodded, struggling to get his gasping under control.

The nurse stepped over to Yveline. "Look, let's just authorize him as a domestic partner. Okay? I'll take full responsibility."

"Thank you." The nurse left while Yveline called up the electronic file, read the latest update. "Mr. Crew?"

He leapt up and came over.

"Your friend is critically injured but alive and is stabilizing," she said in a low voice. "Now if you'll come up and sign this form, I'll authorize you as his domestic partner."

"Thank God!" he cried. "He's alive, thanks be to God!"

The waiting room broke into applause.

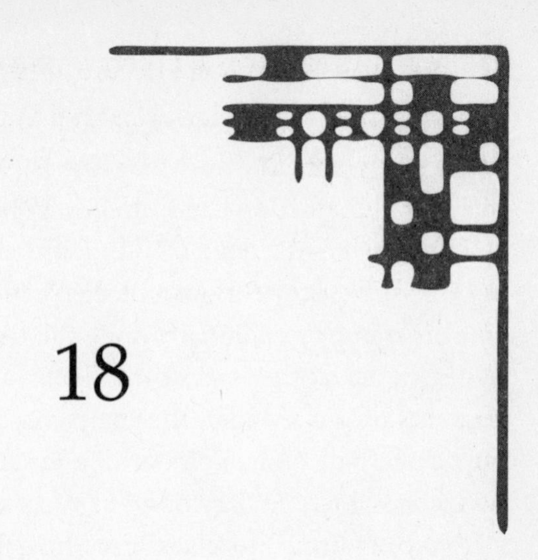

18

Gideon Crew looked around at the room he had booked at the Howard Johnson Motor Lodge on Eighth Avenue. It was surprisingly decent, well appointed, not a trace of blue and orange to be seen. Best of all, it had an iPod dock. He slipped out his iPod, pondered the problem at hand, dialed in Bill Evans's *Blue in Green*, and docked it. The bittersweet chords of "The Two Lonely People" filled the room. He gulped the last of his quintuple espresso and tossed the cup into the trash.

For several minutes, he sat motionless in the chair by the small desk, allowing the moody, introspective music to wash over him, willing himself to relax muscle by muscle, letting the events of the day sort themselves out in his mind. Just fifteen hours earlier, he'd been fishing for trout in Chihuahueños Creek. Now here he was, sitting in a Manhattan hotel room, with twenty thousand dollars in his pocket, a death sentence on his head, and a strange man's blood on his hands.

He stood up, shrugged out of his shirt, and walked into the bathroom to wash his hands and arms. Then he stepped out and put on a fresh shirt. Covering the bed with plastic garbage bags, he carefully spread out Wu's clothes, which had been cut off in the emergency room and already gone into the medical-waste stream. He'd had a devil of a time retrieving them. A heartwarming Christmas story about a broken promise, a Hong Kong tailor, and a lost puppy had finally done the trick—but just barely.

After the clothes were carefully arranged, Gideon laid out the contents of Wu's wallet, the spare change from his pockets, passport, rollerball, and an old-fashioned safety razor in a plastic case, no blade, which he had found in Wu's suit coat pocket. That was all. No cell phone, no BlackBerry, no calculator, no flash drive.

As he worked, dawn broke over the city, the hotel windows shifting from gray to yellow, the city waking up with car horns and traffic.

When everything was laid out in geometric precision, he looked it over, finger pensively placed on his lower lip. If the man was carrying the plans for a new kind of weapon, it was not at all obvious where they were—if he had even been carrying them on his person. Clearly, the list of numbers Wu had gasped out to him at the accident scene couldn't be the complete set of plans—such plans, even in highly compressed form, would take up a significant amount of data. They would have to be stored digitally, which meant he was looking for a microchip; a magnetic or bubble memory device; a holographic image stored on some medium; or perhaps a laser-read storage device such as a CD or DVD.

It seemed logical that the man would have kept the plans on his person—or, more exotically, perhaps embedded within his body. Shuddering slightly, Gideon decided he would deal with the "inside" question later—first he would carefully search all of Wu's few possessions.

From a group of shopping bags dumped by the door, he removed an electronic device he had just purchased—amazing how in Manhattan you could get anything at any time of the night or day, from bombs to blow jobs—opened the box, and began setting it up. Called the MAG 55W05 Advanced Countermeasures Sweep Kit, it was a device used by private investigators, CEOs, and other paranoid people to sweep areas for bugs. Completing the assembly, he perused the manual quickly, then fired it up.

With painstaking slowness, he moved the device's sweeping wand over the clothing spread out on the bed. No hits. The wallet and its contents—money, business cards, family photos—were also negative, except for the magnetic stripe on the single credit card Wu carried. When the sweeping wand went over the magnetic stripe, the MAG 55 bleeped and blinked and bars went flickering up and down the LED screen. It seemed there was data on the stripe, but exactly how much he couldn't be sure: all the MAG 55 told him was that it was less than 64K. He'd have to find some way of downloading and examining it.

Wu's Chinese passport also contained an embedded magnetic stripe along the outer edge of the front cover, just as US passports did. Using the integrated reader of the device, he was able to determine that this stripe held data, and that it, too, was less than 64K. He scratched his head thoughtfully. That seemed too small to credibly detail the workings of a secret weapon. Advanced technology could compress data a great deal, but he wasn't sure just how much.

The passport and credit card would have to be further analyzed.

He threw himself in a wing chair, closing his eyes. He hadn't slept in twenty-four hours. He listened to the rich chord progressions of "Very Early," letting his mind wander through the swirling colors and rhythms. His father had been a jazz aficionado and he remembered him every evening in his easy chair, head bent over the hi-fi, listening to Charlie Parker and Fats Waller, his foot tapping to the music, his bald head nodding. It was the only music Gideon listened to, and he knew it well, very well...

The next thing he knew, he was waking up, the closing bars of "If You Could See Me Now" fading on the player.

He got up, went into the bathroom, stuck his head under the faucet, and turned on the cold water. Toweling his head dry, he emerged with a new spring in his step. Gideon had an ability to get by on very little sleep, and to wake from catnaps feeling completely refreshed. It was now almost nine AM, and he could hear the maids talking in the hall.

Packing away the sweep kit, he began a painstaking visual examination of Wu's clothing with a jewelry loupe, using an X-Acto knife to open up seams and double layers. The clothing was stiff, soaked with blood in places, with bits and pieces of metal, glass, and plastic stuck to it. He removed each piece with tweezers, laying it on a paper towel for further examination. The trousers in particular were bloody and shredded. Where the blood was thick and caked, he carefully soaked the area with wet paper towels, then blotted it dry, picking out every little piece.

Four hours later he had finished. Nothing.

Now for the shoes. He had saved the most likely hiding place for last.

Noon. He hadn't eaten since lunch the day before, a sandwich up in the mountains, and now the only substance inside his stomach was a dozen espressos. It felt like he'd drunk a pint of battery acid. No matter: he picked up the phone and ordered a triple espresso from room service, hot, hot.

He took the shoes out of a paper bag and set them on the coffee table. They were Chinese-made knockoffs of John Lobbs. Both were caked with hardened blood—Wu's legs had been crushed. One shoe was horribly mangled and had been cut off the foot; the other was merely caked in gore. In the summer heat, they had already begun to smell.

Clearing a space, he examined the right shoe with the sweep kit. Nothing. A knock came on the door and he went outside—keeping the door mostly shut—took the coffee, tipped the bellhop, and drank it down with a single gulp.

Ignoring the boiling feeling in the pit of his stomach, he went back to work, taking the shoe apart, methodically, piece by piece, and labeling each with a felt-tipped pen. First the heel came off; then he unstitched the sole and detached it, laying the pegs and stitches in neat rows to one side. With the X-Acto blade, he unstitched all the leather pieces and laid them out. The heel was of leather, built up in layers, and he carefully separated each layer and laid them side by side. A second sweep revealed nothing. Still using the X-Acto knife, he split every piece of leather, examining both sides and sweeping them all again. Yet again, nothing.

He repeated the process on the other shoe without success.

Gideon packed everything away in ziplock bags, labeling each one, and then sorted and stacked it all into a large Pelican case he had bought for the purpose, locking it up tight. He leaned back in the chair. "Sink me," he muttered exasperatedly. This was getting tedious. The thought of all the money Glinn had promised revived him a little.

Now for the inside work. It seemed unlikely, but he had to be thorough. But first: Music to Search Entrails By. Something a little more stretched out. He decided on Cecil Taylor's *Air*.

He picked up a thick manila folder from the bedside table—the complete suite of ER X-rays, head to toe, to which he was entitled as Wu's "life partner." Pulling the shade off the lamp, he held up the first X-ray to the bulb and examined it with the loupe, inch by careful inch. The head, upper chest, and arms were clean, but when he came to the lower midsection his heart just about stopped: there was a small white spot indicating metal. He grabbed the loupe and examined it, and was immediately disappointed. It was indeed a fragment of metal, but nothing more than a twisted piece that had obviously gotten embedded in the car accident. It was not a microchip, or a tiny metal canister, or secret spy gizmo.

There was nothing in the stomach or intestinal tract indicating any sort of container, balloon, or storage device. Nothing in the rectum, either.

It horrified him to look at the X-rays of the legs. Embedded in them were more than a dozen bits of metal—all showing as irregular white spots, along with grayer pieces that he guessed were fragments of glass and plastic. The X-rays had been taken from several directions, and he was able to get a crude idea of the shape of each piece—and none of them even remotely resembled a computer chip, a tiny canister or capsule, or a magnetic or laser storage device.

He had a vision of the owlish man descending the escalators, frightened and peering about, small, serious—and courageous. For the first time Gideon considered the risk the man had taken. Why had he done it? It would be a miracle if the man ever walked again. If he even survived. At the hospital, Wu had remained in a coma; they'd had to cut a hole in his cranium to relieve the pressure. Gideon reminded himself that this hadn't been an accident. It was attempted murder. No, with the death of the innocent cabdriver and half a dozen bystanders it was actual murder—mass murder.

Shaking off these thoughts, he slid the X-rays back into their manila folder and rose, going to the window. It was late afternoon—he'd been at it all day. The sun was already setting, the long yellow light spilling down 51st Street, the pedestrians casting gaunt shadows.

He'd hit a dead end—or so it seemed. What now?

His growling stomach reminded him it was high time to put something in there besides coffee. Something good. He picked up the phone, dialed room service, and put in an order for two dozen raw oysters on the half shell.

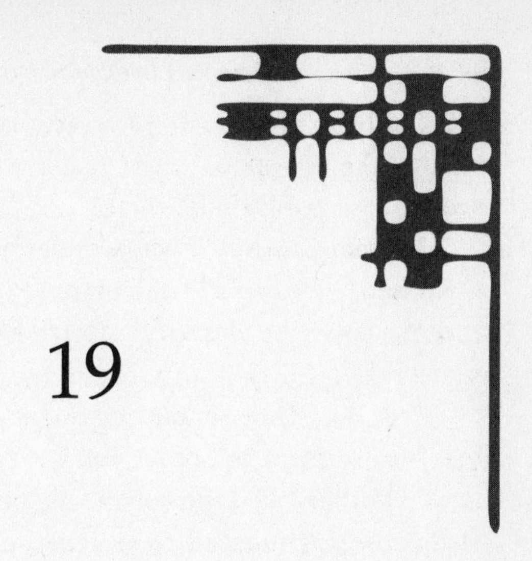

19

The police junkyard was located on the Harlem River in the South Bronx, in the shadow of the Willis Avenue Bridge. Gideon stepped out of the cab to find himself in a bleak zone of warehouses, and industrial lots stacked with old railroad cars, abandoned school buses, and rusting containers. A smell of muck and dead clams came drifting off the river, and the white-noise of evening rush-hour traffic on the Major Deegan Expressway hummed in the air like a hive of bees. He'd lived in a neighborhood not much different from this—the last in a succession of increasingly squalid homes he'd shared with his mother. Even the smell was familiar. It was an intensely depressing thought.

A chain-link fence topped with concertina wire surrounded the facility, fronted by a rolling gate on wheels next to a guardhouse. Beyond the fence sat an almost empty parking lot fringed by dying sumacs, behind which squatted a long warehouse. Beyond that and to the right lay an open-air junkyard of stacked and pancaked cars.

Gideon strolled up to the guardhouse. A swarthy-looking cop

sat behind the plastic windows, reading a book. As Gideon approached, he slid open the street-side window with a hammy arm covered with gorilla hair. "Yeah?"

"Hi," said Gideon. "I was wondering if you could help me?"

"What?" The cop still had his nose in the book. Gideon shifted to see the cover: he was surprised to see it was *City of God* by Saint Augustine.

"Well," said Gideon, putting on his most fawning, obsequious tone, "I'm so sorry to bother you."

"No bother," said the cop, finally putting down the book.

Gideon was relieved to see that, despite the beetling Neanderthal brows and heavy five o'clock shadow, the man had a friendly, open face. "My brother-in-law," Gideon began, "Tony Martinelli, he's the cabbie that was killed in that accident last night. The one where a guy ran him off the road on a Hundred Sixteenth Street—you read about that?"

Now the cop was interested. "Of course. Worst traffic accident in years—it was all over the news. He was your brother-in-law? I'm sorry."

"My sister's really broken up about it. It's just terrible—got two babies at home, one and three, no money, big mortgage on the house."

"That's really tough," said the cop, laying the book aside and appearing genuinely concerned.

Gideon took a handkerchief from his pocket, mopped his brow. "Well," he said, "here's the thing. He had a religious medallion hanging from the rearview mirror. It was a beautiful one, sterling silver, owned it forever. Saint Christopher."

The cop nodded in understanding.

"Tony went to Italy, the Jubilee Year in 2000—and the pope blessed that medallion. Blessed it personally. I don't know if you're Catholic, but Saint Christopher's the patron saint of travelers, and he being a cabbie and all—well, that medallion was the most precious thing he owned. That moment with the pope was the high point of his life."

"I'm Catholic," said the cop. "I know all about it."

"That's good, I'm glad you understand. I don't know if you can do this or not, and I wouldn't want to get you into trouble—but it would mean so much to his widow if she could have that medallion back. To, you know, put in the casket and bury it with her husband. It would give her such comfort to be able to do that..." His voice cracked. "Excuse me," he said, fumbling out a kerchief he had bought for that purpose, blowing his nose.

The officer shifted uncomfortably. "I understand what you're saying. I feel for her and her kids, I really do. But here's the thing."

Gideon waited patiently.

"Here's the thing," the cop repeated uneasily, seeking a way to say it. "The wrecked car is evidence in a homicide investigation. It's locked up right now, nobody can even get to it."

"Locked up?"

"Yeah. Inside an evidence cage in there." He jerked a thumb toward the warehouse.

"But surely someone could just go in there and get the medallion off the mirror? That's not evidence."

"I understand. I really do. But that taxicab's totally locked up. It's in a chain-link cage, with a chain-link roof over it and everything. And the warehouse itself is locked and alarmed. You've got to understand, chain of custody for evidence is crucial in a case like this. The cab is evidence: there are scratches on it, paint from the other vehicle, evidence of ramming. This is a major homicide case—seven people died in that accident and others were badly injured. And they're still looking for the scumbag who did it. Nobody can get in there except authorized personnel, and even then only by filling out forms and going through red tape. And everything they do to the car has to be videotaped. It's for a good reason, to help us catch those responsible and make sure they're convicted."

Gideon's face fell. "I see. That's too bad, it would mean so much." He looked up, brightening, as with a new idea. "Tony won't be buried for a week or two, at least. Will it be locked up very long?"

"The way these things work, that cab will be locked up until the guys are caught, there's a trial, maybe an appeal...It could be years. I wish it wasn't like that." The officer spread his hands. "Years."

"What am I going to tell my sister? You say the warehouse is alarmed?"

"Alarmed and guarded, twenty-four seven. And even if you could get in there, as I said, the vehicle's locked inside an evidence cage way in the back and not even the guard has a key."

Gideon rubbed his chin. "Chain-link cage?"

"Yeah, sort of like those cages they use in Guantánamo."

"The cage is also alarmed?"

"No."

"How's the warehouse alarmed?"

"Doors and windows."

"Motion sensors? Lasers?"

"Nah, there's a guard who makes his rounds every half hour in there. I think it's just the doors and windows that have alarms."

"Video cameras?"

"Yeah, they're all over. The whole area's covered." He paused, his face becoming serious. "Don't even think about it."

Gideon shook his head. "You're right. What the hell am I thinking?"

"Be patient. Eventually you'll get that medallion back, and maybe by then you'll have the satisfaction of seeing the perp doing twenty-five to life at Rikers Island."

"I hope they fry the bastard."

The cop reached out and laid a hammy hand on Gideon's. "I'm very sorry for your loss."

Gideon nodded quickly, pressed the cop's hand, and walked off. When he reached the end of the block, he turned and looked back. He could see, under the eaves of the warehouse's corners, a cluster of surveillance cameras providing full coverage of the outdoor area. He counted them: twelve from this vantage point alone. There would be many more on the other side of the building and an equal number within.

He turned and pondered what he'd learned. The fact was, most of what people called security systems were pastiches, just a lot of expensive electronic shit slapped up willy-nilly with no thought to building a coordinated, comprehensive network. One of Gideon's worst habits, which ruined his enjoyment of museum-going, was his propensity to figure out how many ways he could rip the museum off: wireless transmitters, vibration and motion sensors, noncontact IR detectors, ultrasound—it was all so obvious.

He shook his head with something almost like regret. There would be no challenge here at the police warehouse—none at all.

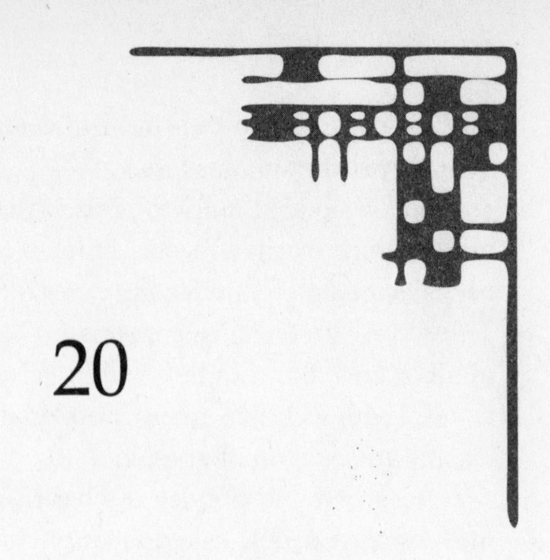

20

Three o'clock in the morning. Gideon Crew sauntered down Brown Place and crossed 132nd Street, weaving slightly, muttering to himself. He was wearing baggy jeans and a thin hoodie sporting a Cab Calloway silkscreen—a nice touch, he thought—which flopped over his face. The fake gut he had purchased at a theatrical supply store hung hot and heavy on his midriff, and it pressed heavily on the Colt Python snugged into his waistband against his skin.

He crossed the street, stumbled on the opposite curb, and continued down 132nd toward Pulaski Park, alongside the chain-link fence surrounding the police warehouse. The sodium lamps cast a bright urine glow everywhere, and the separate security floods around the warehouse added their own brilliant white to the mix. The gatehouse was empty, the gate shut and locked, the rolls of concertina wire at the top of the fence gleaming in the light.

Reaching the point where the fence made a turn toward an old set of railroad tracks across an overgrown and abandoned parking lot, now used for storage of old tractor-trailers, he staggered around the corner, searching here and there as if looking for a place to piss. There was no one in the area he could see, and he doubted anyone was watching, but he felt certain the surveillance cameras were recording his every move; they probably weren't monitored in real time, but they surely would be scrutinized later.

Staggering alongside the fence, he unzipped his fly, took a steaming leak, then continued to the tracks. Turning again, now out of sight from the street, he suddenly crouched, reached into his pocket, and pulled a stocking down over his face. The bottom of the chain-link fence was anchored into a cement apron with bent pieces of rebar and could not be pulled up. Reaching under his baggy sweatshirt, he pulled out a pair of bolt cutters and cut the links along the bottom, then up one side beside a pole. Grasping the cut section of links, he bent them inward. In another moment he was inside. He pushed the flap of chain link back into place and looked around.

The warehouse had two huge doors in the front and back, into which had been set smaller doors. He scooted up to the back door and found, as expected, a numerical keypad with a small LED screen to set or turn off the alarm. No peephole or window—the door was blank metal.

Naturally, he didn't know the code to turn off the alarm. But there was someone who did, inside; all he needed to do was summon him.

He knocked on the door and waited.

Silence.

He knocked again, louder. "Yo!" he called.

And now he could hear, inside, the sound of the guard moving toward the door.

"Who is it?" came the disembodied voice.

"Officers Halsey and Medina," Gideon barked out in a loud,

officious voice. "You okay? We got a silent alarm going at the precinct house."

"Silent alarm? I don't know anything about it." Gideon waited as the guard pressed the password into the keypad on the other side. The numbers came up only as asterisks on the external LED screen.

As the door began to open, Gideon ducked back around the corner, then fled to the outdoor wrecking yard he'd previously picked out as a hiding place. He climbed a stack of pancaked cars and lay down on top, watching and waiting.

"Hey!" shouted the guard at the threshold of the open door, looking about in a panic but not daring to venture outside. "Who's there?" There was real alarm in his voice.

Gideon waited.

An alarm began to whoop—the guard had pulled it, right on cue—and within five minutes the cop cars arrived, three of them screeching up at the curb, the occupants leaping out. Six cops.

Gideon smiled. The more the merrier.

They began a search of the place, three taking the inside of the warehouse, and three searching the wrecking yard. Naturally, most of them being out of shape, they did not attempt to climb the stacks of crushed cars. Gideon watched them poking and shining their lights all over for about thirty minutes, amusing himself by reconstructing the complex bass line of the Cecil Taylor number he'd listened to the previous afternoon. They then inspected the perimeter fence but, as he'd figured, missed the carefully concealed gap he'd created.

Meanwhile, just as he'd hoped, the other three cops and the guard were coming and going from the warehouse without bothering to shut, lock, or alarm the door in their haste. Finally, search completed, the six cops gathered in the parking lot with the guard beside their cars, where they radioed back to the precinct.

Gideon climbed down the heap of flattened cars, ran out of

the junkyard, flitted across the parking lot, and flattened himself against the warehouse wall. He crept up to the door, which was still halfway open, and slipped inside.

Keeping to the shadows, he found a new hiding place inside the warehouse, in a far corner behind two deep rows of chain-link cages, each protecting a car. It was stifling in the building, the muggy dead air redolent of gasoline, oil, and burned rubber.

Another fifteen minutes passed and the guard came back in, shutting and locking the door behind him and resetting the alarm. Gideon watched as the man walked the length of the warehouse and settled into a lighted area at the far end, replete with a chair and desk, a huge bank of CCTV monitors—and a television set.

And sure enough, the guard turned on the set, swung his feet up, and began to watch. It was some old show, and every few moments there was a laugh track. He listened. Was that really the penetrating voice of Lucille Ball and the answering bark of Ricky Ricardo? God bless the unions, Gideon thought, that had fought so hard for the right of municipal employees on night duty to have access to a TV set.

On his hands and knees, Gideon crawled along the row of cages, peering inside, until at last he found the wrecked Ford Escape. He removed the bolt cutters and a thick cotton rag. Winding the rag around the first chain link, he waited for the laugh track; made the cut; rewound the rag around the next link; waited for the laugh track; cut again.

He finished as the show ended with the usual burst of pseudo-Copacabana music. Opening the flap he'd created, he crawled inside.

The car was an absolute mess. It had been pried apart and cut into several pieces that were so mangled they were only vaguely recognizable as belonging to a vehicle. It was still drenched in blood and gore and smelled like a butcher shop on a hot summer's day. Crawling around it, Gideon located the rear passenger area where Wu had been sitting and wormed his way inside. The seat was sticky with blood.

Trying his best to tune this out, he forced his hands into the space behind and groped around. Almost immediately he felt something hard and small. He grasped it, slipped it into a ziplock bag he pulled from his pocket, and sealed the bag with a feeling of triumph.

A cell phone.

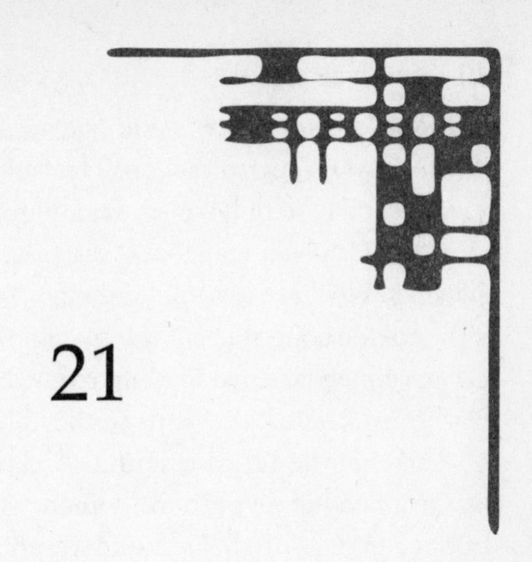

21

In Roland Blocker's four years of working the night shift at the warehouse, nothing had ever happened. Absolutely nothing. Night after night it was the same routine, the same rounds, the same comforting parade of late-night, black-and-white television sitcoms. Blocker loved the peace and quiet of the vast space. He had always felt safe, cocooned in the warehouse with its heavy metal doors and alarms and ceaselessly vigilant cameras, all safely enclosed within a twelve-foot chain-link fence topped by concertina wire. He'd never been bothered, no burglary attempts, nothing. After all, there was nothing to steal either inside or out—except wrecked cars, cars hauled out of the rivers with dead bodies in them, cars found with bodies locked in their trunks, burned-out cars, drug-smuggling cars, shot-up cars. What was there to steal?

But now, after the incident, with the cops gone, he felt spooked for the first time. That had been the strangest damn thing, that voice outside the door. Had he really heard it? A couple of the cops who'd responded to his alarm hinted around that maybe he'd been sleeping and had a dream. That pissed Blocker off—he never slept on the job. The surveillance cameras were always on and God only knew who might check the tapes later.

I Love Lucy had ended and the next show up was *The Beverly Hillbillies*, Blocker's favorite of the night's lineup. He tried to relax as the theme song started, the twang of banjos and the overdone hick accent always making him smile. He bent down to crank up the A/C and adjust the vents so they blew more directly on him.

And then he heard a sound. A clink—as if a piece of metal had dropped lightly onto the cement floor of the warehouse. He dropped his legs off the desk and, fumbling for the remote, muted the TV set to listen.

Clank came the sound again, closer this time. Suddenly his heart was pounding in his chest. First the voice, now this. He scanned the bank of inside CCTV monitors, but they showed nothing.

Should he pull the alarm again? No, the cops would never let him live that down. He considered calling out and realized that was plain stupid—if some intruder was in the warehouse, they wouldn't answer.

Heaving himself out of the chair, Blocker unhooked his Maglite and headed in the direction of the second sound, moving cautiously, his free hand resting easily on the butt of his service piece.

Reaching the area from which the sound had come, he shone the light around. This corner contained stacked pallets of old shrink-wrapped pieces of cars, all labeled—evidence that had been cut from vehicles years before but couldn't yet be tossed.

Nothing. He was just nervous, spooked by the earlier thing—that was all. Maybe rats had gotten into the warehouse. He went back to his little office and sat down, turning the sound of the television up, a little higher than usual this time. The noise comforted him. It was the episode where the banker fakes an attack of wild Indians on the Clampett mansion, one of his favorites. He cracked open a fresh Diet Coke and settled down to enjoy it.

Clank.

He sat up again, muting the television, listening intently.

Clank.

It was such a regular sound, unnatural, almost deliberate, coming from the same damn area. The CCTV monitors remained empty. Once again he rejected the idea of pulling the alarm.

Getting back to his feet, he yanked out the flashlight and shifted it to his left hand, unsnapping the keeper on his sidearm with his right and sliding out the weapon. He walked back to the corner from which the sounds had come and paused, hoping to hear it again. Nothing. He advanced, this time deciding to go behind the stacks of pallets to see if there was something or someone hiding between them and the wall.

He slowly walked down a long aisle between pallets, pausing just before the last one, listening. Still nothing. Weird.

Moving tentatively now, he approached the final stack of pallets and ducked around the corner, shining his light along the wall.

He felt something not unlike a displacement of air behind him and spun around; a black shadow burst out of the darkness but before he could scream there was a flash of steel and he felt a violent tug across his neck, and then everything was tumbling and crazy and red—and then it was over.

22

Gideon Crew waited, listening. There was someone else inside the warehouse who was not the guard: he was sure of it. The guard had heard it, too, and gone to inspect; returned; then investigated again. The second time he had not returned and Gideon had heard a faint scuffling sound, following by the sound of something wet landing softly on the floor.

He waited, absolutely still and unmoving. From his vantage point inside the car, he could see through several breaks in the wreckage, giving him a view of the central, cleared aisle of the warehouse, very broad, that ran to the security area at the far end. The guard was still gone, and he was taking much too long to investigate.

Gideon heard a soft *plop*, and then something rolled out from between two stacks of pallets on the right side and came slowly to rest in the open area.

The guard's severed head.

Gideon's mind kicked into overdrive. He knew instantly it was a trap—a way to flush him out, frighten him, or induce him to investigate. Another person was loose in the warehouse—and now Gideon was the target.

Quickly he reviewed his options. He could stay and fight, stalk his stalker. But his opponent was holding all the cards; he evidently knew exactly where Gideon was, he had worked it all out, he had lured and killed the guard so efficiently that there hadn't even been a sound… Gideon's instincts told him this guy was very, very good, a true professional.

So what to do? Get the hell out. He already had the cell phone, and additional searching had turned up nothing else.

But that was obviously one of the things his opponent—or opponents—expected him to do. *Opponents.* Now that was a chilling thought.

He needed to do the unexpected. But what could be unexpected here? Gideon was well protected inside the twisted car, but any move he made to leave it would potentially expose him.

He was fucked.

As he mulled it over, he realized that the killer, or killers, had been tracking his progress all along. Now they were probably in position, aiming at his cage, just waiting for his appearance. They wouldn't have rolled out the head if they didn't know where he was.

There *was* a way out. It was a huge risk, but at least it had the advantage of leaving him alive. He had no other options.

He glanced at his watch. Then he eased the Colt Python out of his waistband and aimed it carefully at the lock on the door leading outside the warehouse. He squeezed off a shot, which sounded thunderously in the enclosed space, the round clipping the alarm keypad. The siren began to whoop again.

Now it was a question of outwaiting the killer. Because at some point the unknown assailant would have to bolt. And then Gideon would have to get his own ass out.

Who was it? The driver of the black SUV? It had to be—they'd have gotten a good look at him during the chase.

A shot rang out, ripping into the wrecked taxi with a clang, followed by another and another, heavy-caliber rounds that punched through the metal like butter. Gideon realized with dismay that the killer wasn't going to run, at least not immediately. He had, for better or worse, forced the man's hand.

At least he now knew where the shots were coming from. Flattening himself within the wreckage, keeping behind the engine block, he took aim and waited. *Boom* came the next shot; he saw the muzzle flash and quickly returned fire. Already he could hear the sirens. How long had it taken before the police arrived last time? About five minutes.

He glanced at his watch again. It had already been three.

Another pair of rounds banged through the metal, bracketing him, spraying him with paint chips, and he returned fire once again. The sirens were getting louder—and then he heard wheels screeching to a stop outside.

He saw a flash of black behind the pallets—the killer was finally fleeing. Backing quickly out of the ruined rear seat, he jumped up, ready to sprint to the door, when two more rounds suddenly whined past him. As he dove to the floor he realized the son of a bitch had feinted, pretending flight, in order to flush him out. He rolled, fired, and saw the black-clad figure vanish into a dark corner; he evidently had his own method of ingress and egress.

There was a sudden pounding on the forward door of the warehouse; it was still locked, the alarm blaring. To follow the killer out his own exit hole would be suicide; Gideon needed to find another way. He looked wildly around but the only possible escape route lay above, through some louvered vents in the ceiling. Quickly he sprinted across the warehouse to a metal support and began shimmying up it.

"Open up!" yelled the cops. There was more pounding, followed by the crash of a battering ram.

Higher he climbed, using bolts as rungs; he reached a metal collar beam and crawled across it to a gusset, reached up again, grabbed a truss web member, and worked his way up it until he was at the level of the louvered vents.

The battering ram smashed into the metal door again, and again, and Gideon offered a silent prayer of thanks for the fine workmanship.

"Roland! You in there? Open up!"

Crawling up the sloping angle-iron truss on his hands and knees, Gideon gripped the iron, crouched again, and launched himself across the narrow gap, grasping the open louver, his feet swinging free.

A moment later, as the metal door caved in with a great crash, he hoisted himself up, crawled out the louver onto the sloping roof, and lay flat, breathing hard. Would they think of looking up here? They certainly would: as soon as they discovered the decapitated guard, the police warehouse was going to look like Grand Central Terminal.

Sliding down the pitch of the roof, he reached the drip edge along the back and peered over. Good—all the activity was still concentrated at the front. He could hear shouting and expostulations of horror and fury as the police found the guard's decapitated body.

What a balls-up.

Gideon grasped the drip edge, swung over, dropped to the ground, and headed to his previous opening. Then he reconsidered. The killer seemed to know an awful lot about his movements; he might be waiting there in ambush. Instead, Gideon sprinted to another part of the fence, climbed it, and as quickly as he could cut a crude gap through the concertina wire.

"Hey! You!"

Damn. He forced his way through the wire, feeling it slice his clothes and skin, and half climbed, half tumbled down the far side, landing in some bushes.

"Over here!" the cop yelled. "Suspect in flight! This way!"

Boom, the cop fired at him as he darted across the overgrown lot at the rear of the warehouse, dodging between abandoned containers, burned-out cars, and dumped refrigerators. He sprinted toward the railroad tracks running alongside the river; leaping over them and pushing through a sagging fence, he reached the embankment of riprap at the river's edge. An onshore wind brought with it the sulfurous stench of the Harlem River. Hopping and skipping from rock to rock, he dove in.

He swam underwater as far as he could, surfaced to gulp air, swam some more, and then—with as little disturbance as possible—returned to the surface. Jettisoning the heavy weight of the bolt cutters, he let himself drift downstream, floating without treading water, keeping his head as low in the water as possible. He could hear shouts from the shore and an unintelligible screed over an electronic megaphone. A feeble spotlight swung out over the water, but he was already out of reach; nevertheless, he turned his head to show only his black hair. There was quite a lot of flotsam bobbing downstream along with him, and for once he was grateful for the slovenly habits of New Yorkers. He wondered if he'd need to get a battery of shots after this little immersion, then realized it didn't matter—he was a dead man anyway.

He drifted along, letting the river take him downstream toward the fantastical arched and lighted form of the RFK Bridge. Slowly, the sluggish current moved him toward the Manhattan side of the river. Now he was thoroughly out of sight of the cops. Kicking his way over to the riverbank, he crawled up on a riprap boulder and began squeezing the water out of his clothes. He'd lost the Python somewhere in the river; good riddance to it. He would have had to toss it anyway, since shells and rounds had been left back in the warehouse; besides, it was too heavy a gun for his purposes.

He reached into his pocket and extracted the ziplock bag. It was still sealed, the cell phone inside safe and dry.

Balancing on the rocks, he made his way up the embankment, through yet another busted up chain-link fence, and found himself in a huge salt storage yard for the road department, mounds of white rising up around him like snowy mountains in some alien landscape painted by Nicholas Roerich.

The thought of Roerich triggered a rather interesting memory.

He would never get a cab this far uptown at four o'clock in the morning, especially in his sopping condition. He had a long walk back to the hotel, where he'd have to sneak his shit out and find another place to go to ground. And then it would be time to renew his old acquaintance with Tom O'Brien at Columbia.

He wondered what good old Tom would make of all this.

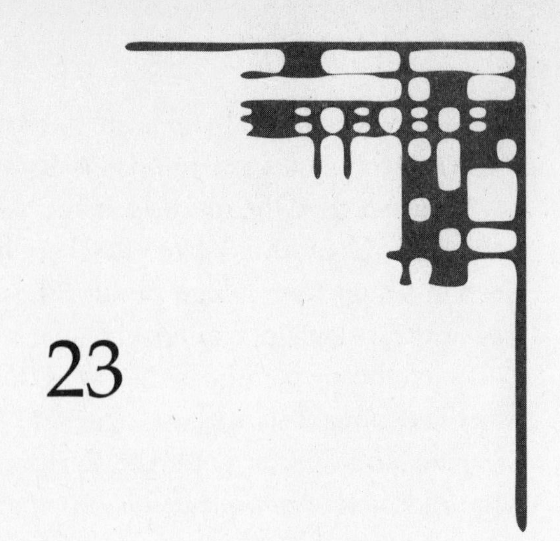

23

Gideon Crew walked east on 49th Street, still slightly damp from his misadventure of the previous night. It was eight o'clock in the morning and the sidewalks were in the full flow of the morning's rush hour, commuters pouring out of the surrounding apartment buildings and heading for taxis or public transportation. Gideon was not normally given to paranoid thinking, but ever since he'd sneaked out of the hotel he'd had the uncanny feeling he was being followed. Nothing he could put his finger on—just a feeling. No doubt it had something to do with lingering worries from the previous evening's shootout. The one thing he couldn't do was allow whoever it was—if there was indeed someone—to follow him to Tom O'Brien's place up at Columbia University. Tom O'Brien was to be his secret weapon in this and nobody—*nobody*—could know.

He slowed his pace until most of the pedestrians—swift-walking New Yorkers, all—were flowing past him. Then he casually paused to look at himself in a window while turning his attention behind. It was as he thought: an Asian man in a tracksuit, face half-hidden by a baseball cap, was a hundred yards back, also slowing down, apparently keeping pace.

Gideon swore under his breath. While it might still be in his imagination, he could take no chances. Even if it wasn't that particular fellow, with all these crowds it could be anyone. He had to assume he was being followed and act accordingly.

He crossed Broadway and entered the subway station, going to the downtown platform. The station was packed, and it was impossible to know if the man in the tracksuit had followed him down. But it didn't matter—there was one surefire way to lose the son of a bitch. Gideon had done it before. It was fun and dangerous and foolproof. He felt his heart quicken in anticipation.

He waited until he heard a faint rumble from the uptown tracks across the way. As he leaned out, he could see the headlights of a local coming up the tunnel, closing in fast on the platform.

Waiting for just the right moment, and making sure no other trains were coming, he leapt down onto the tracks. There was a gratifying chorus of screams, shouts, and loud admonishments from the waiting crowd. Ignoring them, he hopped over the third rail, crossed the uptown local tracks just ahead of the arriving train, and scrambled onto the platform. More screaming, shouts, hollering—*people are so excitable,* he thought. But the platform was unbelievably crowded, no one could move, and as the local pulled in he forced his way inside, mingling with the crush of commuters and instantly rendering himself anonymous.

As the train pulled out he saw, through the grimy window, across the rails, the Asian man in a tracksuit still standing on the downtown platform, staring in his direction.

Screw you, too, thought Gideon, settling in to read the *Post* over the shoulder of the person standing next to him.

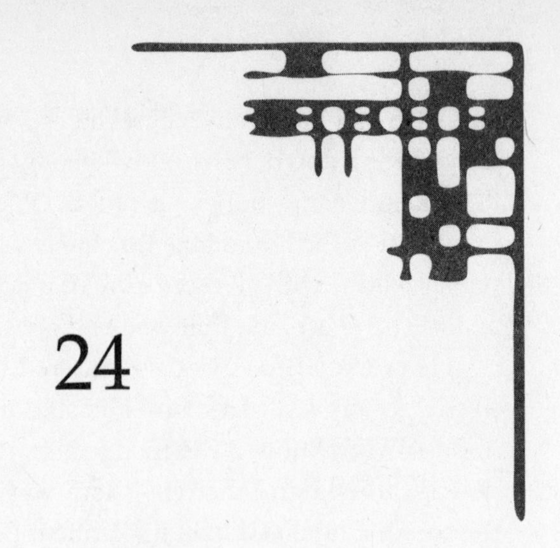

24

Like the whining of a mosquito, the persistent sound of a buzzer intruded into the exceedingly pleasant dream of Tom O'Brien. He sat up with a groan and looked at his clock. Nine thirty in the morning. Who could possibly be disturbing him at this ungodly hour?

The buzzer sounded again, three short blasts. O'Brien muttered, throwing off the covers, pushing the cat to the floor, and picking his way through the strewn apartment to the door. He pushed the intercom button. "Go fuck yourself."

"It's me. Gideon. Let me up."

"Do you have any idea what time it is?"

"Just let me up, you can bitch later."

O'Brien thumbed the door-lock button, unlatched his front door, and wandered back to his bed, sitting down and rubbing his face.

A minute later Gideon came in, carrying a bulky Pelican case. O'Brien stared at him. "Well, well, look what the cat dragged in. When did you blow into town?"

Ignoring this, Gideon set down the case, went to the window, and, standing next to it, opened the curtain with a finger and peered out.

"Cops after you? You still boosting shit out of museums?"

"You know I gave that up a long time ago."

"You look like yesterday's feces."

"You're always so affirmative, that's one of the things I like about you. Where's the coffee?"

O'Brien pointed a finger toward the Pullman kitchen at the back of the studio apartment. Avoiding the moldy dishes in the sink, Gideon rattled around and soon emerged with a coffeepot and mugs.

"Man, you're ripe," said O'Brien, helping himself to a cup. "And your duds are revolting. What the hell you been doing?"

"I've been swimming in the Harlem River and being chased across subway tracks."

"You're kidding?"

"I'm not kidding."

"Want to take a shower?"

"Love to. And also—got any clothes I can borrow?"

O'Brien went into his closet and sorted through a huge pile of suspiciously dirty clothing sitting on the floor, picking out a few items and tossing them toward Gideon.

Ten minutes later, he was cleaned up and dressed in reasonably fresh clothes. They felt a little loose on him—O'Brien hadn't stayed quite as skinny as Gideon—and they were covered with satanic designs and logos of the death metal band Cannibal Corpse.

"You look marvelous," O'Brien said. "But you've got the pants pulled up too high." He reached over and tugged them so they were hanging halfway down Gideon's ass. "That's how it's supposed to look."

"Your taste in music and clothing is atrocious." Gideon hiked them back up. "Look, I need your help. I've got a few problems for you to solve."

O'Brien shrugged, sipped his coffee.

Gideon unlocked the Pelican case and removed a piece of paper. "I'm working on an assignment, undercover. I can't tell you much about it—except that I'm looking for a set of plans."

"Plans? What sort of plans?"

"To a weapon."

"Cloak and dagger, man. What kind of weapon?"

"I don't know. And that's really all I can safely tell you." He handed him the piece of paper. "There is a bunch of numbers here. I have no idea what they mean. I want you to tell me."

"Is it some kind of code?"

"All I know is it has something to do with weapon plans."

O'Brien eyeballed the sheet. "I can tell you right off that there's a theoretical upper limit to the amount of information that could be contained in these numbers, and it isn't even enough to detail the plans for a pop-gun."

"The numbers could be something else, a passcode, bank account or safe-deposit, directions to a hiding place, the encoded name and address of a contact... or, for all I know, a recipe for chop suey."

O'Brien grunted. Over the years, he had gotten used to his friend's vanishings and reappearances, his black moods, his secretive doings and quasi-criminal habits. But this really took the cake. He stared at the numbers, then a smile cracked his face. "These numbers are anything but random," he said.

"How do you know?"

O'Brien grunted. "Just looking at 'em. I doubt this is a code at all."

"What is it, then?"

O'Brien shrugged, laid the paper down. "What other goodies you got in that case?"

Gideon reached in and pulled out a passport and credit card. O'Brien took them; both were Chinese. He stared. "Is all this . . . legal?"

"It's necessary—for our country."

"Since when did you become a patriot?"

"What's wrong with patriotism—especially when it pays?"

"Patriotism, my dear chap, is the last refuge of a scoundrel."

"Spare me your left-wing twaddle. I don't see you packing your bags and moving to Russia."

"All right, all right, stop hyperventilating. So what do you want me to do with the passport and credit card?"

"Both have magnetic stripes containing data. I want you to download that data and parse it, see if anything unusual is hidden in it."

"Piece of cake. Next?"

Gideon reached back into the case and removed, with enormous gravitas, a ziplock bag containing a cell phone. He laid it in O'Brien's palm. "This is really important. This phone belonged to a Chinese physicist. I need you to extract all the information this phone contains. I've already gotten its list of recent calls and contacts, but that's suspiciously short—there might be more that have been hidden or deleted. If he's used it for web browsing, I want the entire history. If there are photos I want those, too. And finally—and most important—I think there's a very good chance the plans for the weapon are hidden in that phone."

"Lucky for you I read and write Mandarin."

"Why do you think I'm here?" said Gideon. "It isn't because I miss your ugly mug. You are a gentleman of singular and diverse endowments."

"And not just in the intellectual department." O'Brien laid the cell phone on a table. "Any money in it for me?"

Gideon extracted from his pocket a massive, sodden roll of banknotes.

"That's a charming Kansas City roll you got there."

Gideon peeled off ten limp bills. "A thousand dollars. I'll give you another thousand when you're done. And I need it, like, done yesterday."

O'Brien collected the wet money and lovingly spread it out on his windowsill to dry. "This is a challenge. I like challenges."

Gideon seemed to hesitate. "One other thing." His voice was suddenly different.

O'Brien looked over. Gideon was removing a manila envelope. "I've got some X-rays and CT scans here. Friend of mine. The guy doesn't feel right, wants a doctor to look these over."

O'Brien frowned. "Why doesn't he ask his own doctor? I don't know shit about medicine. Or take it to your doctor, for Chrissakes."

"I'm busy. Look, he just wants a second opinion. Surely you know some good doctors around here."

"Well, sure, we got a few at the medical school." He opened the file, picked up an X-ray. "Name's been cut out."

"The guy values his privacy."

"Is there *anything* you do that isn't shady? Doctors are expensive."

Gideon laid two more C notes on the table. "Just take care of it, okay?"

"Right, fine, no need to get snippy." He was taken aback by Gideon's sudden short tone of voice. "It's gonna take time. These guys are busy."

"Be careful and for God's sake keep your big mouth shut. No kidding. I'll be back tomorrow."

"Please," groaned O'Brien, "not before noon."

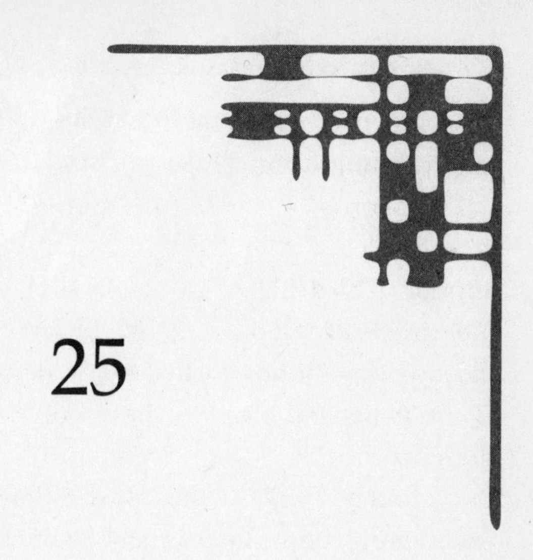

25

The hourly rate hotel room was about as sordid as they came, like something out of a 1950s noir film: the blinking neon light outside the window, elephant stains on the walls, pressed-tin ceiling coated with fifty layers of paint, sagging bed, and smell of frying hamburger in the passageway outside. Gideon Crew dumped his shopping bags on the bed and began unloading them.

"How are we gonna do it if the bed's covered with stuff?" asked the prostitute, standing in the door, pouting.

"Sorry," said Gideon, "we're not doing it."

"Oh yeah? Are you one of those guys who just wants to talk?"

"Not really." He laid out everything on the bed and stared at it, looking for inspiration, his eye roving over the fake paunches, the cheek inserts, the noses and wigs and beards, latex, prostheses, tattoos, pads. Next to this assortment, he spread out some of the clothing he had bought. While he had shaken off his pursuer, it hadn't been easy and the man was a serious professional. He had two places to visit, and it was likely the man, or possibly a compatriot, would be lurking at one or both of them.

It would take more than a disguise to pull this off; it would take creating a new role, and for that the woman was essential. Gideon straightened up and looked at the prostitute. She was nice looking, not drugged out, with a bright-eyed, wiseass attitude. Dyed black hair, pale skin, dark lipstick, slender figure, small sharp nose—he liked the Goth look of her. He sorted through the clothes, picked out a black T-shirt, and laid it aside. Camo pants and black leather boots with thick soles completed the wardrobe.

"Mind if I smoke?" she asked, tapping a cigarette out of a pack and lighting it up. She took a deep drag. Gideon strolled over and slipped the cigarette out of her hand, took a drag himself, handed it back.

"So what's all this?" she said, gesturing at the bed with her cigarette.

"I'm going to rob a bank."

"Right." She blew out a stream of smoke.

Gideon resisted the urge to bum a cigarette from her. Instead, he took another drag from hers.

"Hey," she said, looking at his right hand. "What happened to your finger?"

"Too much nail biting."

"Cute. So what you need me for?"

"You were a good way for me to get this, ah, *inexpensive* hotel room without attracting attention or having to show ID. I need a place to plan the heist."

"You're not really going to rob a bank," she said, but there was a note of concern in her voice.

He laughed. "Not really. I'm actually in the film business. Actor and producer. Creighton McFallon's the name. Perhaps you've heard it."

"Sounds familiar. You got any work for me?"

"Why do you think you're here? You're going to play my girlfriend for a while. To help me immerse myself in a role. It's called Method acting—know about that?"

"Hey, I'm an actress, too. Name's Marilyn."

"Marilyn what?"

"Marilyn's enough. I was an extra in an episode of *Mad Men*."

"I knew it! I'm going to change my looks, but you can be just who you are. In fact, you're perfect."

The woman gave him a quick smile and he saw, briefly, the real person underneath.

"You know, I gotta get paid for something like this."

"Naturally. What would your rate be for, say, six hours?"

"Doing what?"

"Walking around town with me."

"Well, I'd normally make at least a grand for six hours of work, but seeing as how this is the film business, make it two. And I'll throw in a little special something, just for you . . . 'cause you're cute." She smiled and touched her lower lip with a finger.

He took a small bundle of bills out of his pocket and handed them to her. "There's five hundred. You'll get the rest at the end."

She took it a little doubtfully. "I should get half up front."

"All right." He gave her another bundle. "You're going to need a new name. Shall we call you Orchid?"

"Okay."

"Good. For the next six hours, we're going to be in character at all times. That's how Method acting works. But right now I have a few things I have to do, preparation and so forth, so you go ahead and relax."

Gideon sorted through the supplies as he visualized the sort of person he wanted to be. Then he began to create it. When he was done with the makeup, a false nose, cheek inserts, receding hairline, paunch—with the aging-pseudo-rocker clothing to go with it—he turned to Orchid, who had been watching the process with interest, smoking nonstop.

"Wow. That's sad. I liked how you looked before a lot better."

"That's acting," said Gideon. "Now give me a few minutes here, Orchid, and then we'll step out and get into the role."

He took out the list of contacts he had copied from Wu's phone, unfolded his laptop, and booted it up. *Thank God for free Wi-Fi,* he thought, now available even in hourly hotels. He connected to the internet and did a quick bit of research. There was only one phone on the contact list in the United States, and it was labeled "Fa." A quick bit of research indicated that *Fa* was a Chinese character meaning "to commence." It was also a mah-jongg tile called "the Green Dragon." A reverse phone number search indicated the "Fa" phone number belonged to a certain Roger Marion on Mott Street in Chinatown.

Roger. The name the Chinese the scientist had called him.

He began packing away his stuff. With his disguise and Orchid on his arm, he felt pretty sure that nobody, not even his mother, would guess who he was. Whoever was after him was on the lookout for him alone: they wouldn't be interested in an aging rocker with a bimbo in tow.

"What now?"

"We're going to see an old pal in Chinatown, and then we're going to visit a sick friend in the hospital."

"Got time for that little extra I mentioned? You know, to help you get into the role?" Her eyes twinkled as she stubbed out her cigarette.

No, no, no, thought Gideon, but as he looked at her upturned nose, jet-black hair, and fresh, creamy skin, he heard himself say, "Sure, what the hell. I think we can manage it, time-wise."

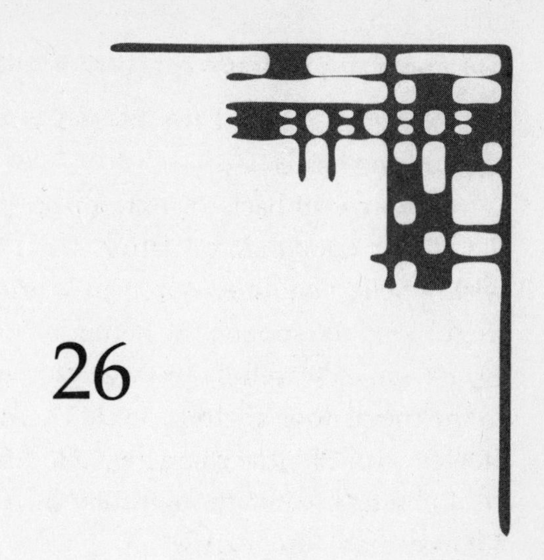

26

The address, 426 Mott, was in the heart of Chinatown, between Grand and Hester. Gideon Crew stood on the opposite sidewalk, giving it a once-over. The Hong Li Meat Market occupied the ground floor, and the upper stories were a typical Chinatown brown-brick tenement, festooned with fire escapes.

"What now?" asked Orchid, lighting up yet another cigarette.

Gideon plucked the cigarette out of her fingers and took a drag.

"Why don't you get your own?"

"I don't smoke."

She laughed. "Maybe we can get some dim sum around here. I love dim sum."

"I've got to see a fellow first. You mind waiting here?"

"What, on the street?"

He suppressed an ironic comment. He slipped out a banknote. God, he thought, it was nice having money. "Why don't you wait for me in that tea shop? I doubt this is going to take more than five minutes."

"All right." She took the bill and sauntered off, derriere twitching, turning heads.

Gideon went back to contemplating the problem at hand. He didn't have enough information about Roger Marion to come up with a believable line. But even a brief encounter might prove useful. And the sooner, the better.

He looked carefully both ways, then crossed Mott and went to the metal door at street level. There was a row of buzzers, all labeled with Chinese characters. No English at all.

Rubbing his chin thoughtfully, he stepped back and stopped a Chinese man. "Excuse me?"

The man stopped. "Yes?"

"I don't read Chinese, and I'm trying to figure out which one of these apartments belongs to my friend."

"What is your friend's name?"

"Roger Marion. But he goes by the nickname Fa—you know, the mah-jongg character they call the Green Dragon?"

The man smiled, pointed to a character beside the label 4C. "That is Fa."

"Thank you." The man walked on and Gideon stared at the character, memorizing it. Then he pressed the button.

"Yes?" came the voice almost immediately, in unaccented English.

He lowered his voice to a conspiratorial hiss. "Roger? I'm a friend of Mark's. Let me in right away."

"Who? What's your name?"

"No time to explain. I'm being followed. Let me in, please!"

The buzzer sounded and he pushed in, climbing a dingy set of stairs to the fourth floor. He knocked on the apartment door.

"Who is it?"

He could see the man's eye in the peephole. "Like I said, I'm a friend of Mark Wu's. The name's Franklin Van Dorn."

"What do you want?"

"I've got the numbers."

The bolt shot open and the door opened to reveal a small, intense Caucasian man in his mid-forties: shaved head, very fit and alert, thin and whippet-muscular, wearing a tight T-shirt and baggy pajama-type pants.

Gideon ducked in. "Roger Marion?"

A sharp nod. "Mark gave you the numbers? Give them to me."

"I can't do that until you tell me what this is all about."

The features immediately creased with suspicion. "You don't need to know. If you were really a friend of Mark's, you wouldn't ask."

"I must know."

Marion looked at him intently. "Why?"

Gideon stood his ground, saying nothing. Meanwhile, he took in the small, crowded, but neat apartment. There were Chinese block prints on the walls, scrolls covered with ideograms, and a curious, colorful tapestry showing a reverse swastika surrounded by yin–yang symbols and spinning designs. There were also various placards and awards that—when he looked more closely—turned out to be for kung fu competitions.

Gideon returned his attention to Marion. The man was looking back at him as if making up his mind. He did not appear in the least bit nervous. There was something about his manner that told Gideon he was not one to push his weight around, but that—if the need arose—he could be violent.

Quite abruptly, the man spoke. "Out," he said. "Get out now." He moved toward Gideon menacingly.

"But I have the numbers—"

"I don't trust you. You're a liar. Get out now."

Gideon placed a light hand on the man's advancing shoulder. "How do you know—"

With frightening speed, the man grabbed the hand and twisted it sharply, spinning him around. "Shit!" Gideon cried out, pain lancing through his shoulder and down his arm.

"Out." He ejected Gideon out the door and slammed it, the bolts shooting back.

Standing in the hall, Gideon rubbed his hurt shoulder thoughtfully. He wasn't used to being smoked out, and it was not a pleasant feeling. He'd assumed making up a story would be worse than nothing—but maybe he'd assumed incorrectly. He hoped he wasn't losing his touch.

He found Orchid in the tea shop, chowing down a plate heaped with pressed duck and white rice. "They didn't have dim sum but this is pretty good," she said, grease dripping down her chin.

"We've got to go."

Overriding her protests, he hustled her out and they walked over to Grand, where they grabbed a cab.

"Mount Sinai Hospital," he told the driver.

"To see your friend?" Orchid asked.

Gideon nodded.

"Is he sick?"

"Very."

"I'm sorry. What happened?"

"Car accident."

At the reception desk, Gideon gave his real name, making sure nobody but the duty nurse heard him speak. Even though he looked very different from the Gideon Crew who had come in after the accident, he was confident he wouldn't run into anyone who had seen him before in the huge city hospital. When he'd called earlier in the day, he'd also learned Wu had been transferred from the ER to the intensive care unit. Even better, he'd been told Wu was coming out of the coma. He wasn't yet lucid, but they felt he might be soon.

Soon would be now.

Gideon had come prepared with a beautifully wrought plan of social engineering. He'd talk to Wu, posing as Roger Marion, and get everything out of the scientist—the location of the plans, the meaning of the numbers, everything. He had gone over his plan in detail and felt at least ninety percent certain it would work. He very much doubted Wu had ever met or seen "Roger," only talked to him on the phone, and Gideon, after his visit, at least had an idea of how the man talked and sounded. Wu would be disoriented, off his guard. The man would have been too devastated at the accident scene to have taken note of his features. He could pull this off. Despite being shot at, despite his dunking in the river, it would be by far the easiest hundred thousand he'd ever earned.

The busy duty nurse didn't even bother to check his ID against his face, just directed them both to a large and comfortable waiting area. Gideon glanced around but saw no one he recognized. Yet he was certain the one who had chased him would not be far behind.

"The doctor will be down to see you in a moment," the nurse told him.

"We can't just go visit Mark?"

"No."

"But they said he was much better."

"You'll have to wait for the doctor," said the nurse firmly.

The doctor arrived a few minutes later, a portly man with woolly white hair and a sad, friendly look on his face. "Mr. Crew?"

Gideon leapt up. "Yes, Doctor, that's me. How is he?"

"And the lady is—?"

"A friend. She's here to support me."

"Very well," he said. "Please come with me."

They followed the doctor into another, smaller waiting room, more like an office, empty of people. The doctor closed the door behind them.

"Mr. Crew, I'm very, very sorry to tell you that Mr. Wu passed away about half an hour ago."

Gideon stood thunderstruck.

"I'm very, very sorry."

"You didn't call me—to be there at the end."

"We tried to reach you at the number you gave us."

Damn, thought Gideon; his cell phone had not survived the swim.

"Mr. Wu gave signs of stabilizing, and we had hopes for a while. But he was severely injured, and sepsis set in. This is not uncommon with severe injuries. We took every possible measure and did the best we could, but it wasn't nearly enough."

Gideon swallowed. He felt Orchid's comforting hand on his shoulder.

"I have here some paperwork, unfortunately necessary, which you as next of kin will need to fill out regarding the disposition of the remains and some other details." He proffered a manila packet to Gideon. "You don't need to do this right away, but we would like to know as soon as possible. In three days, Mr. Wu's remains will be moved to the city morgue to await your instructions. Would you like me to arrange for you to see the body?"

"Um, no, no, that won't be necessary." Gideon took the folder. "Thank you, Doctor. Thank you for all your help."

The doctor nodded.

"By any chance... did Mark say anything before he passed? When I talked to the nurse this morning, she said she thought he was becoming lucid. If he said anything, anything at all, even if it seemed nonsensical, I'd like to know."

"He showed signs of regaining lucidity, but it never actually rose to the level of consciousness. He said nothing. And then the sepsis set in." He looked at Gideon. "I'm terribly sorry. For what it's worth, he didn't suffer at all."

"Thank you, Doctor."

The doctor nodded and left.

Gideon threw himself into a chair. Orchid sat down next to him, her face creased with concern. He reached into his pocket, removed a sheaf of bills, and handed them to her. "This is for you. When we leave the hospital, we'll get in a cab together, but after a while I'll get out of the cab while you continue on to wherever you want to go."

She didn't take the money.

"Thanks for your help," he said. "I really appreciated it."

"Creighton, or Crew, or whatever your name is, I can guess this isn't really about some Method acting gig. You're a nice guy, and it's been a long time since I met any nice guys. Whatever you're doing, I want to help." She pressed his hand.

Gideon cleared his throat. "Thanks, but I've got to do this alone." He knew how lame that sounded even as he said it.

"But... will I see you again? I don't care about the money."

Gideon glanced at her and was shocked at the look he saw on her face.

He thought about lying, but decided the truth was ultimately less painful. "No. I'm not going to call you. Look, the money's yours. You earned it." He gave the bills an impatient shake.

"I don't want it," she said. "I want you to call me."

"Look," said Gideon as coldly as he could. "This was a business arrangement, and you did your job well. Just take the money and go."

She reached out, snatched the money. "You're an asshole." She turned to leave and he tried not to notice she was crying.

"Good-bye," he said, cringing inwardly.

"Good-bye, jerk-off."

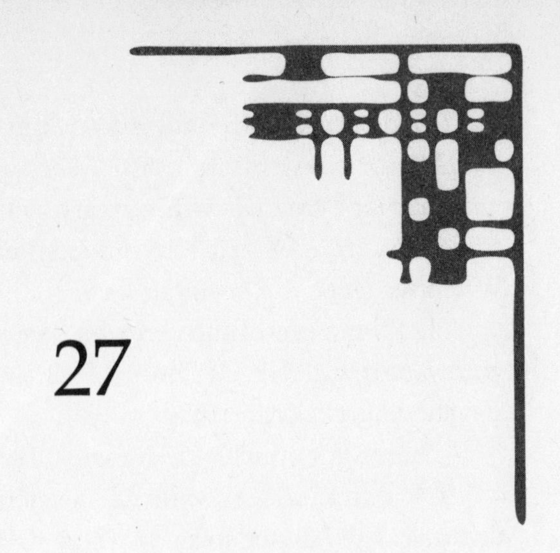

27

Gideon Crew strolled up Fifth Avenue and entered Central Park at the 102nd Street gate. He felt absolutely awful. It was early evening, and the joggers were out in force. He couldn't get Orchid's lovesick look out of his head. And now that Wu was dead—and his assignment had crashed and burned—he found himself replaying Glinn again and again in his mind, pulling out the medical file with a sorrowful look on his face. *Arteriovenous malformation.* The more he thought about it, the less probable it seemed: this mysterious illness that would just happen to strike him dead in a year with no warning, no treatment, no symptoms, nothing. It smelled phony, smacking of psychological manipulation. Glinn seemed the type to tell any kind of fantastic story if it got him what he wanted. Gideon walked aimlessly, not knowing where he was going, cutting across the baseball diamonds, heading west.

This is crazy, he thought, *just forget about Orchid and the file and move on. Focus on the problem.* But he couldn't forget. He pulled out a new cell phone he'd bought—a cheapie with preloaded minutes—and called Tom O'Brien as he walked.

"Yo" came the abrasive voice after an inordinate number of rings.

"Gideon here. What news?"

"Jeez, you told me I'd have twenty-four hours."

"Well?"

"Well, the credit card and passport are just that. No hidden data. The cell phone's the same. It's a brand-new SIM card phone, probably just purchased."

"Damn."

"All that's left on it are the contacts you already got, a few recent calls—and that's it. No other hidden data, no secret microchips, nothing."

"What about the string of numbers I gave you?"

"Those are a lot more interesting. I'm still working on them."

Gideon turned south. It was now dusk, and the park was emptying.

"Interesting why?"

"Like I told you before, lot of patterns in here."

"Such as?"

"Repeated numbers, rows of decreasing numbers, stuff like that. Right now it's hard to say what they mean. I just started in on them. It's definitely not code."

Central Park Reservoir loomed ahead, and he stepped onto the jogging path. The water lay dark and still. Far to the south, over the tops of the trees, Gideon could see the skyline of Midtown, the lights in the buildings glowing against the fading sky.

"How do you know?"

"Any decent code yields a string of numbers that look random. They aren't, of course, but all the mathematical tests for randomness will show that they are. In this case, even the simplest test shows they're not random."

"Test? Such as?"

"Tallying up the digits. A truly random string has roughly ten percent zeros, ten percent ones, et cetera. This one is way heavy on the zeros and ones."

There was a silence. Gideon took a deep breath and tried to speak casually. "And the CT scans I gave you?"

"Oh yeah. I passed them along to a doctor like you asked."

"And?"

"I was supposed to call him this afternoon. I forgot."

"Right," said Gideon.

"I'll call him first thing in the morning."

"You do that," said Gideon. "Thanks." He wiped his brow. He felt like shit.

And then all of a sudden—for the second time that day—he had the distinct impression he was being followed. He looked around. It was almost dark, and he was in the middle of the park.

"Hello? Anyone home?" asked O'Brien.

Gideon realized he hadn't hung up. "Yeah. Listen, I've got to go. See you tomorrow."

"Not before noon."

He closed the phone and stuck it in his pocket. Maintaining a brisk stride, he headed west past the tennis courts, still keeping to the jogging path. What made him feel he was being followed this time? He hadn't heard or seen anything...or had he? Long ago, he'd learned to trust his instincts—and they'd saved his ass again just that morning.

He realized that, by following the jogging path, he was making it easy for his follower—if there was one. Better turn back to the north, get off the paths, and cut through the wooded area around the courts. The pursuer would have to stay closer. And then Gideon could figure out a way to double around and come up behind.

He cut off the path and entered the woods below the courts. There were dead leaves underfoot that rustled as he walked. He continued for a moment, then stopped abruptly, pretending to have dropped something—and heard the crunch of leaves behind him cease abruptly as well.

Now he knew he was being followed, and his stupidity began to dawn on him. He didn't have a weapon, he was in the middle of the empty park—how had he allowed this to happen? He'd been upset about Orchid, who'd turned out to have feelings as tender as a damn teenager's. He'd been worrying about Glinn and his medical folder. And as a result he'd let down his guard.

He started up again, walking fast. He couldn't let them know that he knew. But he had to get out of the park as soon as possible, get among people. He swung around the tennis courts and took a sharp left, walked along the court fence and then, in a bushy area, briefly reversed direction and made a quick ninety-degree dogleg, angling back toward the reservoir.

That would, he hoped, confuse the bastard.

"Move and you're dead," spoke a voice from the darkness, and a figure with a gun stepped out in front of him.

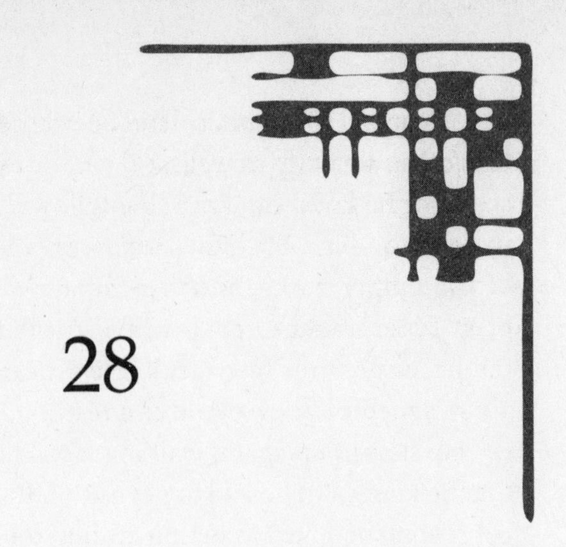

28

Gideon halted, tensed to spring, but held his ground. It had been a woman's voice.

"Don't be stupid. Raise your hands. Slowly."

Gideon raised his hands, and the figure took another step forward. She had a Glock trained on him with both hands, and he could see from her stance that she was thoroughly trained in its use. Slender, athletic, her mahogany hair was pulled back in a heavy, loose ponytail, and she wore a dark leather jacket over a crisp white blouse and blue slacks.

"Put your hands against that tree and lean out, legs apart."

Jesus, thought Gideon. He did as he was told and the woman hooked one foot inside his and patted him down. She stepped back.

"Turn around, keeping your hands raised."

He complied.

"Name is Mindy Jackson, Central Intelligence Agency. I'd show you my ID but my hands are full at the moment."

"Right," said Gideon. "Now, look, Ms. Jackson—"

"Shut up. I'll do the talking. Now, I'd like you to tell me who you're working for and what the hell you think you're doing."

Gideon tried to relax. "Couldn't we discuss this—"

"You don't follow directions well, do you? Talk."

"Or what? You're going to shoot me here in Central Park?"

"Lots of people get shot in Central Park."

"You fire that gun and in five minutes this place will be swarming with cops. Just think of the paperwork."

"Answer my questions."

"Maybe."

There was a tense silence. "Maybe?" she said, finally.

"You want me to talk? Fine. Not at gunpoint and not here. All right? If you're really CIA, we're on the same side."

He could see her thinking. She relaxed, holstered the gun under her thin jacket. "That would work."

"Ginza's over on Amsterdam has a nice bar, if it's still around."

"It's still around."

"So you're a New Yorker?"

"Let's dispense with the chitchat, shall we?"

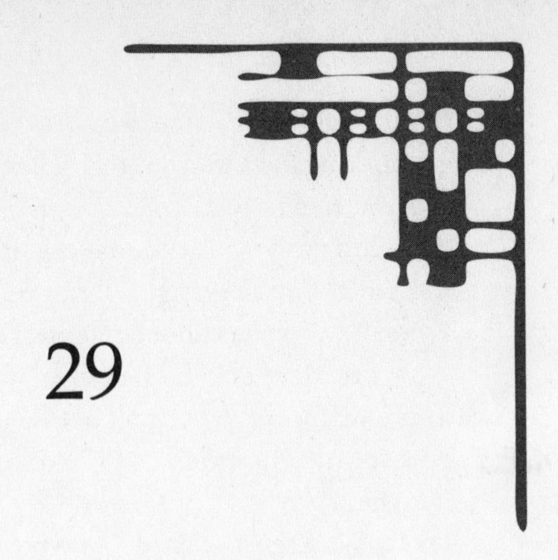

29

Sitting at the bar, Gideon ordered sake, Mindy Jackson a Sapporo. They said nothing while waiting for the drinks to arrive. In the light, with the coat off, he was able to see her better: full lips, a small nose, just a hint of freckles, thick brown hair, green eyes. Thirty, maybe thirty-two. Smart. But maybe too nice for her line of work—although, he reminded himself, you never could tell. The important thing was, even though he had no idea what it might be, she had information he needed—he was sure of that. And to get it, he'd have to give.

The drinks arrived and Jackson took a sip, then turned to him, a hostile look on her face. "All right. Now who are you and why are you interested in Wu?"

"Just as I'm sure you can't tell me all the details of your assignment, I can't tell you mine." The walk over had given Gideon time to work up a story; but he had always felt that the best lie was the one closest to the truth. "I don't even have a badge, as you do. Oh, by the way, as a professional courtesy I'd like to see yours."

"We don't have badges. We have IDs." She brought hers out and quickly flashed it at him under the bar. "So. Who do you work for?"

"I know this is going to frustrate you, Mindy, but I work for a private contractor with the DHS. They wanted me to get the plans for the weapon from Wu."

She stared at him and he could see she was pissed. "DHS? What the hell are they doing meddling in our affairs? With a *private* contractor?"

He shrugged.

"What do you know?" she asked.

"Nothing."

"Bullshit. Wu spoke to you right after the accident. He said something to you. I want to know what it was."

"He told me to tell his wife he loved her."

"That's not even a decent lie. He doesn't have a wife. He gave you some numbers. I want to know what those numbers are."

Gideon gazed into her face. "Um, what makes you think that he gave me numbers?"

"Witnesses. Said they saw you writing down numbers. Look," she said, brushing a stray lock of hair from her face. "You said it yourself. We're on the same side. We should be working together, pooling our resources."

"I haven't noticed you pooling with me."

"You give me the numbers and I'll pool with you."

"That sounds exciting."

"Don't be an ass. Give me the numbers."

"What do the numbers signify?"

She hesitated, and he sensed that maybe she didn't know. But numbers were always stimulating to a CIA agent.

"I've got a question for you," he continued, pushing just a little harder. "What is CIA doing working domestically? Isn't that FBI turf?"

"Wu was coming from overseas. You know that as well as I do."

"That's not answering my question."

"I can't answer your question," she said, looking increasingly irritated. "It's not my place to do so, and it sure as hell isn't any of your business."

"If you want to know anything more, you're going to have to answer it. You can't force me to talk. I haven't broken any laws. Talking to an injured man, inquiring about his condition, isn't illegal." He wondered where Mindy had been during the firefight at the police vehicle yard. Cutting somebody's head off, perhaps?

"If it's in the interests of national security, I can damn well make you talk."

"What, are you going to waterboard me right here at the bar?"

He saw her smile despite herself. She sighed. "This was too sensitive to hand off to the FBI. Wu was our honey pot. We set it up."

"You set up the honey trap?"

She hesitated. "Wu went to a scientific conference in Hong Kong, and we learned he had the plans with him. We set it up."

"Tell me about it."

She hesitated again, seemed to come to a private decision. "Okay. But if you'd like a behind-the-scenes tour of Guantánamo, just try telling somebody—*anybody*—what I'm telling you now. We hired a local call girl to have a chance encounter with Wu in the bar at the conference hotel. She brought him up to her room and satisfied his every fantasy—and we got the goods on him, video and audio and stills."

"And that actually worked? You said the guy wasn't married. What's he afraid of?"

"It works in China. The Chinese are prudish. It wasn't the sex, it was the perversion that, ah, would have destroyed his career."

He laughed. "Perversion? What was it?"

"Dominatrix. Athletic, over six feet, and blond. We had reason to believe he liked that stuff but we had a hell of a time finding one. She whipped his ass good and we got it all on video."

"Ouch. So then what happened to your blackmail scheme?"

"We approached him with the goods. Said we'd trade the pictures for the plans. But he freaked out. Said he needed half an hour to think about it. Instead he took off, got on the first plane here."

"You miscalculated."

She frowned.

"Why here?" he asked.

"We don't know."

"Was he defecting?"

"We have no idea what his intentions were. All we know is, he had the plans when he got on the plane."

"Hidden where?"

"No idea."

"And the car that ran him off the road? Who was that?"

"The Chinese are after him hammer and tongs. They sent an operative over to deal with Wu, immediately and with extreme prejudice. We believe he's a man known as Nodding Crane."

"Nodding Crane?"

"After a certain kung fu stance. We don't know his real name. He was sent to kill Wu and retrieve the plans. He did the first, but since he's still here, we figure the Chinese haven't gotten the plans. They're still floating around out there somewhere." She looked at him pointedly. "Unless *you've* got them."

"No," he said. "You know I don't. Why would I still be running around like this?"

She nodded. "Now: the numbers, please?"

He racked his brains, thinking how he could appear to be reciprocating without actually giving her anything. Could he tell her about the cell phone? But then he'd have to explain where he got it...bad idea. Giving her fake numbers would be an even worse idea. But, he sensed, so would be giving her the real numbers. She'd have no more need of him. And he believed Mindy Jackson could prove an invaluable asset.

"The honest-to-God truth is," he said, "I don't have the numbers with me."

The hostile expression returned immediately, this time with more than a hint of dubiousness. "Where are they?"

"I passed them on to my handlers. They're being analyzed."

"You didn't keep a copy?"

"For security reasons, no. That fellow—what's his name, Nodding Crane—seems to be after me."

"That is really unfortunate for you. You didn't memorize them?"

"It was a long string of numbers. Besides, I figured some things are better not known."

She stared at him. "I don't believe you."

He shrugged. "Look, when I next meet up with my handlers, I'll find a way to get you the numbers. And then I'll share them with you. Deal?" He gave her a big smile.

Her hostile expression softened just a little. "Why did you visit the hospital?"

"I was hoping Wu might have said something before he died."

"I guess you found out he didn't."

He nodded.

"Who was that Goth woman you were with?"

"A hooker I hired to help me go undercover, to sidetrack that assassin."

"It was a good disguise. That theatrical stuff you're wearing fooled me for a while. You are one ugly mother."

"Thank you."

"And now what are you doing?"

"Just what you're doing. Trying to figure out what Wu did

with the plans. Retracing his steps, looking for contacts, people he might have encountered on the way. So far, nothing." He spread his hands. "Look, Mindy, I appreciate you sharing with me, I really do." He tried to sound sincere. "Let's keep sharing. I promise I'll get you those numbers as soon as possible, and anything else I find I'll let you know. Fair enough?" He gave her another big honest grin.

She stared at him suspiciously. Then she scribbled a number on a napkin. "Here's my cell. Call me anytime, day or night. I hope for your sake you're not bullshitting me." She rose to go, dropping the napkin and a twenty on the bar.

"Thanks for pooling with me," Gideon said, with a smirk.

"You wish."

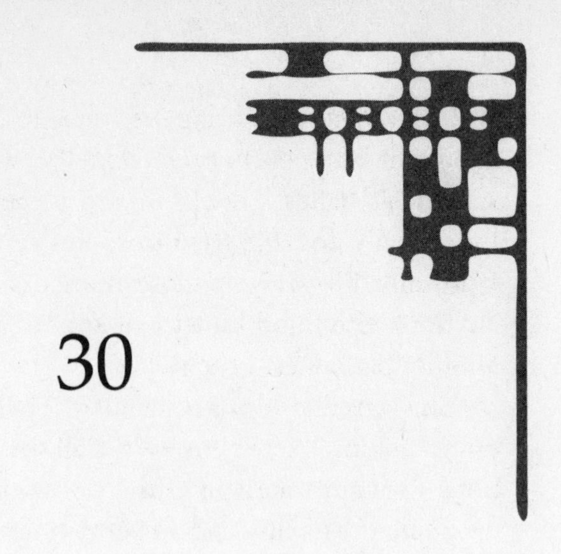

30

Tom O'Brien ate the last of the Chicken McNuggets—cold and stiff—chewing noisily as he perused the latest printout. He washed it down with a swig of kombucha. His tiny office was brilliantly lit by incandescent light—fluorescence left him depressed—and it was packed with papers, books, journals, coffee mugs, plates, and food trash. The lone barred window looked into an airshaft during the day, but at night it turned into a disconcerting mirror of the activity within. Someday, O'Brien thought, he would have to get blinds.

He paused, hearing a squeak, which he instantly recognized as the sticky knob of his office door. He froze as he saw the handle slowly turn. Whipping out his pocketknife, he moved behind the door, heart pounding.

The handle stopped turning, the door began to open. He stood, knife raised, poised to strike.

"Tom?" came the whispered voice.

"Jesus." O'Brien dropped his arm as Gideon Crew entered.

But when he saw the person, it wasn't Crew at all. He yelled, jumped back, brandishing the knife. "Who the hell—?"

"Hey. It's me."

"Christ, you look awful. What the hell do you mean sneaking up on me like this? And how did you get in? The building's locked up for the night. Oh, wait, don't tell me—old skills die hard, right?"

Gideon stepped inside, shut and locked the door behind him, swept some books off a chair, and collapsed. "Sorry about the subterfuge. It's for your own protection, actually."

O'Brien grunted. "You could have called ahead."

"I'm concerned the CIA might be involved," said Gideon. "Might be wiretapping my phone."

"I thought you *were* working for the government."

"In my Father's house are many mansions."

O'Brien folded up the knife and stuck it in his pocket. "You scared the crap out of me." He looked Gideon up and down. "Man, looks like you've been scarfing down corn dogs and shakes twenty-four seven."

"Amazing what they can do with prosthetics. How's the work going?"

"So-so." O'Brien went over to his table, piled with paper, sorted through a stack, and pulled out some sheets. "Take a look at this."

Gideon took the papers.

"Those numbers, they're nothing more than a list." He dropped another piece of paper in front of Gideon. "Here are the numbers, just as you gave them to me. Except I broke them up into three-digit groups. And when I did that, a remarkable pattern emerged. Take a look."

```
871 050 033 022 014 010
478 364 156 002
211 205 197 150 135 101 001
```

```
750 250
336 299 242 114 009
917 052 009 008 007 004 003
500 278 100 065 057
616 384
370 325 300 005
844 092 060 001 001 001 001
```

"Whaddya think?" said O'Brien, grinning at Gideon with amusement. The man didn't see the pattern. Some people were just thick when it came to numbers.

"Ah, yeah?" Gideon said.

"Look. Ten groups of three-digit numbers. Look at 'em. The pattern should be obvious to any idiot."

"Each group of numbers is in descending order?"

"Yes, but that's not the big thing. Look at each group—add 'em up."

A long silence. "Oh my God."

"Right. Each group adds up to a thousand."

"Which means...?"

"I'd guess they're lists of percentages, each one adding up to a thousand—or one hundred percent with one significant digit to the right of the decimal point. This is a formula of some kind: ten formulations set out with the ratios of their various components adding up to one hundred percent."

"One hundred percent of what?"

"It might be some kind of high-explosives formulation, an exotic metallurgy formula, a chemical or isotope formulation. I'm not a chemist or a condensed matter physicist—I'd need to bring in an expert."

"You have someone in mind?"

"Sadie Epstein. She's a professor in the Physics Department, an expert in metastable quasicrystal analysis."

"Is she discreet?"

"Very. But I'm not going to tell her much."

"Give it to her with a false cover story. Dream something up. Say it's a contest of some kind. You could win a trip to Oxford for the Isaac Newton Maths Conference in September."

"Can't you *not* lie? You make up a story even when there's no need."

"I take no pleasure in lying."

"You're the Holy Roman Emperor of liars. And since when are you so flush? Usually it's the poor mouth with you. Where are you staying?"

"I've been moving around town—spent last night at a twenty-dollar-an-hour motel in Canarsie. Tonight I'll crash at the Waldorf. Got a morning flight to Hong Kong."

"Hong Kong? How long are you going to be away?"

"No more than a day. I'll drop in when I return, see what you've found. Don't call me. And for God's sake, make sure this Sadie Epstein keeps her trap shut."

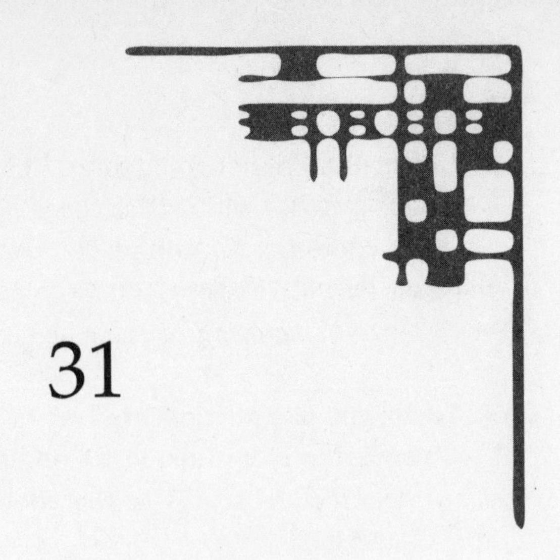

31

Norio Tatsuda had been a flight attendant on Japan Airline's Tokyo–New York run for almost six years, and when he first saw the man sitting in the wrong seat, he instantly recognized the type: one of those inexperienced and combative travelers who were sure they were going to get disrespected and taken advantage of at every turn. The man was wearing an expensive suit and a silly, floppy American hat, and he clutched a plastic carry-on as if it might be snatched away at any moment by one of the many obvious thugs and criminals roaming about the cabin.

With a warm, fake smile, Tatsuda approached the gentleman and gave a little bow. "May I trouble you to see your boarding pass, sir?"

"What for?" the man responded.

"Well, it seems the lady here"—he indicated the woman standing behind him—"has a seat assignment for the seat you are sitting in, and that is why I wanted to check your boarding pass."

"I'm in the right seat," the man said.

"I am not at all questioning that, sir, it could very well be a problem with the booking system, but I need to check nevertheless." He bestowed another broad smile on the scowling ape.

With a frown, the man searched his pockets and finally extracted a crumpled boarding pass. "There it is, if you're so interested in it."

"Thank you so *very* much." Tatsuda saw immediately the man was in the wrong seat; the wrong section, even. "You are Mr. Gideon Crew?"

"That's what it says, doesn't it?"

"Yes, indeed it does. Now, Mr. Crew, according to this boarding pass"—another expansive smile—"you are actually booked in our business-class section, up front."

"Business? I'm not traveling on business. I'm visiting my son."

This man, Tatsuda thought, was almost miraculously stupid. The pugnacious expression on the man's face, the protruding lips, furrowed brow and tilted chin, only confirmed it. "Mr. Crew, business class is not just for business travelers. There's more room up there and a higher quality of service." He waved the boarding pass. "You're supposed to be in a much more expensive seat."

Crew frowned. "My son bought the ticket, I don't know anything about that, but I'm settled in right here, thank you."

Tatsuda had never quite dealt with a situation like this before. He glanced back at the woman whose seat Crew occupied. Being Japanese, she had understood nothing of the exchange. He turned back to the man. "Sir, do you mean to say you would prefer to remain here for the duration of the flight? Your seat in business class will be much more comfortable."

"That's what I said, didn't I? I don't like businesspeople. Bunch of crooks. I want to be right here, in the middle of the plane where I'm safe, not up front in the death zone. That's what I told my son, and that's what I want."

Another bow. Tatsuda turned to the woman and switched to Japanese. "The gentleman," he said, "would like to exchange your seat here in economy class with his business-class seat at the front of the aircraft. Does this meet with your approval?"

It met with her approval.

With a passenger such as Gideon Crew, Tatsuda knew that the ordeal was only beginning, and the next challenge came as soon as the captain turned off the seat belt sign. As Tatsuda passed down the aisle taking drink orders, he found Crew on his feet, hunched over his seat. He had pulled up his cushion and was feeling all along the seams and in the spaces behind the seat.

"May I be of assistance, Mr. Crew?"

"I lost my damn contact lens."

"Allow me to help."

He squinted at Tatsuda with one eye. "Help? How're you going to do that when I can hardly turn around in here?"

Tatsuda could see the passenger next to Crew rolling his eyes in exasperation.

"If you do need help, please let me know. In the meantime, may I have your drink order, Mr. Crew?"

"Gin and tonic."

"Yes, sir." Tatsuda withdrew, but he kept an eye on Crew from the galley. The man had finished searching and palpating the seat cushion and was now fumbling about in the seat compartment. He could see that the man's rough handling had actually caused one of the seams in the cushion to come apart, and the seat covering as well seemed to be falling loose. He would have to carefully monitor the man's alcoholic intake, as he looked exactly like the type who used a long plane journey as an excuse to get drunk.

But Crew did not order a second drink, and after an endless

and obsessive search that even involved several overhead compartments, as if his contact lens might have somehow fallen upward, the man fell back in his seat and went soundly to sleep. And, to Tatsuda's great relief, the difficult passenger proceeded to sleep like a baby all the way to Tokyo.

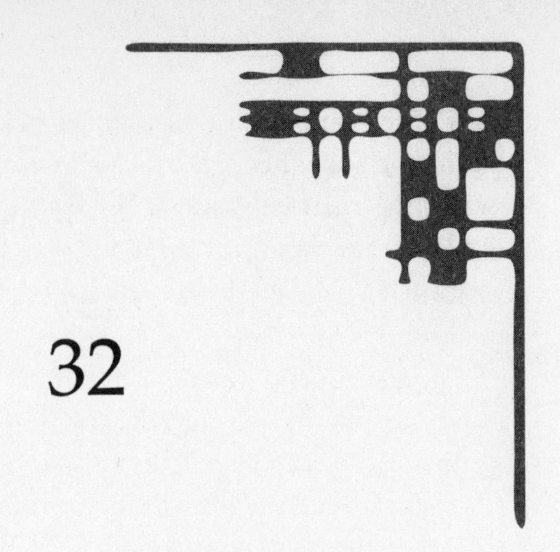

32

Gideon Crew stepped into the vast interior of the Tai Tam Hotel in Hong Kong. He stood still for a moment, looking around while buttoning his suit, taking in the acres of white and black marble, the cold opulence of gold and glass. There did not seem to be anything untoward about his arrival; he had gotten through customs without a hitch and everything had gone smoothly. He was fairly sure he had shaken Nodding Crane and any potential henchmen from his trail long before he left America. Who would imagine a person, being chased by a Chinese agent, getting on a plane and flying to China? The unexpected way was often the safer way.

He approached the desk, gave his name, picked up his room card, and rode an elevator to the twenty-second floor. He had booked an expensive room with a view of Hong Kong's harbor, a necessary part of his cover, and he'd had to spend a considerable amount on some really sharp clothing. The twenty thousand Glinn had given him was almost gone, and he could only hope another infusion of cash would miraculously appear. Otherwise he would be in deep shit.

He threw the stupid hat in the trash, along with the plastic carry-on bag, took a shower, and changed into fresh, crisp clothes. Forty Benjamins' worth, not counting the thousand-dollar shoes.

"A man could get used to this," he said aloud, examining himself in the mirror. He wondered if he should cut his hair, decided against it: the modish length made him look dot-com.

He glanced at his watch. Four in the afternoon—of the next day. After thoroughly searching Wu's plane seat and making sure nothing had been left behind, he'd slept so well he'd be good for another two days. And now he had work to do.

Taking the elevator down to the lobby, he went into the Kowloon Bar, taking a seat and ordering a Beefeater martini, extra dry, straight up, with a twist. The bar's purple light gave his skin a cadaverous look. He drank it down, paid in cash, and made his way back to the lobby. The concierge desk stood to one side; Gideon waited until a few people there drifted away, and then went over. There were two concierges, and he picked the younger one.

"May I help you, sir?" the man said. He was a perfect specimen of neutrality, discretion, and professionalism.

Gideon walked him over to the far end of the desk and leaned forward, speaking in a low, conspiratorial voice. "I'm a businessman, traveling alone."

A faint nod of understanding.

"I'm interested in engaging an escort for the evening. Are you the man I should speak to about that?"

The concierge said, equally quietly but his voice betraying nothing, "We have a gentleman who handles these requests. May I ask you to come with me?"

Gideon followed the man across the lobby and through a

door into a suite of small offices. The concierge ushered him into one. Another man, of identical discretion and almost identical appearance, rose from behind the desk. "Please sit down."

Gideon took a seat while the concierge left, shutting the door behind him. The gentleman reseated himself at the desk, on which sat several phones and computers. "What kind of escort service are you interested in?" he asked.

"Well." Gideon gave a nervous chuckle, making sure to breathe out plenty of martini fumes. "A man traveling, away from his family, gets kind of lonely, you know what I mean?"

"Certainly," the man said, and waited, his hands clasped.

"Well, um..." He cleared his throat. "I want a Caucasian. Blond. Athletic. Over six feet. Young but not too young. You know, late twenties."

A nod.

"Um, is it possible to get special services with the escort?"

"Yes," said the man simply.

"Well, in that case..." He hesitated and then said it all at once: "I'd like a dominatrix. You know what that is?"

"That can be arranged," said the man.

"I want the best. The most experienced."

A slow nod. "The escort services here require cash payment up front. Do you need to visit our private banking facilities before I make the arrangements?"

"No, I'm in the green already," he said, with another nervous laugh, tapping the wallet in his suit coat. Christ, this might use up the last of his money.

The man rose. "And when would you need the escort?"

"Soon as possible. I'd like her for drinks, dinner, then the evening, till, say, midnight."

"Very well. She will contact your room by phone when she arrives."

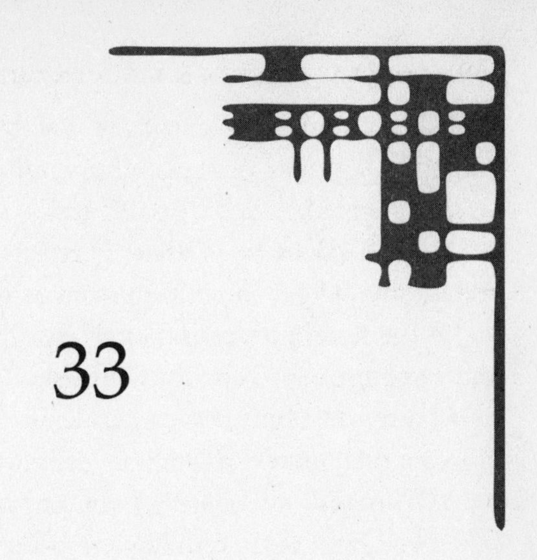

33

Gideon entered the bar and saw her sitting at the end, drink in hand. He was surprised at how attractive she was, tall and willowy, not the muscled roller-derby type he had expected. He, for his part, had shed his suit and changed into tight black jeans, a T-shirt, and Chuck Taylors. He approached her and sat down.

"I'm waiting for someone," she said, in an Australian accent.

"I'm the man you're waiting for. Gideon Crew, at your service." The bartender came over. "I'll have what she's having."

"That would be a Pellegrino."

"Yikes! Get rid of that and bring us a brace of double martinis."

He found her staring at him, and he fancied he saw a look of pleasant surprise in her face.

"I thought I was meeting some fat old suit," she said.

"Nope. I'm a thin, young non-suit. And your name is?"

A smile crept across her face. "Gerta. How old are you?"

"About your age. Where are you from? Coomooroo? Goomalling?"

She giggled. "You're a daft one. You been to Australia?"

He looked at his watch. "Let's take these drinks into the restaurant and get something to eat. I'm famished."

In the hotel restaurant, after plying her with Château Pétrus and sweetbreads, Gideon unburdened himself. He did it slowly, reluctantly, and only under gentle urging. He told Gerta about how he had made a fortune selling his company, how he'd worked so hard he'd hardly ever seen his little son, how his wife divorced him and then they were both killed in a car crash, how he hardly recognized his son's little body in the casket at the wake because it had been so long since he'd last seen him... And now, here he was, a billionaire and so lonely he would trade all of it—all of it—for one hour with his son. One hour of the countless many he had thrown away making all that money while his son waited for him to come home every night, sometimes waiting up with a flashlight under the covers so he wouldn't be asleep when Daddy came home. But he always was asleep, lying there, flashlight still on. Gideon removed a photograph of an adorable blond boy from his wallet and shed a solitary tear over it, and declared himself the loneliest, saddest billionaire on the planet.

He was rewarded with a corresponding tear from Gerta.

Back in the room, Gerta started to bring out her kit with what he noted was a certain reluctance, but as she was unzipping the duffel Gideon told her he'd never met anyone like her before and he wanted her to be his friend and wanted to talk a little more, she was so funny and interesting, and he couldn't imagine now going through that stuff with her—the stuff that helped him forget, just the smallest bit—because he now respected her far too much.

Gideon asked about some of her more interesting experiences and she, reluctantly at first but then more eagerly—stimulated by his fascination—began to tell him about her work. They sat side by side on the bed, Gerta talking. After five or six of her war stories, she finally got to it. It had happened, she said, about two weeks ago. She'd been hired by this fellow from an Australian firm for a special job. Apparently the Chinese had ripped off this firm's technology—did Gideon know China had been stealing from Australian companies for some time?—and they wanted her to get one of the Chinese executives in a compromising position in order to get the technology back. Ten thousand dollars for an evening's work.

"I was expecting some Chinese gangster type," she said, "but he was small and nervous. No bigger than a mozzie. Took him forever to get out what he wanted me to do." She giggled. "But when he got going... here, look out!"

Gideon laughed along with her and went to open a split of Veuve from the minibar. He poured out two glasses.

"Yeah, it was pretty funny. He was like an eager teenager."

"What kind of work did he do?" Gideon asked.

"He made it seem all deep and dark sounding, something to do with electricity. Never even mentioned his real business was ripping off Australia."

"Electricity?" Gideon popped a second split.

"Well, I think that's what he said, electricity or maybe electrons or something like that. Hinted around that it was going to change everything, China was going take over the world. He got pretty drunk, wasn't making a lot of sense."

"Were the Australians who hired you happy with the information?"

"They were more interested in getting it all on videotape. They were going to force him to give back their technology."

"What kind of technology?"

Gerta took a deep swig of champagne. "They wouldn't tell me. Secret."

"This all took place in his room?"

"Oh yeah. I never engage my own room."

"Did you notice if he had a laptop with him? Or a portable hard drive?"

She paused and looked at him. "No. Why?"

Gideon realized he might be pushing it too far. "Just curious. You said he was a scientist—I was thinking maybe the stolen technology might have been in the room."

"Maybe. I didn't notice. The room was very neat, everything put away."

He decided to push it once more. "Did he say anything about a secret weapon?"

"Secret weapon? No, just a lot of talk about China dominating the world, the usual bragging. I get that a lot from Chinese businessmen. They all think in ten, twenty years China's gonna bury the rest of us."

"What else did he say?"

"Not much. Once it was over, he suddenly got really paranoid, looked around the room for bugs, was afraid for me to leave. He sobered up real quick. It was kind of scary, actually, how freaked out he got."

"And they paid you ten thousand?"

"Five up front, five afterward."

"Australians, you said?"

"Right. And from Sydney, where I'm from. It was nice to meet some mates from Oz."

Gideon nodded. The CIA was cleverer than he thought.

"And then," she went on, with a laugh, spilling a bit of champagne, "there was the guy a couple of years ago wanted to bring his pet monkey. Ugh. Monkeys are nasty beasts, and I mean *nasty*! You won't *believe* what he wanted..."

She eventually fell asleep on top of the covers, snoring softly. Gideon carefully tucked her in on one side, then climbed in the other, his own head whirling from the martinis, wine, and champagne.

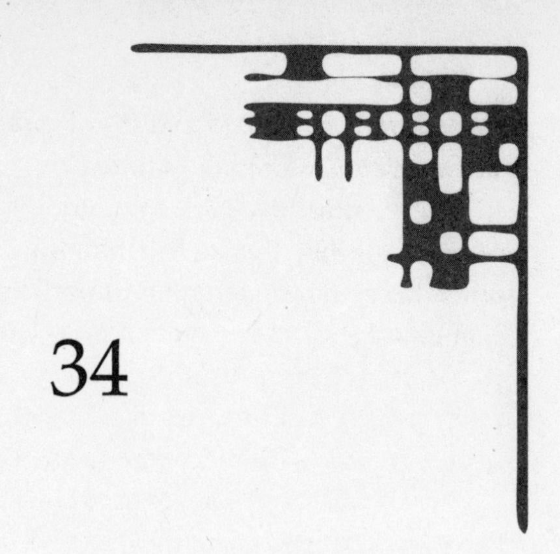

34

They arrived about eight in the morning, dressed in blue suits like a group of Hong Kong real estate developers, unlocking the door with their own key and filing into the room. They stood around politely as their leader spoke.

"Mr. Gideon Crew?"

Gideon sat up in bed, his head pounding. "Um, yes?" This was not good.

"Please come with us."

He stared. The girl, Gerta, was still sleeping soundly next to him. "No, thanks."

The two men flanking the leader casually removed identical nine-millimeter Beretta pistols, letting them dangle.

"Let us please not have trouble. This is a nice hotel."

"May I get dressed?"

"Please."

He got out of bed, all the men staring at him, trying to shake off his hangover and getting up to speed on his situation. He hoped Gerta wouldn't wake up. That would add an element of unpredictability. He had to think of something fast. Once they got him into a car, it would be all over.

"May I shower first?"

"No."

Gideon moved to dress in the walk-in closet.

"Take your clothes out and dress here."

Slowly, thinking all the while, he pulled on the four-thousand-dollar suit and shoes, tie, the works. After spending all that money, he was loath to lose the clothes.

"Walk with us." They closed around him in a tight group. The guns disappeared as they moved out the door and into the corridor. They all got into a waiting elevator. Gideon's mind was running like mad, but he could come up with nothing. Make a scene in the lobby? Start screaming like a madman? Say he was being kidnapped? Run for it? As he played out every scenario, one way or another he ended up either shot or hustled off. The problem was, these men would surely have a better story than his. And official identification. He couldn't win.

The elevator arrived at the lobby level, the doors whispered open, and they stepped into the marbled space. At the far end of the lobby, beyond the wall of glass looking onto the entrance, he could see three black SUVs pulled up in a row, guarded by several additional men in blue suits. His escorts prodded him forward, moving fast.

What if he broke and ran? Would they shoot him? Even if he escaped, where would he go? He knew no one in Hong Kong and had only about two thousand dollars left: chump change around here. They would flag him before he left the country. And he'd been forced to travel under his own name: you couldn't get a fake passport these days.

They shoved him toward the door, toward the trio of idling, black SUVs.

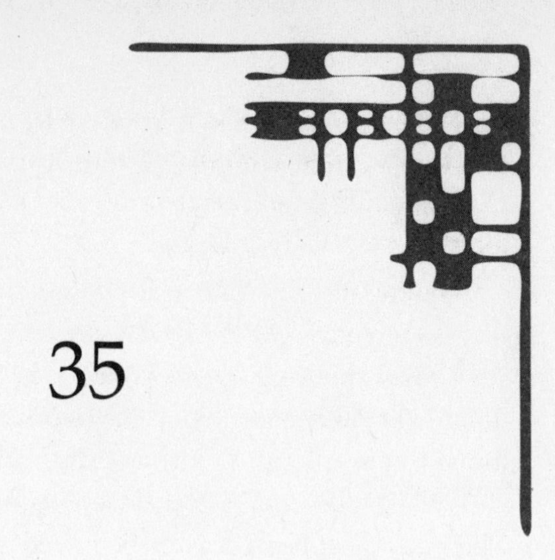

35

Hey!"

He heard a shout from across the lobby and saw a woman charging toward them. Mindy Jackson. She had her CIA wallet out, held open in front of her outstretched arm like a battering ram. "You there! Halt!"

The voice was so loud it brought everyone in the echoing lobby to a standstill.

She busted into the group like a bowling ball into a set of pins, pushing Gideon to one side. Then she wheeled about and shouted at them again. "What the hell do you think you're doing? I'm CIA assistant bureau chief here and this is my colleague. He's got diplomatic immunity! How dare you disrespect diplomatic status!" She seized Gideon and yanked him toward the door.

Half a dozen handguns were immediately out, pointing at her. "You go nowhere!" the lead man shouted, advancing toward her.

Her own weapon came out in a flash, an S&W .38 chief's special. There were sudden screams in the lobby as the guns were drawn, people ducking behind chairs and vases. "Oh yeah?" she cried. "You want a shootout with the CIA right here, right now? Come on! Think of the promotion you'll get for shooting up the lobby of the Tai Tam Hotel!"

As she spoke at high volume, her voice ringing out, she continued hauling Gideon toward the door. The men seemed frozen as the two barged through an emergency exit, where she shoved him into the backseat of a waiting Crown Victoria. She got in behind him and slammed the door and the car screeched from the curb, leaving the group of blue-suited Chinese running to their SUVs.

"Motherfucker," she said, shoving the S&W back into a shoulder holster and leaning back in the seat with a sigh. "Mother*fuck*er. What the hell do you think you're doing here?"

"I owe you thanks—"

"Thanks? You owe me your *life*. I can't believe you walked your ass right into the lion's den like this. Are you crazy?"

Gideon had to admit it seemed, in retrospect, a foolish decision.

She glanced back. "And now they're following."

"Where are we going?"

"Airport."

"They're going to stop us from leaving the country."

"They're confused. They're asking for instructions. It all depends on how fast the intelligence bureaucracy can get their shit together. You know how to handle a handgun?"

"Yes."

She pulled a .32 Walther from her waistband and handed it to him with an extra loaded magazine. "Whatever you do, for God's sake don't *shoot* anybody. Follow my instructions."

"Okay."

She spoke to the driver. "Slow down, let them get closer."

"Why?" the man behind the wheel asked.

"It may reveal their intentions. Are they just following? Or do they want to run us off the road?"

The driver slowed considerably and the lead black SUV came cruising up, fast, in the left lane. It braked to their speed, a smoked window came down, and the muzzle of a gun poked out.

"Duck!"

The round blew out both rear windows, showering them with little cubes of glass. At the same moment their driver made a sickening evasive move, veering across four lanes of traffic on the Eastern Island Corridor, wheels squealing on the diamond-cut surface.

"You ascertained their intentions," said Gideon drily.

"Yeah, and it looks like they got their instructions."

The car was accelerating again along the corridor, weaving through traffic, heading for the exchange leading into the Cross-Harbour Tunnel.

"There's going to be a traffic jam at the tunnel," said the driver. "What'll we do?"

Mindy didn't answer. Gideon looked back. The SUV—and the two others—were whipping through traffic, pacing them.

Thunk! Another round punched through the side of their car with the sound of a sledgehammer on steel. Jackson leaned out the broken window, fired five shots in rapid succession. The SUVs took evasive action, dropping back.

Crouching by the floor, she snapped open the cylinder, shoved in fresh rounds, snapped it shut. "Keep your head down."

"There's no way they're going to let us out of the country," Gideon said.

Thunk! Another round clipped the rear of the car.

Gideon ducked, his hands over his head.

"It's a lot harder than it looks to shoot a handgun from a car," she said. "It isn't like in the movies. Give me your passport."

He fished it out of his pocket. He could hear the roar of the engine, the wheels squealing, the blaring horns of cars rapidly falling away behind—and now the sounds of sirens. She snatched the passport, reached into a bag, and pulled out an embosser and a small circular stamp. Opening the passport, she stamped it, signed it, and embossed it. "You now have diplomatic status," she said as she handed it back.

"Is that CIA standard issue?"

She smiled grimly as the car slowed.

Gideon peeked out. They were entering the sunken approach to the Cross-Harbour Tunnel. The black SUVs, in dropping back, had gotten stuck many cars behind.

The traffic slowed further, bunched, and finally came to a halt.

Gideon peered out the window again and saw the blue suits pouring out of the black SUVs a hundred yards behind. They raced toward the Crown Vic, fanning out among the cars, guns drawn.

"We're screwed," he said.

"Not at all. As soon as I get out, start firing your gun over their heads. Be sure not to hit anyone."

"Wait—"

But in a flash she jumped out, running at a crouch, dodging the lines of stopped traffic. He aimed slightly over the heads of the approaching suits and depressed the trigger, the handgun kicking back, one, two, three shots, deafeningly loud between the enclosed walls of the sunken approach. The suits dove to the ground and a chorus of screams rose up around him, doors flying open, cars emptying.

Instant chaos. Now he saw Jackson's strategy. He fired two more shots, adding to the panic: more doors were flung open, screams, people climbing over cars, shrieking, running like mad in every direction.

The blue suits rose and tried to press their way forward against the fleeing crowd, but it was like fighting an incoming tide. Gideon fired again, high, this time in all directions, *boom boom boom boom!* The panic spread and the suits once again dove for cover. The crowd surged outward, triggering panic in more distant cars, which emptied in turn, in ever-expanding waves. He heard Jackson firing the S&W somewhere behind, the snub-nosed revolver louder than his .32. At the noise, part of the fleeing crowd reversed direction in a panic, people colliding into one another, scrambling under cars. Gideon heard windows breaking, horns blaring. He tried to locate the blue suits but they had completely vanished in the surging mob, pinned down or maybe even trampled.

Suddenly the door was pulled open and he swung around to see Jackson. She passed the back of one hand across her forehead and holstered her weapon. "Time to split."

He jumped out and they ran with the mob, heading back out the sunken approach. It was like an infection, the mob steadily growing as people continued to abandon their cars in a spreading pool of frenzy. It appeared that people were assuming a terrorist attack.

Swept along by the mob, they emerged from the sunken roadway. The crowd spilled over a cement barrier wall, tumbling down a short embankment and onto Hung Hing Road, where they poured in a screaming mass northward into the Hong Kong Yacht Club. The crowd instantly overwhelmed two men in a pillbox at a barrier gate, knocked it down, and scattered down the gracious, tree-lined avenue into the club grounds.

"Stay with me." Jackson split off from the main throng and doubled back down a service road, crossed a set of railroad tracks, and climbed over a chain-link fence. They ended up leaving the crowds behind, running along a promenade overlooking Victoria Harbour. The promenade curved around to a paved asphalt jetty that stood out into the harbor. She had been yelling into her cell phone for a while and now she snapped it shut.

"Out there." She ran down the broad tarmac jetty.

"It's a dead end!" he cried. But then he saw, ahead, a huge yellow *H* stenciled on the tarmac, inside a yellow circle. He looked up and, on cue, heard the sound of a chopper, coming in low and fast. It swung around the jetty, decelerated, then settled, rotors slowing. They ran toward it as a door opened. No sooner had they jumped in than it took off again, sweeping across the harbor.

Mindy Jackson settled into a jumpseat, buckled her seat belt, and turned to him. She eased a notebook out of her pocket, along with a pen. "I just saved your ass. Now you're going to tell me the numbers. And no more bullshit."

He told her the numbers.

36

They boarded the first commercial plane out, an Emirates flight to Dubai, using their diplomatic stamps to bypass passport control. They arrived in Dubai about nine o'clock local time. Their connecting flight to New York wasn't until morning.

"Bur Dubai Hotel is rather nice," Mindy Jackson said as they passed through customs and headed for the taxi queue. "You owe me a stiff one."

He spread his hands. "Drink, or...?"

She colored. "Drink. A stiff *drink*. What a mind you have."

They got into a cab. "The Bur Dubai," she told the driver, then turned to Gideon. "The Cooz Bar is a jazz-and-cigar kind of place. Red velvet chairs, leopardskin bar stools, lots of blond wood."

"Funny, I didn't take you for a cigar smoker."

After crawling through nighttime traffic, the cab finally pulled up in front of the hotel, two curved, ultramodern black-and-white buildings intersecting each other. They went straight to the bar without checking in, just in time to catch the second set.

As they were seated, the big band began to play. Predictably, the opening tune was the Ellington number "Caravan." Gideon listened; they weren't half bad. The waiter came over.

"I'll have an Absolut martini," Jackson said, "dry and dirty, with two olives. And," she went on, eyeing the cigar list, "bring me a Bolívar Coronas Gigantes."

Gideon ordered a beer, going light after his overindulgence the night before. The waiter returned with the drinks and the cigar.

"You going to smoke that?" Gideon asked, eyeing the torpedo-shaped aluminum tube.

"No, you are. I like watching a man smoke a cigar."

Giving in to his baser instincts, Gideon removed the cigar, ran it under his nose. It was very fine. He cut off the end with the supplied trimmer and lit it.

Jackson eyed him sideways. "Like I said. You look good with a cigar."

"Let's just hope I don't get cancer and they have to cut my lips off."

"Such nice lips, too." She sipped her drink, still looking at him. "You know, I've never seen anyone with quite your looks. Jet black hair, bright blue eyes."

"Black Irish. Except I'm not Irish."

"I'll bet you sunburn easily."

"Unfortunately, yes."

Here, so far from home, Jackson seemed like a different person. "You have any idea what those numbers mean?" he asked her.

"Not yet. I've already phoned them in."

"I'd like to know if they find anything."

Jackson remained silent. The band slid into another Ellington classic, "Mood Indigo."

Having given her the numbers, Gideon felt he could push just a little harder. "So tell me more about this Nodding Crane character. He sounds like something out of a Bond movie."

"In a way he is. A bred assassin. We know very little about him—comes from the Chinese far west, of Mongolian extraction, got more than a little Genghis Khan in him. He was raised—so we hear—in a special training unit that immersed him in American culture. Employed by the 810 Office, apparently."

"The 810 Office?"

She looked at him strangely. "For an operative, even a private one, you're unusually ignorant."

"I'm a new hire."

"The 810 Office is the Chinese version of the Gestapo or the KGB, only smaller and more focused. It's under the personal control of a few top Communist Party officials. Nodding Crane is one of their best men, and it appears he's been chemically and hormonally pumped up. He's trained to the max, but he's not the crude killing machine you might think. He's intelligent and, like I said, steeped in American pop culture. I saw one report that says he plays bottleneck guitar. Blues."

"Seems hard to believe. But if he's so good, why did he fuck up with Wu?"

"Fuck up? His orders were to kill Wu and escape. And that's exactly what he did. The collateral damage was of no consequence—to him."

"But he didn't get the plans."

"He didn't expect to—not then. That's phase two. He's working on that now."

"Why's he after me?"

"Come on, Gideon. There are half a dozen witnesses who saw you writing down those numbers. He doesn't need the numbers—his job is to make sure anyone who knows them is dead."

Gideon shook his head, took a small puff from the cigar. "If he's that good, I'd be dead already."

"You've been awfully clever so far. Or maybe it's dumb luck. Thing is, you're unpredictable. Going to Hong Kong—that's the last move anyone would have expected."

"You expected it."

"Not at all. There's a general alert on you at the airports, your exit was flagged. When you return to the States, Nodding Crane'll be waiting for you. I doubt you'll survive." She smiled and fished an olive out of the glass, lobbed it into her mouth.

"Thanks for the vote of confidence. I might point out that now I've told you the numbers, you're a target yourself."

"Don't worry about me."

He took another puff. "How could Wu just walk off with the plans, anyway?"

"Maybe he'd been considering it for some time. He's one of their top people, he'd have had complete access. It could be the honey trap was the final push he needed."

"How do you know he even *had* the plans?"

"That's the intelligence we received. It was expensive, and it's ironclad."

"Could the scientist himself be a red herring? A setup?"

"Doubtful."

"Any specifics about the weapon itself?"

"That's the scariest part. We don't know if it's an enhanced thermonuclear device or something completely new. The mix of scientists at Lop Nor suggests the latter—there's a lack of nuclear physicists and HE experts on site, but a lot of metallurgists, nanotechnologists, condensed matter and quantum physicists."

"Quantum physicists? It sounds like it might be an exotic particle weapon—a laser weapon, mini black hole—or even a matter–antimatter device."

"You're smarter than you look. What exactly do you do at Los Alamos, anyway?"

"I design and test high-explosive lenses."

"What's that?"

"It's classified. Suffice to say they're lenses of conventional high explosive that go into the assemblies used for imploding the cores of nuclear devices."

She took another sip of her drink. "And just how does somebody go about getting background experience for a job like that?"

Gideon shrugged. "Well, in my case, I liked blowing things up."

"You mean, like cars? People?"

"Nah. Started out as kid stuff. I used to make my own pyrotechnical devices, mixed my own gunpowder. Fireworks, sort of. I'd set them off in the woods behind our house and charge neighborhood kids a quarter to watch. Later on they proved to have... other uses." He yawned.

"Quite the renaissance man. Want to order food?"

"I'm too tired to eat."

"Tired? In that case, should we book two rooms?" Her voice trailed off and her lips curled into a suggestive smile.

He looked at her green eyes, glossy hair, freckled nose. He could see the pulse in her throat throbbing softly. "Not that tired."

She dropped a fifty on the table and rose. "Good. I'd hate spending the government's money on a room if no one's going to use it."

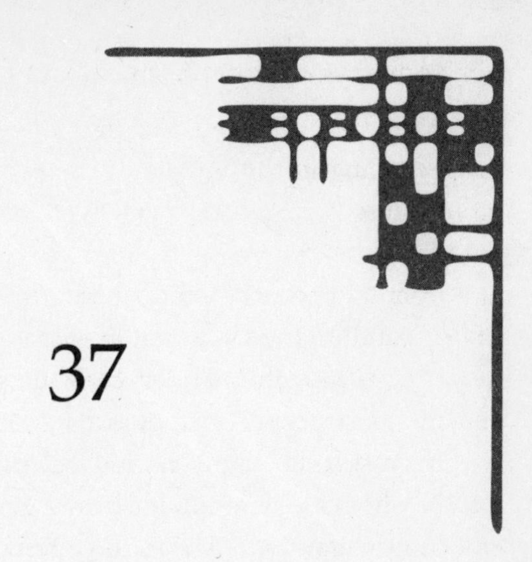

37

Roger Marion locked and bolted the door to his apartment with a sigh. It was a busy Thursday in Chinatown and Mott Street had been awash with humanity, the animal murmur still filtering up into his apartment through the closed and barred windows looking onto the fire escape facing the street.

He paused to collect himself, to reestablish the center of calm destroyed by the city's incessant chaos. He closed his eyes, entered into stillness, and performed the set of movements known as *mile shenyao,* his motions free and unconstrained. He could feel the Law Wheel turning, turning, forever turning.

When the exercises were complete, he went into the kitchen to make tea. Placing the kettle on to boil, he took down the heavy iron teapot and a can of loose white tea, arranging them on the counter. Just before the water came to a boil he removed the kettle, poured some water into the iron pot to heat it, swished it around and dumped it out, spooned in a batch of curly white tea leaves, and covered them with more hot water.

He carried the pot and cup into the living room and found a man standing in the middle of the room, arms crossed, a smile on his face.

"Tea, how lovely," said the man in Chinese. He was dressed in a nondescript suit, white shirt, gray repp tie; his face was as smooth and unlined as a bolt of silk; his eyes cool and empty, his movements graceful. Underneath the clothes, Marion could see he was a perfect specimen of lean athleticism.

"It must steep," said Marion, revealing no surprise, although it astonished and confounded him that the man had been able to enter the apartment. "Allow me to bring another cup in for you."

The man nodded and Marion turned, going back into the kitchen. As he took the cup down from the cupboard, he eased a small knife out of a block on the counter and slipped it behind his back.

Back in the living room, Marion placed the cup beside the pot.

"I prefer white tea to be steeped at least ten minutes," said the man. "Which will allow us time to talk."

Marion waited.

The man clasped his hands behind his back and began a slow perambulation of the room. "I'm looking for something," he said. He stopped in front of the banner hanging on the wall, examined it.

Marion said nothing. He put together in his mind the most efficient set of moves necessary to put the knife in the man's throat.

"Do you know where it is?" the man asked.

"You haven't told me what you're looking for."

"You don't know?"

"I have no idea what you're talking about."

The man waved this comment off as if he were waving away a mosquito. "What were you going to do with it?"

Marion said nothing. All was prepared in his mind. "Tea?"

The man turned. "It hasn't steeped long enough."

"I prefer it on the more delicate side."

"Help yourself, then. I'll wait."

Marion bent forward with an easy motion and picked up the iron pot by the handle. His mind was as clear and bright as a diamond. He tipped the pot up, filling the cup with hot liquid, placed the pot down, brought the cup up in an unhurried motion as if to his lips and then, with a quick flick of the wrist, sent the scalding contents into the man's face while at the same time extracting the knife with a lightning motion, slashing it across the man's throat.

But the man, and the throat, weren't there, and the knife flashed harmlessly through the air. Briefly overbalanced by the motion, Marion's weight went forward, and as he tried to recover, an arm with a clawed hand came shooting out of nowhere; Marion saw what looked like metal talons; he tried to duck but it was too late; he felt a savage tug on his throat and a sudden burning rush of air.

The last thing he saw was the man standing beside him, clutching what he realized was his own bloody, pulsing windpipe.

Nodding Crane took a few steps back from the twitching body as blood pumped out onto the carpet. He dropped the grisly part and waited until all was still, then he stepped around the obstruction and into the kitchen. He washed his hands three times in very hot water and carefully examined his suit. There were no flecks of the *xiǎorén,* the small person, on his clothing. All the force of the movement had been away from his body. There were just a few drops of blood on his left wing-tip shoe, which he meticulously cleaned with a damp rag, followed by a quick polish.

Back in the living room, the blood had ceased to flow. The carpet had absorbed a great deal of it, keeping the bloodstain from spreading. Stepping around it again, he poured himself a cup of tea and tasted it with pleasure. The steeping time had been perfect. He sipped it down and poured another, bringing to mind a particularly appropriate thought from his vast storehouse of Confucian philosophy: *When punishments are not properly awarded, the people do not know how to move hand or foot.*

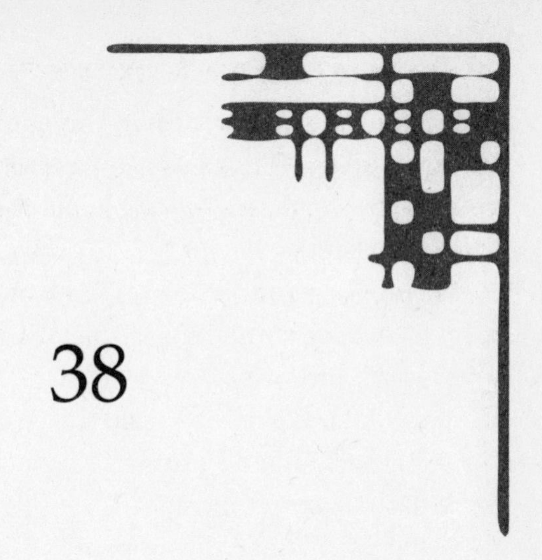

38

Gideon Crew strolled around the baggage carousel, as if awaiting luggage. He had no luggage coming in, of course, but he wanted to check out who else was there. Mindy Jackson's parting words rang in his ears. "Nodding Crane is remarkable only in that he is unremarkable. Except for flat eyes and a perfect physique." There were, of course, many Asians at the carousel, including a number who fit Mindy's rather unhelpful description.

Don't get paranoid, he told himself. *Focus on the next step.*

He extracted his wallet, riffled through the money he had left. About a thousand. Not for the first time, he felt a stab of annoyance at how Glinn and company seemed to have abandoned him.

But when you return to the States, he'll be waiting. I doubt you'll survive.

His next step was obvious. If Wu hadn't passed off the plans after exiting customs, and they weren't on his person, he might have passed them off to someone *before* clearing customs. Conveniently, Gideon was now inside the customs security zone. Even as he pondered his approach, the endless looped warning rang out again on the PA system: *Please report suspicious persons or unattended luggage to the appropriate authority.*

Carpe diem.

He looked about, spied a TSA guard. "Excuse me," he said, "I believe I've seen something suspicious and wish to report it to the appropriate authority."

"I can take the report," said the guard.

"No," said Gideon primly. "I have to report it to appropriate authority. It's very important."

"As I said, I'll take the report."

"But the announcement said *appropriate authority,*" Gideon said, more loudly. "No offense intended, but you're a guard. I want to speak to someone *in authority*—just as the announcement directs. There's no time to waste. I've seen something very startling, and I need to report it immediately." He compressed his lips and put on a truculent expression.

The guard's eyes flickered. "All right, follow me."

He led Gideon through a back door and past a warren of windowless cubicles and passageways to a shut door. The guard knocked, and a voice called them in.

"Thank you," said Gideon, entering, turning, and shutting the door in the guard's face.

He turned back and saw a soft, dough-like man seated behind a large desk completely covered with paper. "What's this?"

The guard tried to enter but Gideon, standing at the door, blocked it with his foot. He tossed his passport on the desk and said, "CIA. Send the guard away."

The man lifted the passport to examine it. The guard knocked again. "Open up."

"Thank you," the man called to the guard. "That will be all. Return to duty."

He turned his attention back to the passport and scowled at

the diplomatic stamps. "Doesn't say anything about CIA. Got a badge?"

"Of course not!" Gideon said sharply. "We don't carry ID when we work under diplomatic cover."

The man put down the passport. "Okay, what's up?"

Gideon gave the man a long, hostile stare. "Captain Longbaugh?"

"That's what the badge says. Now you better tell me what's on your mind, sir, because as you can see I'm pretty busy." What he could see was that Longbaugh was used to dealing with petty bureaucrats and officials. He was going to be a tough nut to crack.

Gideon pulled a notebook from his pocket, consulted it. "On June seventh, at twelve twenty-three AM, a Japan Airlines flight arrived with a passenger on board, Mark Wu. He was followed as he left JFK, and his taxi was forced off the street in Spanish Harlem. Perhaps you read about that accident. Eight people were killed, including Mr. Wu."

"I did."

"We need a copy of the security tapes that captured his movements from the point of debarkation to where he hired the taxi."

Longbaugh stared at him. "I'll need to see some sort of paperwork on this."

Gideon took a step forward. "We've got an ongoing terrorist situation here and you want to 'see paperwork'? Is this where we still are, after 9/11 and two wars?"

"Sir, we have procedures in place..."

Gideon leaned in and screamed into Longbaugh's face like a drill sergeant, hitting him with spittle. "Procedures? *Paperwork?* When people's lives are at stake?"

It was, he realized, a high-risk/high-reward approach. If it didn't work, he was screwed.

But it did. "No need to scream," said Longbaugh, leaning

back, suddenly and thoroughly intimidated. "I'm sure we can work it out."

"Then work it out! Now!"

The man was sweating bullets, clearly in a panic about making the wrong decision. Gideon suddenly took a much softer, kinder tone. "Look, Captain, I know you're concerned about doing the right thing. I respect that. I'll put in a good word up the line about you when this is over. But you've got to understand, paperwork takes time. And we just don't *have* time." He leaned in. "I'm going to share something with you. I'm not supposed to, but I can see you're a trustworthy individual. We've got a flight midway across the Pacific with a known terrorist on board—they let the son of a bitch on in Lagos. We have reason to believe he is planning a terrorist action here."

"Oh my God."

"Oh my God is right. We're way behind the curve on this one, trying to catch up. We're flooding the terminal with undercover people as we speak, but *I've got to see those tapes*. There appears to be a vital link."

"I understand."

"Can we do this really, *really* quietly?" Gideon pleaded. "If we spook this guy or his accomplices..." He let his voice trail off.

Now he had Longbaugh one hundred percent on his side.

"I'm on it." The man rose. "Come with me."

The central security operations room lay in the bowels of the airport, and it was very impressive, walls of video screens and consoles with all the latest gear. The room was dim and hushed, dozens of people staring at monitors, not just of airport locations, but also feeds from bag scanners and X-ray machines and cams observing the taxiways and hangars.

Their efficiency was astounding. Twenty minutes later Gideon was exiting customs with a fresh, piping-hot DVD.

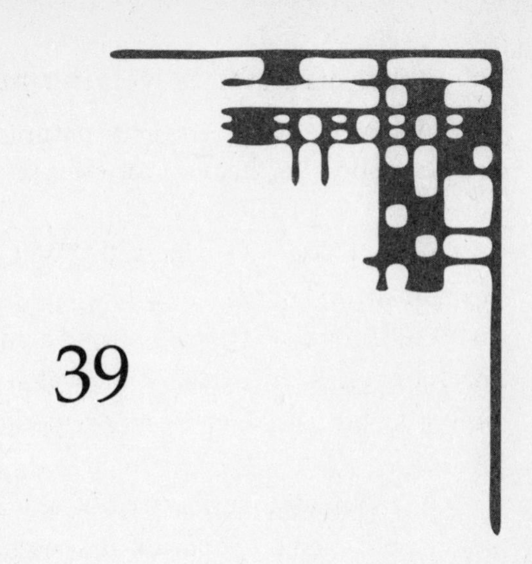

39

Got a movie for us tonight," Gideon said, sliding into the white leather banquette in the Essex House lounge, bestowing a smile on Mindy Jackson. He turned to the waiter. "Bring me what she's having, wet and dirty, two olives."

"What movie?" asked Jackson.

"The Mark Wu show." He laid down the DVD. "Shows him from the time he exited the plane to the taxi stand."

She laughed.

"What's so funny?"

"I've already seen that show. It sucks—nothing on it. Nada."

Gideon felt his face turn red. "You've seen it?"

"Are you kidding? That was the first thing we looked at. How'd you get it?"

The drink arrived, and Gideon took a swig to cover his disappointment. "I used those diplomatic embosses you put on my passport. And a little yelling."

"One of these days you're going to run into somebody who doesn't fall for your bullshit."

"So far, so good."

She shook her head. "Not everyone in the world is stupider than you."

"*I* haven't seen it," he said. "Will you watch it with me—upstairs in our room?"

"Our room?" Her smile turned a little cold. "What happened in Dubai stays in Dubai. We'll watch it in *my* room. You find your own place to sleep. No more pooling, to use your charming phrase."

Gideon made an effort to look as if he didn't care.

She polished off her drink and rose. "You're going to be disappointed."

"I already am."

Up in her room, he fired up the DVD player and slid in the disk. The first shot showed a wide angle of the gate, with a time, date, and location stamp running along the bottom. After a moment Wu appeared, looking much as Gideon remembered him: fringe of hair, domed forehead, mousey, somewhat wan. He walked through the frame, threading a group of passengers waiting for the next flight.

The DVD then cut through a series of rapid frames, one after another, showing Wu walking down the terminal, entering passport control, waiting in the interminable NON-US-CITIZEN line, going through passport control, breezing through customs, then walking out and down the escalators.

"Hey. There's you!" said Jackson. "Like a deer in the headlights."

"Very funny."

The DVD ended outside, with the Escape driving off.

Gideon rubbed his eyes. He felt like a damn fool, taking such a risk at the airport—a risk that might well come back to haunt him—for nothing.

"I'm tired," said Jackson. "I'm jet-lagged, I didn't sleep a wink last night, thanks to you. Do you mind?"

Gideon was staring at the image of the car, frozen on the screen. "There's just one thing I'd like to look at again—"

"Out."

"No, really. Something I'd like to see again. Right at the beginning."

"What?"

"When Wu walks through those waiting people. Did you see there was an Asian woman there with a boy?"

"There were a lot of Asians."

"Yes, but—I want to see it again."

She sighed, turned back to the screen. They watched it again.

"There!" said Gideon abruptly, causing her to jump.

"I didn't see anything."

"Watch again." He retracked the video and went through it in slow motion.

"I still didn't see anything. Trust me, our experts have examined this tape in detail."

"Quiet and watch... *There!*" He froze the frame. "A classic sleight. A reverse palm-out manip."

"A what?"

He felt himself blush. "I studied magic." He didn't go into the reasons why he had studied magic. "You learn how to manipulate smallish pieces of paper. Magicians call such moves 'manips.' Usually they're for cards." He backed up the DVD and went through it again, frame by frame. "Check it out. The boy drops the teddy bear as Wu approaches... she leans over to pick it up... anyone watching would be following her hand picking up the teddy bear. But look at her *left* hand... you see her left palm is facing out, wrist straight... Then Wu goes past, and afterward her left hand is closed and the wrist slightly bent."

He ran it through it yet again, frame by frame.

"I think I saw it," she said doubtfully. "He passed her something."

"No, *no*! It's a reverse—she passed *him* something. And she did it in a way to hide it from anybody watching from any angle."

"Why would she pass *him* something?"

"No idea." Stopping the replay and getting a small piece of hotel notepaper, he demonstrated the move.

"I'll be damned. But if she passed him a piece of paper, where is it?"

"Who knows? I expect he destroyed it when he realized he was being pursued."

"That woman," said Jackson, "is key. We've got to find her."

Gideon nodded.

She turned to him. "We'll split up the job. You look for the boy, I'll look for the woman."

"How in the world could I find the boy—?" But then he stopped, having noticed something else in the video; something that she, and everyone else, had apparently overlooked.

Jackson was already putting on her coat, gathering her wallet. "Call me if you find anything. I'll do likewise."

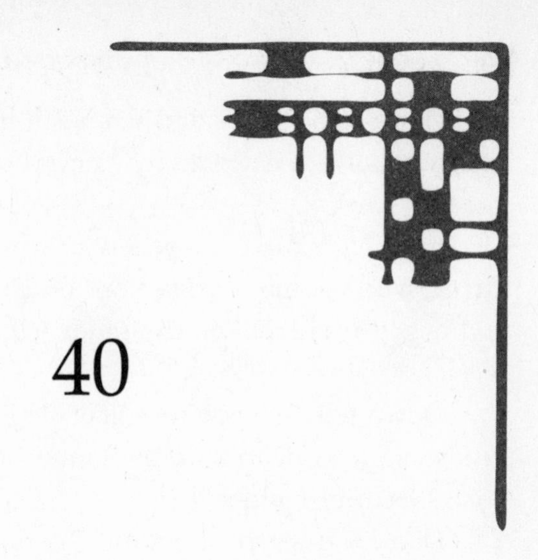

40

Tom O'Brien's stubbled face slipped away from his supporting palm, and he awoke with a jerk. He glanced blearily over at the clock: just past ten. He'd been asleep at his desk for several hours and both his legs were tingling. It had happened again: he'd gotten so engrossed in the Python data-handling extension he'd been coding that he'd "wrapped around" the previous night and totally forgotten to sleep.

He stood up with a groan and massaged his legs. Food: that would wake him up.

Sliding a Sacramentum CD into the player and cranking it up, he padded into the kitchen. Pushing away piles of dirty dishes to make a work space, he pulled a baguette from its paper sheath and cut it lengthwise. Quickly he assembled a sandwich: peanut butter, sliced banana, mini marshmallows. A few slices of deli pickle added the final touch. He pressed the two halves of the sandwich together, tucked it under one arm, plucked a liter bottle of Dr Pepper from the fridge, and headed back toward his office.

He neighed in surprise and dismay at the sight of a man in

his living room. Bottle and sandwich fell to the floor in unison, marshmallows and pickles flying everywhere. Then he saw it was Gideon Crew.

"Stop *doing* that!" he yelled at his friend. "If I die of a heart attack, who's going to solve your little problem?" He knelt down and began reassembling the sandwich, picking cat hairs off the pickles.

"Don't tell me you're still eating peanut-butter-and-pickle sandwiches," Gideon said. "Not interested in living to enjoy your Social Security, I guess."

"Don't you worry about me. I'm not the one being chased by half the spooks in Langley." He scowled. "I haven't had time to do any more work on those numbers."

"No? Why not?"

"Unlike some people, I have to work for a living."

"Yeah. Assistant lecturer at Columbia. When are you going to stop being a perennial grad student and actually earn that degree?"

"And face the real world?" He took a bite of the sandwich and headed into his office, Gideon following. "Look, it's not just my work. It's the nature of your problem. I told you, it's like having a recipe without the ingredients. Three tablespoons of X, two ounces of Y, and a pinch of Z. Without the ingredients, I can't do squat!"

"There's something else I need your help on."

"Do I get another thousand?"

Gideon ignored this, reaching into his coat and pulling out a DVD. "There's a video capture on this. I need you to blow up and enhance an image for me."

O'Brien took it and felt his face light up. "Oh. That's easy."

Gideon pointed at the music player with a pained expression. "Before we get started, mind turning that off? If any music could be carcinogenic, that's it."

O'Brien glanced at him in mock horror. "You don't like blackened death metal?"

"Not even when it's the blue plate special." Gideon looked around for a place to sit, but there was only one chair in the tiny, impossibly crowded office and O'Brien was already in it. "I've never seen so much junk crammed into so little space. When are you going to clear some of this crap out?"

"Junk? Crap?" O'Brien sniffed as he turned down the volume of his player. "Everything in here is absolutely necessary to my work. For instance." And wheeling his chair around, he plucked a gray metal device the size of a shoe box from its precarious perch atop an ancient UNIX terminal, placed it on his desk, plugged it in, and attached it to his PC.

"What's that?" Gideon asked.

"It's a VDT."

"I repeat: what's that?"

"A virtual digital telecine. Normally used to transfer different kinds of video stock from one format to another. But this particular model is very useful for forensic video work." Turning it on, he pressed a few buttons on the tiny LED screen, then slid Gideon's DVD into the slot. As the machine whirred, he took a huge bite of his sandwich, double-clicked an icon on the computer desktop. "I'm firing up the VDT's host application."

A large window appeared on the screen, surrounded by several smaller windows that included fine-grained transport controls, gamma correction, and utilities for image manipulation. "Where is it?"

"Just start playback. I'll tell you when you reach the target image."

O'Brien clicked the forward button in the transport control window, and an image appeared on the screen. "An airport," O'Brien said. "Shit. It's a security tape."

"So?"

"Their quality sucks. Heavily compressed, too."

They watched in silence for a minute as a worried-looking Asian man crossed the screen and made his way through a tangle of passengers.

"It's been hard-telecined," O'Brien said, staring at the monitor. "A hair under thirty fps—"

"There." Gideon pointed at the screen. "Back up just a bit, then go forward, frame by frame."

O'Brien returned playback to the moment the man encountered the group of passengers, then moved forward again.

"Slower, please."

O'Brien took a lengthy pull of the Dr Pepper, worked the transport controls. "One frame per second."

They watched together as a boy in the crowd dropped a teddy bear, a woman beside him picked it up, handed it back.

"Pause," said Gideon. "Now, you see the satchel that boy is carrying?"

"Yup," O'Brien said, peering at the flickering screen.

"I want you to find the clearest frame of that satchel, then enhance it. It's got a blurry logo of some kind. I want to know what it is."

"Sure thing." O'Brien went backward through the frames, then forward, until he found the clearest shot of the satchel.

"Blurry as hell," he muttered. "Whoever demultiplexed this for you did a lousy job."

"They were in a hurry."

"I'll have to de-interlace the image or the combing will kill us." O'Brien's fingers ran over the keyboard. The image in the main window faded, grew larger.

"What are those bars across the image?" Gideon asked.

"That's 2:3 pulldown. I'm trying to compensate." Again he typed a rapid-fire series of commands. The image brightened, stabilized. "That's better. Let me apply some unsharp masking." O'Brien moused through a series of sub-menus.

"It's a shield with a motto," Gideon said, staring.

O'Brien worked the machine, further refining the image.

"*Pectus Est Quod Disertos Facit*," Gideon read from the screen.

"What the hell's that? Latin?"

"It is the heart that makes men eloquent," said Gideon.

"What a crock," said O'Brien, shaking his head sadly at the supreme idiocy of the sentiment. "Who the hell said that?"

"It's from Quintilian's *Orations*. But it's just pompous and vacuous enough that it might be a private school motto." He stood up. "Thanks, Tom."

"Hey. What about that other thousand bucks?"

"Enjoy your sandwich. I'll be in touch." He paused just before going out the door. "You haven't heard from that doctor yet, I suppose?"

"Oh yeah. I did. I meant to tell you about that."

"And?"

"I hope the guy in those X-rays isn't really a friend of yours."

Gideon looked at him. "Why do you say that?"

"According to the doc, he's *fucked*."

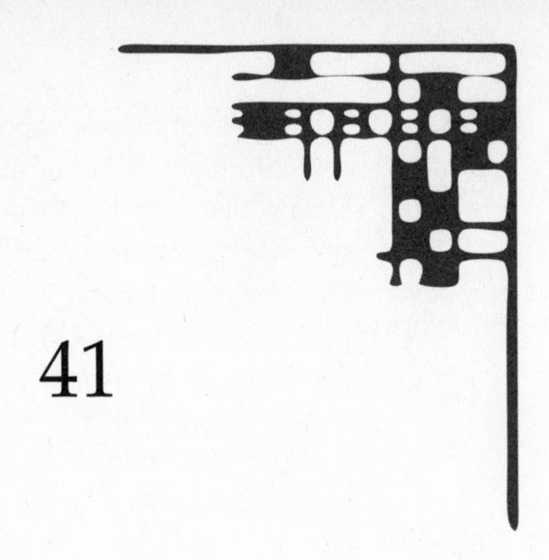

41

Gideon slid onto the vinyl stool of the all-night diner and ordered coffee, poached eggs, hash browns, toast, and marmalade. The waitress, her zaftig figure bursting out of a 1950s uniform, took his order and bawled it into the back.

"You should sing opera," he said distractedly.

She turned to him with a brilliant smile. "I do."

Only in New York. He nursed his coffee, feeling numb.

I hope the guy in those X-rays isn't really a friend of yours. Maybe O'Brien's doctor was wrong. It wouldn't be the first time. But this was the third opinion.

Would he have been happier not knowing? Just enjoying his final year of life in blissful ignorance? But no—this changed everything. Gideon felt a strange sense of dissociation, as if he were already out of his body, away from the living world. Suddenly, very suddenly, his priorities had shifted. No point anymore in meeting someone, raising a family. No point in advancing his career. No point in not smoking or worrying about his cholesterol count. No point, really, in anything.

He took another sip of coffee, trying to shake the odd feeling of nerveless disbelief. *One thing at a time.* There'd be plenty of opportunities to think about this later. Right now, he had a job to finish.

He forced his thoughts back to Throckmorton Academy. He'd been correct about the private school motto. Having perused the school's website, he'd gleaned some important, if inadvertent, information about the place. It was very exclusive, highly protective of information regarding its students and staff, and sophisticated in the management of such information. But every person and organization had a weakness, and Throckmorton Academy's was written all over its site: overweening self-regard. *Pectus Est Quod Disertos Facit.* Yeah, right.

The question was how to devise a social engineering plan to exploit that weakness. These were not idiots. He couldn't go busting in there as a hyper-successful, self-important billionaire hedge fund manager seeking to enroll his son. They would undoubtedly have seen that type before, many times. They would be immune. He couldn't pose as a celebrity, phony or real: Google had ended that game. Something just the opposite would be required: something that would play more subtly on their hopes, assumptions, and—perhaps—prejudices. As he mulled it over, an approach began to take shape in his head. Unfortunately, it would take two to pull it off. Jackson wouldn't do: she was off trying to scare up her own leads, and besides, she wasn't the type. No, it would have to be Orchid. Orchid would be perfect. He pushed away the sting of guilt at using her again, telling himself the ends were worth the means. After all, hadn't she said she wanted him to call her?

A man slid onto the stool next to his, laying a folded *Post* down on the counter. Gideon was irritated that, in an empty diner at three o'clock in the morning, some asshole had to sit down right next to him.

The waitress came out with his plate, laid it down, and turned to the other man. He ordered coffee and Danish.

She poured it, brought him the Danish, and retired into the kitchen.

"How's it going?" the man murmured, opening his paper.

Gideon glanced sideways in irritation, decided to ignore him.

"You must be almost out of cash," the man murmured, perusing the front page.

Gideon felt something touch his leg and glanced down to see the man proffering a fat roll of cash under the counter. Before Gideon could react, the man had slid it into Gideon's jacket pocket, all the while reading his paper. Gideon raised his head, got a better look at the face.

Garza. Eli Glinn's right-hand man at EES.

An unpleasant mixture of shock and irritation coursed over him. So much for his facility at staying below the radar.

"It's about time!" he said, turning on the man, suddenly snarky in his embarrassment at being caught unawares. "I wondered when Glinn would be sending a messenger boy."

Garza frowned, his previous unflappability fading slightly. "That's how you say *thank you*?"

"Thank you? Obviously you people at EES knew a lot more about this situation than what you briefed me on. I feel like I've been hung out to dry."

Garza took a sip of coffee, pushed the Danish away, rose, and placed a few dollars on the counter. "You're doing okay—at least until now. If I were you, instead of complaining I'd be worried as hell that we were able to locate you. If we can find you, so can Nodding Crane."

The man slipped back out into the night, leaving the paper unfolded on the counter, its headline displayed.

MURDER ON MOTT

Chinatown Resident's Throat Ripped Out by Assailant

Below was a picture of Roger Marion.

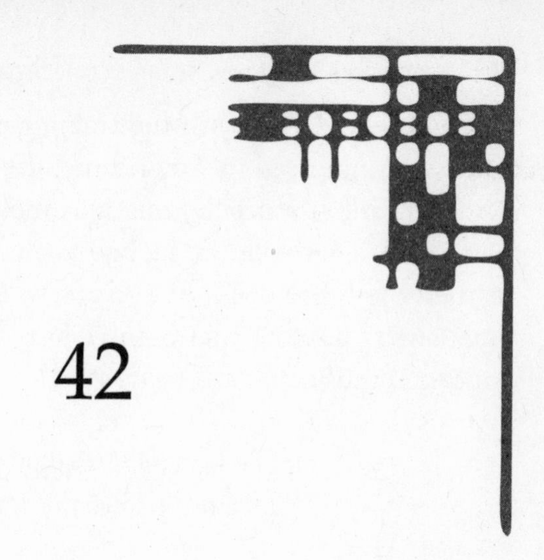

42

The man known as Nodding Crane moved slowly, painfully along the sidewalk outside the diner. Crew was still in there, talking to the fat waitress. The man who had passed him money had come and gone. He wasn't interested in that man. He was interested in Crew.

Coming to a halt next to the stoop of an abandoned brownstone, he eased himself onto it, placing the beer can wrapped in a greasy paper bag beside him, and lowered his head. A set of garbage cans, stacked in a row for morning pickup, cast a long shadow, further hiding his face. A group of noisy young people crossed the street at the corner of Avenue C and went on into the night, laughing and hooting. All became silent once again.

Right hand in the pocket of his old raincoat, he flexed his fingers, the razor-sharp picks clicking lightly against one another. He had been trained in the use of many exotic weapons—double sai, sweepers, flutes, walking canes, fire wheels, tiger forks, moonteeth—but the fingerpicks had been his own innovation. They were, in fact, genuine Dunlops he had modified, sharpened, and polished. As a boy in the training temple back in China, he had been immersed in American culture—movies, books, video games, music. Especially music, as music was the soul of a people. On his own volition, he had taken up bottleneck guitar and learned the tunes of Big Bill Broonzy, Blind Willie Johnson, and Skip James. "Hard Time Killing Floor Blues." Now, that was real American music.

If I ever get off this killin' floor
I'll never get down this low no more

As he hummed the music under his breath, his fingers, hidden in his voluminous coat pocket, picked out the imaginary notes, the sharpened picks making a clicking sound not unlike knitting needles.

He saw a movement in the diner out of the corner of his eye and, while continuing to hum, shifted his attention. It was Crew. The man exited the diner, crossed the street—walking with that characteristic loping stride of his—and turned, coming along the sidewalk toward Nodding Crane, moving toward Avenue C. Keeping his head down, the low brim of his old cap hiding his face, Nodding Crane waited for Crew to arrive. His humming continued, the fingers clacked.

Crew passed by and Nodding Crane let him go on, smiling to himself at how easy it would have been. But there were reasons not to kill him now—excellent reasons. As the man reached Avenue C, he held out his hand for a cab, and one almost immediately stopped. Nodding Crane noted the hack number, went back to humming.

Half an hour later, he stood up, stretched, and shuffled down the street, removing his cell phone. He called the Taxi and Limousine Commission hotline, explained he had left a PDA in the cab he had flagged down on Avenue C and 13th, about three thirty AM, the ride ending at Grand Central Terminal. He waited while the cabbie was contacted. The driver had not seen the lost PDA; but there was confusion over which fare was which, since the trip record indicated that the fare in that hack number had not ended at Grand Central, but instead at Park Avenue and 50th—in front of the Waldorf-Astoria Hotel. Nodding Crane thanked the person, apologized for the confusion, and shut the phone.

Discarding the shapeless raincoat in one of the garbage cans, Nodding Crane walked over to Avenue C and caught his own cab.

"The Waldorf," he said crisply as he settled in.

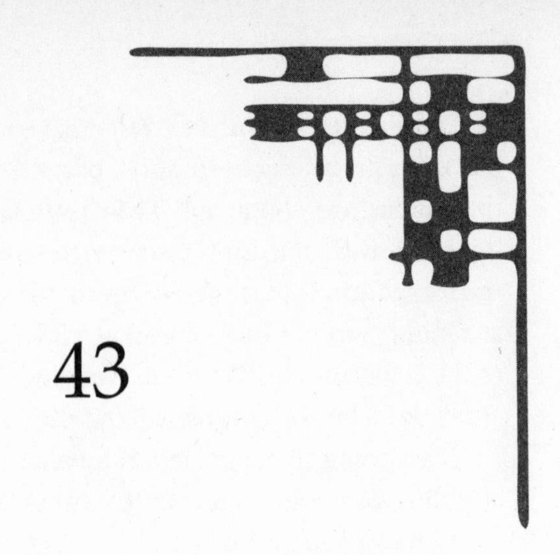

43

Gideon Crew tossed the thick roll of money onto the bed of his suite. Then he pulled out his cell and called Orchid.

"What the fuck do you want?"

Many derogations, animadversions, and apologies later, she agreed to the elaborate plan he described.

He hung up and went to the window, which faced Park Avenue, and looked carefully up and down the wide boulevard in front of the hotel. He couldn't shake the feeling he was being followed, but that was probably due to Garza's making him paranoid. He'd given the taxi driver special directions to make sure no one was following, and he couldn't imagine that anyone had. So why did he feel like an ant under a magnifying glass?

He called his Pelican case up from the Waldorf baggage storage room, where he had deposited it before going off to Hong Kong. After laying out his kit, he sorted through the disguises and settled for the *Death of a Salesman* role—a quietly desperate middle-class suburban persona—assembled it, then stepped into it. Examining himself in the floor-length mirror on the closet door, he found it most satisfactory.

He checked his watch. A little after four. Still wearing his disguise, he exited the Waldorf through the back door and made his way east down 51st Street, where he spied Orchid loitering outside the vest-pocket Greenacre Park, as per his instructions.

"Excuse me, miss?" he said, approaching her.

She turned on him and said, in a voice as cutting as dry ice, "Get lost. I'm waiting for someone."

"Yes, but you see that's just the point, I *am* lost..."

She practically spat at him. "Beat it. Now. Or I'll kick you so hard in the balls I'll sterilize your whole family."

Gideon laughed, pleased at the effectiveness of his deception. "It's me. Gideon. Nice disguise, eh?"

She gasped, leaned closer. "God, that's worse than before." She dropped her cigarette and angrily ground it into nothing on the sidewalk. "You've got a lot of nerve, calling me up like that after the way you acted."

"I'm staying at the Waldorf," he said, hooking her arm and hauling her along the street. "Listen." He pressed a wad of money into her hand. "I want you to book a room at the Waldorf for Mr. and Mrs. Tell. Go to the room, get into bed, turn off the lights, but leave the door unlocked. I'll join you in thirty minutes."

"Listen, you—"

But he released her and peeled off down 51st Street, walked into the Metropolitan Hotel, changed out of his disguise in an upper hallway, exited, then reentered the Waldorf as Gideon Crew. He went to his previous room, changed back into his disguise, showed up at the front desk, introduced himself as a Mr. Tell meeting his wife, moved through the empty corridors to the room Orchid had booked, eased open the door, shut and locked it.

She sat up in bed, the sheet falling partway off her nude body.

"I'm not going to take much more of your crap, I can tell you that."

He sat on the bed, took her face in his hands. "I know I've been a jerk, but bear with me just a little longer. Tomorrow we're going to dress up as Mr. and Mrs. Middle Class and try to enroll our brilliant son in Throckmorton Academy. I guarantee you, it'll be fun. And there's some good money in it for you."

She stared at him. "I don't like the way you're treating me. And I'm sure this isn't more Method acting—that's bullshit. I want to know what's really going on."

"I know you do, but we've got to get some sleep now, because we've got a big day ahead of us."

She looked at him askance. "Sleep?" She put her arms around him and drew him down on to the bed. "Get rid of that stupid face paint and I'll show you what kind of 'sleep' we're going to be getting."

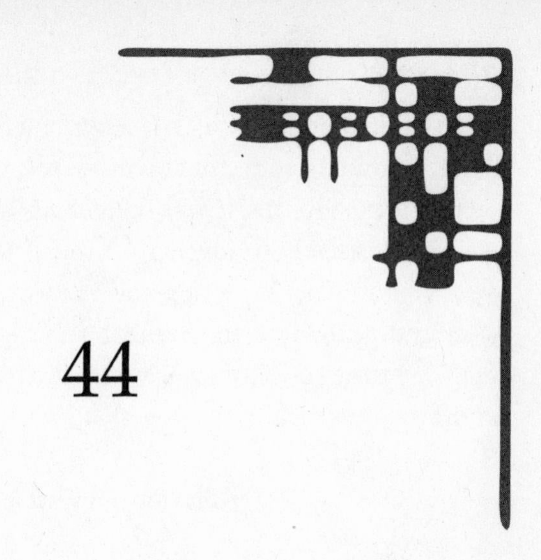

44

Nodding Crane sat in front of Saint Bartholomew's Church, strumming his Beard Road-O-Phonic with the case open in front of him, collecting small change. It was nine o'clock in the morning and most of the sidewalk was full of bankers and brokers on their way to work, rushing past without a second glance.

I'm looking funny in my eyes

He plucked the strings, singing in a low, rough voice, a voice he had practiced from years of listening to Bukka White. He felt calm after his near panic earlier that morning, when Crew had almost slipped away from him. That was some trick with the rooms and the sudden appearance of the woman. He had almost been fooled. Almost. If it hadn't been for Crew's characteristic loping walk, he *would* have been fooled.

And I believe I'm fixing to die

Crew had gone off with her, and he had decided not to follow them, knowing that they would return. Nodding Crane had learned long ago that it was dangerous and often counterproductive to obsessively follow your prey. And unnecessary: everyone lived by patterns, by loops and returns; better to learn the patterns and anticipate the returns than follow every useless footstep. The time to follow was when the pattern broke and the prey set off on a new path.

I'm looking funny in my eyes

The suits hustled by, bent on money matters. He began to resent that nobody was dropping money in his guitar case—these masters of the universe were passing him by without even a glance. And then, out of the blue, someone dropped in a twenty.

And I believe I'm fixing to die

That was better. America. What a wonderful country. Too bad it was doomed to fail.

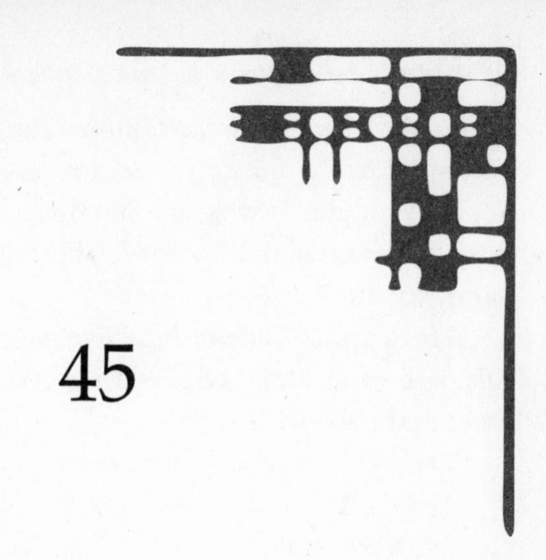

45

Gideon Crew stepped out of the car and looked up at the admissions building of Throckmorton Academy. It loomed before them, a nineteenth-century Romanesque Revival structure of gray granite, rising from perfectly tended shrubbery, flower beds, and clipped lawns. A brass plaque screwed into the wall told them the structure was known as the SWITHIN COTTAGE, following the WASPish self-deprecating habit of calling gigantic and expensive houses "cottages." It fairly exuded money, privilege, and smug superiority.

"This is really stupid," said Orchid, standing in the parking lot, tugging down the jacket of her tacky orange pantsuit. "I don't get it. We look like idiots. They're going to toss us out on our asses."

"Perhaps," said Gideon, clutching a thick folder of papers that had taken him hours of sustained and careful labor to prepare. He smoothed down his checked pants and jacket, adjusted his polyester tie, and headed toward the front door.

"I don't know why you dressed us like this," Orchid whispered furiously. "We don't fit in *at all* here."

He took her arm reassuringly. "Just follow my lead. All will become clear, I promise."

They entered a well-appointed waiting room, and the receptionist looked at them. "May I help you?" The tone was studiously neutral.

"Hello," said Gideon heartily, approaching and shaking her surprised hand. "Mr. and Mrs. Crew. We're here to enroll our son Tyler in the school."

"Do you have an appointment?"

"Yes."

"With whom?"

Gideon liked that *whom*. Here was someone punctilious with her grammar. He shuffled through his papers. "Mr. Van Rensselaer." It was one of those old New York names and he mispronounced it badly.

She rose and disappeared into an inner sanctum. A moment later she emerged again. "Mr. Van *Rensselaer* will see you now," she said, emphasizing the correct pronunciation.

The admissions officer was exactly as Gideon had hoped: tall, relaxed, friendly, dressed understatedly. The slightly longish hair and modish glasses indicated a man who, if not exactly open-minded, thought of himself as tolerant and moderate.

Perfect.

Van Rensselaer greeted them warmly, his eyes betraying only momentary alarm as he professionally covered up his reaction to their dress and manner.

"Thank you so much for meeting with us," said Gideon, after the introductions. "We'd like to enroll our son, Tyler, in the second grade. He's a very special boy."

"Of course. Naturally, we have a fairly comprehensive process here at Throckmorton Academy, involving interviews with the parents and child, teacher references, and a battery of age-appropriate testing. We have many more applicants than we can accept, unfortunately. And I am afraid to say, as I believe I explained on the telephone, there are currently no openings in the second grade."

"But Tyler is *special.*"

Van Rensselaer had not seated himself. "So as I mentioned, while we're glad to give you a quick tour of the campus, it would be unfair to take up more of your valuable time without any hope of admission for your son. If something opens up, of course, we'll be in touch. Now, we'd be glad to arrange that tour."

"Thank you. But I just thought I would leave this folder of Tyler's work—" Gideon brandished the folder of papers toward Van Rensselaer, who eyed it with the faintest whiff of distaste.

"That won't be necessary at this time."

"At least let me leave you the symphony."

"The . . . excuse me?"

"The symphony. Tyler composed a symphony."

A long silence. "How old did you say Tyler was?"

"Seven."

"And he had help composing this . . . symphony?"

"Oh heavens, no!" said Orchid, suddenly, her raspy cigarette-cured voice echoing in the hushed confines of the office. "What do we know about classical music!" A laugh followed.

Suppressing a smile, Gideon slid out the sheet music. After a moment, Van Rensselaer took it.

"He used GarageBand," said Gideon. "It sounds great, lots of trumpets. The CD is taped there, too. You should listen to it."

Van Rensselaer began flipping through the printed-out symphony. "Surely someone helped him do this."

"No one. Really. We didn't even know he was doing it."

"Um, neither of you is musical?"

"I like Lady Gaga," said Orchid, with a nervous laugh.

"Where does . . . Tyler get his musical interest?"

"No idea. He was adopted, you know, from Korea."

"Korea," Van Rensselaer repeated.

"Sure. Some of our friends were adopting kids from Asia and so we thought it would be cool, since, well—we can't have children. And it was something we could have in common with them, you know, talk about. But the symphony isn't the only thing. Here are some of his drawings. You can keep them—they're copies."

He slid out the drawings. It was amazing what you could find on the web. He'd added a little signature to the bottom of each one, *TYLER CREW*, before copying them.

Van Rensselaer took the drawings and looked at them.

"That's our dog. Tyler loves the dog. And that's some old church he found in a book."

"Chartres," murmured Van Rensselaer.

"What?" It had been devilishly difficult finding the right drawings from the vast selection available online; they had to combine childishness with artistic genius in just the right way.

"These are amazing," said Van Rensselaer softly, paging through them.

"Tyler is *special*," repeated Orchid. "He's already smarter than I am." She put a Chiclet in her mouth and began to chew. "Gum?"

Van Rensselaer didn't answer. He was absorbed in the drawings.

"I gotta tell you," said Gideon, "Tyler's also just an ordinary kid. He's not one of those stuck-up types. He loves to watch *Family Guy* with us, he laughs so hard. He especially liked the episode where Peter gets drunk and drops trou in the front yard, just as the cops are driving by."

Orchid burst into a peal of laughter. "That one was the *best*."

"*Family Guy*?" A look of horror bloomed on Van Rensselaer's face.

"Anyway, in this folder are a bunch of Tyler's sonnets, more drawings, and a bunch more musical compositions."

"All done by himself?"

"I helped him with the cartoons," said Gideon proudly. "But, well, we don't know much about music, literature, or drawing. I own a sports bar, see. In Yonkers."

Van Rensselaer looked from him to Orchid.

"He's also good at mathematics, I don't know how the heck he learned the stuff. Just like when he taught himself to read when he was two and a half. Also, I've got some letters from his teachers in there." He pawed through the folder and extracted a couple of letters he had carefully composed and printed on faked school letterhead. "There's one from his math tutor—he's way ahead of his grade—and another from the principal." The letters waxed eloquent about Tyler's transcendental genius and some made carefully veiled illusions to his home environment.

"Oh, and here are his test results. Somebody gave him an IQ test."

Van Rensselaer examined the results. His face became very still, almost blank, and the paper shook slightly. "I think..." he began slowly. "Under the circumstances...we may be able to find a place for Tyler here at Throckmorton. Of course, we'd still have to meet him and go through the application process."

"Wonderful!" cried Orchid, clapping her hands. She was really getting into it.

"Please," Van Rensselaer said, "have a seat."

"Just a minute," said Gideon as he sat down. "There are a few things I want to make sure of. First of all, will there be other Asian students in his class? I don't want him to feel left out."

"Absolutely," said Van Rensselaer briskly, switching into full salesmanship mode.

"Like, how many? Not just in the second grade, but in the elementary school. I want to know numbers."

"Let me get the class lists." Van Rensselaer called in the receptionist, issued the request. She returned a moment later with a piece of paper. The admissions officer glanced through it, slid it across his desk. "She's checked the ones of Asian descent."

Gideon took the paper.

"I'm afraid I can't let you keep that. We are naturally very protective of our families' privacy."

"Oh, sure, sure." He examined it. Fifteen students. That was his universe. He committed the names to memory.

"I also heard," he said sternly, laying down the paper, "that there was a serious outbreak of flu on campus."

"Flu? I don't think so."

"That's what I heard. In fact, I heard that on June seventh, just before graduation, more than three-quarters of the elementary school was out sick."

"I hardly think that's possible." Van Rensselaer called the receptionist back in. "Get me the attendance records for the lower school on June seventh."

"Very well."

"How about some coffee?" asked Gideon, eyeing a pot in the corner.

"What? Oh, please excuse me! I should have offered it to you earlier. How negligent."

"No problem, I'll take it with extra cream and three sugars."

"Extra cream and four sugars for me," said Orchid.

Van Rensselaer rose and fumbled with the coffee himself. As he did so, the receptionist came back. She laid the document on the desk just as Van Rensselaer returned with the coffee. Gideon reached for it as he rose from his chair, and the combined movement somehow caused him to knock the cups and spill coffee all over Van Rensselaer's desk.

"Oh, I'm so sorry!" he cried. "What a klutz I am!" Pulling a handkerchief from his pocket he began mopping up the liquid, wiping the papers, fussing about, shoving everything this way and that.

They all joined in cleaning up the mess, the receptionist returning with paper towels.

"So sorry," repeated Gideon. "So sorry."

"No problem," said Van Rensselaer, his voice tight, surveying the mess of damp, stained papers. "It could happen to anyone." He brightened up again immediately. "We'd love to see Tyler as soon as possible. Shall we schedule the interview now?"

"I'll call you," said Gideon. "Keep the file. We gotta run."

A few minutes later they were out in the car, driving through the wrought-iron gates. Orchid was almost helpless with laughter. "Jeez, you're funny, you know that? I couldn't believe the look on that guy's face. He thought we were just awful people. *Awful.* I know all about guys like that—they always want blow jobs, 'cause their wives don't like to get a—"

"Right, right," said Gideon, hoping to head the conversation in another direction. "He wanted to save poor Tyler from us, that much was obvious."

"So what's the point? Why the charade? And don't give me any more shit about Method acting."

The class lists and June 7 attendance records were now safely in Gideon's jacket pocket, and they would show exactly which Asian child was absent on the day after Wu's plane landed at JFK. Because, Gideon expected, a child in the international terminal waiting area at JFK after midnight would not likely be attending school the next day.

"Method acting," said Gideon Crew. "On my word of honor, it's all about Method acting. And you're a star."

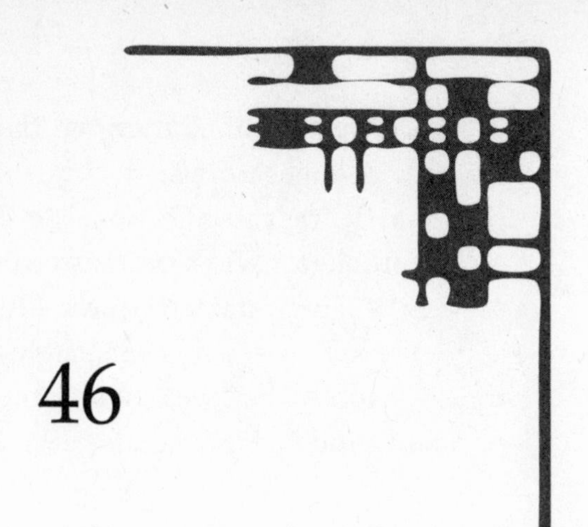

46

I just wish you'd tell me what the hell's *really* going on!" Orchid said as they rounded the corner of 51st and Park. Gideon walked fast. He'd been avoiding her questions all the way back, trying to focus on his next move. And she was getting increasingly pissed at his evasions.

She struggled to keep up. "Damn it, why won't you talk to me?"

Gideon sighed. "Because I'm tired of lying to people. Especially you."

"So tell me the truth, then!"

"It isn't safe." They walked past the iron gates of Saint Bart's park and Gideon heard a brief strain of old Blues music from a street musician. He suddenly halted and listened. The faint strains of the guitar floated to him over the sounds of midday traffic.

He placed a hand on her arm. "Wait."

"You can't keep me in the dark—"

He gave her arm a light warning squeeze and she stopped talking. "Just be cool," he murmured. "Don't react."

He listened to the faint music, the raspy singing.

In my time of dyin'
Don't want nobody to mourn

"What is it?" Orchid whispered.

Gideon answered with more gentle pressure. He turned and pretended to answer his cell phone, giving them an excuse to be standing there, listening.

All I want for you to do
Is to take my body home.

Gideon recognized it as a Blind Willie tune, "In My Time of Dyin'." It aroused in him a faint sensation of déjà vu, and he searched his mind for where he had recently heard that same bottleneck guitar.

Bottleneck guitar.

It was on Avenue C. It wasn't a guitar, but a bum humming that same old Blues tune. When he was leaving the diner. He pictured the dark street and he remembered a bum sitting on a stoop, humming—just humming.

Well, well, well so I can die easy
Well, Well, Well
Well, Well, Well so I can die easy

Now he listened with care. The guy was good. More than good. Not flashy, not technical, but playing easy and slow, as a real Delta Blues tune should be played. But as Gideon listened, he realized that some of the lyrics were different from the version he knew best; this was another version, one he wasn't as familiar with.

Jesus gonna make up
Jesus gonna make up
Jesus gonna make up my dyin' bed.

The revelation struck him hard. Disguising his surprise, he shut his phone as if the call were over and urged Orchid forward by the arm, toward the awning of the Waldorf. As soon as they were inside he quickened his pace, propelling her through the lobby, past the giant urn of flowers, toward Peacock Alley.

"Hey! What the hell?"

They swept past the maître d', brushing aside his proffered menus, walked through the restaurant to the back, and pushed through the double doors into the kitchen.

"Where are you going?" The voice of the maître d' was drowned out by the clatter of pots and shouts. "Sir, you can't—"

But Gideon was already moving fast toward the rear of the kitchen. He pushed through another set of double doors into a long hallway lined with giant walk-in refrigerators.

"Come back here!" came the maître d's distant voice. "Someone call security!"

Gideon took a sharp turn, blew through a third set of doors, and ended up in an inner receiving bay. Continuing on, a protesting Orchid following in his wake, he trotted through the bay and onto the outside receiving dock, clambered down the steps, and ran down a short alley to 50th Street, still hustling Orchid along. He swiftly crossed the street through blaring traffic, trotted two blocks uptown, entered the Four Seasons Restaurant, ran up the stairs to the upper level of the Pool Room, and entered the kitchen.

"Again?"

Racing through the kitchen to more protests and shouts, they emerged onto Lexington Avenue opposite the 51st Street subway entrance. At Gideon's urging, they ran across the street and jogged down the stairs. He swiped his card through the turnstile twice, and they emerged onto the platform just as an uptown train was pulling in. Orchid in tow, Gideon boarded the train. The doors closed.

"What the *hell*?" Orchid said, gasping for breath.

Gideon sank back into a seat, thinking fast. He'd heard the same voice humming and singing on Avenue C. And today, the man had been playing a very rare version of a Blind Willie tune—a version that had only been released on vinyl in Europe and the Far East.

If we can find you, Garza had said, *so can Nodding Crane.* And now it seemed he had.

Gideon exhaled slowly, looked carefully around the car. Surely it was impossible that Nodding Crane had followed them onto the uptown train.

"I'm sorry." He took her hand, still recovering his breath.

"I've just about had it with your shenanigans," said Orchid, yelling.

"I know. I know." He patted her hand. "I've been really unfair to you. Look, Orchid: I've dragged you into something that's a lot more dangerous than I realized. I've been a real idiot. I need you to go back to your apartment and lie low—I'll contact you later when all this blows over."

"No *way*! You're not gonna leave me again!"

Now she was really shouting, turning heads all the way down the car.

"I promise I'll call you. I *promise*."

"I won't be treated like shit!"

"Please, Orchid. I really like you, I really do. That's why I can't drag you into this trouble." He looked at her carefully. "I *will* call you."

"Why don't you just say it?" she cried, the tears suddenly springing into her eyes and rolling down her face. "You're in some kind of trouble, aren't you? You think I can't see that? Why don't you let me help you? Why do you keep pushing me away?"

He didn't have the heart to deny it. "Yes, I'm in trouble, but you can't help. Just go back to your place. I'll come back for you, I promise. It'll be over soon, one way or another. Look—I've got to go."

"*No!*" She clutched at him like a drowning woman.

This was futile. He needed to get away from her—for her own safety. The subway rolled into 59th Street, halted with a groan, and the doors slid open. At the last moment, making a sudden decision, Gideon twisted free and ran out. He stopped and turned to apologize again, but the doors slammed shut, and he had a glimpse of her devastated face through the window as the train pulled out of the station.

"I promise I'll call you!" he cried, but it was too late and the train was gone.

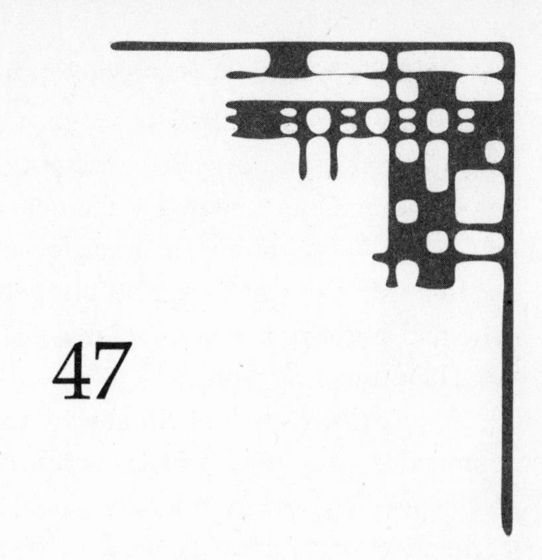

47

Gideon drove moodily through the midafternoon Jersey traffic. He'd crossed over through the Holland Tunnel, then pointed the rented Chevy northward through the old, tired urban tangle, one town blending seamlessly with another: Kearny, North Arlington, Rutherford, Lodi. The streets all looked the same—narrow, busy, dense with three- and four-story brick buildings, their shopfronts dingy, heavy clusters of telephone wires hanging claustrophobically overhead. Now and then, through the urban accretion, he could catch glimpses of what had once been a downtown: the marquee of a movie theater, now disused; the plate-glass window of an erstwhile soda joint. Fifty or sixty years ago, these places had been separate little towns, bright and sparkling, full of bobby soxers and guys with derbies and ducktails. Now they were just ghostly pentimentos beneath an endless procession of salumerias, mercados, discount stores, and cell phone shops.

He crossed into Bergen County, passing through another half a dozen sad-looking towns. There were much faster ways to reach his destination, of course, but Gideon wanted to lose himself for a while in a mindless act such as driving. He was full of uncomfortable and unwelcome emotions: agitation at discovering Nodding Crane, shame and embarrassment at his treatment of Orchid. He told himself it was for her own good, for her protection; that she was better off not getting involved with a man who had a year to live. It didn't make him feel any better. He had used her, used her cynically.

As he drove farther north, toward the New York State line, the cramped streets grew broader and leafier, and the traffic eased. Residences became grander and farther apart. He glanced down at the sheet of paper he'd placed on the passenger seat. *Biyu Liang, Bergen Dafa Center, Old Tappan,* he'd scrawled on it. With the attendance records unwittingly supplied by Van Rensselaer, it had been a trivial undertaking to single out the Asian boy who'd been at JFK—Jie Liang—and from there to learn the identity of his mother. He didn't know what a Dafa Center was, but that was the woman's place of employment—and his destination.

Fifteen minutes later, he pulled into what to his surprise appeared to be an old estate: not huge, but well manicured, a large puddingstone mansion, a separate garage, and an adjoining gatehouse, the whole now converted into a small campus of sorts. A sign set back from the road read BERGEN DAFA CENTER.

Gideon parked his car in the lot beside the main building and trotted up the steps to the twin doors, decorated with wrought-iron filigree. He stepped through into an ornate front hall that had been converted into a reception area. A tasteful sign on one wall read: FALUN GONG EXERCISES 3–5 WEEKDAYS, TEACHINGS WEEKNIGHTS 7–10. It was flanked by other signs covered with symbols and Chinese ideographs.

A young Asian woman was seated behind a desk. She smiled as he approached.

"May I help you?" she asked in unaccented English.

Gideon smiled back. "I'd like to speak with Biyu Liang, please."

"She's conducting a session at the moment," the woman said, extending her hand toward an open door through which Gideon could hear a mixture of music and speech.

"Thank you, I'll wait for her to finish."

"Feel free to observe."

Gideon stepped past her and into a spacious room of Zen-like simplicity. A woman was leading a group of people in a series of slow exercises, all of them moving gently in unison to the hypnotic sound of five-tone music, tinkling bells, and percussion. The woman was apparently giving instructions in melodious Mandarin. He looked at her carefully. She was younger than the woman in the airport had been, but resembled her enough that he concluded the woman in the video had probably been the child's grandmother.

Gideon waited for the session to end. As he did so, he was increasingly struck by what he was seeing; there was something ineffable in the movements, something beautiful, almost universal. *Falun Gong,* he mused. He had heard of it, vaguely, and recalled it was some form of Buddhist practice from China. Clearly, he needed to learn more.

The session continued for another ten minutes. As the group dispersed, chatting quietly, Gideon remained standing at the entrance, waiting. The woman who had been leading the session noticed him and came over. She was small with what could only be described as a round, shining face.

"Can I help you?" she asked.

"Yes." Gideon gave her a big smile. "My name's Gideon Crew, and my son, Tyler, is entering Throckmorton Academy in the fall—we've just moved here from New Mexico. He's going to be in your son Jie's class."

"How nice," she said, smiling. "Welcome." They shook hands and she introduced herself.

"He's adopted," Gideon continued, "from Korea. We just

wanted to make sure he'd feel at home—he's still having some difficulty with English—which is why my wife and I were pleased to learn there would be other Asian children in the class. It's hard to come into a new school in a new place. That's why I was hoping to meet you and a few of the other parents."

"I'll talk to Jie about your boy. Jie's very kind and I know he'll make a special effort to be friends with your son right away."

Gideon felt embarrassed. "Thank you, I know that will make a real difference." He moved to leave but then, as if on impulse, he turned back. "I'm sorry if this is a bother. I couldn't help but watch what was going on here while I was waiting to speak with you. I was struck by it, the music, the movements. What is it, exactly?"

Her face lit up. "We are practitioners of Falun Gong—or, more properly, Falun Dafa."

"I'm very curious, and... well, I thought it was quite beautiful. What's it for? Physical conditioning?"

"That's only a small part. It's a total system of mind and body cultivation, a way to recapture your original, true self."

"Is it a religion?"

"Oh no. It's a new form of science. Although it does involve Buddhist and Taoist principles. You might call it a spiritual and mental path, as opposed to a religion."

"I'd like to learn more."

She responded warmly, with a well-rehearsed description. "Dafa practitioners are guided by universal principles: truthfulness, compassion, and restraint. We strive continuously to harmonize ourselves with these, through a series of five simple exercises and meditation. Over time, the exercises will transform your body and mind and connect you to the deepest and most profound truths of the universe—and in this way you eventually find the path of return to your true self."

This was clearly a topic dear to her heart. But in an odd way,

Gideon found himself genuinely impressed. There might actually be something to this; he had felt it just listening and watching the movements. "Is it open to anyone?"

"Of course. We welcome everyone. As you saw, we have all kinds of practitioners, from every walk of life and background—in fact, here most of our practitioners are Westerners. Would you like to join a session?"

"I would. Is it expensive?"

She laughed. "You can come, listen, do the exercises as long as you like. Most of our English-language sessions are in the evenings. If in the future you feel it is helping you, then of course we would welcome support for the center. But there are no fees."

"Does it originate in China?"

At this, the woman hesitated "It's connected to ancient Chinese traditions and beliefs. But it's been suppressed in China."

This would be an extremely interesting thread to follow up on. But right now he had to find the older woman—the grandmother. "Thank you for sharing that with me," he said. "I'll certainly join a session. Now, getting back to the school: they mentioned Jie had a grandmother he's very close to."

"That might be my mother. She's the founder of the Bergen Dafa Center."

"Ah. May I meet her?"

Even as he asked it, he realized he had pushed a little too far. Her face lost a bit of its openness. "I'm sorry, she's working on other Dafa business and is no longer involved on a daily basis with the center." She paused. "If I may ask, why would you want to meet her?"

Gideon smiled. "Since they're so close... and she takes him to school... well, I just thought it would be good to meet. But of course it's not at all necessary..."

Now he realized he had made another mistake. The woman's expression grew a little chilly. "She never takes him to Throckmorton. I'm surprised the school even knows of her." A pause. "I wonder how *you* know of her?"

Sink me, Gideon thought ruefully. He should have shut up while he was ahead. "They mentioned her at the school... Perhaps Jie's talked about her?"

Her face softened just a bit. "Yes. I imagine he would."

"I don't want to take up your time any longer," said Gideon, backing off and giving her an innocent smile. "You've been most kind."

Mollified, she fetched him a brochure. "Here's the schedule of introductory sessions. I hope to see you soon. And I'll tell Jie about your son Tyler. Maybe we can have him over for a playdate before school begins in the fall."

"That would be most kind," said Gideon, with a final farewell smile.

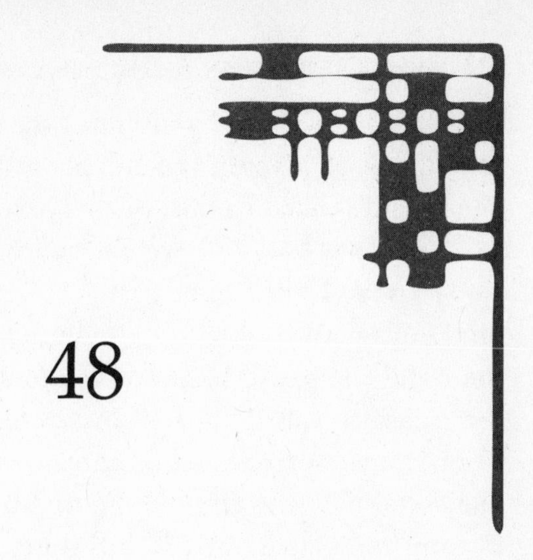

48

Orchid stepped out of the 51st Street deli and marched quickly down the sidewalk toward Park Avenue, opening the pack of cigarettes she'd just purchased and tossing the wrapper into the trash. Instead of going back to her apartment, she'd just walked the streets, her mind whirling. She was furious and determined. Gideon was just awful, a real bastard, but at the same time he was in desperate trouble. She realized that now. He needed help—and she would help him. She would save him from whatever was chasing him, tormenting him, driving him to do all these bizarre things.

But how? How could she help?

Swinging around the corner, she charged up Park Avenue. The uniformed doorman at the Waldorf opened the door for her as she swept in. She paused in the stupendous lobby, breathing hard. Finally getting herself under control, she went up to the reception desk and used the fake names they had registered under. "Has Mr. Tell returned? I'm Mrs. Tell."

"I'll ring the room." The receptionist placed the call, but no one answered.

"I'll wait in the lobby for him," she said. He'd have to be back sometime—all his stuff was still here. She opened the pack of cigarettes and shook one out, stuck it between her lips.

"I'm sorry, Mrs. Tell, we don't allow smoking in the lobby."

"I know, I know, I'm going outside." She lit the cigarette on the way out, just to spite them. On the sidewalk in front of the hotel she paced back and forth, smoking furiously. When the cigarette was done she threw the butt on the sidewalk in front of the doorman, fished another out of her purse, and lit it. She could hear the faint sound of guitar music from that bum in front of Saint Bart's. To kill time, she crossed the street to listen.

The man, dressed in a thin shapeless trench coat, strummed on his guitar and sang. He was sitting cross-legged, plucking the strings with his fingerpicks. His case lay open beside him, and a number of crumpled bills lay within it.

Meet me Jesus meet me
Meet me in the middle of the air
If these wings should fail me Lord
Won't you meet me with another pair

This guy was pretty damn good. She couldn't see his face—it was bowed over his old guitar and he wore a brown fedora—but she could hear his voice, kind of gravelly, full of sorrow and the hard life. She could identify with that. It made her feel sad and happy at the same time. On impulse, she reached into her bag, pulled out a dollar bill, dropped it in the case.

He nodded, not interrupting his music.

Jesus gonna make up
Jesus gonna make up
Jesus gonna make up my dyin' bed

The last mournful chord sounded and the song was over. He laid the guitar aside and raised his head.

She was surprised to see he was Asian, and young, quite handsome, his face lacking the usual signs of alcoholism or drug addiction, his eyes clear and deep. In fact, despite the shabby outfit, her own street instincts told her he wasn't a street person at all—probably a serious musician. The raggedy clothes and filthy old fedora were for show.

"Hey, you're pretty good, you know that?" she said.

"Thank you."

"Where'd you learn to play like that?"

"I'm a disciple of the Blues," he said. "I live the Blues."

"Yeah. Sometimes I feel that way myself."

He gazed at her until she began to flush. He then began to collect the pile of money from his guitar case, stuffed it in his pocket, and put away his guitar. "Done for the day," he said. "I'm going to grab a cup of tea at the Starbucks around the corner. Would you care to accompany me?"

Would you care to accompany me? This guy was a student at Juilliard, probably, out here paying his dues, living the life. Yes, that had to be it. His formal way of asking pleased her, and she liked his semi-undercover shtick. Part of her was still mad at Gideon. She hoped he would see them together; that would teach him a lesson.

"Sure," she said. "Why not?"

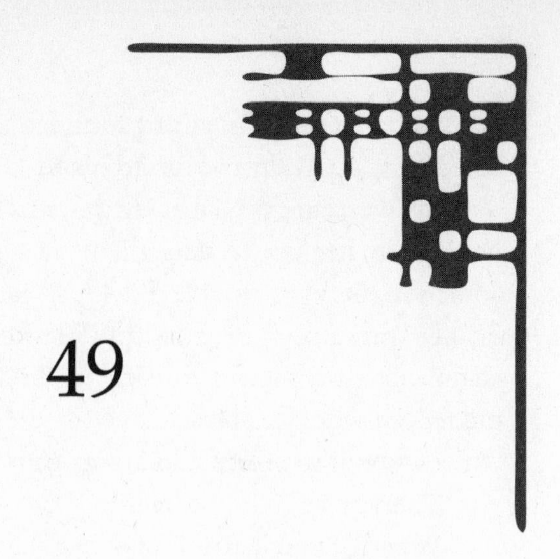

49

Nodding Crane sat at the little table, sipping green tea and listening to the woman talk. This opportunity had been dropped right in his lap, and he knew exactly how to exploit it, to flush Crew out, to destabilize him, to throw him back on the defensive.

A marvelous opportunity, actually.

"You went by earlier today," he said. "I noticed you immediately."

"Oh well, yes, I did."

"You were with a man—your husband?"

She laughed. "He's just a friend." She leaned forward. "And you. You're no street person—am I right?"

Nodding Crane remained very still.

"You don't fool me." She winked. "Although, I must say, it's a pretty good act."

He sipped his tea as if nothing had happened. Inside, he was deeply perturbed. "A friend? Your boyfriend?"

"Well, not really. He's kind of a weird guy, actually."

"Oh? How so?"

"Said he was an actor, a producer. He gets dressed up in wild costumes, goes out and pretends to be someone else, drags me along. Totally crazy. He said he was a Method actor but I think he's in some kind of trouble."

"What kind of trouble?"

"I wish I knew! I'd like to help him, but he won't let me. He dragged me up to Riverdale to this really tony private school. We pretended to be parents of some genius kid and he stole some papers from the school—God only knows why. And we did this crazy room switch at the Waldorf in the middle of the night."

"How strange."

"Yeah, and then we went to visit this friend of his in the hospital and it turned out the guy had died."

Nodding Crane sipped his tea. "Sounds to me like he might be involved in some sort of illegal activity."

"I don't know. He seems pretty honest. I just can't figure it out."

"Where's he now?"

The girl shrugged. "He, like, abandoned me on the subway, just jumped out, said he'd call me later. He'll be back. All our stuff is in the room."

"Stuff?"

"Yeah. He carries around a suitcase full of disguises. And one of those hard cases, all locked up. No idea what's in that one, he guards it pretty carefully."

"A hard case? In the room?"

"Hard molded plastic. He keeps it locked up in the Waldorf's baggage room."

She chattered on, oblivious. When Nodding Crane had gotten out of her all the important information he needed, he brought the subject back to himself. "You implied you thought I was in disguise. What did you mean?"

"Come on. Look at you." She laughed, teasing him. "I know who you really are."

He rose and checked his watch. "It's almost time for vespers at Saint Bart's."

"What? You're going to church?"

"I go to hear the music—I love the Gregorian chants."

"Oh."

"Would you care to come with me?"

Orchid hesitated. "Well . . . sure. But don't think this is a date."

"Of course not. I would enjoy your company. As a friend."

"All right, why not?"

A moment later they had entered the church. The doors were unlocked but the sanctuary was empty and, in the gathering twilight outside, it was dark.

"Where's the music?" she asked. "Nobody's here."

"We're a little early," said Nodding Crane. He took her arm and gently led her down the aisle into the darkest of the choir stalls near the front. "We can get a good seat here."

"Okay." There was a doubtful sound in her voice.

Nodding Crane had kept his right hand buried in his coat pocket. The picks were still on his fingers. As they entered the shadowy chancel, he slipped his hand from the pocket.

"I can hear your fingerpicks clicking away," she said.

"Yes," he said. "I'm always hearing music. I'm always hearing the Blues." He raised his hand, his fingers waving before her face, the picks gleaming faintly in the dim light, and began to sing ever so softly.

In my time of dyin'
Don't want nobody to mourn
All I want for you to do
Is to take my body home

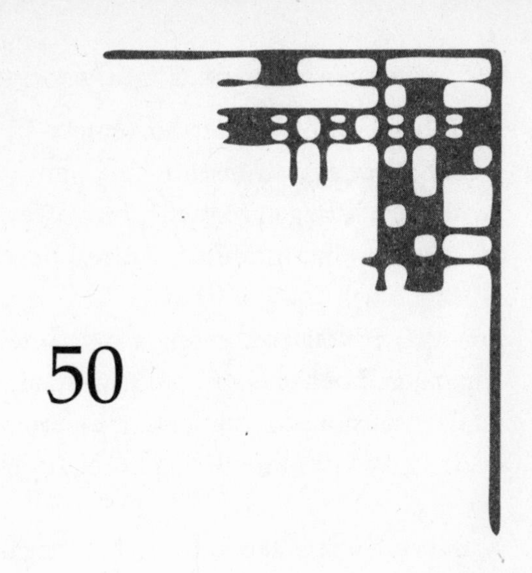

50

Gideon left the center, but instead of returning to his car he strolled across the campus lawn toward the gatehouse of the old estate, now clearly a small private residence. Some sixth sense told him it was the house of an orderly old woman—with its neat brick walkway, the tiny flower beds flanking the door, the lace curtains and unusual ornaments visible through the windows.

He approached the door as nonchalantly as possible, but even before he reached it two Asian men in dark tracksuits appeared from nowhere.

"May we help you?" one asked as they stepped in front of him. The tone was polite, but they were careful to block his way.

Gideon didn't even know the name of the grandmother. "I'm here to see the mother of Biyu Liang."

"I'm sorry—is Madame Chung expecting you?"

He was gratified to see, at least, that he'd picked the right house. "No, but I'm the father of a boy starting at Throckmorton Academy this fall—"

They didn't even let him finish. In the politest way possible, but without any ambiguity, they approached him and, taking him by the arms, began to escort him away. "Come with us."

"Yes, but her grandson Jie will be in my son's class—"

"You will come with us."

As they started moving away, Gideon noticed that he was being taken, not to his car, but toward a small metal door in the side of the mansion. An unpleasant memory flashed through his head: waking up in a Hong Kong hotel, his bed surrounded by Chinese agents.

"Hey, wait a second—" He struggled, dug his heels into the ground. The two men stopped, tightened their grip, then began dragging him toward the door.

A voice sounded from the small house. The two stopped. Gideon turned to see an elderly Chinese woman on the steps of the gatehouse, gesturing at the guards with a withered hand. She said something in Mandarin.

After a moment, the guards reluctantly loosened their grasp. First one took a step away, then the other.

"Come in," said the old woman, gesturing. "Come in, now."

Gideon glanced from the guards to the woman, and wasted no time in complying. She ushered him inside, leading him into the parlor.

"Please. Sit down. Tea?"

"Yes, please," said Gideon, rubbing his arms where the guards had held him.

A servant appeared in the door. Madame Chung spoke to him briefly, and he withdrew once again.

"Forgive my guardians," she said. "Life is rather dangerous for me right now."

"Why is that?" Gideon asked.

The woman merely smiled in reply.

The servant returned with a small, cast-iron teapot and two

diminutive round china cups. As she poured out the tea, Gideon took the opportunity to scrutinize her. She was indeed the old woman in the security video—he felt a kind of awe in her presence, thinking of the long and strange journey of discovery that had brought him to this place. And yet, in person, she seemed very different. There was a kind of life energy that the grainy airport video had been unable to capture. He didn't think he had ever met a livelier or more vigorous elderly person in his life. She was like a bright-eyed bird, alert, quick, joyful.

She handed him one of the cups, then—settling in the chair opposite him—she folded her hands on her knees and looked at him so intently, he almost blushed. "I see you have something you want to ask me," she said.

Gideon didn't answer right away. His mind started to race. He had worked up several stories, of course, several possible phony scenarios, for extracting the information from her. But sitting opposite Madame Chung like this, now, face-to-face, he realized that she was not one to be taken in. By anything. All his careful constructs, his machinations, his ploys and stratagems and cons were—quite suddenly—emasculated. He was strangely afraid; he didn't know what to say. He frantically cast about for a better story, a better concatenation of lies and half-truths to tell her, realizing even as he did so that it was a hopeless effort.

"Just tell me the truth," she said, with a smile, as if reading his mind.

"I..." He couldn't go on. If he told her the truth, all would be lost. And now he did blush, coloring in confusion.

"Let me ask you some questions, then."

"Yes, thank you," he said with enormous relief.

"Your name?"

"Gideon Crew."

"Where are you from and what do you do?"

He hesitated, again casting about for a suitable lie, but for perhaps the first time in his life he came up blank. "I live in New Mexico and work at Los Alamos National Lab."

"Your place of birth?"

"Claremont, California."

"And your parents?"

"Melvin and Doris Crew. Both gone."

"And your reason for being here?"

"My son Tyler will be in Jie's class at Throckmorton this fall—"

She folded her hands. "I'm sorry," she gently interrupted, peering at him with her bright black eyes. "I think you're a professional liar," she said. "And you've just run out of lies. That's what I think."

He had no answer.

"So, as I said before, why not try the truth for a change? You might just get what you want."

He felt like he'd been backed into a corner by this old woman. There was no way to turn, he was unable to escape. How had this happened?

She waited, hands folded, smiling.

What the hell. "I'm a... a sort of special operative," he said.

Her carefully painted eyebrows went up.

He took a deep, shuddering breath. He could latch on to nothing save the truth, and in an odd way he felt relieved. "My assignment is to find out what Mark Wu was bringing into this country and to get it."

"Mark Wu. Yes, that makes sense. Who do you work for?"

"I work for the United States. Indirectly."

"And where do I fit in?" the old woman asked.

"You gave something to Mark Wu at the airport, just before he got into a car and was chased down and killed. I want to know what you gave him. Beyond that, I'd like to know if he really was carrying plans for a new weapon, what that weapon is, and where those plans are now."

She nodded very slowly. She took a sip of tea, replaced the cup. "Are you left-handed or right-handed?"

Gideon frowned. "Left-handed."

She nodded again, as if this explained quite a bit. "Please extend your left hand."

After a moment, Gideon complied. The woman took it gently with her right. For a moment, Gideon was aware only of the feel of her dry, withered skin against his. Then he almost cried out in surprise and dismay. Her hand seemed to be burning his own.

He jerked in his chair, and she released her grip.

"I will try to answer all your questions," she said, hands once again folded on her knees. "Even though you are a professional liar, that is evidently part of your job. I see—I *sense*—that you are at heart a good person. And I think that by helping you, we can help ourselves."

She took another sip of tea.

"Mark Wu was a scientist working on a secret project in China. He was also a devotee of Falun Dafa." She nodded slowly, several times, letting the silence build. "As you may or may not know, Falun Dafa has been brutally suppressed in China. For this reason, Dafa has had to go underground in China. Deep underground."

"Why have the Chinese done this?"

"Because we pose a threat to their monopoly on power. China has a long history of empires being brought down by charismatic spiritual movements. They are right to be afraid. Because Dafa not only challenges their assumptions about communism and totalitarian rule—but also challenges their new notions about the value of materialism and unbridled capitalism."

"I see." And Gideon did in fact see: here would be a prime motive for Wu's defection. But then, what of the CIA honey trap?

"Because of the persecution, Dafa adherents in China must practice underground, in secret. But we remain linked with our

Chinese brethren. We are all in touch with one another. Dafa requires a communal spirit. The government tried to block our websites and silence us—but they failed."

"Is this why you said you're in danger?"

"It is part of the reason." She smiled. "You're not drinking your tea."

"Oh. Sorry." Gideon raised the cup, took a gulp.

"Many Dafa adherents are scientists and computer engineers. We developed a powerful software program called Freegate. Perhaps you've heard of it."

"It rings a bell."

"We distributed it worldwide. It enables internet users from mainland China—and other countries—to view websites blocked by their governments. And it allows users to penetrate those firewalls certain governments use to block websites and social networking sites."

Listening, Gideon took a more careful sip, found it excellent.

"Freegate servers disguise true IP addresses, so people can roam freely online. Right here at the Bergen Dafa Center, we have a massive Freegate server cluster. There are other locations across the world."

Gideon finished his tea. "What does this have to do with Mark Wu?"

"Everything. You see, Mark Wu was bringing us a secret from China. A huge, huge secret."

"Us? You mean, Falun Gong?"

She nodded. "It was all in place. He was going to pass it to us, and we were going to put it on our Freegate servers. We were going to broadcast this secret to the entire world."

Gideon swallowed. "So. What is this huge secret?"

She smiled again. "We don't know."

"What do you mean? How could you not know? I don't believe you." The words tumbled out before he could stop himself.

Madame Chung let this pass. "Wu couldn't, or wouldn't, tell us. Our job was to disseminate the information. That's all."

"And it was a super-weapon?"

"Perhaps. But I doubt it."

Gideon stared at her. "Why?"

"Because that isn't quite how Wu described it. He said it was a new technology that would allow China to conquer the world—to *rule* the world, I think he said. But we didn't get the impression it was necessarily dangerous. Besides, I doubt he would have wanted the plans for a new weapon to be broadcast everywhere—that would put the information into the hands of terrorists." She paused. "How unfortunate they murdered him first."

"If he had the plans with him, where are they now?"

"We don't know that, either. He was very secretive."

"Surely he must have indicated to you where and when he'd pass you the plans."

"We took the precaution of choosing which person should take possession. One of our technical contacts, Roger Marion, was to pick them up at a hotel room. We passed him Roger's name when he arrived at the airport." She paused, as if recollecting. "During the negotiation process, Wu did say something odd. He said he would need a few moments in his room to extract the information."

"Extract? I don't understand."

"He used the Chinese phrase *cai jian*, which means 'to extract or cut out.' I had the impression the information was buried in something and that it had to be removed."

Immediately Gideon thought back to the dirty X-rays. Maybe Wu *had* placed the information inside his body. "Wu also had a list of numbers that he'd memorized. What were those?"

She looked at him. "How do you know about the list of numbers?"

For a moment, Gideon held his breath. "Because I followed him from the airport. I saw his cab get rammed by the SUV. I dragged him free. He thought I was Roger Marion, he told me the numbers. I tried to save him. I failed."

There was a lengthy silence. Finally, the old woman spoke again.

"We don't know what the numbers mean, either. All he told us was the numbers had to be combined with the thing he was bringing to us. The two had to be put together for the secret to be complete. One without the other wouldn't work—both were necessary. It was his way of protecting the secret. He was to give them both to Roger."

"And you did all this for Wu—just on the basis of his assurances, without knowing what it was?

"Dr. Wu was a very advanced Dafa practitioner. His judgment was completely sound."

He was close—very close, maddeningly close. "How did he describe this secret information? Was it a set of plans, a microchip—what?"

"He referred to it as an object. A thing."

"Thing?"

"He used the word *wù*, which means 'thing, object, solid matter.' It's also the Chinese word for 'physics.' Not the same word as his name, by the way. It's pronounced *wù*, with the lower tone."

Again Gideon's thoughts returned to the X-rays of Wu's lower body. They showed his crushed legs full of bits and pieces of metal and plastic from the accident. He had looked carefully over all those specks and marks—but could he have missed something? Could one of those irregular spots have been the object? He'd been looking for a set of plans, a microchip, a micro-canister. But it might have been something else entirely. Maybe it was a piece of metal.

A piece of metal...

O'Brien had said his physicist friend, Epstein, told him the numbers looked like a metallurgical formula. That was it. *That was it.*

"You have to understand," said Madame Chung. "Dr. Wu wasn't planning to defect to the United States or anything like that. He's a loyal and faithful citizen of China. But as a scientist, he felt in this case he had a moral imperative. His intention was for us to broadcast this great secret to the entire world, through our servers, in such a way that it could never be hidden again. It was to be a gift, you see—a gift to the world. From us."

So Mindy was wrong about his motives, Gideon thought. But he had more important concerns at the moment. His mind was racing. Wu's legs were full of metal, and his body was still in the morgue. Waiting for him, as next of kin, to claim. Good God, all he had to do was go down there and cut it out.

But first he had to get the X-rays and figure which piece of metal to cut out. He needed to visit Tom O'Brien first, and his friend the physicist.

He found Madame Chung staring at him. "Mr. Crew," she said. "You realize that when you retrieve whatever it is Dr. Wu was bringing us, you'll have to bring it back to me."

He stared back at her.

"You do realize that, don't you? It is an obligation you *cannot escape.*" And her musical voice cheerfully emphasized these final words as she gave him another bright smile.

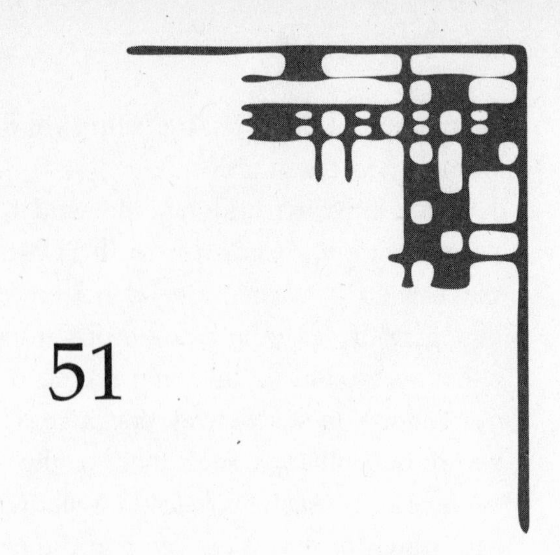

51

Gideon Crew arrived back at the Waldorf around eleven in the evening, slipping in via the staff entrance and avoiding Saint Bart's, where he feared Nodding Crane might still be waiting with his guitar. Thinking about it on his drive back from New Jersey, he realized that, from the steps of Saint Bart's, Nodding Crane had a clear view of the windows of both his rooms, as well as both the main hotel entrance and the 51st Street entrance. Gideon couldn't be sure the man knew of both rooms—but he had to assume he did. Nodding Crane had picked his location well.

Cursing his stupidity, Gideon punched the button for one of the service elevators and rode it up to the floor of his backup room. Once there, he carefully slipped in, not turning on the light in case Nodding Crane was still watching from below. Then again, maybe the man was waiting for him in the room. Gideon paused, listening. For the first time, he wished he hadn't lost his handgun in the river or, at least, had asked Garza for another.

What unnerved him most about Nodding Crane wasn't that

the man had been tailing him so successfully. No—it was how damn good the man was on Blues guitar. Despite what Jackson had told him, he'd assumed Nodding Crane was a sort of Chinese contract killer, a caricature out of a kung fu movie, an expert in martial arts but unfamiliar with American culture, hobbled by his foreignness and lack of familiarity with the city. Now he realized these assumptions were false.

Gideon shivered. The room was silent, the air still. At last, he moved toward the bed and pulled out the Pelican case from underneath. In the reflected light from the window it looked undisturbed. He dialed the combination and opened it, slid out the manila folder containing Wu's X-rays and medical report, then closed and locked it again. He removed his coat, slid the folders under his shirt, put his coat back on.

He momentarily thought of his own X-rays and CT scans, then forced the thought away. He would surely fail if he lost his focus now.

A growing hubbub of sirens sounded on the street out front. Gideon sidled up to the window and peered out. Something was going on at Saint Bart's. Several ambulances and a slew of cop cars had pulled up, blocking the northbound lanes of Park Avenue, and a crowd was growing. The cops were setting up barricades and pushing the crowd back. Nodding Crane and his guitar were nowhere to be seen, and it was likely that, with all the activity, he'd moved off. But he would still be around, watching—Gideon was certain of that.

He slipped out of the room, easing the door shut behind him. The brightly lit hallway was quiet. He had to get up to see Tom O'Brien, and he had to do it in such a way as to make absolutely sure he wasn't followed. The subway trick was a pretty good one, but Nodding Crane might be ready for it a second time. And he was pretty sure Nodding Crane was wise to his disguises by now.

He gave it some thought. The Waldorf had four exits, one on

Park, one on Lex, and two on 51st Street. Nodding Crane could be watching any one of them. He might even have seen Gideon enter the hotel.

Damn. How was he going to get up to Columbia?

He had an idea. The crowd in front of Saint Bart's just might, ironically enough, be a good place in which to lose a pursuer. He would find his opportunity in the crowd.

He took the elevator downstairs, walked through the lobby, and exited through the main door.

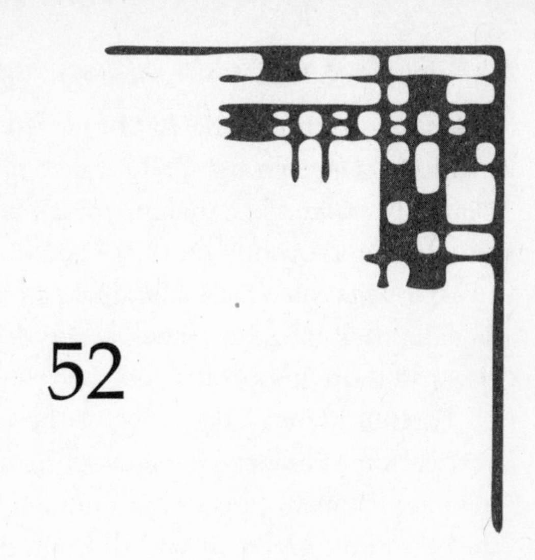

52

Gideon walked briskly toward the crowd, which was now spilling into Park Avenue, blocking traffic. Amazing how in New York a crowd could develop at any time of the day or night. He glanced about again, but Nodding Crane was nowhere in sight—at least, not in any way that he recognized. He wasn't surprised; he knew now he was dealing with an exceptionally clever adversary.

He merged into the fringes of the crowd and began forcing his way through. If he could get to the other side fast enough, his pursuer—if there was one—would be forced to do the same. And that would render him visible.

As he reached the middle of the crowd, there was a collective gasp. EMTs had appeared in the door of the church with a stretcher, wheeling it down the handicapped ramp. A body bag lay on it. Somebody had evidently died—and, given the large police presence, it would appear that somebody had been murdered.

The crowd pressed forward with murmurs of excitement.

Wheeling the body, the EMTs passed through the church park and down a temporary corridor through the crowd that had been cleared by barricades, making for a waiting ambulance. A perfect setup. Gideon pushed up to the barricades, vaulted them, sprinted across the open area, and ducked under the barricades on the far side, back into the crowd. A cop shouted at him, but the officials had more important things on their mind and let it go.

Forcing his way back out of the crowd, ignoring angry expostulations, Gideon emerged on the far side and ran down Park Avenue. He glanced over his shoulder to see if anyone had leapt the barrier or forced his way through the crowd. But no one had. He turned right, darted across the avenue against the light, and there—perfectly placed—was a cab disgorging its customer. He jumped in.

"West Hundred and Twentieth between Broadway and Amsterdam," he said. *"Go!"*

The cabbie pulled out and Gideon watched the crowd as they sped away, but again no one appeared to be following or trying to hail another cab.

He glanced at his watch. Almost midnight. He pulled out his cell phone and dialed Tom O'Brien's number.

"Yo," came the sarcastic voice. "Finally you're calling at a decent hour, my man. Whassup?"

"I found out the secret Wu was carrying. It's some special compound or alloy. And it's embedded in his leg."

"Cool."

"I'm on my way to you with his X-rays. There's a lot of crap in the legs from the car accident. I need your help pinpointing which spot it might be."

"I'll need to bring in Epstein—she's the physicist."

"I expected as much."

"And then?"

"What do you mean?"

"What happens when we identify the piece of metal?"

"I go to the morgue and cut it out."

"Nice. How're you going to manage that?"

"I've already established myself as Wu's 'next of kin,' and they've been waiting for me to claim the body. It'll be a piece of cake."

A long, low wheezy laugh sounded over the cell phone. "Jeez, Gideon, you're a piece of work, you know that?"

"Just be ready. I don't have any time to waste."

He hung up and dialed Orchid's number. He hoped she'd be happy to hear he'd almost worked through the "trouble" he was in and that he would see her, if not tomorrow, then surely the day after.

Orchid's cell was turned off.

He settled back in the seat with the sour thought that she was probably with a customer.

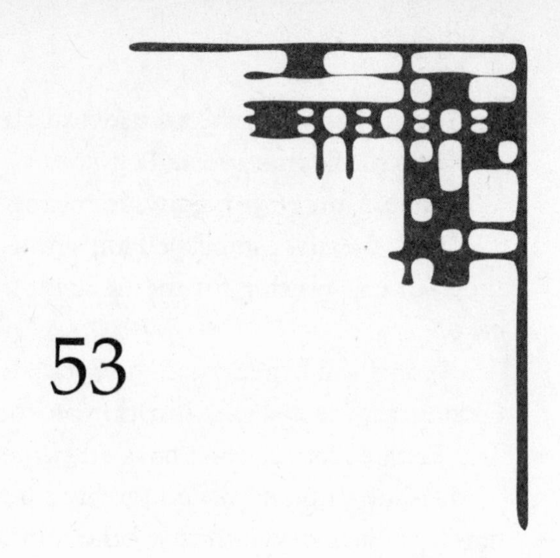

53

Merry Christmas to you, too," said O'Brien, watching Gideon let himself in without knocking, as usual.

"Is this the guy you told me about?" said Epstein, half sitting, half lying on a small sofa, cranky at having been roused from her bed at such a late hour. Her hair was askew and she was in a particularly foul mood because, O'Brien realized, she'd been expecting something quite different when he woke her up in the middle of the night. She was always ready for a good shagging, it had to be said.

"Gideon, meet Epstein. Epstein, Gideon."

"O'Brien called you Sadie," said Gideon, shaking her hand, which she proffered limply.

"Anyone who calls me Sadie," she drawled sleepily, "gets a bang on the ear. This better be good."

"It is good," said O'Brien, hurriedly launching into the lie he'd prepared. "You remember those numbers I gave you? Well, we've got X-rays of this smuggler, see, he got in an accident but he was carrying some contraband substance embedded in his leg to get it through customs—"

Epstein cut him short with a wave of her hand. She turned to Gideon. "*You* tell me what it's all about."

Gideon glanced at her. He looked too flat-out exhausted to lie. "For your own safety, it's better you not know anything."

She waved her hand. "Whatever. Let's just get on with it."

Tom O'Brien rubbed his hands together with excitement. He loved intrigue. "Bring on those X-rays."

Gideon pulled them out from beneath his shirt. O'Brien swept a light table clean of clutter, laid them on it, snapped on the light. After a moment, Epstein roused herself and leaned over the table from her sitting position, glanced at them, then sat back. "Yuck."

"Let's recap," said O'Brien, rubbing his hands together again. "This guy's carrying something stuck in his leg, a piece of metal or something, and he's memorized the ratios of the various elements it's made up of. That's what Epstein here thinks about those numbers you gave us. Right?"

She nodded.

"Right. So now we've got some X-rays, and we've got to figure out which one of these blots or spots is what we're looking for. Want to take a closer look, Epstein?"

"No."

"Why not?" O'Brien was starting to get irritated.

"Because I've got no idea what you're looking for. Is it an alloy? An oxide? Some other compound? Each would react differently to X-rays. It could be anything."

"Well, what do you *think* it is? You're the condensed matter physicist here."

"If you two bullshitters gave me some idea of what's going on, maybe I could take a guess."

O'Brien sighed and looked at Gideon. "Should we tell her?"

Gideon was silent for a moment. "Fair enough. But this is

classified information—and it would endanger your life if others found out you knew of it."

"Spare me the spy-versus-spy crap. I'm not going to say anything—nobody would believe me, anyway. Just tell me."

"For some years," said Gideon, "the Chinese have been working on a top-secret project at one of their nuclear installations. The CIA thinks it's some kind of new weapon, but what I've learned doesn't jibe with that. Instead, it appears to be some kind of technological discovery that would, allegedly, allow China to dominate the rest of the world."

"Sounds unlikely," Epstein said. "But go on."

"A Chinese scientist was bringing this secret into the United States—not to give it to us, but for other reasons."

Epstein had finally sat up and was displaying a certain interest. "And is this secret the thing that's embedded in his leg?"

"Exactly. The secret came in two parts: the thing in his leg and those numbers we gave you. As I guess you've surmised, the two go together: you can't figure out one without the other. The scientist was killed in a car accident. Those are the X-rays from the emergency room."

Epstein scrutinized the X-rays with fresh interest. "The numbers," she said, "indicated to me that we're dealing with a composite material made of a number of complex chemical compounds or alloys." She turned to O'Brien. "Do you have a magnifying glass?"

"I've got a loupe." O'Brien rummaged around in a drawer, finally fishing it out. Examining the lens, he grimaced and wiped it clean on his shirttail before handing it to her.

She put it in her eye and bent over the X-rays once again, examining the white spots one after the other. "He really got creamed. Look at all this shit inside his legs."

"It was a bad accident," said Gideon.

Slowly, she moved from spot to spot on the X-ray. The minutes ticked off. After what seemed forever, she moved to the second film, and then the third. Almost immediately she stopped, examining one small fleck in particular. She looked at it a long time, and then straightened up, letting the loupe drop from her eye. Her whole face was shining, a transformation so complete that O'Brien took an involuntary step backward.

"What is it?" he asked.

"Unbelievable," she breathed. "I think I know what we're dealing with. Everything suddenly makes sense."

"What?" both men asked at the same time.

She smiled broadly. "You really want to know?"

"Come on, Epstein! Don't play games." O'Brien could see her eyes glittering. He'd never seen her so excited.

"This is only a guess," she said, "but it's a *good* guess. It's the only thing I can think of that fits the facts you've told me—and the peculiar thing I see on the X-ray."

"What?" O'Brien asked again, more urgently.

She handed him the loupe. "You see that thing, there—the one that looks like a short, bent piece of wire?"

O'Brien leaned over and looked at it. It was about nine millimeters long, a medium-gauge piece of wire, irregularly bent.

"Look at the tips of the wire."

He looked at the tips. Two black shadows with diffused ends. "Yeah?"

"Those shadows? Those are X-rays leaking out the ends of the wire."

"Which means—?"

"That the wire somehow absorbed the X-rays and channeled, or redirected, them out through its ends."

"And?" O'Brien looked up, took out the loupe.

"That's almost unbelievable. A material that can capture and channel or focus X-rays? There's only one material I know of that could do that."

O'Brien exchanged glances with Gideon.

Epstein smiled mischievously. "I would direct your attention to the fact that it's a *wire*."

"Jesus, Epstein," O'Brien cried. "You're giving us a nervous breakdown! So what if it's a wire?"

"What do wires do?" she asked.

O'Brien took a deep breath and glanced again at Gideon. He looked as impatient as O'Brien felt.

"Wires conduct electricity," Gideon said.

"Exactly."

"So?"

"So this is a special kind of wire. It conducts electricity—but in a different sort of way."

"You've completely lost me," O'Brien said.

"What we're dealing with here," she said, triumphantly, "is a room-temperature superconductor."

A silence.

"Is that all?" O'Brien asked.

"Is that all?" She rounded on him incredulously. "It's only the Holy Grail of energy technology!"

"I was expecting something that would... change the world," O'Brien said lamely.

"This *would* transform the world, you dolt! Look. Ninety-nine percent of all electricity generated in the world is lost to resistance as it flows from source to use. *Ninety-nine percent!* But electricity flows through a superconducting wire without *any* resistance. Without *any* loss of energy. If you replaced all the transmission lines in America with wires made out of this stuff, you'd reduce electrical energy usage by ninety-nine percent."

"Oh my God," mumbled O'Brien as the impact sank in.

"Yeah. You could supply all US energy needs with just one percent of what it takes now. And that one percent could easily be supplied by existing solar, wind, hydro, and nuclear installations. No more coal and oil generating plants. Transportation and manufacturing costs would drop enormously. Electricity would be virtually free. Cars that ran on electricity would cost almost nothing to operate—they'd sweep away the gas-powered vehicle industry. The oil and coal industries would fold. We're essentially talking the end of fossil fuels. No more greenhouse emissions, no more OPEC holding the world by the short hairs."

"In other words," Gideon said, "the country that controls this discovery would blow everyone else out of the water economically."

Epstein laughed harshly. "Worse than that. The country that controls this material would *control* the world's economy. It would rule the world."

"And everyone else would be fucked," O'Brien said.

She looked at him. "That is the technical term for it, yes."

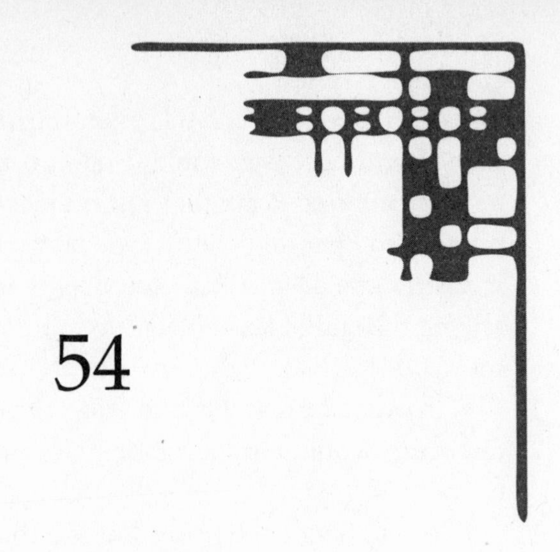

54

LET CONVERSATION CEASE, LET LAUGHTER FLEE. THIS IS THE PLACE WHERE DEATH DELIGHTS IN HELPING THE LIVING.

It was two o'clock in the morning and Gideon Crew was getting tired of reading that same motto above the door into the morgue, over and over again. It irritated him; it managed to be macabre and smug at the same time. As far as he could see, there wasn't anything delightful about this grim and noisome place—or about death, for that matter.

He'd been waiting for forty-five minutes, and his impatience had almost reached its limit. The receptionist seemed to be moving as if underwater, shifting a piece of paper here, another there, taking a call, murmuring in a low voice, her long red fingernails clicking and clacking as she shuffled her paperwork.

This was ridiculous. He stood up, walked over. "Excuse me? I've been waiting almost an hour."

She looked up. The nails ceased clacking. Black roots showed through the bleached-blond tease. She was a hard New Yorker of the old school. "We had a homicide come in. Tied up our personnel."

"Homicide? Wow, that must be a rarity in New York City." Gideon wondered, through the fog of irritation, if that was the one he'd seen at Saint Bart's earlier. "Look, my...*partner* is in some cold drawer in there, and I just want a few minutes alone with him." He put an aggrieved whine into his voice. "Just a few minutes."

"Mr. Crew," she said, unfazed, "you realize, don't you, that the remains of your partner have been sitting here for five days, awaiting your instructions? You could have come in at any time. The file here says we've tried to contact you at least—" She checked her computer. "—half a dozen times."

"I lost my cell phone," he said. "And I've been traveling."

"Okay. But you can't expect to drop in at one in the morning and have everything ready and waiting, now, can you?" She gave him an uncompromising look.

Gideon felt sheepish and defeated. She was right, of course. But the box cutter was burning a hole in his pocket; the X-rays were doing the same in his shopping bag; and he couldn't stop thinking of Nodding Crane and what he might be doing right now, whether he was around, whether he had staked out the morgue. The longer he had to wait, the more time he was giving Nodding Crane.

"How much longer?" Gideon asked.

The red nails went back to clacking and moving paper. "I'll let you know when someone's free."

He sat back down and stared moodily at the motto again. He could hear faint sounds coming from behind the stainless-steel double doors, well dented by the incessant pounding of stretchers. Something was going on in there—the homicide, no doubt. Now he felt sure it was the one at Saint Bart's. That would be big: someone murdered in one of the oldest and most venerable churches in New York, with one of the wealthiest congregations, to boot.

"What's through those doors?" Gideon asked.

The woman looked up again. "Autopsy, coolers, offices."

There was more noise from beyond the double doors, a vague murmur of excitement and activity. He glanced at the clock. Almost two thirty now.

The intercom on the receptionist's desk squawked. She answered it in a hushed voice, then looked over at him. "Someone's coming to help you now."

"*Thank* you."

A man, dressed in none-too-clean whites, bumped out through the doors. He was badly shaven, little dots and pimples of blood on his neck. He raised a clipboard, read from it. "George Crew?"

"That's Gideon. Gideon Crew."

Without another word he turned, and Gideon followed him through the doors. "I'd like to have a moment with him—alone," he said to the man's back.

No reply.

They walked down a long, bright, linoleum corridor that ended in another set of doors leading, it seemed, into the autopsy room itself. Through the door windows he had a glimpse of a row of stainless-steel and porcelain tables, several orange medical-waste bins, stacks of Tupperware containers. He could see a group around one of the tables, including detectives and cops. Must be the murder victim.

"This way, please."

Gideon turned to follow the man through another door, down another corridor, and finally into a long room, lined on either side with metal drawers. A company logo identified them as SO-LOW, INC. equipment. The "coolers."

The aide consulted his clipboard, his lips moving silently, and then, lips still moving, looked down the rows of drawers until he found the right one. He unlocked it with a key on a spiral cord held around his waist and slid the drawer out. A gray plastic body bag appeared, zipped up tight. The bitter-cherry smell of formaldehyde bit into Gideon's nostrils, not even coming close to covering the smell of dead human meat.

"Um. You sure this is Mark Wu?" Gideon found himself unaccountably nervous.

"What it says here." The man compared his clipboard with a number on a tag clipped to the bag.

Gideon could feel the hard plastic handle of the box cutter in his pocket. Despite the chill air of the morgue, the handle was slick from his sweaty hand. This was going to be an ordeal. He swallowed, tried to steel himself for it.

"I want a moment alone with him," Gideon said, ending the request with a quick little fake sob. It didn't come off well, sounding more like a hiccup.

This time, a nod. It seemed the aide was no more eager to stay in here than Gideon was. "Five minutes?"

"Um, how about ten?" Another sob, this one better.

A grunt of approval. "I'll wait in the hall."

"Thank you."

The man went out and the door swung shut behind him. The fluorescent lights buzzed faintly; the forced-air system hissed; the smell in the room was so strong, Gideon felt like it was coating him.

Ten minutes. He'd better get his ass moving. Pulling out the X-rays, he rechecked the location of the wire. It was on the inside of the left thigh, where Wu could have gotten to it readily. For the same reason, it wouldn't be deep. With luck, the mark or scab of its insertion would still show—assuming the skin hadn't deteriorated that badly over the last five days. He took a deep breath, then reached over and grabbed the zipper. It felt like a little cold worm between his thumb and finger. He hesitated, took another breath. And then he drew down the zipper, exposing the face, the naked hairless chest, its Y-incision crudely sewn back together after the autopsy. The body had been sponged off badly, leaving behind streaks and bits of clotted blood, various strings of one thing or another. There were numerous cuts and lacerations that had been sewn up more carefully, obviously during the time Wu was still alive.

The smell was overpowering.

With his left hand he pulled the box cutter from his pocket, wiped it dry, thumbed open the blade. It was time. With a final jerk he pulled the zipper all the way down—and stared. Shocked. Speechless.

"The legs!" he cried. "What the hell? *What happened to the legs?*"

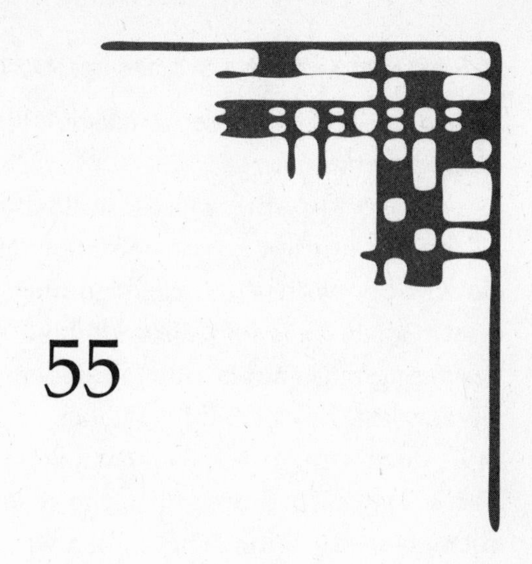

55

A few blocks north of the Port Authority Bus Terminal and hard by the Hudson River stood a massive, nearly windowless ten-story structure of brown limestone, covering an entire city block. It had originally been the mill and headquarters of the New Amsterdam Blanket and Woolen Goods Corporation. Later, when the company went out of business, an enterprising firm purchased the building and retrofitted it into self-storage facilities. When this failed and was seized for nonpayment of taxes, the city converted the storage units, with few modifications, into "temporary" shelters for homeless persons. Known officially as the Abram S. Hewitt Transitional Housing Facility, unofficially as the Ant Farm, it was a vast cliff dwelling for thousands of the disillusioned and disenfranchised.

Nodding Crane's own storage-unit-*cum*-studio was on the seventh floor of the Ant Farm. It suited him perfectly. In his grimy coat and hat, head hanging low, he was almost indistinguishable from the other inmates, the battered guitar case being the only thing that gave him a certain distinction in this shabby and miserable environment.

At two forty-five AM, he walked along the narrow corridor of the seventh floor, past unit after unit, each just a closed roll-down door with a stenciled number, his guitar case knocking gently against his legs. From behind the metal doors, he could hear coughing; snores; other, less identifiable noises. Reaching his own at last, he opened its padlock with a key, raised the curtain wall, ducked in, lowered it again, and barred it shut with a police brace. He reached up, pulled the cord to turn on the bare bulb, then glanced around. The slit of a window peeped into the blackness of an airshaft.

He knew the tiny room had not been burgled: he had replaced the supplied padlock with a much better one he'd purchased, with a five-pin tumbler and a stainless-steel shackle, and it had not been disturbed. And yet with him such an examination was as instinctive as breathing. There was little to take in: a futon, neatly made; a battered leather suitcase; a rice-paper mat; a case of liter-size bottles of springwater; a few rolls of paper towels. In one corner was a portable music player and a stack of well-used Blues CDs; in another, a small neat row of popular paperback books. Nodding Crane favored Hemingway, Twain, and the martial arts literature of the Tang dynasty: *Fengshen Yanyi*; *Outlaws of the Marsh*.

There was only one item in the little space that could be considered decorative: a photograph, badly creased and faded, of a brown and desolate-looking mountain range—the Pamir Plateau in the Xinjiang Autonomous Region. Putting his guitar carefully aside and hanging his coat and hat on a metal hook, Nodding Crane sat on the rice-paper mat and gazed at the photograph with an intense concentration, for five minutes exactly.

He had been born on that plateau, in the shadow of those mountains, far from any village. His father had been a poor herder and smallhold farmer who died when Nodding Crane was less than a year old. His mother had tried to carry on with the farm. One day, when Nodding Crane was six, a man stopped by. He looked very different from any man Nodding Crane had ever seen, and he spoke Mongolian haltingly, with a strange accent. The man said he was from America—Nodding Crane had vaguely heard of that place. He said he was a missionary, traveling from village to village, but to Nodding Crane he looked more like a beggar than a holy man. In exchange for a meal, he would pray with them and teach the word of God.

His mother invited the man in to share their supper. The man accepted. While they ate, he talked of faraway places, of his strange religion. He was a little clumsy with chopsticks and wiped his mouth on his sleeve, and he kept taking quick drinks from a flask. Nodding Crane did not like the way he kept staring at his mother with wet eyes. Now and again he broke into song: a dolorous, mournful kind of music that was new to Nodding Crane. After dinner, as they were drinking tea, the man began pawing at Nodding Crane's mother. When she pulled away, he knocked her to the floor. Nodding Crane threw himself on the man and was shoved violently away. When the man began to rape his mother, again he tried to defend her. But the man was powerful and beat him senseless with a brick. When he woke, he found his mother strangled.

A few days later, Shaolin monks took him away to live in their temple. Other than the kung fu training, however, monastic life ultimately proved not to his liking, and when he had mastered all they could teach he ran away, traveling first to Hohhot and then to Changchun, where he lived on the street and became a master thief. That was before the state police picked him up and, seeing his talent, sent him to the 810 Office for special training.

Every day, without fail, Nodding Crane performed this bitter reflection while gazing upon the faded photograph of his distant home. It was his meditation. He stood up, went through a lengthy series of breathing exercises and limbering drills. Then—in perfect silence—he performed the twenty-nine ritual steps of the "flying guillotine" kata. Breathing a little harder, he sat down again on the rice-paper mat.

Gideon Crew had almost reached his goal. Nodding Crane was now certain he would lead him to what he sought. As Crew closed in on his goal, he would be excited, rushed. It was the correct time for the feint, the unexpected jab at the flank. The girl would serve that purpose well.

Give your enemy no rest, Sun Tzu had written. *Attack where he is unprepared, appear where you are unexpected.*

Since that night on the Pamir Plateau many years ago, Nodding Crane had never smiled. Nevertheless he felt a warm glow inside himself now: a satisfied glow of violence performed, an expectant glow of more violence to follow.

Slipping his hand into a tear in the seam of the futon, he pulled out a small carrying case made of hard, ballistic plastic, hidden in a cavity excavated from the stuffing. He disarmed the explosive device protecting the case, then unlatched it. Inside were six cell phones; Chinese, Swiss, British, and American passports; many thousands of dollars in a variety of currencies; a Glock 19 with a silencer; and a single handkerchief, pale silk with complex embroidery.

Carefully, lovingly, he drew out the handkerchief. It had been his mother's. Draping it over his knees, he reached his other hand into the pocket of his overcoat and pulled out his set of picks: four fingerpicks and a thumbpick. They were coated with blood and matter and had lost their characteristic gleam.

He took one of the bottles of springwater, cracked it open, and dampened a paper towel with it. Then he arranged the picks before him, one by one. Long ago he had given them names, calling them after mythological deities, and now as he cleaned each one in turn he pondered its name and the individual personality of that pick. Pinkie: *Ao Guang*, dragon king of the east sea, who had once unleashed chaos onto the sinful world. Ring: *Fei Lian*, Flying Curtain, god of the wind. Middle: *Zhu Rong*, god of fire. Index: *Ji Yushyu Xuan*, god of the endless outer darkness. And master of them all, the thumbpick, *Lei Gong*, "duke of thunder," tasked with punishing mortals who strayed from the true path.

Nodding Crane used the thumbpick to anchor the windpipe of his victims as the others did their slicing work; this last pick was particularly dirty and required a second application of water to clean satisfactorily.

At last the picks shone brilliantly again, their peace and equilibrium restored through loving attention. They would rest now, in preparation for fresh exercise to come. And Nodding Crane would follow their lead.

He carefully wrapped the picks in his mother's handkerchief and placed them in a small wooden box. Then, stretching out on the futon, he quickly fell asleep amid the fitful night sounds of the Ant Farm.

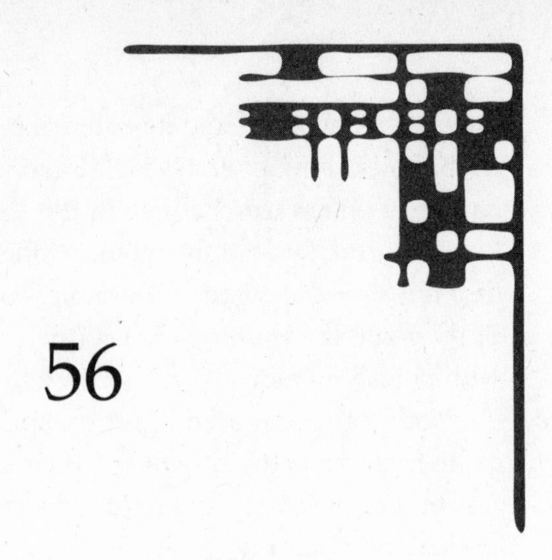

56

Where are the legs?" Gideon rarely lost it, but he lost it now. He was beside himself, absolutely furious.

The aide came running in. "Hey, man, take it easy—"

"No one told me! No one asked my permission!"

"Look, stop shouting—"

"Fuck you! I won't stop shouting!" His voice echoed and re-echoed down the stark corridors. There was the sound of running feet.

"You can't shout in here," said the aide. "I'm going to call security if you don't calm down."

"Go ahead! Call security! Ask them who stole the—my *lover's* legs!" Even in his fury, he had to remain in character.

Another aide burst through the double doors, followed by a security guard. Gideon turned on them. "I want to know where Mark's legs are!"

"Excuse me," said a man, pushing his way in through the stupefied group. He had the air of authority, of calmness in the face of panic. "I'm a med tech. Sir, you've got to calm down." He turned to the aide. "Go get the deceased's medical records."

"I don't need the medical records, I need the legs!"

"The medical records will tell what happened to the legs," the man said. He laid a steadying hand on Gideon's arm. "You understand? We're going to find out what happened to them. I suspect—" He hesitated, then went on. "—they may have been amputated."

The word *amputated* hung in the air like a bad smell.

"But..." Gideon stopped. He realized immediately this was what must have happened. The legs had been crushed, ruined, beyond medical repair. They would have been amputated as part of the effort to save Wu's life. He should've realized it the moment he first saw the X-rays.

The aide returned, followed by the blond receptionist, holding a freshly printed sheet of paper. The med tech took it, scanned it, handed it to Gideon.

It confirmed that the legs had been amputated a few hours after the accident, no doubt shortly after the X-rays were taken. Gideon scanned the sheet again. That had been almost a week ago. Now they were gone forever. He swallowed. The disappointment was so crushing that he was temporarily unable to speak.

"I think we've got everything under control here," said the med tech. The others began to disperse.

Gideon recovered his voice. "What... what happened to them?"

The med tech continued to steady Gideon with a kindly arm. "They would have entered the medical-waste stream. Been disposed of."

"Medical-waste stream? And what happens to that, goes into a landfill or something?"

"No. Medical waste is disposed of by burning."

"Oh." Gideon swallowed. "And... and how long does it take for it to be burned?"

"They don't let it sit around, obviously. Look, I'm really sorry, but the legs are gone. I know it must've been a shock, but... well, your friend is dead." He waved down at the body. "What you see here is just a discarded shell. Your friend has gone somewhere else, and where he is now he won't be missing his legs. At least that's what I believe, if you don't mind my saying so."

"No. No, I don't mind. It's just that..." Gideon fell silent. He couldn't believe it was over. He had failed.

"I'm very sorry," the man said.

Gideon nodded.

"Can I help you with anything else?"

"No," said Gideon wearily. "I'm done here." He zipped up the bag, slid the drawer shut. He wondered what Eli Glinn would have to say.

As they turned away, he noticed, for the first time, a very large and imposing African American woman standing in the doorway, wearing surgical scrubs, her mask pulled down. She cleared her throat. "I couldn't help but overhear," she said. "I'm Dr. Brown, one of the MEs around here."

The med tech greeted her, and there was a silence.

Dr. Brown began to speak, very gently. "What was your name again, sir?"

"Gideon Crew."

"I have some information, Mr. Crew, that might give you some small comfort."

Gideon waited for another exposition of religious views.

"Mr. Correlli here is correct that it is standard procedure in this country for body parts from surgery to enter the medical-waste stream. But in this case, that would not have happened."

"Why not?"

"Here in New York City we have an unusual system, perhaps

even unique. When a limb is removed in surgery, if the patient doesn't have specific directions for its disposal, that limb, after it leaves pathology, is placed in a box and delivered to New York's potter's field for burial."

Gideon stared at her. "Potter's field?"

"That's right. It's the place where the indigent are buried. The name comes from the Bible, the field where Judas was buried."

"New York City has a potter's field?"

"Correct. When a person dies and the body isn't claimed, or if the family can't afford a burial, the city buries the remains in their potter's field. Same thing for, ah, unclaimed limbs. That's where your friend's legs would be buried."

"And just where is this... potter's field?"

"On Hart Island."

"Hart Island?" Gideon repeated. "Where's that?"

"As I understand, it's an uninhabited island in Long Island Sound."

"And the legs were buried there?"

"Undoubtedly."

"Is there a way to... relocate them?"

"Yes," the ME said. "After going through pathology, all the bodies, limbs, and so forth are placed in numbered, labeled boxes and buried in such a way that they can be retrieved for pathological or forensic reasons. So you needn't worry. Your friend's legs received a decent burial."

"I'm so relieved." Gideon made an effort to cover up his racing pulse. This was incredible, unbelievable news.

The med tech gave Gideon a kindly pat on the shoulder. "Well, I hope that gives you some small comfort."

"Yes," Gideon said. "Yes, it does. Although—" Here Gideon turned a pair of soulful, pleading eyes toward the ME. "—I'd like the opportunity to visit them. Mourn them. Surely you understand?"

For all her self-possession, Dr. Brown seemed disconcerted. "Well, I would think the remains here would be sufficient for mourning purposes."

"But this is only *part* of him." Gideon let his voice quaver a little, as if he might break down at any moment.

Brown considered this, and then spoke. "On a few rare occasions, an ME has had to retrieve human remains. It's always a huge ordeal, lots of paperwork, taking weeks. A court order is required. You've got to understand, Hart Island is completely off-limits to all visitors, period. The burial work is done by prisoners from Rikers Island."

"But if they can retrieve a limb, how do they know where it's buried? Do they keep track?"

"I believe the numbered boxes are stacked in their trenches in order. When they fill a trench, they place a cement marker at the end and start a new one."

"How would I find out the number and location? Do you have that information?"

Brown took the printout from the med tech and consulted it, her brow wrinkling. "The files, here, have the number."

Gideon extended a hand. "May I?"

She handed Gideon the printout and, fumbling a pen out of his pocket, he wrote down the indicated number: 695-998 MSH.

"Thank you. Thank you so much."

"Is there anything else I can help you with?" the ME asked. "I'm overdue in the autopsy room, if you don't mind. We're a little short-staffed at the moment."

"No, this is all I need. Thank you, Dr. Brown. I can find my way out."

"I'll have to escort you as far as the waiting room."

Gideon followed her solid and reassuring form into the corridor and past the autopsy room, which was still filled with activity. At least a dozen homicide detectives and police officers remained in the room; others had moved out into the corridor, almost blocking it. Even as they pushed through, Gideon could see that members of the press had now gathered outside the double doors, shouting and pushing.

"Must be a big deal, that homicide," said Gideon.

"It was particularly brutal," said Brown, tersely. "Excuse me," she said, pushing through the doors and trying to get past an especially aggressive camera crew. As soon as the press saw her doctor's scrubs, they surged forward with a chorus of shouted questions.

"Good luck." She retreated behind the doors as the crowd peppered her with questions.

"Suspects," someone shouted. *"Are there any suspects?"*

"Where in the church was the body hidden?"

Gideon tried pushing through the crowd as they continued to yell questions at the closed doors.

". . . any witnesses or leads?"

He elbowed a burly soundman aside and made for the exit.

". . . true that the throat was ripped out again, like the last one in Chinatown?"

Gideon halted abruptly, turned. Who had said that? He looked about the seething crowd and grabbed a reporter, hanging at the fringes of the crowd, tape recorder in hand.

"This murder—what was that I heard about the throat ripped out?"

"You're a witness?" the man asked, suddenly eager, sticking out his hand. "Bronwick of the *Post*."

Gideon stared at the man, his yellow ferret-teeth pushing out his lower lip. He had an incongruous Cockney accent.

"Maybe. Answer my question: *was the throat ripped out?*"

"Yes, it was. An 'orrible murder. Up at Saint Bart's, they found her body hidden beneath some pews. Almost decapitated she was, just like the chap in Chinatown. Now then: your name, sir? And your connection to the case?"

Gideon gripped him harder. "Did you say *her*? The victim was a woman? What was her name?" He felt a sudden indefinable, hideous sensation, like insects eating at his nerves.

"A girl, yes, in her late twenties—"

"Her name!" He shook the man. "I need her name!"

"Take it easy, guv. Her name was Marilyn..." He consulted his notes. "Marilyn Creedy. Now I'd like to hear what *you* know, sir."

Gideon pushed the man away and ran. And kept running.

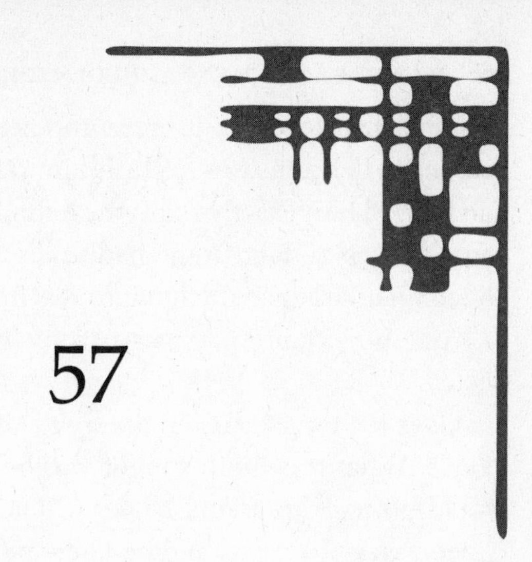

57

Dawn broke over the Central Bronx, a dirty yellow stain that crept into the sky above Mosholu Parkway. Gideon Crew stared out the scarred window of the Lexington Avenue Express, seeing nothing, hearing nothing, feeling nothing. He had been on the train for hours, going from its southern terminus at Utica Avenue in Queens to its northern terminus at Woodlawn in the Bronx and back, traveling beyond emotion into the gray territory of mere existence.

It had been years since he'd last cried, but he had found himself crying—with fury, with sorrow, with his own stupidity and selfishness.

But now he was beyond that. He had come through the other side and—slowly but surely—his mind had begun to function again.

He understood certain facts. Nodding Crane had murdered Orchid, then hidden her body so it would not be found immediately, giving him time for a clean getaway. He'd killed her for two reasons. First, there was the possibility she knew something and therefore had to die. But more importantly, Nodding Crane had murdered her as a way to flush him out. In this Nodding Crane had figured him exactly right: the killing would flush him out. Because now, Nodding Crane had to die. There was no other way. Gideon had dragged Orchid into this horror; he owed it to her.

And no doubt that was exactly what Nodding Crane expected.

Over the long hours on the train, Gideon had worked out the details. What they both sought was buried on Hart Island. Both would go to Hart Island to get it. Only one would return. But Gideon was not crazy, and he knew he needed to stack the deck in his favor. And this was where Mindy Jackson came in. She had proven herself; she would be his secret weapon.

He took out his cell phone and dialed her number.

To his great surprise, she actually answered. "Gideon?"

"Where are you?" he asked.

"Downtown. No luck yet on the woman. How about you? Found anything?"

"Everything."

A silence. Then a cool, "Tell me."

"First, I want your promise. We handle this my way."

A pause. "Okay. Fine. Your way."

"Wu wasn't smuggling the plans to a weapon—he was carrying a piece of wire embedded in his leg. This wire is of a revolutionary new material. The numbers are the formula, the recipe for it. Put the two together and you've got it all."

"What kind of new material?"

"A room-temperature superconductor." He explained the significance of it and was impressed at how quickly she understood the ramifications—and the dangers.

"The legs," he went on, "were amputated after the accident. They're buried in a mass grave on Hart Island—New York's potter's field. I've got a few things to take care of, and then tonight

I'm going to Hart Island to dig up those legs."

"How are you going to find them?"

"Body parts are tagged and buried in numbered boxes, in sequence. I've got the number. We might have to do a little... sorting. I've got it all worked out. There's a place where you can rent outboard skiffs on City Island, past the bridge on the right. Murphy's Bait and Tackle. Meet me there at ten PM."

"How far offshore is this island?"

"About a mile northeast of City Island, in the middle of Long Island Sound opposite Sands Point. Bring a sniper rifle."

"This is stupendous. How did you—?"

He interrupted her. "Nodding Crane will be there."

"Oh. Jesus."

"Remember the agreement. We run this my way. No CIA army descending on the island and scaring Nodding Crane off. Just you and me."

He snapped the phone shut. Then he collected a piece of trash lying on the floor of the subway car and began to write on it.

Nodding Crane sat across the street from Saint Bart's, strumming his battered guitar. The police had come and gone, the barriers had been taken down, the cleaning crews had fixed the church. Everything had returned to normal. It was a beautiful morning, just a few fluffy clouds scudding across the field of blue. Now all he had to do was wait.

I wants my lover, come and drive my fever away

He saw Crew come up from 49th Street, going against the crowds of commuters, and turn the corner onto Park. Right on time. Nodding Crane took no little satisfaction in seeing that the man looked like death warmed over: haggard, disheveled, his eyes two pools of shadow. He crossed Park Avenue and walked directly up to where Nodding Crane had laid his open guitar case collecting tips. Nodding Crane kept playing, his voice soft. Crew stood over him, on the far side of the case, as he continued to strum and sing. The morning crowds streamed past; he knew Crew wouldn't do anything rash.

Doctor says she'll do me more good in a day

Crew dropped a crumpled piece of paper into the case, where it joined a smattering of bills and coins. He did not move. Nodding Crane finished the song and finally raised his head, and their gazes locked. For almost a minute they stared at each other, and Nodding Crane could feel the implacable hatred in Crew's eyes, which warmed him as well as a fire. Then the man abruptly broke eye contact, turned, and walked back the way he had come, toward Lexington Avenue.

When he was gone, Nodding Crane picked up the wadded paper and opened it, to reveal a scribbled note.

We will meet on Hart Island at midnight tonight. This is where Wu's amputated legs are buried. The exact location of the legs will be written on a slip of paper in my pocket. To get it, or the wire, you will have to kill me. Or I will kill you. Either way, one of us will die on Hart Island.

That is the way you planned it and that is the way it must be.

G. C.

Nodding Crane slowly balled up the paper in his fist as a look of deep satisfaction settled on his face.

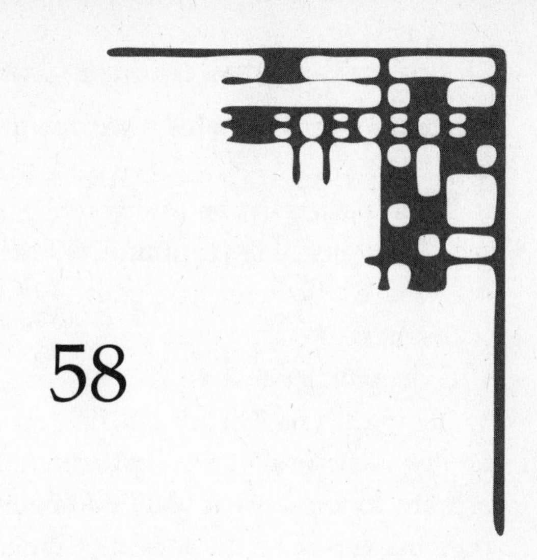

58

Wherever there were drug dealers there were guns. And the center of drug dealing in New York City, at least at the street level, could be found in the ironically named Mount Eden neighborhood of the South Central Bronx. Gideon sat on the D train rocketing northward from Manhattan, a wad of cash burning a hole in his pocket. This was not the most intelligent way to acquire a firearm, but he was in a hurry and it had the advantage of efficiency.

As the D train pulled out of the 161st Street Yankee Stadium stop, a man who had just gotten on angled over to sit down beside him. It took Gideon a few moments to realize it was Garza, tricked out as an artist in black beret and peacoat.

"What, exactly, are you doing?" Garza asked. His tone had lost much of its initial affability.

"My job."

"You're out of control. You've got to cool it, slow down, and come in to discuss the next step with us."

"This has nothing to do with you anymore," said Gideon, not

even bothering to keep his voice down. "It's my gig now. It's personal."

"That's just what I mean: you're getting too close to this. I've never seen anything so unprofessional. Eli was wrong to trust you. You're in danger of compromising the mission with your recklessness."

Gideon didn't answer.

"Going up to Throckmorton Academy, pretending to be a parent—what kind of a crazy damn move is that? From now on, we want to know what you're doing and where you're going. If you think you can beat Nodding Crane, you're a fool."

Gideon sensed Garza knew nothing of Hart Island. It gave him a certain satisfaction to be ahead of Glinn and his smooth-operating sidekick for once. "I'll handle it myself."

"No, you won't. You'll need backup. Don't be a damn idiot."

Gideon scoffed.

"Where are you meeting him?"

"None of your business."

"You go rogue on us, Crew, and we'll shut you down, I swear to God we will."

Gideon hesitated. This was a complication he didn't need. "Corona Park. Queens."

A beat. "Corona Park?"

"You know. Where the old World's Fair was. We're meeting at the Unisphere."

A silence. "When?"

"Midnight tonight."

"Why there?"

"Just a place to meet."

Garza shook his head. "A place to meet."

"Nodding Crane murdered my friend. Now it's either him or me. Like I said, this has nothing to do with you. When I get done with this business, I'll take care of yours. Don't try to stop me."

Garza was silent for a while, then he nodded. As the train pulled into the next stop, he rose and left, a disgusted look on his face.

Crew got off at 170th and the Grand Concourse. He walked eastward toward the park, passing a row of abandoned buildings. Reaching the park—a sad affair with dirt instead of grass and trash everywhere—he slowed his walk to a loiter, glancing around, just another suburban guy looking for drugs. Almost immediately he was accosted by a dealer, who passed him murmuring *smoke, smoke*.

He stopped, turned. "Yeah."

The dealer swerved and came back. He was a short, stooped kid with a comb stuck in his hair, pants hanging south of his ass. "What you need?" he asked. "Got smoke, blow, horse..."

"A pistol."

Silence.

"I'll pay big money," Gideon went on. "But I need something heavy-caliber, best quality."

The dealer didn't seem to hear at first. Then he muttered something that sounded like "wait here" and rambled off.

Gideon waited. Twenty minutes later the kid was back. "Follow me," he said.

Gideon followed him out of the park and into an abandoned building on Morris Avenue, an old brownstone with bashed-out windows and a dark, urine-fragrant interior. As dangerous as this was, it was better than asking Garza for another gun on bended knee. He didn't want to be any more beholden to the man than necessary. He knew he should be nervous, even scared, and yet he felt nothing. Nothing but rage.

The dealer went to the dismal stairwell, whistled up it. A whistle returned.

"Second floor," he said.

Gideon mounted the stairs, stepping over a scattering of used condoms, crack vials, and vomit. He reached the second floor. On the landing, two men waited, both dressed in expensive gym clothes with puffy white sneakers. They were Hispanic and well groomed. The taller one, obviously the leader, had a carefully clipped five-day stubble, plenty of rings and gold chains, and smelled strongly of Armani Attitude. The shorter one sported several cold sores.

"Let's see the money," said the tall one, flashing a self-assured grin.

"When I see the gun."

The leader shoved his hands in his pockets and leaned back, looking down at Gideon. He was tall and used his height to intimidate. His eyes, however, were stupid. "We got the gun."

"Let's see it. I don't have all day."

The short one with the cold sores reached into his jacket, pulled a gun halfway out. "Nine-millimeter Beretta."

"What's the price?"

"How much you got?"

Gideon felt his rage, already close to the boiling point, rise. "Listen, sucker. Name your price. Then I'm going to check out the piece. If it's good, I pay. If not, I walk."

Tall Man nodded, puckering his lips. "Show it to him."

Cold Sores removed the gun, handed it to Gideon. Gideon took it, looked it over, snapped the rack a few times. "The magazine?"

Out came the magazine. Gideon took it, frowned. "Rounds?"

"Look, man, we can't have no shooting here."

Gideon thought about that. They were right, of course. He would have to field-test it later. He took the magazine, slapped it in, hefted the gun, pulled the trigger. It appeared to be in excellent condition. "I'll take it."

"Two thousand."

That was a lot for a seven-hundred-dollar pistol. He looked at it closely. The serial number had been filed off, which probably meant nothing. Acid would bring it up again. He felt in his jacket pocket, where he had put his cash, done up in rubber-banded blocks of five hundred. He selected four, brought them out. He put the gun in his pocket and gave the packets to Tall Man.

He turned to go and heard a voice. "Just a minute."

He turned back to find both men with pistols aimed at him. "Give me the rest of your money," Tall Man said.

Gideon stared. "You robbing me? A customer?"

"You got it, boy."

Gideon had another two thousand in his pocket. He made a quick decision, pulled out the money, tossed it on the ground. "That's all of it."

"Pistol, too."

"Now, that's going too far."

"Then kiss your white ass good-bye." They both grinned, aiming their guns.

"My *white* ass?" Gideon asked, incredulously. He reached in, removed the pistol, aimed it at the men.

"You're forgetting it ain't loaded, you punk-ass bitch."

"If I give you the gun back, promise to let me go," Gideon whined, holding it out.

"Sure thing." Two shit-eating smiles followed this assurance.

Gideon's hand shook so much they began to laugh. Tall Man reached over to get the pistol and, just at that moment of distraction, Gideon lashed out at Cold Sores, smacking the gun out of his hand while at the same time jamming his foot against the side of his knee and twisting himself out of the way of Tall Man's line of fire. As Cold Sores went down with a howl, Tall Man fired, and Gideon felt the bullet tug the shoulder of his jacket. With a furious scream he fell on Tall Man. He went down like a rotten tree and Gideon landed on top of him, wresting the gun from him in one violent motion and jamming it in his eye, pressing it hard against the eyeball.

"No, no, *oww!*" the man screamed in pain, trying to twist his head, but the barrel was pressed so hard against his eye, he was forced to stop moving. "Stop, please, oh shit, don't! My eye!"

Cold Sores was up again, having retrieved his gun. He aimed it at Gideon.

"Drop it or I fire!" Gideon screamed like a lunatic. "And then I'll kill you!"

"Drop it!" shrieked Tall Man. "Do what he says!"

Cold Sores backed out of the room, limping, not dropping it. Gideon could see he was going to run. Hell, let him go. Cold Sores broke and ran. Gideon could hear his footsteps clattering down the stairs, and then a crash as he fell in panic. More lopsided running and then silence.

"Looks like it's just us," said Gideon. He could feel warm blood running down his arm. The bullet had evidently grazed his shoulder. A tuft of material stood out. The actual wound was dead, without feeling.

Tall Man blubbered incoherently. Keeping the barrel pressed hard into his eye socket, rendering him immobile, Gideon felt inside the man's jacket, removed the money. There was another, much bigger brick of cash in there—at least five thousand. He took that as well, along with a knife. Then, as an afterthought, he ripped the gold jewelry from the man's neck, yanked off his diamond rings, and took his wallet. Feeling around in the pockets, he collected car keys, house keys, loose change, and half a dozen nine-millimeter rounds that had evidently been removed from the Beretta's magazine.

He pulled the pistol out of the man's eye. Tall Man lay on the floor, blubbering like a baby. "Listen to me, Fernando," said Gideon, looking at the man's driver's license. "I've got your keys. I know your address. You try any shit and I'm coming to your house and I'm going to kill your family, your dog, your cat, and your goldfish."

The man let out a wail, covering his face with his hands, rocking on the floor.

As Gideon left the building, he made sure Cold Sores wasn't lurking around, then began heading for the Grand Concourse subway station. Along the way he dropped the keys, bling, and wallet down a storm drain, keeping the money and guns.

Now he had two pistols. He ducked into a doorway and examined his haul. The second was a Taurus Millennium Pro in .32 ACP caliber with a full magazine. He loaded the 9mm rounds into the magazine of the Beretta, slapped it into place, and tucked both firearms into the rear of his belt. Then he took off his jacket and examined his shoulder. It wasn't quite as superficial as he'd thought, but it was still only a flesh wound. He put his jacket back on and glanced at his watch. Ten AM.

On the way to the subway, he stopped at a drugstore, where he purchased a butterfly bandage and applied it to his shoulder in the restroom. Next, on impulse, he dropped into a variety store, where he bought a notebook, some paper, pens, and a thick manila envelope. Finally, he repaired to a nearby coffee shop to write his last will and testament.

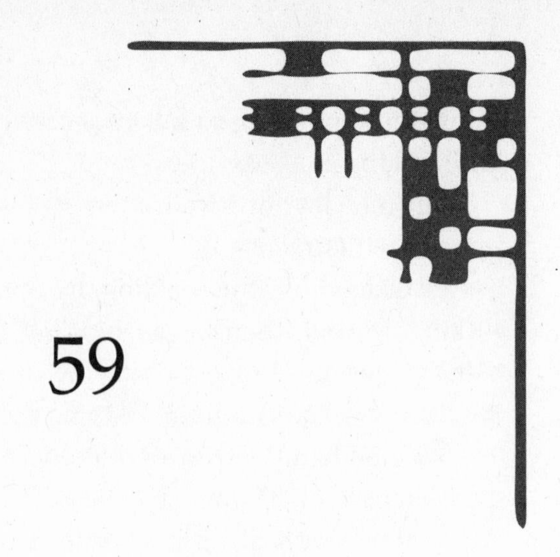

59

The coffee shop was a cheerful place, a sturdy holdout against the grime and hopelessness outside. A battleax waitress, at least sixty but spry as a teenager, with bobbing hair and pancake makeup, came bustling over.

"What can I get you, hon?"

She was perfect. For the first time in a long while, Gideon felt an emotion that wasn't dark. He tried to smile. "Coffee, eggs over easy, bacon, white toast."

"You got it."

She went off and he opened the notebook, thinking. There were two things he loved in the world: his fishing cabin in the Jemez Mountains and his Winslow Homer drawing. The drawing would have to go back to the Merton Art Museum in Kittery, Maine, from which he'd appropriated it years before. But the cabin... He wanted to make sure it went to someone who would love it as he did, who would not let it go to wrack and ruin. Or sell it to a developer. Even if he defeated Nodding Crane—and that was a big if—he knew now that he would still be staring death in the face.

The waitress slid his breakfast in front of him. "Writing the great American novel?" she asked.

He gave her his best smile and she went off, pleased. As Gideon contemplated his own mortality—which he'd been doing a lot of lately—he realized he had nobody. He'd spent most of his adult life pushing people away. He had no family, no true friends, and no colleagues he was friendly with from work. The closest thing he had to a pal was Tom O'Brien—but their relationship had always been transactional, and the guy lacked integrity. His only real friend had been a prostitute—and he'd gotten her killed.

"Top off that coffee?" the waitress asked.

"Thanks."

And then a name came to him. Someone he could trust. Charlie Dajkovic. He hadn't been in touch with the man since the death of General Tucker. The fellow had spent some time in the hospital, but last Gideon had heard he was recovering nicely. They weren't friends—not exactly. But he was an honest man, a good man.

Gideon began to write, trying to control the faint shake in his hand. It was not easy. Dajkovic would get the cabin and everything in it, with the exception of the Winslow Homer. He appointed Dajkovic his executor and charged him with returning the drawing (anonymously) to the Merton Art Museum. In life he had escaped all suspicion; he sure as hell didn't want to be fingered after death.

It didn't take long to complete the document. As he read it over, his mind drifted to his secret fishing hole on Chihuahueños Creek. It had taken him years of lashing the waters of the creeks that drained the northern Jemez Mountains to find that one place—the most beautiful on earth. After a moment's consideration, he turned over the letter and drew a map for Dajkovic, showing him how to get there, along with suggestions for what sort of flies to use at what times of the year. That would be his biggest bequest.

He hoped to hell Dajkovic liked to fish.

When he was done, he called the waitress over.

"More coffee?" she asked.

"A favor."

She immediately brightened.

"This letter," said Gideon, "is my last will and testament. I need two witnesses."

"Aw, hon, you can't be over thirty, what you thinking about that for?" The waitress filled up his mug anyway. "I got thirty years on you and I still ain't thinking about that."

"I've got a terminal illness." As soon as he said it, he wondered why in the world he was confiding in this stranger.

The waitress laid a gentle hand on his shoulder. "I'm sorry. Nothing's engraved in stone. Pray to the Lord and he'll deliver you a miracle." She turned. "Gloria? Get over here, this gentleman needs our help."

The shop's other waitress came over, a chubby girl of perhaps twenty, her face shining with happiness at being of service. Gideon felt moved by these two random strangers with big hearts.

"I'm going to sign this," Gideon said, "and then I'd like the two of you to witness it and sign your names here, then print them below."

He signed, they signed, and then, as Gideon rose, the old waitress gave him a spontaneous hug. "Pray to the Lord," she said. "There's nothing He can't do."

"Thank you so much. You've both been really kind."

They moved away. Gideon wrote a cover note to Eli Glinn, asking him to make sure Dajkovic received the letter; he then sealed it and addressed it to Glinn at Effective Engineering Solutions on Little West 12th Street. He removed the brick of cash he had stolen from the drug dealer, slipped it under his overturned plate, and quickly left the coffee shop.

On his way to the subway he dropped the letter into a mailbox, feeling a huge wave of self-pity at his lonely, screwed-up existence, which was soon to end one way or another. Maybe the waitress was right: he should try prayer. Nothing else had worked in his sorry life.

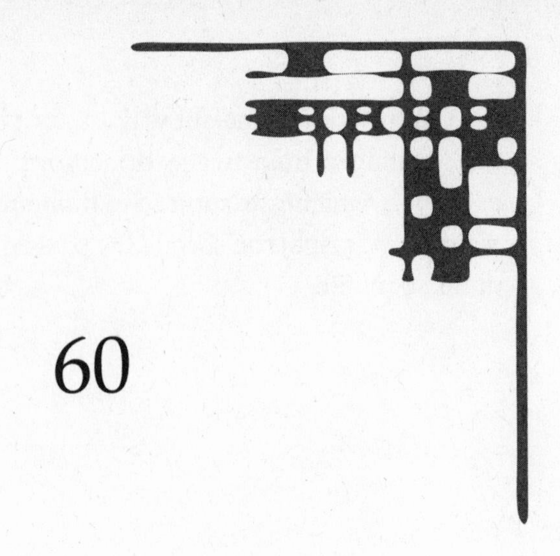

60

Gideon took the subway to the end of the line and caught the bus for City Island. By noon he found himself standing outside Murphy's Bait and Tackle on City Island Avenue, seabirds wheeling overhead. It was hard to believe this sleepy fishing village was part of New York City.

He pushed in to find himself in a narrow shop with glass cases on three sides and a gigantic man in a T-shirt at the far end.

"What can I do for you?" the man boomed out in a genial Bronx accent.

"Are you Murphy?"

"The one and only."

"I want to rent a boat."

The rental was quickly arranged, and the man escorted him through the shop to the docks behind. There a dozen open fiberglass skiffs were tied up, each with a six-horsepower outboard, anchor, and gas can.

"Got a storm coming in," Murphy said as he readied the boat for departure. "Better be back by four."

"No problem," Gideon replied as he stowed the fishing rod and bait box he'd purchased as a cover.

A few minutes later he set off, soon passing under the City Island Bridge and entering the open water of Long Island Sound. Hart Island lay about half a mile to the northeast, a long, low mass, indistinct in the haze, dominated by a large smokestack that rose easily a hundred fifty feet into the air. The wind had picked up and the small boat ploughed through the chop, water slapping against the hull. Dark clouds scudded across the sky and gulls rode the air currents, crying loudly.

Gideon consulted the marine chart he had purchased earlier and identified the various landmarks by sight: the Execution Rocks, the Blauzes, Davids Island, High Island, Rat Island. He tried to get a feel for the waypoints of the journey: the next time he came this way it would be dark.

The boat, with its puny engine, moved through the water at a walking pace. Gradually, the island solidified out of the haze.

Almost a mile long, it was covered with a scattering of trees interspersed among clusters of ruined brick buildings. When he was about a hundred yards offshore, he turned the tiller and began making a circuit of the island, examining it with binoculars. The large smokestack rose from a ruined complex on the eastern shore that appeared to have once been a power plant. Reefs and outcroppings were everywhere. Giant, billboard-like signs placed every few hundred yards along the shore warned visitors away:

New York City Correction Department
RESTRICTED AREA
NO Trespassing NO Docking NO Anchoring
VIOLATORS WILL BE PROSECUTED

As he reached the northern end of the island, he saw some activity and threw the engine into idle, scrutinizing the scene with his binoculars. Through a screen of oak trees, he could make out a group of convicts in orange jumpsuits laboring in the middle of a field. A backhoe idled nearby. They were unloading pine coffins from the rear of a truck and laying them out beside a freshly dug trench. A group of well-armed corrections officers stood around, watching the activity, gesturing and shouting directions.

Allowing the boat to drift, Gideon continued his observations, occasionally making notes.

Satisfied at last, he fired up the engine again and continued down the western shore of the island. About midway, a long sandy beach came into view, covered with various jetsam, including trash, driftwood, and old boat hulls. The beach ended at a concrete seawall, behind which rose the old power plant complex and the great smokestack. Painted on the brick façade of the main building was a message at least a hundred feet long and thirty feet high:

PRISON
KEEP OFF

He decided to land his boat beside the seawall, next to a salt marsh and beyond a treacherous-looking series of reefs.

Gideon brought the boat in, angling it through the reefs, moving slowly. A moment later he cut the engine, hopped out of the boat into the chop, and, wading, pulled it up on the beach.

He checked his watch: one o'clock.

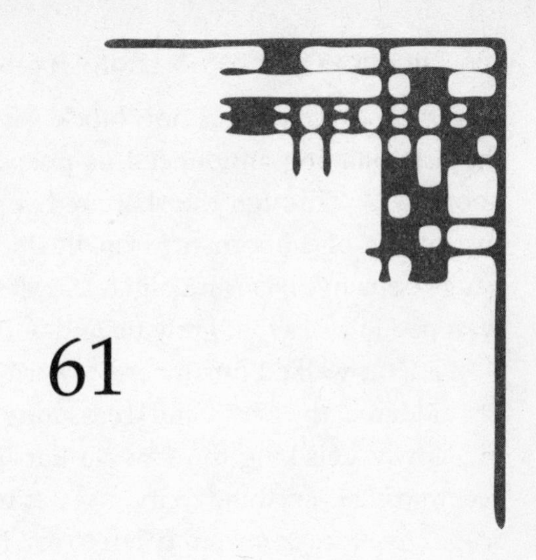

61

Gideon walked up the beach, climbed over the low seawall, slipped into the cover of some trees, then paused to take stock. To his left lay an open field, beyond which stood the ruined power plant. On the right, set back from the shore, stood a neighborhood of modest bungalow houses, complete with streets, streetlights, driveways, and sidewalks. It looked like an ordinary, old-fashioned suburban neighborhood—except that everything lay in ruins, the houses crumbling, window frames broken and black, roofs caved, vines smothering the streetlights and choking the houses, the street itself a web of cracks through which sprouted weeds and stunted trees.

He waited, senses on high alert. In the distance, toward the end of the island, he could hear the faint rumble of the backhoe digging a mass grave. But this middle section of the island seemed deserted. He took from his pocket a Google Earth image he'd printed and spent a few minutes reconnoitering. Then he began moving cautiously along an overgrown street and across the broad field toward the ruined complex of buildings he'd noticed earlier. A carved limestone block set into the brick façade of the first building announced its purpose and the date: DYNAMO ROOM 1912. Through the shattered windows, he could see massive pieces of equipment: iron flywheels, rotting belts, broken gauges, steam pipes, and a giant, riveted iron furnace and boiler wrapped in vines that grew up and out of a roof open to the sky.

Gideon walked northward toward the burial grounds, keeping hidden in the brush and trees along the side of the road, moving slowly, checking the Google Earth image and taking notes, committing everything to memory. It was a postapocalyptic landscape, an entire community left to rot. Nothing had been boarded up or secured; it was as if, perhaps half a century ago, everyone had just walked away and never returned. There were parked cars sunken in weeds, a general store with moldering goods still on the shelves, houses with sagging door frames, inside of which he glimpsed decaying furniture, peeling wallpaper, an umbrella sitting in a stand by the door, an old hat on a table. He passed a ruined chapel, gaping and open to the elements; a butcher shop with rusting knives still hanging on a pegboard—and lying in the central square, an ancient, headless Barbie doll. At the edge of town he came to an old baseball field, bleachers draped in vines and the field a small forest.

Gideon skirted the ruins of a tubercularium and rows of dormitories for a juvenile workhouse, with the motto GOD AND WORK carved into the decaying lintels. There were several pits in the ground, old basements and foundations, some exposed, others covered with rotting flooring. Everything was on the verge of collapse. Consulting the Google Earth image again, he located, beyond the dormitories, a huge, circular open area covered with concrete with several decaying metal trapdoors—the subterranean remains of the old Nike missile base.

As he neared the northern end, buildings gave way to large overgrown fields, dotted with cement markers, numbered and whitewashed. The sounds of the backhoe grew louder. He crept into some dense woods bordering the fields and continued moving north. Within a quarter mile, the woods petered out into yet another overgrown field, and here Gideon dropped and crept forward on his belly, peering through binoculars at the scene of activity, about a hundred yards away, in a freshly dug area of the field.

Rows of coffins had been lined up on the edge of a long trench, and the convicts were busily handing them down to others within the trench, who were stacking them in rows, six deep and four across. He watched as they laid down two courses of coffins, forty-eight in all. Each coffin had a number scrawled on the side and lid in a black felt-tip marker.

A trusty with a clipboard kept track of the work, backed up by several guards armed with pistols and shotguns. When the coffins had all been lowered, the men climbed out, laid pieces of corrugated tin over the top layers, and stood by as the backhoe fired up, ejected a dirty cloud of diesel smoke into the air, and pushed a wall of earth onto the tin, covering up the fresh coffins with dirt to ground level. The wind was blowing hard, tossing the treetops, and Gideon could smell, from time to time, the scent of fresh earth, mingled with an acrid odor of formalin and decay. At the far end of a field stood an open-sided brick shed, in which sat a second backhoe.

Gideon circled the field, seeking a better vantage point, trying to locate where the small boxes containing limbs might be buried. He found what he was looking for in a second, parallel trench, farther down the field. It had been partially covered with dirt, keeping the most recent boxes exposed and ready for more stacking; his binoculars revealed that these boxes were small—the right size for body parts—and also marked by scrawled numbers. A piece of corrugated tin had been laid over the exposed rows of mini coffins, weighed down with dirt at one end, evidently protecting them from the elements until the stacks could be finished.

He would need a better inspection. The trench was deep, and from his vantage point he couldn't see to its bottom. He'd have to get close enough to peer in—very close. And there was no way to do that without being caught.

He stood up, shoved his hands in his pockets, and casually strolled into the open field.

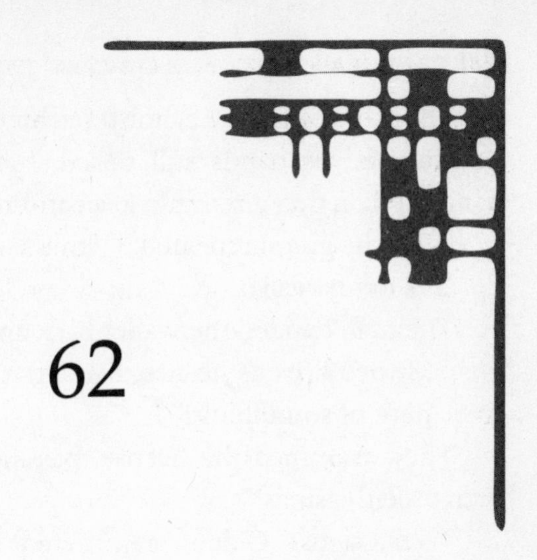

62

They spotted him immediately.

"Hey! Hey, you!" Two of the guards drew their guns and came running toward him across the field. Gideon kept walking, moving quickly to the trench before they could stop him. By the time they reached him he was standing at the edge, looking down.

"Hands in sight! Keep your hands in sight!"

Gideon looked up, as if surprised. "What's going on?"

"Don't move! Hands in sight!" A guard dropped to one knee and covered him with his service pistol while the other approached cautiously, shotgun at the ready. "Hands behind your head."

Gideon obeyed.

One was white, the other black, and both were pumped up and fit. They wore blue shirts with NYC CORRECTION SSD printed on the backs in white letters. One of the guards patted him down and emptied his pockets, removing the Google Earth map, the notebook, his wallet, and a piece of parchment Gideon had prepared earlier.

"He's clean."

The other officer rose, holstered his Glock. "Let's see some ID."

Gideon, his hands still raised, spoke in a voice high with panic. "I didn't do anything, I swear! I'm just a tourist!"

"ID," the guard repeated. "Now."

"It's in my wallet."

The man handed the wallet back and Gideon fumbled out his New Mexico driver's license, handed it over. "Am I not supposed to be here or something?"

They examined the license, passing it back and forth. "You didn't see the signs?"

"What signs?" Gideon stammered. "I'm just a tourist from—"

"Cut the crap." The black officer, who was evidently in charge, frowned. "The signs on the shore. Everywhere. You telling me you didn't see them?"

The officer's radio burst into life, a voice demanding to know what was going on with the intruders. The guard unholstered his walkie-talkie. "Just some guy from New Mexico. We got it under control."

He holstered the radio and stared at Gideon with narrowed eyes. "Care to tell us how you got here and just what the hell you're doing?"

"Well, I was... just out in the boat fishing, decided to explore the island."

"Oh, yeah? You blind or something?"

"No, I really didn't notice any sign... I was worried about the chop, I wasn't paying attention, I swear..." He made his whine singularly unconvincing.

The white guard held up the parchment. "What's this?"

Gideon turned red. He said nothing. The two officers exchanged amused glances.

"Looks like a treasure map," said the white officer, dangling it in front of Gideon.

"I... I...," he stammered and fell silent.

"Cut the bullshit. You were hunting for buried treasure." The officer grinned.

After a moment's hesitation, Gideon hung his head. "Yeah."

"Tell us about it."

"I was here on vacation from New Mexico. This guy down on, um, Canal Street sold me the map. I'm an amateur treasure hunter, you see."

"Canal Street?" The two officers exchanged another glance, one rolling his eyes. The black officer struggled to keep a straight face as he examined the map. "According to this map, you're even on the wrong island."

"I am?"

"The X on this map here is on Davids Island. That's the island over there." He jerked his chin.

"This isn't Davids Island?"

"This is Hart Island."

"I'm not used to the ocean, I must've gotten mixed up."

More laughter, but it was more amused than derisive. "Man, you are one lost dude."

"I guess so."

"So who's the pirate who's supposed to have buried this treasure? Captain Kidd?" More chuckling, then the black guard's face became serious again. "Now look, Mr. Crew, you knew you were trespassing. You saw the signs. Don't bullshit us."

Gideon hung his head. "Yeah, I saw them. I'm sorry."

His radio burst into life again, another voice inquiring about the intruder. He responded. "Captain, the guy was hunting for buried treasure. Got a map and everything. Bought it down on Canal Street." He paused and Gideon could hear the crackle of laughter on the other end. "What should I do?"

He listened for a while and then said, "Right. Over." He grinned. "Today's your lucky day. We aren't going to arrest you for criminal trespass. Where's your boat?"

"On the beach down by that big smokestack."

"I'm going to escort you back to your boat, understand? For your information, this island is totally off-limits to the public."

"What, ah, do you do here?"

"Landscaping," said the guard, to more laughter. "Now let's go."

Gideon followed him across the field and down to the road. "Really, what are you doing back in that field, burying all those boxes? They look like coffins."

The officer hesitated. "They are coffins."

"What is this, some kind of burial ground?"

"Yeah. It's the public burial ground for New York City. Potter's field."

"Potter's field?"

"When someone dies in the city, and they don't have any family or money to pay for a burial, they get buried here. We got Rikers Island inmates doing the work, so we can't have visitors landing in boats, you understand?"

"Yeah? How many bodies are there?"

"Over a million," said the guard, with no little touch of pride.

"Holy cow."

"Largest burial ground in the world. Been going since the Civil War."

"That's incredible. And you give them all a Christian burial?"

"Interfaith. We got all kinds of religious figures coming here blessing the dead—priests, ministers, rabbis, imams. Every religion gets its turn."

They walked past the old power plant. The ruined Dynamo Room loomed above the tangled vegetation, adjacent to a broad field.

"Where's your boat?" asked the guard, peering across the field toward shore.

"It's down on the beach over there beyond that seawall."

Instead of walking straight across the field, the guard walked north along the road, making a loop.

"Why are we going this way?"

"That field's off-limits," said the guard.

"What for?"

"Don't know. There's a lot of places on the island that are dangerous."

"Oh really? How do you know where they are?"

"We got a map, shows the no-go areas."

"On you?"

The guard pulled it out. "We're required to carry it."

Gideon took the map and scrutinized it for as long as he dared before the guard folded it up and put it away. After making a broad detour around the field, they arrived at the beach and walked over to the boat.

"Um," said Gideon, "can I have my stuff back?"

"Guess it isn't a problem," the guard said, pulling the map, notebook, and other papers from his pocket, handing them over.

"Is Davids Island open to the public?" Gideon asked.

The guard laughed. "It's a park but, ah, if I were you I wouldn't go digging holes over there." He hesitated. "Mind if I give you a little advice?"

"Please."

"That map you bought? It's fake."

"*Fake*? How do you know?"

"Canal Street? You see all those Rolexes, Vuitton bags, Chanel perfume, and Prada shit they're selling down there? That's counterfeit central. Although I got to admit a fake treasure map is taking it to another level." He issued a not unkindly laugh, laying a friendly hand on Gideon's shoulder. "I'd hate to see you waste your time and get into trouble. Trust me, that's no treasure map."

Gideon put on his most crestfallen face. "I'm sorry to hear that."

"I'm sorry we've got so many scumbags in New York City ripping off the tourists." The guard glanced up at the sky, which had grown almost black with roiling clouds. The wind was gusting, and the bay was covered with whitecaps. "If I were you, I'd forget Davids Island and get my ass off the Sound. We get some serious riptides and shit around here when there's a storm, and there's a big one coming in."

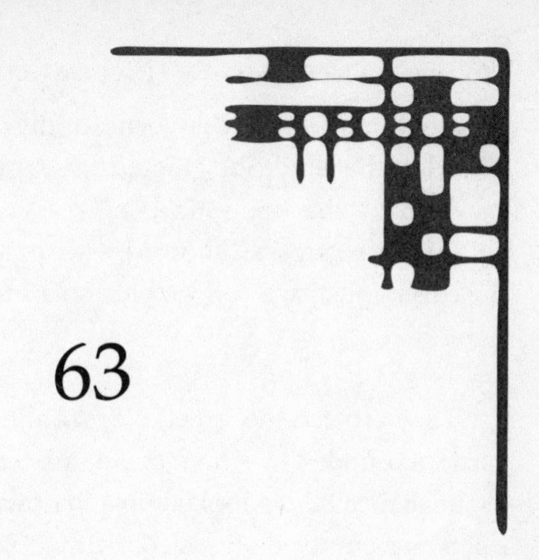

63

At ten o'clock that evening, Gideon, dressed as a college-aged backpacker, loitered on City Island Avenue, observing Murphy's at a distance. In his backpack he carried the two illegal firearms, boxes of extra rounds, a knife, a headlamp, a flashlight, a folding shovel, folding pick, rope, Mace, bolt cutters, two pairs of night-vision goggles, maps, and the notebook. The gusts of wind coming off the Sound set Murphy's old wooden sign swinging back and forth on creaky hinges. The air smelled of salt water and seaweed. The southern horizon was alive with distant flashes of lightning, blooming inside towering thunderheads, approaching fast.

He could see no sign of Mindy. It was a few minutes past their rendezvous time, but he assumed she had arrived early and was probably hanging back somewhere, waiting for him to show.

And as if on cue, he heard her low voice from the darkness of the small park behind him. "Hello, Gideon."

She stepped out, looking trim and athletic, carrying her own backpack, a woolen beret worn jauntily on her head, her short hair stirred by the wind. She greeted him with an affectionate kiss.

"What a charming surprise."

"Don't be an ass," she said with an arch smile. "That's part of the cover—just two college kids on a summer trip—like you said, right?"

"Right."

They crossed the street. Next to the boat rental was a marine yard surrounded by a high chain-link fence, which blocked access to the piers. Gideon looked up and down the street, satisfied himself it was empty, then scaled the fence and dropped down on the other side. Mindy landed softly beside him. They scooted across the yard, scaled another fence, and ended up on the pier leading to the floating docks.

"The outboards are kept in here," Gideon said, indicating a locked shed. He attacked the lock with the pair of bolt cutters, and in a moment they had hauled out a six-horsepower Evinrude with a full gas can, fuel lines, and a pair of oars. They jumped into a boat; Gideon bolted the engine to the stern and connected the fuel lines while Mindy untied and pushed off.

Gideon started rowing. In a few minutes they'd moved out of the protective slip and into the teeth of the rising wind.

Mindy shielded herself from the blowing spume. "You got a plan yet?"

"Of course. Nodding Crane is already on the island. It's essential for him to think I'm coming alone. So get down and stay down while I explain."

"Sure thing, boss." She curled up below the gunwale.

Beyond the docks, Gideon lowered the engine, fired it up, and headed down the protected channel toward the dark outline of the City Island Bridge. Beyond lay the open water of Long Island Sound. Even in the darkness, he could make out the whitecaps. It was going to be a rough crossing.

"Let's hear it," said Mindy from the bottom of the boat.

"I'm going to drop you off at the southern end of the island. I'll land midway on the island and make my own way to where the burial ground is. On foot, you'll follow the map I've sketched for you. Stick to the route I've drawn—the island's a veritable death trap. By the time I reach the burial ground you'll already be in position in the trees, covering me. I go in, find the limb, cut out the wire, we split."

"What about Nodding Crane?"

"He's going to show, no way to predict when. The field around the burial site is wide open—there's no way for him to cross it without you seeing him. When he appears, shoot him dead. Don't mess around."

"Not very sporting."

"The hell with sporting. Got a problem with shooting a man in the back?"

"Not a man like him."

He nodded at her backpack. "You got a good sniper rifle in there like I said?"

"It's not a sniper rifle but it'll do, a Kel-Tec SUB-2000 nine-millimeter semi-automatic. Kevlar vest, too. What about you?"

"Two handguns, body armor—I'm ready." Gideon pulled out a map enclosed in a ziplock bag. "You won't have any problem finding your way, but as I said, the whole island's an accident waiting to happen, so follow the route I marked on this map—no shortcuts. There's a timetable here, too. Stick to it."

"What if he's already waiting for you in the burial trench? You step out in the field and he guns you down?"

"I'm going to cross the field in a backhoe. Two are parked in a shed beside the field, and they're built like tanks."

The boat puttered along, nearing the City Island Bridge and

the opening to the Sound. The wind howled, whipping the relatively calm channel water into whitecaps.

"Tell me about the island."

"The place started out as a POW camp for Civil War soldiers. A lot of them died and were buried there. New York City bought it for a public burial ground in 1869. But that only took up about half the island. The rest was used for other things at various times: a women's lunatic asylum, boys' workhouse, tubercularium, yellow fever quarantine, prison. During the 1950s the military used it as a base for a battery of Nike Ajax missiles, stored in silos. Now it's uninhabited and just used for burials. But nothing's been removed or boarded up, it was all just left to disintegrate."

"And the burials?"

"They lay them in two parallel trenches, one for amputated limbs, the other for the, ah, complete corpses. The limbs are buried at a rate of, I figured, about seven to ten a day. Each box has two numbers: the medical file number and a sequential number added by the inmates as they bury them, so they can be located again if necessary. The body part is also tagged inside the box with the identifying information. It's been about a week since Wu's legs were amputated, so I figure we need to go about sixty, maybe seventy boxes back. The boxes are stacked in the trench four across and eight high, thirty-two in a row, so I figure it'll be in the second or third row deep."

"And then?"

Gideon patted his backpack. "I've got the X-rays with me. We'll have to do a little dirty work to get the wire out."

"When do you expect Nodding Crane to appear?"

"He's going to be unpredictable. That's why you'll remain hidden throughout and only appear when he shows himself or the fight is joined. Maximize your element of surprise. You understand?"

"Perfectly. And you've got a plan B?"

"And C and D. The very unpredictability of the island works to our advantage." Gideon smiled grimly. "Nodding Crane behaves like a chess player. We're going to give him a craps game instead."

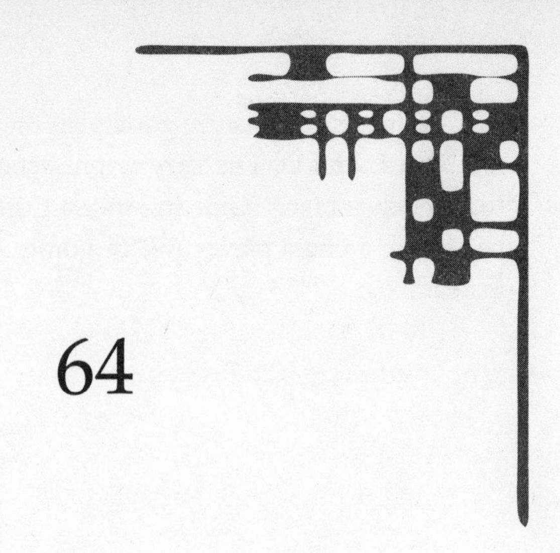

64

As the boat entered the broad Sound, the storm hit them with a blast, raising a vicious chop that battered the hull and slopped into the boat. The lightning front was closing in, the distant booms rolling across the water like artillery.

Gideon steered the boat into the wind. "Start bailing."

Keeping low, Mindy picked up an old Clorox-bottle bailer in the bow and began scooping up water and tossing it out. As she did so, a large wave slammed the gunwale and shoved the boat sideways, drenching them.

"My God," Mindy said as she bailed. "This boat is like a bathtub."

The lights of City Island wavered on the horizon, but ahead all was blackness. Gideon pulled a compass from his pocket, took a bearing, corrected course. While the chop was bad, the swell was worse, surprisingly strong for protected waters. The engine sputtered and hiccupped; if it quit, they'd be finished.

But it did not quit, and the boat pushed on through the gale, Mindy bailing almost continuously. It was not a long crossing—half a mile—but the boat was heading into the wind, moving at a crawl, and a strong current was sweeping the boat northward, past the island and out to sea.

If they missed the island, their next stop would be Execution Rocks.

Gideon took another reading and compensated for the current by heading farther south. Another wave slammed into their flank, throwing them to one side and almost swamping the small vessel. The weak engine coughed as Gideon struggled to bring the boat back into the wind.

"We're going to drown before we even get there," said Mindy.

But even as she spoke, the faintest outline of the island began to materialize in the dark, fringed by a dim line of breaking water. Gideon angled in toward the southern end. They were on the lee side of the island, and as they approached the dangerous swell subsided.

"Be ready to jump," he said in a low voice, pulling a pair of night-vision goggles from his backpack and handing them to her. "Use these. No lights. Follow the timetable I laid out. Be in position at the appointed time. And for God's sake, wait for your opportunity."

"I've been at this a lot longer than you," she said as she fitted the goggles to her head.

The surf loomed up, the chop boiling up onto a strand of large cobbles.

"Now," he murmured.

She jumped into the surf and Gideon slammed the shift into reverse, the propeller shaft almost bucking out of the water with the effort. In a moment she had vanished into the darkness. Gideon turned back into the gale, making a loop far from shore where the boat couldn't be seen or heard from the island. He struggled to bail and steer at the same time, the rain coming down hard, the waves smacking into the boat.

Navigating by dead reckoning, he turned northward, paralleling the eastern shore of the island, and then angled in when he felt he was nearing the island's midpoint. As he neared the shore, he could just see the outline of the giant smokestack against the dim sky—his landmark. He picked his spot along the shore, the location of the small salt marsh, and ran the boat full speed up on the beach. He hopped out and pulled the boat into the dense marsh grass.

Crouching in the cover, he prepared himself for the trek up-island, fitting on his night-vision goggles, checking his sidearms, and giving his own map a final look. To decrease predictability, he had chosen an unlikely and inefficient route, one that went through the most dangerous and unstable areas of the ruins.

Nodding Crane would have arrived early, scouted around, and taken up position—the spider waiting for the fly. And Gideon believed, although he had not mentioned it to Mindy, that he knew exactly where that position was. There was one place on the island he himself would have chosen: a superior vantage point in all respects. If he understood Nodding Crane—and he believed he did—the man would not be able to resist occupying the strongest offensive position.

The rain was now lashing down in sheets, the booms of thunder following hard on the flashes of lightning. Another stochastic element in his favor. He checked his watch: ten thirty. He had another twenty minutes before Mindy was in position.

He crept through the sodden grass and into some heavy bayberry bushes, the goggles displaying his surroundings in a sickly green light, the rain blurring and obscuring the outline of the trees and bushes. It was like moving, half blind, through a ghostscape.

He worked his way through the heaviest brush until he came up behind a ruined building: the boys' workhouse complex. He slipped through a broken window frame into the moldy interior, water pouring down from holes in the upper floors and the roof. The boys' primary task had been to make shoes, and old pairs lay everywhere, thousands of them, curled up like autumn leaves, scattered about among broken glass, tools, iron shoe stands, and rotting wooden forms. He moved along the edge of the wall, gun at the ready, taking care not to step on glass.

In a moment he was in the long, echoing central corridor of the workhouse. The muffled sounds of the storm penetrated the walls.

Down the corridor, he came to the rear door, which was hanging on a single hinge. From the door, he made a quick dash through weeds into the workhouse dormitory. Passing rows of rusting iron bedsteads and graffiti-scratched walls, he paused to let an especially intense barrage of lightning and thunder pass. Each flash illuminated the interior in spectral light, the rusting bed frames casting flickering shadows onto the walls, a single graffito scratched in large letters above one bed: I WANT TO DIE.

He hurried on. At the far end of the building, he passed several small rooms heaped with broken filing cabinets, burst cardboard boxes, bundled records and file folders, soaked and rotting. A large rat, sitting on top of a heap of paper, watched him pass by.

He was soon back out in the storm, the rain harder than ever. He had gotten past the ruins and into the oldest section of burial grounds, now returned to forest. As he made his way through the densest stand of trees, he came across old grave markers sunken in leaves and vegetation, row upon row of them, delineating ancient mass graves. Here and there, bones peeped from the leaf litter and tangles of ground cover.

Keeping to the woods, he approached at last the back of the shed in which the two backhoes were stored. On his previous foray to the island, he'd noted they were almost brand-new Caterpillar 450E backhoe loaders. Earlier in the day, he'd studied how to hotwire and operate this particular model, but he'd hoped to find the keys in the ignition.

He waited, well hidden, listening and looking. Each flash of lightning allowed him a hard-edged glimpse of his surroundings, and there was no sign of Nodding Crane. Which meant nothing. He knew in his gut the man was close.

Now Gideon slowly circled the shed, keeping hidden in the surrounding cover, moving with infinite caution, examining the edge of the roof as he did so. It was made of timbers laid onto the old brick walls, and covered with corrugated tin sheets screwed to sleepers laid across the rafters. Everything was rotting, but not yet to the point of collapse.

It confirmed a key fact: the roof would support the weight of a man.

He approached the back corner of the shed, where the bricks had tumbled, leaving a hole. One quick darting move and he was through the hole, inside the shed. The two loaders glowed bright green in his goggles.

Keeping flat against the rear wall, he crept up to the closest Cat, reached up and eased open the cab door, which had been left ajar. With one quick movement he swung himself up and ducked inside, silently closing the door.

The key was in the ignition.

He checked his watch: Mindy had now been in place for at least ten minutes.

Time for round one. He set the controls, placed his hand on the key, and turned the ignition.

The machine sprang to life with a deep-throated rumble. Very good. It had an easy joystick control that almost any idiot could use, or so the literature claimed. He quickly lowered the stabilizers and raised the loader bucket into a vertical position, above the cab, as protection against what was about to happen.

Then he activated the backhoe joystick controller and took a deep breath.

With a smooth movement of his fingers, he raised the massive quarter-ton bucket fast and hard, like a man pumping his fist over his head. It struck the inside of the roof with a crash, bucking it upward with a groan of rotten timbers and a shower of water. For a moment it seemed as if the whole roof would come off; then the bucket punched up through the rotting timbers and rusted tin and the roof slammed back into position with a crash, showering him with debris.

With another violent motion he jammed the bucket sideways, the boom tearing a long hole in the roof. Then he retracted it, closing the bucket on a roof beam and pulling down hard. Everything came crashing down: rotten timbers, boards and twisted pieces of corrugated tin, along with a gush of water. A couple of wild pistol shots clanged off the loader bucket, indicating he had guessed exactly right: Nodding Crane had taken position on the roof of the shed, where he not only commanded a bird's-eye view of the burial field and the trenches, but also could fire on anyone coming for the backhoes.

Without hesitation Gideon folded the boom into traveling position, raised the stabilizers, jammed the shift into forward, and drove the machine out onto the field, swinging the loader rearward to form a shield against small-arms fire. Almost immediately, a fusillade of shots ricocheted off the back of the loader, ringing it like a bell, but protecting Gideon inside the cab.

The bastard must've gotten the surprise of his life when the backhoe punched through the roof. A damn shame he hadn't broken his neck. But it proved Nodding Crane wasn't the invulnerable, all-seeing killing machine Garza had described.

Gideon drove the backhoe across the muddy field at full throttle. The fire from behind grew more accurate, bullets snapping through the roof of the cab, spraying him with plastic and insulation. He crouched low, driving blind as more bullets blew holes in the windshield. The loader couldn't provide one hundred percent cover.

He ducked up briefly to check his position, saw he was almost there. Two more bullets went past, one practically parting his hair. Another moment—and then Gideon halted the machine, flung open the door, and jumped out, taking a flying leap from the edge of the trench and falling over the lip. He tumbled down and landed in a wallow of mud and water at its bottom, then scrabbled back up to the rim, sweeping the field with his night vision. The shooting had finally stopped.

He had possession of the trench; Mindy had not yet revealed herself; his adversary had miscalculated and—with any luck—might even be hurt.

A feeling of something like euphoria swept over Gideon. So far, he was kicking Nodding Crane's ass.

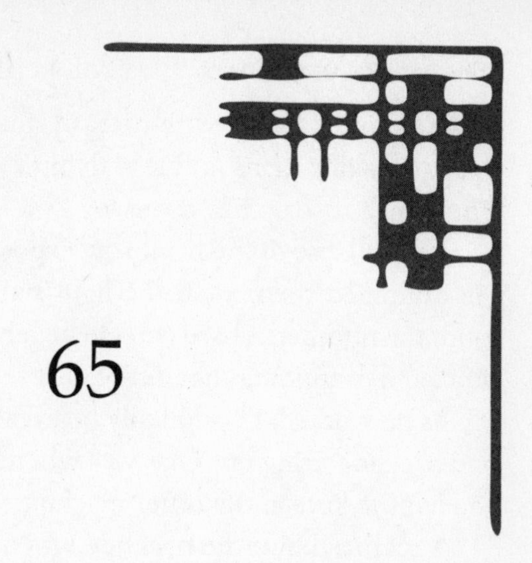

65

He turned his attention to the exposed wall of boxes. Down here in the trench, he was safe from fire—and Mindy, he hoped, was in position in the trees, ready to take down Nodding Crane if he tried to advance over the field. Nevertheless, there was no time to waste. He pulled off the goggles, stuffed them in his backpack, donned a headlamp, and switched it on. A wall of pine boxes greeted his eye, ten boxes high and five wide. Once fresh, the little coffins were already streaked with mud. Lightning split the sky and the rain continued to pour down. The stench was almost unbearable: it reminded Gideon of a combination of rotting meat, dirty socks, and liquid cheese.

He examined the numbers of the top row: 695-1078 MSH, 695-1077 SLHD, 695-1076 BGH. He thought: *1076 minus 998 equals 78.* So Wu's legs would be seventy-eight boxes back. A quick glance told him the number he was looking for wasn't in the exposed row of boxes. He yanked a pickax out of his pack and swung it at a box at the bottom of the row, piercing it with the point. Prying the box from the wall, he caused the entire row to come toppling down with a crash, many of the boxes breaking open, decaying arms and legs flying everywhere, tags fluttering. The stench rose up like a wet fog.

The collapse of the front row exposed the next wall of coffins. He examined them with the light but most were covered with mud, the numbers obscured. He began wiping them off, one at a time, and examining the numbers.

As he worked, he suddenly heard an ominous sound: the second backhoe firing up. That was when he realized his mistake: he had left the keys in the other machine.

A roar told him the backhoe was out of the garage and coming down the field at full speed.

He put on the goggles and scrambled back up to the lip of the trench. The second backhoe was approaching, mud flying, wheels churning, bucket raised like the stinger of a scorpion. Nodding Crane had positioned the loader in front as a shield, using it just as Gideon had.

He had perhaps a minute before it arrived.

There was only one thing to do. Grasping a root at the edge of the trench, Gideon pulled himself out and scrambled into his own backhoe, still idling nearby. A volley of bullets tore through the cab as he lowered the loader, protecting him but blinding him at the same time.

He adjusted the loader so he could just see the top edge and then headed directly for the other backhoe, throttle shoved in forward, twenty tons of steel lumbering down the muddy field. He jammed his backpack on the accelerator, keeping it floored, so he could stand up and lean out with his Beretta, squeezing off a few shots. But his shots weren't accurate and the rounds clanged harmlessly off the shovel of the approaching Cat. They were closing fast on a collision course, each moving twenty miles an hour. Nodding Crane returned fire with his more accurate weapon, sending Gideon scrambling back for cover.

They were now fifteen, maybe twenty seconds from collision. Gideon braced himself for the impact, frantically buckling himself in, his mind calculating a hundred possible responses to follow.

The collision came with a tremendous jolt, a deafening clash of steel against steel, throwing him forward, buckling his cab and shattering the already-holed windshield. He instantly threw the machine into reverse, backing and turning frantically as he fingered the joystick controller. Nodding Crane was doing the same with his backhoe, the wheels churning as he maneuvered into position.

Gideon extended the boom and, wielding the backhoe bucket like a club, pivoted it sideways at the other machine's cab; the quarter-ton piece of steel swung around with a whine of hydraulics. But Nodding Crane anticipated the move, raising his own backhoe to block it, and the two booms struck each other with a violent, deafening crash.

The blow knocked Gideon's backhoe sideways, spraying hydraulic fluid, and almost immediately a fusillade of shots tore through his cab. One struck the Kevlar vest that covered his chest, kicking him back, knocking his wind out.

Gasping for breath, struggling with the controls, Gideon saw the blow had by chance rotated his machine back into a striking position; he raised the bucket and brought it down hard on the other machine's cab; but again the assassin saw it coming and lurched forward, striking Gideon's machine with his own loader and tipping him back. Gideon's bucket glanced off the corner of the cab with a spray of sparks and he frantically worked the controls, throwing out the stabilizers, trying to keep his backhoe from tipping over.

Nodding Crane raised his loader higher, readying it for a violent blow. As he did so he exposed himself. Gideon dropped the controls and, firing with both hands, emptied the Beretta into

Nodding Crane's cab, the rounds blowing out the glass windows and turning the interior into a flurry of broken plastic. But Nodding Crane had dropped to the floor, behind the protection of the lowered loader, an angle Gideon couldn't target.

Seizing the controls again, Gideon jammed the accelerator forward, ramming the other machine while raising the backhoe to smash the other's cab. Nodding Crane blocked the move by raising his loader, and they clashed with a shower of sparks. At the same time, he extended his bucket high on its boom, then brought it down on Gideon's cab with a terrific crunch, half-collapsing the cab in a burst of crackling metal and plastic, sprung wires and insulation.

Gideon threw himself to the floor, avoiding being pulverized at the very last moment. But his backhoe was now useless, the seat crushed, the controls gone. And he could hear Nodding Crane lifting his bucket for another massive blow. He had to get out.

He threw himself against the buckled door. It wouldn't open.

Nodding Crane's bucket came down with another shuddering crash, almost trapping Gideon in the wreckage, but when it lifted a tooth caught on part of the frame and tore open a hole in the tangled cab. Seeing his chance, Gideon dove through the hole, simultaneously pulling out the Taurus and firing up at Nodding Crane. He landed in the muck, rolled. Nodding Crane raised the bucket again, obviously intending to crush him like a bug. Gideon struggled to his feet and ran for the cover of the trench, fifty yards away.

A flurry of shots kicked up the mud around him and one slammed into his Kevlar-covered back, knocking him down. He wallowed in the muck, unable to rise, pain ripping through him. He could see more shots walking along the ground, sweeping toward him, and then he heard the roar of the backhoe as it bore down on him, full speed. He would never make the cover of the trench...

…And then he heard a distant *pop pop pop* from the trees and the clang of bullets on metal. Mindy. The shots drew Nodding Crane's fire away, forcing him to halt the backhoe and turn it to cover himself. Gideon seized the opportunity to struggle to his feet and stagger toward the trench, diving in.

He turned and started firing from the lip of the trench, raking Nodding Crane. Magazine empty, he reloaded with trembling hands and slammed it back into place, maintaining a steady fire.

The crossfire hemmed in Nodding Crane. He swung the loader around, trying to use it as a shield, but was unable to effectively block fire from two directions as the rounds tore through his cab. He backed the machine with a furious diesel roar, retreating across the field, moving out of handgun range. Gideon stopped firing and used the moment to once again reload the Beretta. As he did so he saw Mindy's dark figure come running across the field, firing while she ran. He emptied his magazine, covering her, and a moment later she leapt into the trench as more gunfire erupted from the far end of the field.

"You're supposed to stay in the trees!" he yelled over the storm.

"You need covering fire while you find the leg."

Gideon realized she was right.

She positioned herself at the lip, firing steadily, the return fire kicking dirt off the edge of the trench or slamming into the walls of the trench behind them. Gideon quickly turned back to the wall of boxes, shining his light on each one in turn, frantically wiping off the mud. And there it was, halfway down: 695-998 MSH.

"Got it!" he exclaimed.

"Hurry!" Mindy kept firing from the edge of the trench.

He frantically pulled the covering boxes down, throwing them to one side, until he had exposed the right one. Grasping it by the edges, he hauled it free. Both his chest and back throbbed violently at the effort: the shots had broken a rib, maybe two. Raising the pickax, he swung it full-force into the lid, splitting it. With another fierce motion he ripped the pieces away and then probed inside with his light.

"Son of a *bitch*!" he cried. "It's an arm!"

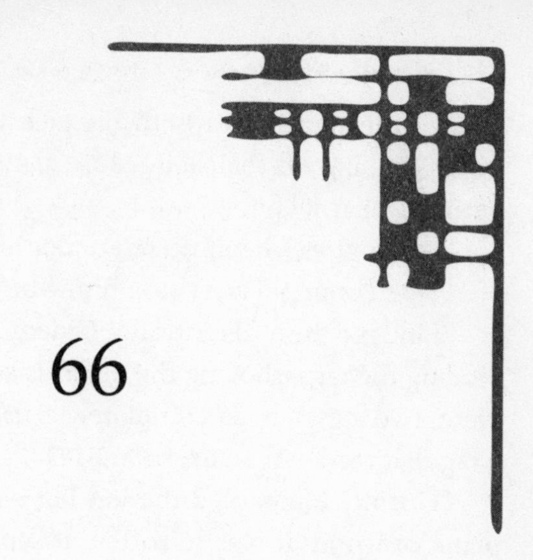

66

Gideon grabbed the tab tied to one finger, read off the patient data. MUKULSKI, ANNA, ST. LUKE'S DOWNTOWN 659346C-41. "These bastards mixed up the body parts!" he cried.

"Keep looking!" Mindy yelled back.

She ducked as more bullets raked the lip of the trench, showering them both with mud.

Gideon surveyed the jumble of boxes, chose one at random, swung his pick at it and ripped off the lid, spilling out what appeared to be a diseased lung. Kicking it aside, he attacked another box, then another, ripping open the lids, ignoring all but the legs and reading the tags on those. Many of the boxes had broken open in the confusion and he sorted through the piles of body parts and less recognizable organs, checking the tags and putting the rejects aside. They had been days, even weeks, in the warm summer ground, and most of them were rotting, soft, bloated.

"He's returning with the backhoe," Mindy said.

"Keep him at bay!" Gideon pushed the discarded offal to one

side of the trench and with his pick toppled another series of boxes, ripping off their lids. More arms and legs tumbled out, a veritable charnel pit.

"Sorry, guys," he muttered under his breath.

"He's coming! I can't stop him—he's got his loader up!"

"Find me time!" Frantically, Gideon sorted through the limbs, reading the tags, shoving the discards aside. And then, there they were: two legs, almost completely crushed, in the same box with a tag that read: WU, MARK. SINAI 659347A-44.

"Got it!" He hauled the left leg out of the box, laid it on a plank of wood. It was so rotten, it separated at the knee. But it was the thigh he needed. He yanked the box cutter out of his backpack and pulled out the X-rays. Laying his flashlight down, he held up the X-rays, compared them with the leg, identifying the place to cut.

"For God's sake, hurry! He's dropped his loader and he's pushing a wall of dirt toward us! I can't fire through it!"

Gideon drew a deep breath. Then he sank the cutter into the flesh and drew a long line; retracted the scalpel; drew another parallel line a centimeter away; then another. The wire was just beneath the surface, but the leg was so mangled, so rotten, and so full of debris from the accident that it was hard to identify the correct place to cut.

"Hurry!" Mindy screamed.

He could hear the roar of the backhoe approaching, the deep vibration in the ground.

Another long cut, this one at a ninety-degree angle.

"Oh my God!" She was firing almost continuously. The roar was almost on top of them.

The scalpel was deflected by something. Gideon reached in with his fingers, grasped it, drew it out: a heavy piece of wire, bent in a U shape, about a centimeter long.

"Got it!" He shoved it in his pocket.

But the roar was now on top of them. An enormous pile of dirt, mingled with bones, crashed down on them like a tidal wave, knocking Gideon to the ground and burying Mindy. Her scream was abruptly cut off as blackness rose to meet him...

Gideon swam back into consciousness buried almost up to his chest, pinned in a mess of muck and water. He could feel his broken ribs grinding against each other. He shook the dirt away from his head, sucked in air, tried to pull himself out.

A heavy boot came down slowly on his neck, pressing him into the mud. "Not so fast, my friend," came the cool, accentless voice. "Give me the wire."

Gideon lay there, breathing hard. "Help her. She's buried—"

The boot jammed his neck and the voice said, "Don't worry about her. Worry about yourself."

"She's suffocating!"

Nodding Crane dangled the tag from Wu's leg in front of him. "I know you have the wire. Give it to me." A hand searched his shirt pocket, pushing away dirt. Feeling through the dirt, the hand located the Beretta and the Taurus. The box cutter came next.

"Let me up, for God's sake!"

The boot came off his neck and Nodding Crane stepped back, night-vision goggles swinging around his neck. "Get yourself out. Slowly."

Gideon tried to crawl out from under the dirt. "The shovel," he gasped.

Nodding Crane picked up Gideon's shovel and tossed it over.

Frantically, Gideon shoveled away the dirt, wincing with pain. Finally he got enough of the weight from his lower body to allow himself the use of his legs. He shook off the dirt and dragged himself free. Rising to his feet, he took a shuddering breath, then immediately attacked the slide of dirt that had buried Mindy.

"The wire," Nodding Crane said, jamming his gun—a TEC-9—against Gideon's head.

"For God's sake, we've got to dig her out!"

"You're a fool." Nodding Crane struck him a lashing blow across the head with the butt of his gun, wrenched the shovel from his hand, and screwed the barrel of the TEC-9 into his ear. "The wire."

"Fuck you."

"I will take it from your dead body, then." He gave the warm muzzle of the pistol another screw into Gideon's ear and whispered, "Good-bye."

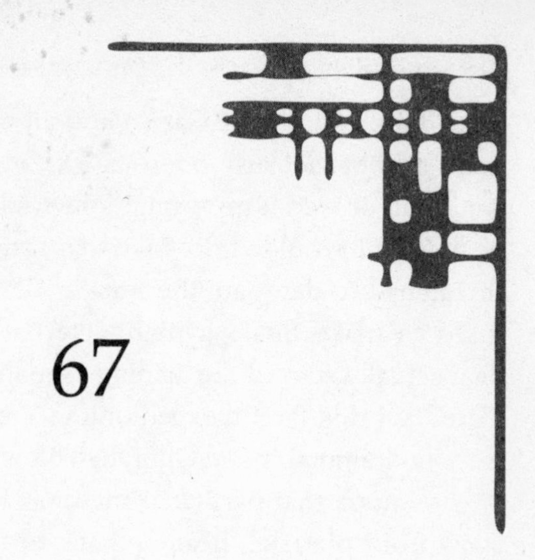

67

Manuel Garza, dressed in a frayed Department of Sanitation uniform he'd appropriated from the vast wardrobes of EES, walked along the bicycle path that circled the north end of Meadow Lake. In the distance, he could hear the hum of the Van Wyck Expressway. It was past eleven; the joggers, bikers, and mothers with strollers had gone home hours ago, and the sloops on the lake were tied in their berths.

With the retractable trash spear he held in one hand, he jabbed at a stray piece of rubbish and stuck it into the plastic bag hanging from his utility belt. Cover like this had been much easier back in the 1980s, when New York had been a filthy place. These days, with the city squeaky-clean, park sanitation crews weren't nearly as invisible as they had once been. He considered that EES should brainstorm some new covers: commuters, maybe, or homeless persons, or marathon trainers.

He speared another piece of trash, his expression darkening. The thought of EES brought Eli Glinn back to his mind. No matter how long he worked for the guy, Garza had never understood him. Every time Garza thought that age had mellowed the man, or a particularly onerous op had reformed him, Eli Glinn went and proved him wrong. You could just never predict what he'd do—or wouldn't do. Like that time in Lithuania, when he'd threatened to detonate the nuclear device because the client refused to make final payment. He hadn't been kidding, either, he'd actually started the arming sequence before the client capitulated. Or that fateful expedition in Tierra del Fuego, when they were under pursuit and Glinn had blown up an iceberg to...

He shook that particular memory from his mind and turned away from the lake, heading back to the electric Parks Department cart that sat nearby. Just this morning, after the encounter on the subway train, Glinn had refused Garza's request that they assign several teams to shadow Crew during the final stage of his mission. Glinn listened carefully, then simply shook his head. "We're not doing that," he'd said.

We're not doing that. Garza rolled his eyes. A typical Glinn answer, containing no reasons, no explanation. Just fiat.

He eased himself into the cart, put the trash spear away, and unlocked a metal equipment locker bolted into one wall of the vehicle. He made a quick visual inventory of the contents: nine-millimeter Glock with silencer, sawed-off shotgun, taser, police radio, night-vision goggles, emergency paramedic kit, half a dozen federal, state, and local ID badges in assorted sizes. Satisfied, he closed the locker, then eased the cart north, toward the Queens Museum of Art.

Glinn had nixed assigning teams to Gideon Crew. So Garza had come here on his own initiative. This was a critical mission, a world-altering mission. There was no way Garza was going to let Crew go it alone—especially when somebody as dangerous as Nodding Crane was involved.

The Unisphere, Crew had said. Garza could see it ahead in the distance: a huge, gleaming silver globe, fringed at its base by fountains, on the far side of the Long Island Expressway. The problem was, Crew hadn't said whether they were meeting right *at* the Unisphere, or just somewhere in the general vicinity. The fact that the damn thing was located smack in the middle of Flushing Meadows Corona Park—the second largest park in New York City—didn't make Garza's job any easier. If it had been up to him, he'd have had police, real and imitation; EMS workers, public and private; snipers, fire-suppression teams, hijacking specialists, getaway drivers, journalist interdictors, and a partridge and a pear tree, all fanned out through the park in carefully assigned locations. As it was, he was alone and had his work cut out for him.

It had made absolutely no sense right from the get-go. Why assign such an important mission to someone like Crew: untested, unproven? Glinn could have selected any number of operatives who had proven themselves under fire. It just wasn't right to pick a screwup like Crew, someone who hadn't made his bones, who hadn't started small, worked his way up through the ranks—the way that, say, Garza himself had. Gideon Crew was impulsive; he operated on anger and adrenaline more than steely-eyed caution. Garza was a pretty levelheaded guy, but the very thought made irritation bubble up in him like so much acid.

He glanced at his watch again: eleven thirty. Ahead, the Unisphere glowed against the night sky like a streaking meteor. Not much time—he'd do one last reconnoiter, then pick the optimal spot from which to monitor the unfolding situation. He pointed the cart toward the vast globe and pushed down hard on the accelerator.

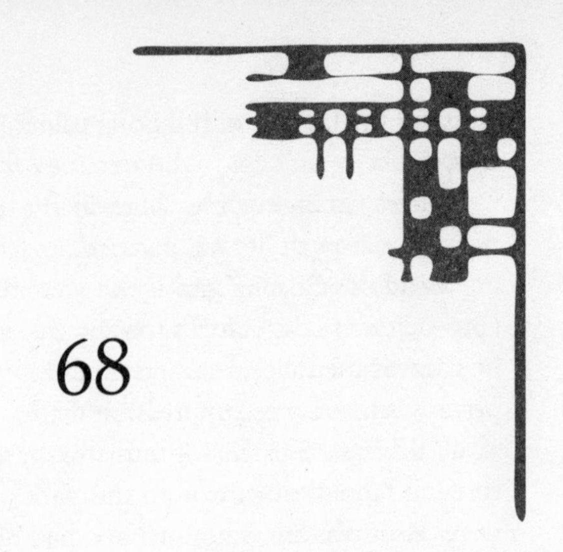

68

Gideon knew he was going to die but felt absolutely nothing. At least this way would be quicker and less painful.

There was a sudden yell and a fusillade of shots. Turning toward the sound, Gideon saw a monstrous apparition—a form covered in mud—erupting from the slide of dirt, firing and screaming like a banshee. Nodding Crane was punched violently back by the bullets. He sprayed return fire wildly as he went down.

"I'm out of ammo!" she screamed, tossing the rifle aside and scrabbling in the muck for her handgun.

Gideon fell on Nodding Crane, grasping the man's gun and trying to wrench it from his hands, hoping he was dead. But he was not—it seemed he, too, had body protection. The two wallowed in the muck, locked in a struggle for the TEC-9. But Nodding Crane was incredibly strong and he threw Gideon off, bringing his weapon up.

Mindy swung in with a board, attempting to slam it against Nodding Crane's head, but the assassin pirouetted away, deflecting the blow with his shoulder and raising his weapon unsteadily.

Gideon staggered back, realizing they had only one option now: to get away. "Out!" he cried.

Mindy leapt over the lip of the trench as Gideon followed. Another burst came from the TEC-9, but they were already racing across the field in the blackness of the storm and the rounds went wild.

For a moment the sky was split by an immense blast of lightning, followed by the roar of thunder.

"Bastard's reloading," Mindy gasped as they ran, reaching the line of trees as a fresh burst of fire ripped through the leaves around them, spraying them with vegetation. They crashed through the undergrowth, running until they could run no more.

"Your weapon?" Gideon gasped.

"Lost it. Got my backup." She pulled out a military-issue Colt .45. "The wire?"

"In my pocket."

"We've got to keep moving." She turned and headed south at a jog, Gideon following, pushing away the pain as best he could. He had lost his night-vision goggles and flashlight in the fight, and they were moving in pitch black, blundering through the woods, thrashing aside heavy brush and brambles. He had no doubt Nodding Crane was following.

"This isn't going to work," gasped Gideon. "He's got night vision. We need to get out in the open where we can see."

"Right," said Mindy.

"Follow me." Recalling the map, Gideon headed due east. The woods thinned and they passed through another field of bones, their feet crunching over skulls half-hidden under the leaves, and emerged at a broad, overgrown road with long, low buildings along one side: the boys' workhouse complex. There was just enough light coming from the southern sky—the lights of New York City—for them to see. Gideon broke into a run and Mindy did the same.

"Where's the boat?" she gasped.

"Near the beach by the smokestack," he said.

A sudden burst of fire came at them from behind, and Gideon instinctively threw himself down. Mindy landed beside him, rolled, returned fire with the .45. There was a sharp scream, then silence.

"I got him!" she said.

"I doubt it. He's a wily bastard."

Scrambling to their feet again, they ran for the ruined dormitories, leaping over a shattered doorway. Gideon kept going, running almost blind through one ruined room after another, tripping over mangled bed frames and broken plaster. Coming out the far end, he took a sudden turn into the ruined chapel, ran its length, leapt out the broken rose window at the end, then doubled back.

"What are we doing?" Mindy called softly from behind. "You said the boat was the other way—"

"*Random* is what we're doing. We need to lose him, go to ground."

Gasping, ribs on fire, he led the way through a dense stand of woods toward the opposite shore, moving more slowly now, trying to be as silent as possible. The trees thinned and they stepped out onto the overgrown baseball field he had seen earlier, bleachers covered with vines and trees, the diamond having vanished under a riot of weeds and saplings.

They pushed through the field. Gideon stopped and listened. The wind howled, the rain came down in stinging sheets—it was impossible to hear.

"I'm pretty sure we lost him," Mindy whispered, digging rounds out of her pocket and reloading. She nodded at the bleachers. "That looks like a good place."

Gideon nodded. On their hands and knees, they crawled under the old bleachers. They were covered with a heavy mat of vegetation; within, it was like a cave. The rain drummed on the metal seats above.

"He'll never find us here," she said.

Gideon shook his head. "He'll eventually find us anywhere. We'll wait for a bit, then make a dash for the boat. It's not that far."

He listened. Over the roar of the storm he could hear the sound of the surf in the distance.

"I think I really did hit him back there."

Gideon didn't answer, thinking instead of the route they now had to take to get to the boat. He had no confidence that Nodding Crane had been hit—or that they'd shaken him.

"You don't have a light or the map?" he asked.

"Everything was in my pack. All I saved was the gun."

"How did you get out of the dirt?"

"It was loose and I wasn't far under the surface. You shoveled off most of the weight. Give me the wire."

"For God's sake," he hissed, "we'll deal with that later."

The gun came around and pointed at him. Mindy rose slowly, taking a step back. "I said, *give me the wire.*"

For a moment, Gideon's mind went black as he stared at the gun. And then he recalled Nodding Crane's comment. *You're a fool.* It had seemed like a random insult at the time. But now, too late, he realized that nothing Nodding Crane said or did was random.

"What the hell are you doing?" he asked.

"Just give me the wire."

"Who are you? You're not CIA."

"I was. They didn't pay worth shit."

"So you're freelance."

She smiled. "Sort of. I'm doing this particular job for OPEC."

"OPEC?"

"Yeah. And I'm sure you're smart enough to figure out where OPEC comes in."

"No," he said, buying time.

"What do you think that piece of wire would do to their business? You could kiss the petroleum market good-bye. Along with the gas-powered car. So give me the wire, big boy. I really don't want to kill you, Gideon, but I will if you don't do what I say."

"So how much are they paying you?"

"Ten million."

"You sold yourself short." He thought back to Hong Kong, how she'd just happened to have a diplomatic embosser in her bag. That alone should have made him suspicious. He recalled how she always seemed to be working alone, no backup, no partner. Very un-CIA.

Nodding Crane was right—he'd been a fool.

She stuck out her hand. Of course, she might kill him anyway. But maybe, just maybe, the memory of their time together would stop her...He reached into his pocket and handed her the wire.

"That's a good boy." Still covering him, she held it up, scrutinizing it. Then she balled it in her fist and took fresh aim.

"Wow," she said. "I'm really sorry to do this."

And Gideon realized she meant it: she truly was sorry. But she was going to do it anyway.

He closed his eyes.

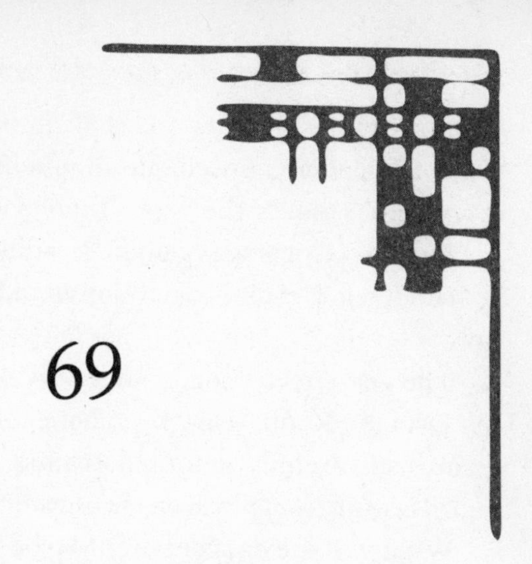

69

A single shot rang out from the darkness. Gideon felt nothing: no pain, no impact of a bullet. His eyes flew open. At first, nothing seemed to have changed. Then he saw the blank look on Mindy's face, the clean bullet hole between her eyes. For a moment she stood there. Then she toppled backward into the dirt.

Gideon snatched the wire from her twitching hand and ran.

More shots ripped through the seats, spraying him with wood chips and vegetation. He burst out the rear of the bleachers and made a beeline for the boat. It was his only chance for survival.

Ahead stretched the post-Armageddon suburban neighborhood. He sprinted down the leafy, ruined streets, turned a corner, then another. He could hear Nodding Crane pounding along behind him, slowly catching up.

To go into a house would mean being trapped. He couldn't outrun his enemy. And he realized now he was never going to make the boat.

He doubled back at the next street, turning corners to keep

from giving his pursuer a clear field of fire. He had no gun, no way of defending himself. He should have taken Mindy's .45, but it was either that or the wire—there hadn't been time for both.

Nodding Crane was gaining steadily. And Gideon was gasping so hard it felt as if his broken ribs would puncture his lungs. What now?

The last street ended. Ahead lay the open field adjacent to the Dynamo Room. He'd been here before. This was the area the guard had carefully detoured around. *That field's off-limits,* he'd said. *There's a lot of places on the island that are dangerous.*

What was the danger here? Maybe this was an opportunity. It sure as hell was his last chance.

He sprinted across the field, zigzagging as he went. He could hear Nodding Crane still closing the gap, not bothering to stop and fire but instead using the opportunity to get close enough so that he couldn't miss. Gideon glanced back: sure enough, there was the running figure, only fifty yards away now.

Halfway across the field Gideon realized he had made a serious mistake. He would never make it to the other side and there was nothing here that offered any chance of escape, no unexpected danger, no evidence of pits or old structures. Just a big damn open field without cover. The ground was solid and level. It was a race—and Nodding Crane was the faster runner.

He glanced back, his legs churning. Nodding Crane was now only thirty yards behind.

As Gideon turned his head toward the unattainable far end of the field, his eye caught the monstrous, crumbling smokestack rising from the Dynamo Room. Abruptly, he understood. The danger wasn't in the field itself—it was that smokestack. It was old and unstable. That was the reason the guard had detoured: the damn stack looked like it might fall at any moment.

An old iron stairway spiraled up to the top.

He veered off, running toward the smokestack. Clawing his

way through the undergrowth, he reached its base. He hesitated just a moment: this was a one-way trip to nowhere.

Fuck it.

He leapt onto the rusting stairs and began climbing. A trio of shots sounded from behind, smacking the bricks around him, spraying him with chips and dust. But the stairs spiraled around the curve of the stack, providing cover.

The stairway was old and rusted, and as Gideon climbed it rumbled and screeched, sagging and swaying with his every step, the rust raining down on him from the sudden strain. A step broke and he seized the railing, swinging briefly out into space before recovering, grasping the next step and hauling himself back up.

As he continued, climbing recklessly higher and higher, he heard a groan of metal below and felt a new vibration. Nodding Crane was coming up after him.

Naturally. This was a stupid move. Nodding Crane would chase him to the top and then shoot him from below.

As Gideon mounted higher, he could feel the stack vibrating in the buffeting winds, with an accompanying grinding and crackling sound of crumbling mortar.

Now the true insanity of what he had done began to hit home. The storm was shaking the entire stack, which felt like it was going to collapse at any moment. There was no outcome he could imagine in which he survived this chase to the top.

A single shot rang out, the bullet snipping the railing by his hand. He scrambled upward faster, keeping the turning of the staircase as cover. A flash of lightning illuminated the ghastly scene: the island, the ruins, the crumbling stack, the rotten stair, the storm-tossed sea beyond.

"Crew!" came a call from below. "Crew!" Nodding Crane's peculiar, flat voice pierced the howling wind.

He paused, listening. The stack groaned, crackled, swayed in the wind.

"You're trapped, you fool! Bring me down the wire and I'll let you live!"

Gideon resumed his climb. Another shot rang out, but it went wild and he knew Nodding Crane must be having a hell of a time firing accurately, given the swaying of the stack, the howling wind and rain. And there was something else: he thought he detected a note of fear in Nodding Crane's voice. And no wonder. That was progress of a kind. Strangely, Gideon felt no fear himself. This was the end—there was no way he was coming down off this smokestack alive. What did it matter? He was already a dead man.

The thought gave him a strange feeling of relief. That had been his secret weapon, the one Nodding Crane was unaware of: he was a man living on borrowed time.

As he climbed higher, heavier wind gusts boomed around him, so strong at times that they almost tore him from the stairway. Another lightning bolt split the sky, the crash of thunder following instantaneously. He heard a screech of metal as a section of the stairway detached from the stack, the bolts popping loose like gunfire, and the detached section swung out over the void, with Gideon clinging to the railing. He gripped the metal with all his might as the wind swung him back, slamming him against the bricks. The iron held until the wild oscillations of the stair finally calmed down. He found purchase, his feet back on the shaking iron steps, and resumed climbing.

He looked up as lightning flashed. He was about halfway to the top.

He had to go on, to prevent his weight from remaining too long on any one rotten step, while simultaneously keeping to the far side of the stack from Nodding Crane.

"Crew!" came the shout from below. "This is suicide!"

"For both of us!" Gideon screamed back. And it *was* suicide. Whether the smokestack fell or not, he couldn't go back down that stair; it was too damaged now, and besides, he was trapped by Nodding Crane. He had no weapon. Once he reached the top Nodding Crane would close in on him and that would be it.

"Crew! You're crazy!"

"You can count on it!"

The stack shuddered under a particularly fierce gust, and a fresh shower of bricks rained down. He pressed himself against the side of the stack as they clattered and bounced off the stairs. He looked down but Nodding Crane was out of sight around the curve of the stack. The lightning was now almost continuous, providing a glimpse every few seconds.

He looked up. He was almost at the top now. A narrow iron catwalk circled the rim of the great chimney, half of its braces gone. It slanted perilously to one side. He pressed on, one foot after the other, clinging to the railing with all his might.

Quite suddenly he was at the top, in the howling storm. He crawled through a hole onto the platform grate, clinging hard because of the slant. Bricks had broken away from the lip, giving it the look of ragged black teeth. The top of the stack was covered by a heavy grate to trap fly ash, and two brass dampers stood open, like giant bat wings. A strange hollow moaning rose up from inside the stack, as if out of the throat of some primitive, antediluvian monster.

There was nowhere to go.

One of us will die on Hart Island. That is the way you planned it and that is the way it must be.

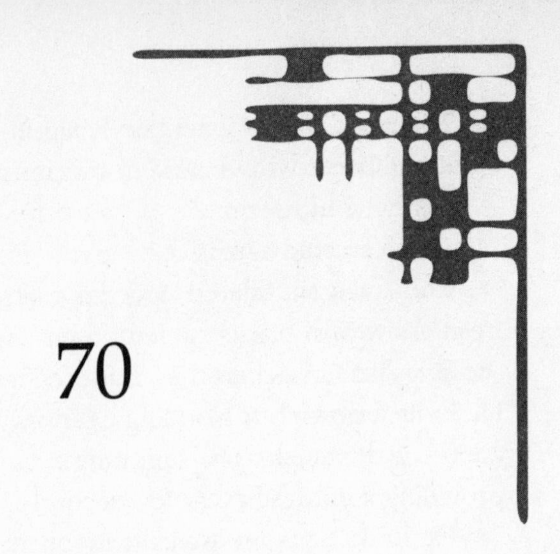

70

Laughter echoed up. "End of the line!" came the voice from below, suddenly sarcastic.

What now? Gideon had gone up the stack blindly, with no plan.

A gust struck, and the top of the smokestack swayed, more bricks crumbling and popping off the edge. At this rate, the whole damn stack could collapse at any minute.

Suddenly he had an idea. Working a brick loose, he peered down, waiting for the next bolt of lightning.

It arrived with a boom of thunder, illuminating Nodding Crane, clinging to the ladder about fifty feet below. Gideon hustled around and threw the brick into the void.

A fusillade of shots followed, punching holes through the metal platform, and Gideon almost fell off in his effort to get back. More laughter echoed up.

Dropping bricks on Nodding Crane was a waste—he was easily able to dodge them with his night-vision goggles, while Gideon had to wait for a flash of lightning. He would only get himself shot.

The wind cut around the open dampers, making a singing noise. He peered down the interior of the smokestack, but it was so dark he could see nothing. It muttered and groaned restlessly. The wind blasted across the top, the iron platform shaking, and the stack swayed. The damn thing really was about to fall.

About to fall…

For some reason, an image of Orchid formed in his mind. *You're in some kind of trouble, aren't you? Why don't you let me help you? Why do you keep pushing me away?*

He looked at the damper system. It was all brass and still in good condition, a long lever operating a set of gears that raised and lowered the semicircular dampers. Grasping the lever, Gideon pulled on it. The heavy dampers creaked and shuddered but appeared frozen in place. He gave the lever a hard yank: still nothing. Grasping the platform with both hands, he raised his foot and gave the lever a kick.

The lever flipped up and the dampers fell shut with a massive boom, sending a shock wave vibrating down the entire length of the smokestack. A dozen bricks peeled off the top, dropping into blackness, and the stack rocked violently.

"What are you doing?" Nodding Crane cried from below, his disembodied voice filled with horror.

A grim smile briefly crossed Gideon's features.

Grasping the handle, crouching on the trembling platform, he leaned in with all his might and forced the dampers open again, the bass wheels turning, flaking verdigris. The two dampers rose back up like a drawbridge.

He pulled the lever and dropped them again.

This crash sent an even more violent shudder down the smokestack. A flurry of crackling, grinding noises came up the flue as the entire stack shook.

"You're insane!" cried Nodding Crane. A flash of lightning revealed that he was now just below the lip of the platform and

Gideon could hear his heavy gasps, the iron stairway groaning with his steps. He was amazed the man had the courage to get so far. Bizarrely, he could see fingerpicks gleaming on the fingers of Nodding Crane's right hand.

Gideon forced the dampers open again. "Say good night!" he yelled, letting the lever drop again with a thunderous boom.

"No!"

He forced the dampers open once more, dropped them again—and this time the entire stack seemed to shift on its rotten base. A grinding noise came from far below.

"You fool!" In a flash of lightning Gideon got a glimpse of Nodding Crane gripping the stairway twenty feet below—clearly terrified—and now *descending*.

A maniacal laugh erupted from Gideon. "Who's the fool?" he shouted. "I'm the one who's not afraid to die! You should have stayed down there, waited me out!"

He let the dampers crash shut again. The platform shuddered, tilted abruptly with the crack of snapping steel, and Gideon began to slide. He seized the damper lever and held on. With a great popping of iron stays, the platform leaned sideways, the wind catching it like a sail and jamming it over; with a final screech it broke loose and plunged down into the darkness, leaving Gideon clinging to the brass lever at the ruined mouth of the chimney, his legs dangling in space.

Another flash of lightning. Nodding Crane was descending the ladder as fast as he could. If he reached the bottom, Gideon would lose his chance at revenge. And he would still die.

With a strength he didn't know he had, he hoisted himself up and swung his leg over the lever. From there he was able to climb onto the rim of the smokestack, clinging to the ash grating. He could feel it shifting and moving beneath him, the grinding noise rising in volume up the flue. Something was happening and it sounded like a runaway process of failure. He brought down the dampers again with another mighty crash, sending one more shock wave down the stack.

With a strange grinding, moaning noise, the immense stack listed one way, then the other, pausing, stopping—and then, in extremely slow motion, it began to lean more and more away from the direction of the wind.

This time it didn't move back to vertical. It continued to lean, the wind pushing it over. The top shook violently, once, twice.

"Nooo!" came a scream from below.

There was a rumble of bricks splitting and grinding under the shifting weight of the smokestack. It was going over, no question about it. Both of them would die. Gideon only hoped his end would be quick.

A crack of livid lightning exposed Nodding Crane. He wasn't quite halfway down.

"This is for Orchid, you bastard!" Gideon screamed down into the darkness.

The stack leaned out, falling faster, gathering speed. Another arc of lightning cut the sky, illuminating the turbulent sea below.

And that was when Gideon realized all was not lost. The stack was falling toward the water.

Faster and faster it fell, the wind roaring in his ears, as he clung to the lever, riding the crumbling smokestack down. His senses were assaulted by the deafening thunder of the collapsing structure; the air that rushed in his ears; the howling wind; the approaching roar of the sea. Through the flickers of lightning he could see the lower sections of the smokestack exploding against the ground in a running cloud of bricks, drawing a line of ruin in the direction of the water. As the sea came rushing up, Gideon braced himself. Just before the mouth of the stack crashed into the sea he leapt up and out, shedding some of his downward momentum while stiffening his body and clenching his stomach muscles and hands, seeking to hit the water in a rigid, vertical position.

He struck with tremendous force and was instantly plunged deep. He quickly spread out his legs and arms, slowing, then stopping, his descent into the depths. Then he swam upward, struggling in the chill water. Up and up he went, but the surface seemed too far to reach.

Just when he thought his lungs would burst, he broke through, gasping and heaving, sucking in air, treading water in the teeth of the storm. All was blackness. But then, as he rose on a swell, he could just make out the lights of City Island, and that oriented him.

Treading water, he tried to recover his breath, his strength. Then he struck out for the cobbled beach and his boat, swimming through the violent, heaving seas, the water breaking over his head and forcing him under every few seconds. His broken ribs were like veins of fire in his chest. But he kept on, the darkness complete, the boom and roar of the storm all around him like a violent womb. What little strength remained was rapidly ebbing. It would be ironic, he thought, if he survived all this only to drown.

But he was going to drown. He could hardly move his arms and legs anymore. He couldn't keep his head above water. A big wave shoved him under and he realized he just didn't have the strength to struggle back up.

That was when his feet struck the underwater cobbles of the beach and he was able to stand.

He didn't know how long he lay on the beach or even how he found the strength to crawl above the booming surf. But he came back into consciousness on the high part of the strand. Next to him he could see the shattered mass of the great smokestack lying across the beach and going down to the water. Pulverized bricks lay everywhere, amid pieces of twisted metal.

Metal. He clasped at his pocket in sudden fear. The wire was still there.

Dragging himself to his hands and knees, he crawled over the rubble, using the lightning as his guide. There, after a brief search, he found the body of Nodding Crane nestled among the broken bricks, not five feet from the sea. In his fear, he had tried to descend. And that was what had killed him: he struck the ground instead of the water.

The body was a hideous, pulped mess.

Gideon crawled away and—finally—managed to rise to his feet. With a sense of emptiness, of utter physical and spiritual exhaustion, he stumbled away from the crushed remains of the smokestack to the salt marsh where he had hidden his boat.

He still had one very important thing left to do.

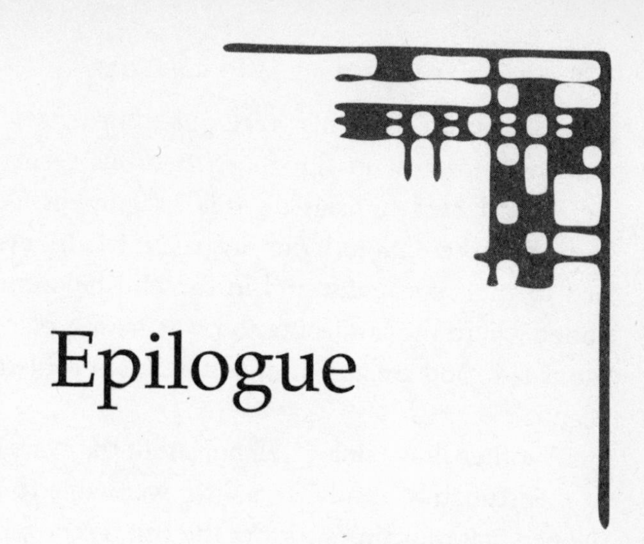

Epilogue

Gideon Crew followed Garza into the confines of the EES building on Little West 12th Street. Garza had said nothing, but Gideon could feel anger emanating from the man as if from a heat lamp.

The interior of EES looked unchanged: the same rows of tables covered with exotic models and scientific equipment; the same technicians and lab workers shuttling busily from here to there. Once again, Gideon wondered whom he was really working for. His phone call to DHS had confirmed, beyond doubt, that Glinn and his outfit were legit. But it nevertheless seemed surpassing strange.

They entered the spare conference room on the fourth floor. Glinn sat again at the head of the table, his one good eye as gray as a London sky.

Nobody said anything. Gideon took a seat without being asked, and Garza did the same.

"Well," said Glinn, his one eye making a slow blink that seemed to give Garza permission to speak.

"Eli," said Garza, his voice quiet but tense, "before we start I wish to protest in the most vigorous terms the way Crew here conducted himself on this assignment. Almost from the beginning he ignored our instructions. In every meeting he lied to me, repeatedly, and in the end he went rogue. He lied about where the confrontation was taking place, took an enormous risk, and created a huge potential problem for us on Hart Island."

Another slow blink. "Tell me about the Hart Island problem."

"Fortunately," said Garza, "we were able to pinch it off." He slapped that morning's copy of the *Post* on the table. The headline screamed VANDALS STRIKE POTTER'S FIELD, TWO DEAD.

"Summarize."

"The article says that Hart Island was struck by vandals last night. They stole a boat from City Island, tore up a bunch of graves, desecrated human remains, and vandalized some equipment. And then one of the vandals took it upon himself to climb the smokestack, which fell in the storm, killing him. He hasn't yet been identified. Another one, a woman, was shot and killed by persons unknown. The others escaped and are being sought by police."

"Excellent," said Glinn. "Mr. Garza, once again you have proven your usefulness to this organization."

"No thanks to Crew over there. It's a damn miracle he pulled it off."

"A miracle, Mr. Garza?"

"What would you call it? From my perspective, it was a cluster-fuck from beginning to end."

Gideon saw a smile play briefly over Glinn's colorless lips. "I would beg to differ."

"Yeah?"

"As you know, here at EES we have many proprietary software algorithms that quantify human behavior and analyze elaborate game-theory simulations."

"You don't need to tell me that."

"Apparently I do. Haven't you asked yourself why we didn't send a kill-team after Wu? Why we didn't assemble formal, six-on-six surveillance teams to monitor Dr. Crew, here? Why we didn't furnish him with additional information or weaponry? Why we didn't engage police or FBI backup for him? We have ample resources to do all those things, and more." He sat forward slowly. "Did you ever wonder why we didn't attempt to kill Nodding Crane ourselves?"

Garza was silent.

"Mr. Garza, you know the computing power we have here. I ran *all* those scenarios—and many more. The reason we didn't go those routes was because they all ended in failure. If Nodding Crane had been killed, the Chinese would have reacted—on a colossal scale. That *prematurity* was the event we had to avoid. The arc of the lone operator offered the highest probability of success. The arc in which Dr. Crew operated on his own, with no support; in which Nodding Crane remained alive to the very end, reporting back positive, reassuring news to his handlers."

"You know that I think some of your programs are a lot of horsefeathers," said Garza.

Glinn smiled. "I do. You're a straight engineer—the best I've got. I'd be concerned if you weren't suspicious of my psychoengineering methods."

He turned toward Gideon. "Dr. Crew, here, has unique talents. And he labors under the most liberating psychological environment a human being can have: he knows when and how he'll die. The Native Americans understood the power of this knowledge. The greatest vision a warrior could receive was to see his own death."

Gideon shifted uncomfortably in his chair. He wondered if Glinn would be so smug and self-satisfied when he learned the final outcome of the op.

The gray eye turned on him, examining him with unblinking intensity. A crippled hand rose from the wheelchair, cupped, ready to receive. "The wire, Dr. Crew?"

Here it came. "I don't have it."

The room settled into a strange, listening stasis. All was silent.

"And why not?"

"I gave it to Falun Gong. Along with the numbers. I completed Wu's mission. Soon the technology will be available to the entire world—free."

For a moment, the self-assured mask left Eli Glinn's face and something unreadable—some strong emotion—passed across it. "I am afraid our client will be *most* dissatisfied to hear that."

"I did it because—"

As soon as it had come, the mysterious expression vanished and the faint smile returned. "Say no more, please. I know perfectly well why you did it."

There was a brief silence.

"Highest probability of success!" Garza exploded. "Was *this* part of your computer simulation? I told you from the very beginning not to trust this guy. What are we going to tell our client?"

Glinn looked from one to the other, not speaking. There was something not entirely dissatisfied in his expression.

The silence stretched on until, finally, Gideon rose. "If we're finished here," he said, "I'm going back to New Mexico to sleep for a week. Then I'm going fishing."

Glinn shifted in his wheelchair and sighed. The withered hand reappeared from under the blanket shrouding his knees. It contained a brown-paper package. "Your payment."

Gideon hesitated. "I figured you weren't going to pay me. After what I did."

"The fact is, based on what you've told me, our payment structure has changed." Glinn opened the package envelope, counted out several banded bricks of hundreds. "Here is half of the hundred thousand."

Gideon took it. *Better than nothing,* he thought.

Then, to his surprise, Glinn handed him the other half. "And here's the rest. Not as payment for services rendered, however. More in the way of, shall we say, an advance."

Gideon stuffed the money into his jacket pockets. "I don't understand."

"Before you go," Glinn said, "I thought you might like to drop in on an old friend of yours who's in town."

"Thanks, but I've got a date with a cutthroat trout in Chihuahueños Creek."

"Ah, but I was so hoping you'd have time to see your friend."

"I don't have any friends," Gideon replied drily. "And if I did, I sure as hell wouldn't be interested in 'dropping in' on them right now. As you pointed out, I'm living on borrowed time."

"Reed Chalker is his name. I believe you worked with him?"

"We worked in the same Tech Area—that's not the same as working *with* him. I haven't seen the guy around Los Alamos in months."

"Well, you're about to see him now. The authorities are hoping you could have a little chat with him."

"The authorities? A chat? What the hell's this about?"

"At this moment Chalker's got a hostage. Four of them, actually. A family in Queens. Held at gunpoint."

Gideon felt this sink in. "Jesus. You sure it's Chalker? The guy I knew was a typical Los Alamos geek, straight as an arrow, wouldn't hurt a fly."

"He's raving. Paranoid. Out of his mind. You're the only person nearby who knows him. The police are hoping you can calm him down, get him to release those hostages."

Gideon didn't reply.

"So I'm sorry to tell you, Dr. Crew, but that cutthroat trout is going to be enjoying life just a little bit longer. And now we really do need to go. That family can't wait."